THE MONK WHO VANISHED

A Sister Fidelma Mystery

Also by Peter Tremayne
and featuring Sister Fidelma

Absolution by Murder
Shroud for the Archbishop
Suffer Little Children
The Subtle Serpent
The Spider's Web
Valley of the Shadow

THE MONK WHO VANISHED

A Sister Fidelma Mystery

Peter Tremayne

HEADLINE

First published in 1999 by
HEADLINE BOOK PUBLISHING

10 9 8 7 6 5 4 3 2

British Library Cataloguing in Publication Data

Tremayne, Peter, 1943–
The monk who vanished
1. Detective and mystery stories
I. Title
823.9′14[F]

ISBN 0 7472 2017 4

Typeset by Palimpsest Book Production Limited,
Polmont, Stirlingshire
Printed and bound in Great Britain by
Antony Rowe Ltd.

HEADLINE BOOK PUBLISHING
A division of Hodder Headline PLC
338 Euston Road
London NW1 3BH

For Mary Mulvey and the staff at the Cashel Heritage Centre in appreciation of their enthusiasm and support for Sister Fidelma.

HISTORICAL NOTE

The Sister Fidelma mysteries are set during the mid-seventh century A.D.

Sister Fidelma is not simply a religieuse, formerly a member of the community of St Brigid of Kildare. She is also a qualified *dálaigh*, or advocate of the ancient law courts of Ireland. As this background will not be familiar to many readers, this foreword provides a few essential points of reference designed to make the stories more readily appreciated.

Ireland, in the seventh century A.D., consisted of five main provincial kingdoms: indeed, the modern Irish word for a province is still *cúige*, literally 'a fifth'. Four provincial kings – of Ulaidh (Ulster), of Connacht, of Muman (Munster) and of Laigin (Leinster) – gave their qualified allegiance to the *Ard Rí* or High King, who ruled from Tara, in the 'royal' fifth province of Midhe (Meath), which means the 'middle province'. Even among these provincial kingdoms, there was a decentralisation of power to petty-kingdoms and clan territories.

The law of primogeniture, the inheritance by the eldest son or daughter, was an alien concept in Ireland. Kingship, from the lowliest clan chieftain to the High King, was only partially hereditary and mainly electoral. Each ruler had to prove himself or herself worthy of office and was elected by the *derbfhine* of their family – a minimum of three generations gathered in conclave. If a ruler did not pursue the commonwealth of the people, they were impeached and removed from office. Therefore the monarchial system of ancient Ireland had more in common with a modern-day republic than with the feudal monarchies of medieval Europe.

Ireland, in the seventh century A.D., was governed by a system of sophisticated laws called the Laws of the *Fénechas*, or land-tillers, which became more popularly known as the Brehon Laws, deriving from the word *breitheamh* – a judge. Tradition has it that these laws were first gathered in 714 B.C. by the order of the High King, Ollamh Fódhla. But it was in A.D. 438 that the High King, Laoghaire, appointed a commission of nine learned people to study, revise, and commit the laws to the new writing in Latin characters. One of those serving on the commission was Patrick, eventually to become patron saint of Ireland. After three years, the commission produced a written text of the laws, the first known codification.

The first complete surviving texts of the ancient laws of Ireland are preserved in an eleventh-century manuscript book. It was not until the seventeenth century that the English colonial administration in Ireland finally suppressed the use of the Brehon Law system. To even possess a copy of the law books was punishable, often by death or transportation.

The law system was not static and every three years at the Féis Temhrach (Festival of Tara) the lawyers and administrators gathered to consider and revise the laws in the light of changing society and its needs.

Under these laws, women occupied a unique place. The Irish laws gave more rights and protection to women than any other western law code at that time or since. Women could, and did, aspire to all offices and professions as the co-equal with men. They could be political leaders, command their people in battle as warriors, be physicians, local magistrates, poets, artisans, lawyers, and judges. We know the name of many female judges of Fidelma's period – Bríg Briugaid, Áine Ingine Iugaire and Darí among many others. Darí, for example, was not only a judge but the author of a noted law text written in the sixth century A.D. Women were protected by the laws against sexual harassment; against discrimination; from rape; they had the right of divorce on equal terms from their husbands with equitable separation laws and could demand part of their husband's property as a divorce settlement; they had the right of inheritance of personal property and the right of sickness benefits. Seen from today's perspective, the Brehon Laws provided for an almost feminist paradise.

This background, and its strong contrast with Ireland's neighbours, should be understood to appreciate Fidelma's role in these stories.

Fidelma was born at Cashel, capital of the kingdom of Muman (Munster) in south-west Ireland, in A.D. 636. She was the youngest daughter of Faílbe Fland, the king, who died the year after her birth, and was raised under the guidance of a distant cousin, Abbot Laisran of Durrow. When she reached the 'Age of Choice' (fourteen years), she went to study at the bardic school of the Brehon Morann of Tara, as many other young Irish girls did. Eight years of study resulted in Fidelma obtaining the degree of *anruth*, only one degree below the highest offered at either bardic or ecclesiastical universities in ancient Ireland. The highest degree was *ollamh*, still the modern Irish word for a professor. Fidelma's studies were in law, both in the criminal code of the *Senchus Mór* and the civil code of the *Leabhar Acaill.* She therefore became a *dálaigh* or advocate of the courts.

Her role could be likened to a modern Scottish sheriff-substitute, whose job is to gather and assess the evidence, independent of the police, to see if there is a case to be answered. The modern French *juge d'instruction* holds a similar role.

In those days, most of the professional or intellectual classes were members of the new Christian religious houses, just as, in previous centuries, all members of professions and intellectuals were Druids. Fidelma became a member of the religious community of Kildare founded in the late fifth century A.D. by St Brigid.

While the seventh century A.D. was considered part of the European 'Dark Ages', for Ireland it was a period of 'Golden Enlightenment'. Students from every corner of Europe flocked to Irish universities to receive their education, including the sons of the Anglo-Saxon kings. At the great ecclesiastical university of Durrow, at this time, it is recorded that no less than eighteen different nations were represented among the students. At the same time, Irish male and female missionaries were setting out to reconvert a pagan Europe to Christianity, establishing churches, monasteries, and centres of learning throughout Europe as far east as Kiev, in the Ukraine; as far north as the Faroes, and as far south as Taranto in southern Italy. Ireland was a byword for literacy and learning.

However, the Celtic Church of Ireland was in constant dispute with Rome on matters of liturgy and ritual. Rome had begun to reform itself in the fourth century, changing its dating of Easter and aspects of its liturgy. The Celtic Church and the Eastern Orthodox Church refused to follow Rome, but the Celtic Church was gradually absorbed by Rome between the ninth and eleventh centuries while the Eastern Orthodox Churches have continued to remain independent of Rome. The Celtic Church of Ireland, during Fidelma's time, was much concerned with this conflict.

One thing that marked both the Celtic Church and Rome in the seventh century was that the concept of celibacy was not universal. While there were always ascetics in both Churches who sublimated physical love in a dedication to the deity, it was not until the Council of Nicea in A.D. 325 that clerical marriages were condemned but not banned. The concept of celibacy in the Roman Church arose from the customs practised by the pagan priestesses of Vesta and the priests of Diana. By the fifth century Rome had forbidden clerics from the rank of abbot and bishop to sleep with their wives and, shortly after, even to marry at all. The general clergy were discouraged from marrying by Rome but not forbidden to do so. Indeed, it was not until the reforming papacy of Leo IX (A.D. 1049–1054) that a serious attempt was made to force the western clergy to accept universal celibacy. In the Eastern Orthodox Church, priests below the rank of abbot and bishop have retained their right to marry until this day.

The condemnation of the 'sin of the flesh' remained alien to the Celtic Church for a long time after Rome's attitude became a dogma. In Fidelma's world, both sexes inhabited abbeys and monastic foundations which were known as *conhospitae*, or double houses, where men and women lived raising their children in Christ's service.

Fidelma's own house of St Brigid of Kildare was one such community of both sexes in Fidelma's time. When Brigid established her community at Kildare (Cill-Dara = the church of oaks) she invited a bishop named Conlaed to join her. Her first biography, written in A.D. 650, in Fidelma's time, was written by a monk of Kildare named Cogitosus, who makes it clear that it was a mixed community.

It should also be pointed out that, showing women's co-equal role with men, women were priests of the Celtic Church at this time. Brigid herself was ordained a bishop by Patrick's nephew, Mel, and her case was not unique. Rome actually wrote a protest in the sixth century at the Celtic practice of allowing women to celebrate the divine sacrifice of Mass.

To help readers locate themselves in Fidelma's Ireland of the seventh century, where its geo-political divisions will be mainly unfamiliar, I have provided a sketch map and, to help them more readily identify personal names, a list of principal characters is also given.

I have generally refused to use anachronistic place names for obvious reasons although I have bowed to a few modern usages, eg: Tara, rather than *Teamhair*; and Cashel, rather than *Caiseal Muman*; and Armagh in place of *Ard Macha*. However, I have cleaved to the name of Muman rather than the prolepsis form 'Munster', formed when the Norse *stadr* (place) was added to the Irish name Muman in the ninth century A.D. and eventually anglicised. Similarly, I have maintained the original Laigin, rather than the anglicised form of Laigin-*stadr* which is now Leinster.

Armed with this background knowledge, we may now enter Fidelma's world. The events of this story occur in September, the month known to the Irish of the seventh century as the middle month (*Meadhón*) of the harvest (*Fogamar*), which is still known in Modern Irish as *Meán Fhómhair*. The year is Anno Domini 666.

The story of the Uí Fidgente plot and rebellion are told in *The Subtle Serpent*.

Readers might like to known that hardly anything remains of the great abbey and cathedral of St Ailbe at Imleach Iubhair – 'The Borderland of Yew-Trees', or Emly (Co Tipperary) as it is now anglicised. Today it is just a little village lying just over eight miles west of the county town of Tipperary (the 'Well of Ara'). A church still stands on the site. Emly stayed a 'Cathedral City' until 1587, remaining the principal ecclesiastical See of Munster until it was combined with the See of Cashel. Catholic and Protestant bishops of the See take their titles from both Emly and Cashel.

The ancient abbey buildings were replaced by a thirteenth-century cathedral which was destroyed during the wars of 1607. The church was rebuilt by the end of that century, consecrated as an Anglican cathedral, but it soon fell into disrepair. In 1827 it was rebuilt again but pulled down within forty years mainly due to the disestablishment of the Anglican Church in Ireland. An offer to buy it by the Catholic Church was refused and many of its stones were taken to build the new Anglican Church of Ireland at Monard. The modern Catholic church was built in 1882 which is worthy of a visit if only for its fine stained-glass windows, one of which commemorates the famous King-Bishop of Cashel, Cormac Mac Cuileannáin (A.D. 836–908), poet, writer and lexicographer. Within the churchyard, which still has a Yew Tree growing in its centre, is St Ailbe's Well and the remains of an ancient weathered stone cross which, it is said, marks the saint's grave. You may still find worshippers, faithful to the memory of the patron saint of the great Eóghanacht kingdom, visiting the well on Ailbe's feastday of September 12 to ask for his holy intercession.

There are no less than five ancient holy well sites at Emly but Tobair Peadair (Peter's Well) became dangerous and is now covered over. It is from here that an underground passage is reputed to lead from the well head to the hill of Knockcarron (Hill of the Cairn).

Principal Characters

Sister Fidelma of Cashel, a *dálaigh* or advocate of the law courts of seventh-century Ireland
Brother Eadulf of Seaxmund's Ham, a Saxon monk from the land of the South Folk

At Cashel

Colgú of Cashel, King of Muman and Fidelma's brother
Donndubháin, *tanist* or heir-elect to Colgú
Donennach mac Oengus, Prince of the Uí Fidgente
Gionga, commander of Donennach's bodyguard
Conchobar, an astrologer and apothecary
Capa, captain of the bodyguard to Colgú

Brehon Rumann of Fearna
Brehon Dathal of Cashel
Brehon Fachtna of Uí Fidgente

Oslóir, a groom
Della, a recluse

At Ara's Well

Aona, the innkeeper
Adag, his grandson

At Imleach

Ségdae, abbot and bishop of Imleach, Comarb of Ailbe
Brother Mochta, Keeper of the Holy Relics
Brother Madagan, the *rechtaire* or steward
Brother Tomar, the stableman
Sister Scothnat, *domina* of the guests' hostel
Finguine mac Cathal, Prince of Cnoc Áine
Brother Daig
Brother Bardán, the apothecary
Nion, *bó-aire* (petty-chief) and smith
Suibne, his assistant
Cred, a tavern keeper
Samradán, a visiting merchant of Cashel
Solam, *dálaigh* of the Uí Fidgente

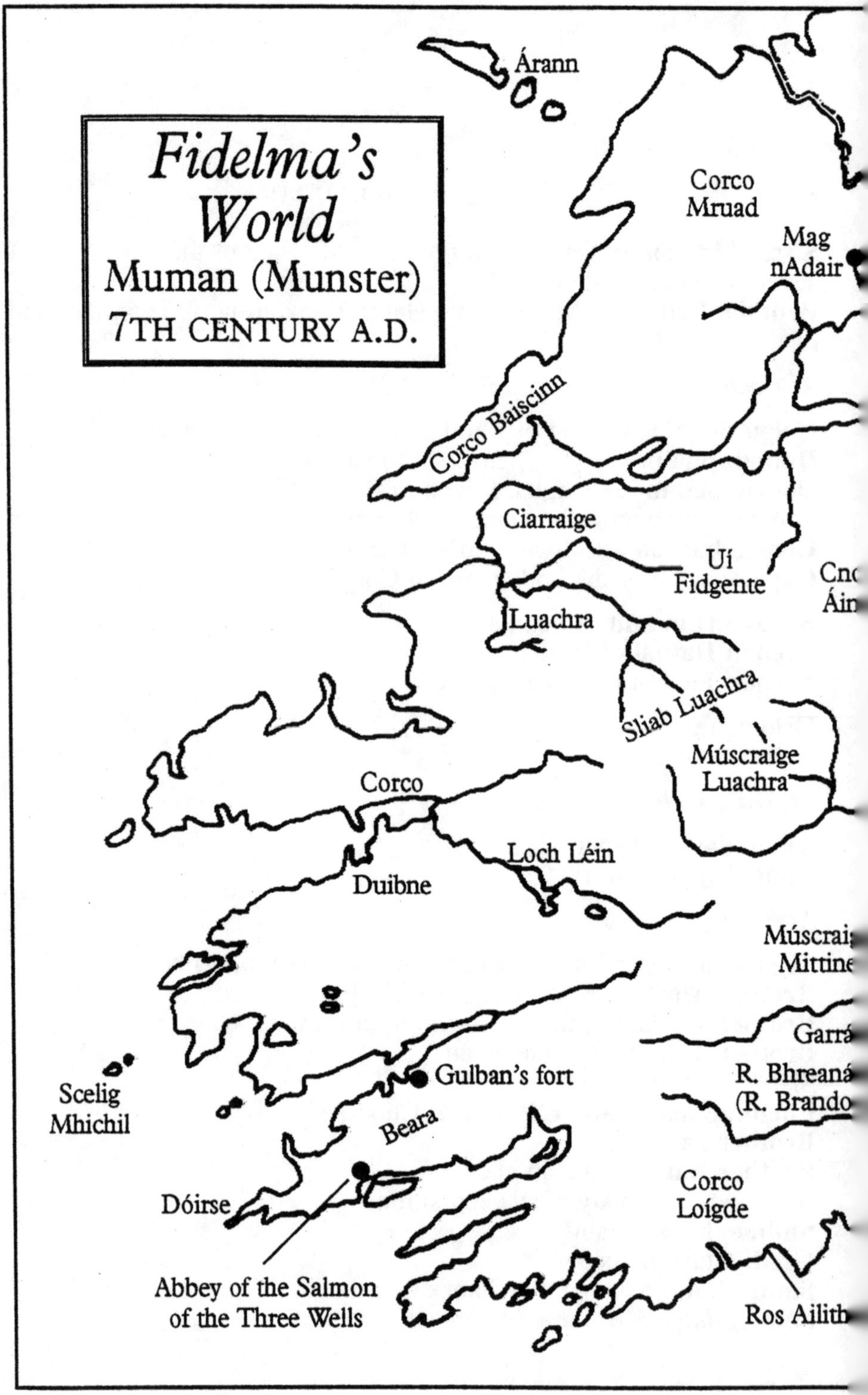
Fidelma's World
Muman (Munster)
7TH CENTURY A.D.
Árann
Corco Mruad
Mag nAdair
Corco Baiscinn
Ciarraige
Uí Fidgente
Luachra
Sliab Luachra
Múscraige Luachra
Corco
Loch Léin
Duibne
Gulban's fort
Scelig Mhichil
Beara
Dóirse
Abbey of the Salmon of the Three Wells
Corco Loígde
Ros Ailith
R. Bhreaná
(R. Brando

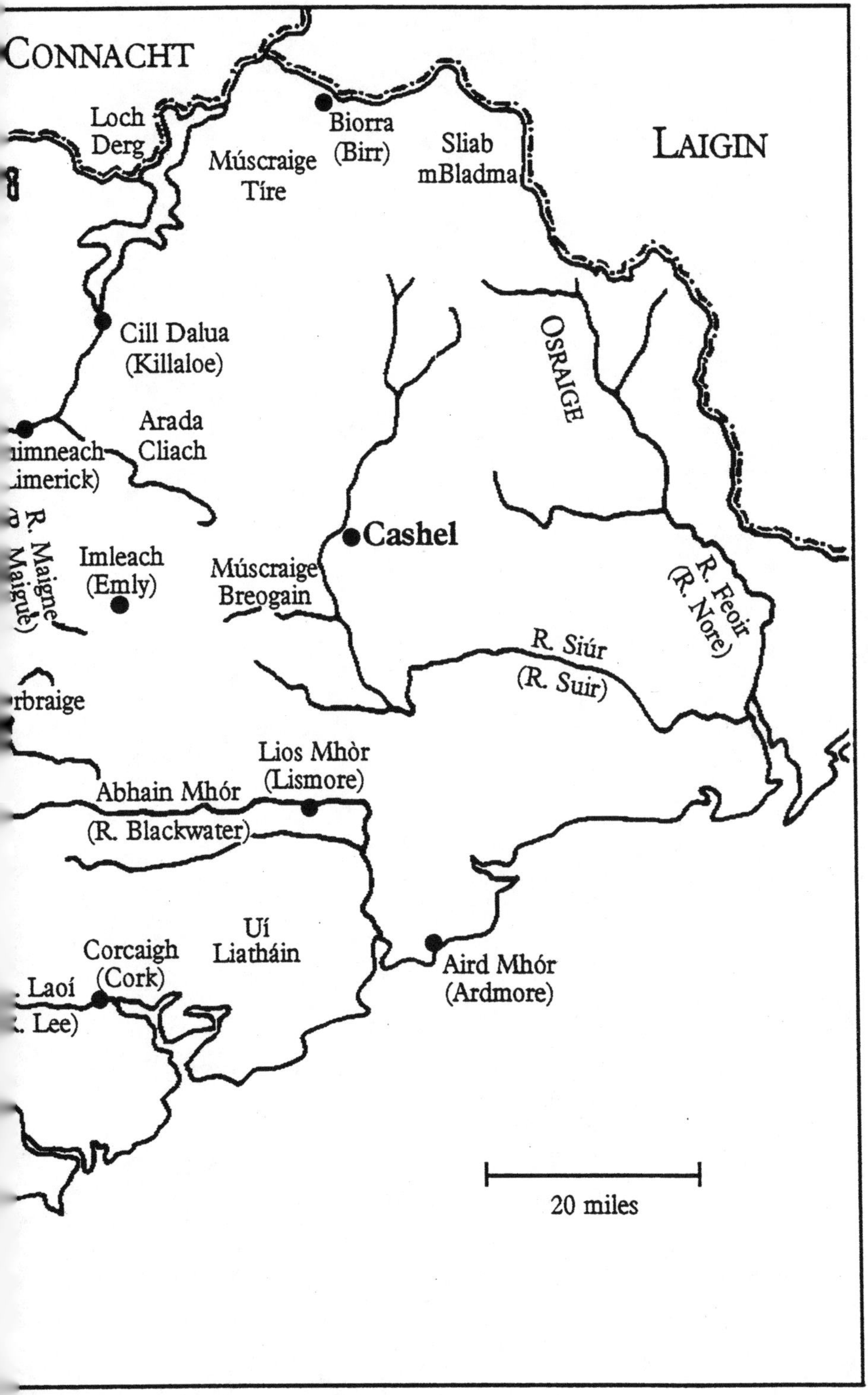
CONNACHT
LAIGIN
Loch Derg
Biorra (Birr)
Sliab mBladma
Múscraige Tíre
Cill Dalua (Killaloe)
OSRAIGE
Arada Cliach
imneach
imerick)
R. Maigne
Maigue)
Imleach (Emly)
Cashel
Múscraige Breogain
R. Feoir (R. Nore)
R. Siúr (R. Suir)
rbraige
Lios Mhòr (Lismore)
Abhain Mhór (R. Blackwater)
Uí Liatháin
Corcaigh (Cork)
Laoí
Lee)
Aird Mhór (Ardmore)
20 miles

Chapter One

The tall figure of the cowled religieux was hurrying down the darkened corridor, the soles of his sandals slapping against the granite flagstones with sharp cracking sounds which one might have believed would rouse the entire abbey from its slumbers. The man held a thick stub of tallow candle in front of him, its flame flickering and dancing in the draughty passageways but providing just enough gloomy illumination to light his way. It reflected on his gaunt features, etching them and distorting them to make his face appear like some nightmarish vision of a demon conjured from hell rather than a servant of God.

The figure came to a halt before a stout wooden door and hesitated for a moment. Then he clenched his free hand into a fist and pounded twice upon it before, without waiting for any response, he swung open the round iron latch and entered.

Inside, the room was in darkness, for night's mantle still shrouded the abbey. He hesitated on the threshold and held up the candle to illuminate the room. In one corner, a recumbent figure lay on a small bed covered in a blanket. The religieux could tell by the continued heavy, regular breathing, that his knocking and abrupt entry had failed to rouse the room's sole inhabitant.

He moved towards the bed, placing his candle on the bedside table. Then he leant forward and shook the shoulder of the sleeper roughly.

'Father Abbot!' he called urgently, his voice almost cracking in suppressed emotion. 'Father Abbot! You must awake!'

The sleeping man groaned a moment and then came reluctantly awake, eyelids blinking rapidly and trying to focus in the gloom.

'What . . . ? Who . . . ?' The figure turned and looked up, seeing the tall religieux standing over his bed. The man flung back his cowl in order to be recognised and a frown crossed the hawk-like features of the disturbed sleeper. 'Brother Madagan. What is it?' The figure struggled to sit up, his eyes observing the night sky at the window. 'What is it? Have I overslept?'

The tall monk shook his head in a quick, nervous gesture. His face was grim in the candlelight.

'No, Father Abbot. It still lacks an hour until the bell tolls the summons for lauds.'

Lauds marked the first day hour of the Church when the brothers of the Abbey of Imleach gathered to sing the psalms of praise which opened the day's devotions.

Ségdae, abbot and bishop of Imleach, Comarb, or successor to St Ailbe, eased himself up against his pillow with the frown still furrowing his features.

'Then what is amiss that you should rouse me before the appointed time?' he demanded petulantly.

Brother Madagan bowed his head at the sharp tone of rebuke in the abbot's voice.

'Father Abbot, are you aware what day this is?'

Ségdae gazed at Brother Madagan, his frown of annoyance giving way to bewilderment.

'What sort of question is this that you must awake me to ask it? It is the feastday of the founder of our abbey, the Blessed Ailbe.'

'Forgive me, Father Abbot. But, as you know, on this day, following lauds, we take the Holy Relics of the Blessed Ailbe from our chapel to his grave in the abbey grounds where you bless them and we offer thanks for Ailbe's life and work in converting this corner of the world to the Faith.'

Abbot Ségdae was increasingly impatient. 'Get to the point, Brother Madagan, or have you awakened me simply to tell me what I already knew?'

'*Bona cum venia*, by your leave, I will explain.'

'Do so!' the abbot snapped irritably. 'And your explanation better be a good one.'

'As steward of the abbey, I was making the rounds of the watch. A short while ago I went to the chapel.' The monk paused as if to give dramatic effect to his words. 'Father Abbot, the reliquary of the Blessed Ailbe is missing from the recess wherein it was kept!'

Abbot Ségdae became completely alert and swung out of his bed.

'Missing? What's this you say?'

'The reliquary is gone. Vanished.'

'Yet it was there when we gathered for Vespers. We all saw it.'

'Indeed, it was. Now it has been removed.'

'Have you summoned Brother Mochta?'

Brother Madagan drew his brows together as if he did not understand the question. 'Brother Mochta?'

'As Keeper of the Holy Relics of the Blessed Ailbe he should have been the first to be summoned,' pointed out Ségdae, his irritation growing again. 'Go . . . no, wait! I'll come with you.'

He turned and slipped his feet into his sandals and took down his woollen cloak from a peg. 'Take the candle and precede me to Brother Mochta's chamber.'

Brother Madagan took up the tallow candle and moved into the corridor, closely followed by the agitated figure of the abbot.

Outside, a wind had started to rise, whispering and moaning around the hill on which the abbey stood. The cold breath of the wind penetrated through the dim corridors of the building and Abbot Ségdae could almost feel the rain it was bringing with it. With a sense born of experience the abbot could tell the wind was sweeping up from the south, bringing up the clouds that had lain across the Ballyhoura Mountains on the previous evening. By dawn it would be raining. The abbot knew it from long experience.

'What can have happened to the Holy Relics?' Brother Madagan's voice interrupted his thoughts almost like a wail of despair as they hastened along the corridor. 'Can some thief have broken into the abbey and stolen them?'

'*Quod avertat Deus!*' intoned Abbot Ségdae, genuflecting. 'Let us hope that Brother Mochta was simply early abroad and decided to remove the relics in preparation for the service.'

Even as he spoke the abbot realised that it was a vain hope for everyone knew the order of the service of remembrance for the Blessed Ailbe. The relics remained in the chapel until after lauds and were then taken out, carried by the Keeper of the Holy Relics. They would be followed in procession by the community firstly to the holy well, in the abbey's grounds, where the abbot would draw fresh water and bless the relics, as Ailbe had once blessed his new abbey over a hundred years ago. The reliquary, and a chalice of the blessed water, would then be carried to the stone cross which marked the grave of the founder of the abbey and there the service of remembrance would be conducted. That being so well known, why would the Keeper of the Holy Relics have removed them from the chapel at such an early hour?

The abbot and the anxious steward halted before a door and Brother Madagan raised his fist to knock. Abbot Ségdae, with a sigh of impatience, pushed him aside and opened the door.

'Brother Mochta!' he cried as he entered the small chamber. Then he halted, his eyes widening. He paused for a few moments, while Brother Madagan tried vainly to peer over his shoulder to see what was amiss in the gloom. Without turning, the abbot said in a curiously quiet tone: 'Hold the candle higher, Brother Madagan.'

The tall steward did so, holding the candle high above the abbot's shoulder.

The flickering light revealed a tiny cell. It was in total disarray.

Items of clothing lay discarded on the floor. It appeared that the straw mattress had been almost dragged from the tiny wooden cot that provided the bed. A stub of unlit candle lay in a small pool of its own grease on the floor with its wooden holder a short distance away. A few personal toilet items were scattered here and there.

'What does this mean, Father Abbot?' whispered Brother Madagan aghast.

Abbot Ségdae did not reply. His eyes narrowed as they fell on the mattress. There appeared to be a discolouration on it that he could not account for. He turned and took the candle from Brother Madagan's hand and moved forward, bending to examine the stain more closely. Tentatively, he reached forward a finger and touched it. It was still damp. He took his fingertip away and peered at it in the flickering candlelight.

'*Deus misereatur* . . . ,' he whispered. 'This is blood.'

Brother Madagan did not hide the shiver that passed abruptly through his body.

Abbot Ségdae stood frozen for several moments. It seemed a long time before he stirred himself.

'Brother Mochta is not here,' he said, stating the obvious. 'Go, Brother Madagan, arouse the abbey. We must start a search immediately. There is blood on his mattress, his cell is in disorder and the Holy Relics of Blessed Ailbe are missing. Go, ring the alarm bell for there is evil stalking this abbey this night!'

Chapter Two

The figure of the religieuse paused on the last step, before ascending to the walkway behind the battlements of the fortress, and peered up at the morning sky in disapproval. Her young, attractive features with the rebellious strands of red hair blowing across her forehead, the bright eyes which now mirrored the sombreness of the grey skies, were drawn in an expression of censure as she viewed the morning weather. Then with an almost imperceptible shrug, she took the final step onto the stone walkway which surrounded the interior of the towering walls of the fortress that was also the palace of the Kings of Muman, the largest and most south-westerly kingdom of Éireann.

Cashel rose, almost threateningly, some two hundred feet on a great limestone peak which dominated the plains around it. The only approach to it was by a steep road from the market town which had grown up in its shadow. There were many buildings on the rock as well as the palace of the Kings of Muman. Sharing the rock was a great church, the *cathedra* or seat of the bishop of Cashel, a tall circular building, for most churches were built in such a fashion, with its connecting corridors to the palace. There was a system of stables, outhouses, hostels for visitors and quarters for the bodyguard of the King as well as a monastic cloister for the religious who served the cathedral.

Sister Fidelma moved with a youthful agility that seemed at odds with her calling in life. Her religious habit did nothing to conceal her tall but well proportioned figure. With an easy gait she moved to the battlement, leaning against it, and continued her study of the skies. She felt a slight shiver catch her as a cold wind gusted across the buildings. It was obvious that it had rained sometime during the night for there was an atmosphere of dampness in the air and there was a slight silver sheen across the more shaded fields below which showed the early morning light sparkling on droplets of water.

The weather was unusual. St Matthew's Day, which heralded the autumn equinox by the first morning frosts and a drop in night temperature, had not yet arrived. The usually fine daytime weather of the month was chill. The sky was covered in a uniform grey layer of cloud and there was only a faint brightness as, now and then, the sun tried to penetrate it. It was a troubled sky. The clouds lay thick across the tops of the mountains to the south-west, on the far side of the interceding valley where the broad ribbon of the River Suir twisted its way from north to south.

Fidelma turned from her examination and, as she did so, espied an elderly man standing a short distance from her. He, too, was apparently meditating on the morning sky. With a smile of greeting, she walked to where the old man stood.

'Brother Conchobar! You wear a mournful look this day,' she exclaimed brightly, for Fidelma was not one to let the weather dictate her moods.

The old religieux raised his long face to Fidelma and grimaced sadly.

'Well I might. It is not an auspicious day today.'

'A cold one, I grant you, Brother,' she replied. 'Yet the clouds may clear for there is a south-westerly wind, albeit a chill one.'

The old man shook his head, not responding to her bright tone.

'It is not the clouds that tell me that we should beware this day.'

'Have you been examining your charts of the heavens, Conchobar?' chided Fidelma, for she knew that Brother Conchobar was not only the physician at Cashel, whose apothecary stood in the shadow of the royal chapel, he was also an adept at making speculations from the patterns of the stars and spent long, lonely hours in contemplation of the heavens. Indeed, medicine and astrology were often twins in the practice of the physician's art.

'Don't I examine the charts each day?' replied the old man, his voice still kept to a mournful monotone.

'As I do recall even from my childhood,' affirmed Fidelma solemnly.

'Indeed. I once tried to teach you the art of charting the heavens,' sighed the old man. 'You would have made an excellent interpreter of the portents.'

Fidelma grimaced good-naturedly. 'I doubt it, Conchobar.'

'Trust me. Did I not study under Mo Chuaróc mac Neth Sémon, the greatest astrologer that Cashel has ever produced?'

'So you have told me many times, Conchobar. Tell me now, why is this day not an auspicious one?'

'I fear that evil is abroad this day, Fidelma of Cashel.'

The old man never addressed her by her religious style but always referred to her in the manner denoting that she was the daughter of a king and the sister of a king.

'Can you identify the evil, Conchobar?' asked Fidelma with sudden interest. While she placed no great reliance on astrologers, for it was a science which seemed to rely solely on the ability of the individual, she accepted that much might be learnt from the wisest of them. The study of the heavens, *nemgnacht*, was an ancient art and most who could afford to do so, had a chart cast for the moment of their children's birth which was called *nemindithib*, a horoscope.

'I cannot be specific, alas. Do you know where the moon is today?'

In a society living so close to nature it would be an ignorant person or a complete fool who did not know the position of the moon.

'We are on a waning moon, Conchobar. She stands in the house of The Goat.'

'Indeed, for the moon squares Mercury, conjuncts Saturn and sextiles Jupiter. And where is the sun?'

'Easy enough, the sun's in the house of The Virgin.'

'And is opposed by the moon's north node. The sun is squared by Mars. And while Saturn is conjunct the moon in Capricorn it is squared by Mercury. And while Jupiter is conjunct the midheaven, Jupiter is squared by Venus.'

'But what does this mean?' pressed Fidelma, intrigued, and trying to follow what he was saying from her meagre knowledge of the art.

'It means that no good will come of this day.'

'For whom?'

'Has your brother, Colgú, left the castle yet?'

'My brother?' frowned Fidelma in surprise. 'He left before first light to meet the Prince of the Uí Fidgente, at the Well of Ara as arranged, in order to escort him here. Do you see danger for my brother?' She was suddenly anxious.

'I cannot say.' The old man spread his arms in a negative gesture. 'I am not sure. The danger may apply to your brother, although, if this be so, and harm approaches him, whoever causes that harm will not be triumphant in the end. That is all I can say.'

Fidelma looked at him in disapproval.

'You say too much or too little, Brother. It is wrong to stir up someone's anxieties but not tell them sufficient in order to act to dispel that anxiety.'

'Ah, Fidelma, isn't there a saying that a silent mouth is most melodious? It is easier for me not to say anything and let the stars follow their courses rather than try to wrest their secrets from them.'

'You have vexed me, Brother Conchobar. Now I shall worry until my brother's safe return.'

'I am sorry that I have put this worry before you, Fidelma of Cashel. I pray that I am entirely wrong.'

'Time will tell us that, Brother.'

'By time is everything revealed,' agreed Conchobar quietly, quoting an ancient proverb.

He inclined his head in a gesture of farewell and turned to make his careful way from the battlements, his back bent, leaning on a thick blackthorn staff for his support. Fidelma stood staring after him with her sudden feeling of unease not dispelled. She had known old Brother Conchobar since her birth thirty years ago. In fact, he had assisted at her birth. He appeared to have dwelt at the ancient palace of Cashel for ever. He had served her father, King Failbe Fland mac Aedo, whom Fidelma could not really remember for he had died in the very year of her birth. He had also served her three cousins who had succeeded to the kingship in their turn. Now he served her own brother, Colgú, who had been proclaimed as King of Muman hardly a year previously. Brother Conchobar was considered one of the most learned of those who studied the heavens and made maps of the stars and their courses.

Fidelma knew enough of Conchobar to realise that one didn't take the old man's prognostications lightly.

She gazed up at the melancholy sky and shivered before turning down from the battlements into one of the many courtyards of the large palace complex which rose on the rock of limestone peak. Interspersed here and there were tiny courtyards and even smaller gardens. The entire network of buildings was surrounded by the high defensive walls.

Fidelma began to walk across the paved courtyard towards the large entrance of the royal chapel. The sound of children's playing caused her to glance up as she walked. She smiled as she saw some young boys using the chapel wall to play a game called *roth-chless*, the 'wheel-feat'. It had been a favourite game of her brother's when they were young because it was the one game that Colgú knew he could beat her at. It was a game that relied on the strength of the arm because it consisted of throwing a heavy, circular disc up a tall wall. Whoever managed to cast the disc up farthest was the winner. According to ancient legend, the great warrior Cúchullain hurled a disc up so high that it went up beyond the wall and roof of the building.

There was a scream of delight from the children as one of their number made a particularly good cast with the disc. A grizzled hostler passing near the children stopped to reprimand them.

'A silent mouth sounds sweetly,' he admonished, wagging his finger and using almost the same proverb that Brother Conchobar had just quoted to her. The servant turned and, observing Fidelma, saluted. Behind him, Fidelma saw a couple of the young boys pulling faces at his back but pretended that she had not observed them.

'Ah, my lady Fidelma, these young ones,' sighed the elderly servant, deferring to her royal status, as did everyone in Cashel. 'Truly, my lady, their noise pierces the tranquillity of the hour.'

'Yet they are merely children at play, Oslóir,' she returned gravely. Fidelma liked to know the names of all the servants at her brother's palace. 'A great Greek philosopher once said, "Play so that you may become serious". So let them play while they are young. There are plenty of years ahead of them in which to be serious.'

'Surely silence is the ideal state?' protested the hostler.

'That depends. Too much silence can be painful. There can be a surfeit in all things, even honey.'

Smiling at the children, she turned towards the doors of the royal chapel and was about to ascend the steps when one of the doors swung open and a young religieux in a brown woollen homespun habit emerged. He was a thickset young man whose abundance of curly brown hair was cut into the *corona spina*, the circular tonsure of St Peter of Rome. His dark brown eyes carried a humorous twinkle and were set in pleasant and almost handsome features.

'Eadulf!' Fidelma greeted him, 'I was just coming to find you.'

Brother Eadulf of Seaxmund's Ham, in the kingdom of the South Folk, had been sent as an emissary to the King of Cashel by no less a dignitary than Theodore, Archbishop of Canterbury. He grimaced pleasantly in salutation.

'I was expecting to find you at the services this morning, Fidelma.'

Fidelma grinned, one of her rare mischievous grins. 'Do I hear a criticism in your voice?'

'Surely one of the first duties of a religieuse is to attend the Sabbath morning service.' The Irish Church held to Saturday as the Sabbath day.

'Indeed, I attended lauds first thing this morning,' rejoined Fidelma waspishly. 'That was before first light when, so I was told, you were still sleeping.'

Eadulf flushed slightly.

Fidelma immediately felt contrite and reached out a hand to touch his sleeve.

'I should have warned you that on the feastday of Saint Ailbe, it is the custom of our house to attend lauds in order to give special thanks for his life. Besides that, my brother had to leave Cashel before first light to ride to the Well of Ara. We were early abroad.'

Eadulf was not mollified but he fell in step with Fidelma as they turned to walk back across the courtyard towards the entrance to the Great Hall of Cashel.

'Why is this feastday so special?' he asked, somewhat peeved. 'Everyone is giving praise for St Ailbe, though, I freely confess, I know nothing of his life nor work.'

'No reason why a stranger to this land would know about him,' observed Fidelma. 'He is our patron saint, the holy protector of the kingdom of Muman. This is the day when the Law of Ailbe is proclaimed to our people.'

'I see,' acknowledged Eadulf. 'I understand why this day is made special. Tell me, why he is regarded as the protector of Muman and what is this Law of Ailbe?'

They walked together through the palatial reception room, across the Great Hall of the palace building which, at this hour of the morning, was almost deserted. Only a few servants moved discreetly about, laying fires in the great hearth or cleaning the chamber, sweeping the paved stone floors with brushes of twigs.

'Ailbe was a man of Muman, born in the north-west of the kingdom in the household of Crónán, a chief of the people of Cliach.'

'Was he the son of this chief?'

'No. He was the son of a servant to the chief who had become pregnant and died giving birth. There is argument over who his father was. The chief was so enraged that his birth had killed a favourite servant that he would have smothered the child. The story goes that the baby was taken from Cliach and left to die in the wild but was found by an old female wolf who raised him.'

'Ah, I have heard many such stories,' observed Eadulf cynically.

'Indeed, you are right. We only know that when Ailbe grew to manhood he went abroad and converted to the New Faith in Rome and was baptised there. The Bishop of Rome gave him a present of a beautiful silver crucifix as a symbol of his office and sent him back to Ireland to become bishop to the Christians. This was even before the Blessed Patrick set his feet on our shores. My ancestor, the first Christian King of Muman, Oenghus mac Nad Froích, was converted to the Faith by Ailbe. And Ailbe and Patrick both took part in the baptismal ceremony of the King here on this very Rock of Cashel. King Oenghus then decreed that Cashel would henceforth be the primacy of Muman as well as continuing to be the royal capital and Ailbe would be first shepherd of the flock in the kingdom.'

They took a seat by a window in the Great Hall which overlooked the western end of the township below, giving an outlook across the plains to the distant south-western mountains. Eadulf stretched himself and found he had to quickly smother a yawn in case Fidelma might feel insulted. She did not notice for she was gazing towards the shimmering forests in the distant valley. Part of her mind was still thinking about old Brother Conchobar and his gloomy prediction. She wondered if it did relate to the safety of her brother, Colgú. It was no secret that he had gone to the Well of Ara, a ford on the River Ara, to meet the arch-enemy of the Kings of Cashel. The princes of the Uí Fidgente had been enemies to her family for as long as she could remember. True, Colgú had taken his personal bodyguard, but could harm really threaten him? She became aware that Eadulf was asking something.

'How is it, then, that he is called Ailbe of Imleach? Not Ailbe of Cashel? And what is this Law of Ailbe?'

Eadulf was always eager to pick up what information he could about the kingdom of Muman.

Fidelma brought her gaze back to him and smiled apologetically for her drifting.

'The Kings of Cashel accepted that only Ailbe held ecclesiastical authority in our kingdom. Armagh, which is in the northern Uí Néill kingdom of Ulaidh, is now trying to assert that it is the primacy of all Ireland. We, in Muman, maintain that our primacy is Imleach. That is what makes Ailbe important to us.'

'But you said that the primacy was Cashel,' Eadulf pointed out in confusion.

'It is said that as Ailbe grew old, an angel appeared to him and told him to follow to Imleach Iubhair, which is not too far distance from here, and there he would be shown the site of his resurrection. This was symbolic because Imleach was once the ancient capital of the kingdom before King Corc chose Cashel in pagan times. It takes its name from the sacred yew-tree which is the totem of our kingdom.'

Eadulf made a clicking sound with his tongue to express his disapproval of pagan symbolism. A convert to Christianity himself, he, like most converts, had become vehement in his new belief.

'Ailbe left Cashel and went to Imleach and built a great abbey there,' continued Fidelma. 'There was an ancient sacred well which he blessed and converted to God's use. He even blessed the sacred yew-tree. When Ailbe's abbey was set up there, a flourishing community sprang up. When Ailbe's work was done, the saintly man passed to heaven. His relics still remain at Imleach where he is buried. There is a legend . . .'

Fidelma paused, smiled and shrugged apologetically. If the truth were known she was really talking for the sake of keeping her thoughts occupied against the anxiety that kept gnawing in her mind for the safety of her brother at the Well of Ara.

'Go on,' pressed Eadulf, for he enjoyed the effortless way Fidelma recalled the legends of her people, making the ancient gods and heroes seem to come to life before his fascinated eyes.

Fidelma glanced across the valley again, towards the road which led across the great River Suir and then further across the valley where the road led towards the Well of Ara. There was no sign of any movement on the road. She turned her attention back to Eadulf.

'It is a fact not to be approved of, but many of our people believe, with an extraordinary faith, that should Ailbe's relics be stolen from us, there would be nothing to save this land from falling to our enemies. Ailbe's name in ancient legends was given to a hound which guarded the borders of the kingdom. Some say that Ailbe the saint was named after that mythical hound so that the people look to our saint as being the embodiment of the hound, always protecting our borders. If his relics were taken from Imleach, then the Eóghanacht dynasty would fall from Cashel; the kingdom of Muman would be rent in twain and there would be no peace in the land.'

Eadulf was clearly impressed by the legend.

'I had no idea that such beliefs were still held by your people,' he commented, with a slight shake of his head.

Fidelma grimaced wryly.

'I am not one to countenance such superstitions. But the people believe it so strongly that I would hate to put it to the test.'

She glanced up and caught sight of a movement at the edge of the distant forest. She focused carefully and then her features broke into a broad smile of happy relief.

'Look Eadulf! Here comes Colgú and the Prince of the Uí Fidgente with him.'

Chapter Three

Eadulf peered through the window, towards the expanse of green cultivated fields which lay between the outskirts of the town and the river some four miles or more away. Halfway along the road was a woodland and from its edge he could only just make out a column of riders emerging. He glanced quickly at Fidelma, silently admiring her eyesight, for he could, as yet, make out few details beyond the fact that they were horsemen. That she could recognise the approach of her brother was more than he was able to manage.

They watched in silence for a moment or two as the column moved along the road which led towards the town below the castle walls. Now Eadulf was able to pick out the brightly coloured banners of the King of Muman and his followers, together with banners which he did not recognise but presumed belonged to the Prince of the Uí Fidgente.

Fidelma suddenly grabbed his hand and pulled him up and away from the window.

'Let us go down to the town and watch their arrival, Eadulf. This is an exciting day for Muman.'

Eadulf smiled softly at her sudden bubbling enthusiasm and allowed himself to be pulled after her across the Great Hall.

'I confess, I do not understand this. Why is the arrival of the Uí Fidgente prince so important?' he asked as he followed her into the courtyard of the palace.

Fidelma, assured of his following her, dropped her hand and assumed the more sober gait of a religieuse.

'The Uí Fidgente are one of the major clans of Muman dwelling west beyond the River Maigne. Their chieftains have often refused to pay tribute to the Eóghanacht of Cashel, refusing even to recognise them as Kings of Muman. Indeed, they claim a right to the kingship of Muman by the argument that their princes descend from our common ancestor Eóghan Mór.'

She conducted the way quickly across the courtyard, passing the chapel, and through the main gates. The warriors on sentinel duty there smiled and saluted her. The sister of Colgú was well respected among her own people. Eadulf walked easily beside her.

'Is their claim true?' he asked.

Fidelma pouted. She was proud when it came to her family which, Eadulf knew from experience, did not make her unusual from most of the Irish nobility he had encountered. Each family employed a professional genealogist to ensure that the generations and their relationship with one another was clearly and accurately recorded. Under the Brehon Law of succession which delineated who should succeed by means of the approval of an electoral college made up of specified generations of the family, called the *derbfhine*, it was important to know the generations and their relationships to one another.

'Prince Donennach, who arrives with my brother today, claims that he is the twelfth generation in male line from Eóghan Mór whom we look to as the founder of our house.'

Eadulf, missing the subtle sarcastic tone, shook his head in amazement as he wondered at the ease with which the Irish nobility knew the status of their relatives.

'So this Prince Donennach descends from a junior branch of your family?' he asked.

'If the Uí Fidgente genealogists are truthful,' Fidelma replied with emphasis. 'Even so, junior only in terms of the decisions of the *derbfhine* which appoint the kings.'

Eadulf sighed deeply.

'It is a concept that I still find hard to understand. Among the Saxons it is always the eldest male child of the senior line of the family, the first born male, for good or ill, who inherits.'

Fidelma was disapproving.

'Exactly. Good or ill. And when that first born male proves an unsuitable choice, is crippled in mind, or rules with ill-counsel, your Saxon family have him murdered. At least our system appoints the man who is best fitted for the task, whether eldest son, uncle, brother, cousin or youngest son.'

'And if he proves an ill-governing king,' Eadulf was stung to reply, 'don't you also have him killed?'

'No need,' rejoined Fidelma with a shrug. 'The *derbfhine* of the family meet and dismiss him from office and appoint another more suitable. Under the law, he is allowed to go away unharmed.'

'Doesn't he then incite rebellion among his followers?'

'He knows the law as do any potential followers and they know that they would be regarded as usurpers for all time.'

'But men are men. It must happen.'

Fidelma's face was serious. She inclined her head in agreement.

'Indeed, it does happen – sometimes! That is why this reconciliation with the Uí Fidgente is so important. They have been constantly in rebellion against Cashel.'

'Why so?'

'Their justification is the very reasons that we are discussing. Our family, the family of Colgú and my father Faílbe Fland, trace our descent from Conall Corc, who was son of Luigthech, son of Ailill Flann Bec, the grandson of Eóghan Mór, the founder of our house.'

'I will accept your word for that,' smiled Eadulf. 'These names are beyond me.'

Fidelma was patient.

'The Uí Fidgente line claim descent from Fiachu Fidgennid, son of Maine Muincháin, another son of Ailill Flann Bec, grandson of Eóghan Mór. *If* their genealogists are truthful, as I say.' She pulled a wry expression. 'Our genealogists think that their pedigrees were forged in order that they might have a claim on the kingship of Cashel. But, if this be a happy day, we shall not argue with them.'

Eadulf struggled to follow her.

'I think I understand what you are saying. The split between your family and these Uí Fidgente began between two brothers, Luigthech, the eldest, and Maine Muncháin, the youngest.'

Fidelma smiled sympathetically but shook her head.

'If their genealogists are correct, Maine Muncháin, the progenitor of the Uí Fidgente, was the eldest son of Ailill Flann Bec. Our ancestor Luigthech was his second son.'

Eadulf threw up his arms in despair.

'It is hard enough to follow your Irish names but as to your precedents of generations . . . You are now saying that the Uí Fidgente have a better claim over the kingship because they descend from the eldest son?'

Fidelma was annoyed at his lack of understanding.

'You ought to appreciate our laws of kingship succession by now, Eadulf. It is a simple enough matter. Maine Muncháin's line was deemed, by the *derbfhine* of the family, to be unsuitable to be kingship material.'

'I still find it hard to follow,' admitted Eadulf. 'But from what you say, the Uí Fidgente descend from a senior line, in primogeniture terms, and this makes them reluctant to accept your family's authority at Cashel?'

'Senior line or not, your primogeniture does not enter into our law system,' Fidelma pointed out. 'And this happened nearly ten generations ago. So long ago that our genealogists, as I say, maintain that the Uí Fidgente are not really Eóghanacht at all but descend from the Dáirine.'

Eadulf raised his eyes to the heavens.

'And just who are the Dáirine?' he groaned in despair.

'An ancient people, who nearly a thousand years ago were said to have shared the kingship of Muman with the Eóghanacht. There is still a clan called the Corco Loígde to the west who claim they are descended from the ancient Dáirine.'

'Well, my simple brain has taken in enough genealogy and too many names.'

Fidelma chuckled softly at the comic look of woe on his face but her eyes remained serious.

'Yet it is important that you should know the general politics of this kingdom, Eadulf. You will recall how last winter we came across a plot by the Uí Fidgente to foment rebellion here and how my brother had to lead an army to face them in battle at Cnoc Áine? That was scarcely nine months ago.'

'I do remember the events. How can I forget them? Was I not captured by the conspirators at that time? But wasn't the ruler of the Uí Fidgente slain in battle?'

'He was. Now his cousin Donennach is Prince of the Uí Fidgente and among his first actions was to send messengers to my brother and seek to negotiate a treaty with him. Donennach comes to Cashel to negotiate the peace. This is the first peace between the Uí Fidgente and Cashel in many centuries. That is why today is so important.'

They had walked from the gates of the fortress down the steep path which led to the bottom of the Rock of Cashel and followed the road round until it entered the outskirts of the market town below. The town itself lay less than a quarter of a mile from the great Rock of Cashel.

They found the people of the town were already gathering to witness the entry of their King with the Prince of the Uí Fidgente and his retinue. The column of riders had arrived at the western gateway to the town as Fidelma and Eadulf reached the eastern gate to take up their positions with a group standing to one side of the broad market square.

A group of seven warriors on horseback led the column. Then came Colgú's standard bearer. The fluttering blue silk bore the golden royal stag of the Eóghanacht of Cashel. Following the standard, the King of Muman sat his horse well. He was a tall man with red, burnished hair. Not for the first time Eadulf was able to mentally remark on the similarity of facial features between him and his sister. There was no mistaking that Fidelma and Colgú were related.

Next came another standard bearer. The banner he held aloft was a fluttering white silk on which there was a mystical red boar in the centre. Eadulf presumed this was the standard of the Uí Fidgente Prince. Behind this standard rode a young man with thickly set features which were dark but as handsome as the red-haired King of Muman. In spite of claims to a common ancestry there was nothing that reminded Eadulf of any form of relationship between the Prince of the Uí Fidgente and the King of Muman.

The leading horsemen were followed by several warriors, many bearing the emblems of the Order of the Golden Chain, the élite bodyguards of the Eóghanacht kings. At the head of these warriors rode a young man, not much younger than Colgú himself. He bore a vague similarity to Colgú, though his features seemed a little coarser, and his hair was black, even as the Prince of the Uí Fidgente. He sat on his horse with ease but there was a pride to his bearing. His dress spoke of conceit in his appearance as well. He wore a long blue dyed woollen cloak which was fastened at the shoulder by a glittering brooch. It was silver and in the shape of a solar emblem, its five radiating arms marked at each end by a small red garnet stone.

Donndubháin, as Eadulf knew well, was the *tanist* or heir-apparent of the King of Cashel. He was cousin to Colgú and Fidelma.

There was no doubting the pleasure of the people at the sight of the company as they began to cheer and applaud their arrival. For most the sight of the King of Cashel and the Prince of the Uí Fidgente riding together meant the end of the centuries of feuds and bloodshed; the start of a new era of peace and prosperity for all the people of Muman.

Colgú was relaxed and acknowledged the cheers with a wave of his hand although Donennach sat rigidly and it seemed that he was extremely nervous. His dark eyes flickered from side to side as if watching warily for signs of hostility. Only now and then did a quick smile cross his features as he inclined his head stiffly, from the neck only, to acknowledge the applause of the demonstrative crowd.

The horsemen were crossing the market square to approach the path which led upwards to the rocky outcrop of the seat of the Cashel kings. Even Donennach of the Uí Fidgente's eyes widened a little as he gazed upwards to the dominating fortress and palace of Cashel.

Donndubháin raised his arm as if to signal the column of warriors to swing round in order to approach the fortress road.

Fidelma had pushed her way forward to the edge of the crowd, followed by the anxious Eadulf, meaning to greet her brother.

Colgú caught sight of her, his face splitting into a grin of urchin-like quality which was so like Fidelma at moments of intense amusement.

Colgú drew rein on his horse and leant forward abruptly to greet his sister.

It was that action which saved his life.

The arrow impacted into his upper arm with a curious thud, causing him to cry out in pain and shock. Had he not halted his horse and bent down, the arrow would have impacted in a more mortal target.

In the shock of the moment, everyone seemed to stand as if turned into stone. It seemed a long time but it was less than a couple of seconds before another cry of pain rang out. Donennach, the Prince of the Uí Fidgente, was swaying in his saddle, a second arrow sticking in his thigh. In horror, Eadulf watched him sway and then topple from his horse into the dust of the road.

The impact of the falling body caused everyone to burst into a frenzy of activity and commotion.

One of the Uí Fidgente warriors drew forth his sword with a cry of 'Assassins!' and urged his mount forward towards a cluster of buildings a short distance away across the square. A moment later, some of his men were following him while others hurried to their fallen Prince and stood over him with drawn swords as if expecting an assault on him.

Eadulf saw Donndubháin, Colgú's heir-apparent, also with drawn sword, go racing after the Uí Fidgente warriors.

Fidelma was among the first to recover her wits. Her mind was racing. Two arrows had been shot at her brother and his guest and both, miraculously had missed. Obviously, the Uí Fidgente warrior had seen the path of their flight and pinpointed the buildings as hiding the bowman who wished to strike down the King of Cashel and the Prince of the Uí Fidgente. Well, there was no time to consider that now. Donndubháin had also gone in chase of the assassins.

'See to Donennach,' she cried to Eadulf, who was already pushing his way through the Prince's reluctant bodyguard. She turned to where her brother was still sitting astride his horse, a little in shock, clutching at the arrow which was embedded in his arm.

'Get down, brother,' she urged quietly, 'unless you want to continue to make yourself a target.'

She reached forward and helped him dismount, which he did, trying not to groan aloud from the pain of his wound.

'Is Donennach hurt badly?' he asked between clenched teeth. He still held one hand clutching at his blood-soaked, pain-racked arm.

'Eadulf is looking after him. Now sit down on that stone while I remove the arrow from your arm.'

Almost reluctantly her brother sat down. By this time, two of Colgú's men, including Capa, the captain of the bodyguard, had hurried forward but their drawn swords were superfluous. People were crowding round their King with a mixture of advice and questions. Fidelma waved them back impatiently.

'Is there a physician among you?' she demanded, having examined the wound and realised that the arrow head went deep. She was afraid to pry it loose for fear of tearing the muscle and creating more damage.

There was a muttering and shaking of heads.

Reluctantly, she bent down and hesitantly touched the shaft. It would take too long to send someone to find and bring old Conchobar hither.

'Hold on, Fidelma,' cried Eadulf, pushing his way back through the crowd.

Fidelma almost sighed with relief for she knew that Eadulf had trained in the art of medicine at the great medical school of Tuaim Brecain.

'How is Donennach?' Colgú greeted him, his face grey with pain as he struggled to remain in control.

'Concentrate on yourself for the time being, brother,' admonished Fidelma.

Colgú's features were set grimly.

'A good host should see to his guest first.'

'It is a bad wound,' Eadulf admitted, bending forward to examine where the arrow head had embedded itself in Colgú's arm. 'Donennach's wound, I mean, though your own is no light scratch. I have ordered a litter be constructed so that we can carry Prince Donennach up to the palace where we may attend him better than here in the dust of the road. I suspect the arrow has entered Donennach's thigh at a bad angle. But he was lucky . . . as, indeed, you are.'

'Can you remove this arrow from my arm?' pressed Colgú.

Eadulf had been examining it closely. The Saxon smiled grimly. 'I can but it will hurt. I would prefer to wait until we can take you back to the palace.'

The King of Muman sniffed disdainfully.

'Do it here and now in order that my people may see that the wound is no great one and that an Eóghanacht King can bear pain.'

Eadulf turned to one of the crowd. 'Whose house is nearest in which there is a glowing fire?'

'The blacksmith's stands across the street there, Brother Saxon,' replied an old woman, pointing.

'Give me a few moments, Colgú,' Eadulf said, turning and making his way to the smith's forge. The smith himself was one of the crowd, having left his forge to see what the commotion was about. He now accompanied Eadulf with interest. Eadulf took out his knife. The smith looked on in surprise as the Saxon monk turned the knife for a while in the glowing coals before returning to Colgú's side.

Colgú's jaw was set and there were beads of sweat on his forehead. 'Do it as quickly as you can, Eadulf.'

The Saxon monk nodded curtly.

'Hold his arm, Fidelma,' he instructed quietly. Then he bent forward and taking the shaft of the arrow, he eased it with the tip of the knife and pulled quickly. Colgú gave a grunt and his shoulders sagged as if he were going to fall. But he did not do so. His jaw clenched so hard that they could hear his teeth grinding. Eadulf took a clean linen cloth, which someone offered, and bound the arm tightly.

'It will do until we get back to the fortress.' There was satisfaction in his voice. 'I need to treat the wound with herbs to prevent infection.' He added quietly to Fidelma, 'Luckily the tip of the arrow made a clean entry and exit.'

Fidelma took the arrow from him and examined it with a frown. Then she thrust it into her waist cord and turned to help her brother.

The young flush-faced heir-apparent pushed his way back through the crowd. He was now on foot. He examined Colgú, standing supported by Fidelma, with an anxious glance.

'Is the wound bad?'

'Bad enough,' replied Eadulf on the King's behalf, 'but he will survive.'

Donndubháin exhaled slowly.

'The assassins have been run to earth by Prince Donennach's men.'

'They can be dealt with once we have removed my brother back to the palace together with the Prince of the Uí Fidgente,' Fidelma said sharply. 'Here, help me with him.'

Eadulf had turned away to where a litter had been constructed for the wounded Prince of the Uí Fidgente. The man lay in pain on it. Eadulf had placed a tourniquet around the top of the thigh. He checked the litter and then signalled to the Uí Fidgente warriors to lift it carefully and follow him and the group escorting Colgú up the path to the palace.

They had not even began to proceed before there came the sound of horses and an outcry.

The mounted members of Donennach's bodyguard came riding back across the square. Behind their horses, dragging along the ground, were two limp forms, their wrists secured by rope to the pommel of the leading horseman.

Fidelma had spotted them and turned from her brother with an angry cry on her lips to criticise such barbarity. To see any man, even a would-be assassin, so ill-treated, was a cause of anger. But the protest died away on her lips as the riders halted. Even a cursory glance at the blood-stained bodies showed her that both men were already dead.

The leading warrior, a man with a bland oval face and narrowed eyes, swung off his horse and strode to the litter of his Prince. He saluted swiftly with the blood still staining his sword.

'My lord, I think you need to look at these men,' he said harshly.

'Can't you see that we are carrying your Prince to the palace to have his wound tended?' demanded Eadulf angrily. 'Do not bother us with this matter until the more urgent task is complete.'

'Hold your tongue, foreigner,' snapped the warrior haughtily, 'when I am speaking to my Prince.'

Colgú, who had halted a short distance away, turned back, leaning on Donndubháin, his face distorting in annoyance now as well as pain.

'Do not presume to give orders on the slopes of Cashel, where I rule!' he grunted through clenched teeth.

The Uí Fidgente warrior did not even blink. He deliberately kept his gaze on the pale, pain-racked face of Donennach of the Uí Fidgente, laying on the litter before him.

'My lord, the matter is urgent.'

Donennach raised himself on one elbow, in a pain equally shared with his host.

'What is it that you wish me so urgently to see, Gionga?'

The warrior named Gionga waved to one of his men, who had cut loose the two bodies. He dragged one over to the side of the litter.

'These are the dogs who shot at you, my lord. Observe this one.'

He held the man's head up by the hair.

Donennach leaned forward from the litter. There was a tightness at the corners of his mouth. 'I do not recognise him,' he grunted.

'Nor should you, lord,' replied Gionga. 'But perhaps you will recognise the device that he wears about his neck.'

Donennach looked hard and then he pursed his lips in a soundless whistle.

'Colgú, what does this mean?' he demanded, glancing to where Donndubháin had helped the King of Muman move forward to view the body.

Painfully Colgú peered at the dead man. Fidelma and Eadulf stood with him. No one recognised the dead man but it was obvious what the cause of the concern was.

The man was wearing the collar and emblem of the Order of the Golden Chain, the élite bodyguard of the Kings of Cashel.

Donennach's harsh tones suddenly rang out in agitation. 'This is a strange hospitality which you observe, Colgú of Cashel. Your élite warriors have shot me. They have tried to kill me!'

Chapter Four

There was a long silence after the Prince of the Uí Fidgente had made his accusation.

It was Fidelma who finally broke the menacing stillness by inclining her head towards her brother who was standing with his face barely masking the pain of his wound.

'If Colgú's warriors shot and tried to kill you, Donennach, then they also tried to shoot down the King of Cashel.'

Donennach's keen dark eyes examined her searchingly.

It was his chief warrior, Gionga, who articulated his unasked question.

'Who are you, woman, who dares to speak in the presence of princes?' His voice was still arrogant.

Colgú answered quietly although his voice was tight in pain. 'It is my sister, Fidelma, who speaks and has more right to do so than any in this company for she is a *dálaigh* of the courts as well as a religieuse. She is qualified to the degree of *anruth*.'

Gionga's eyes widened visibly, realising that only an *ollamh*, the highest degree ever bestowed by the secular and ecclesiastical colleges of Ireland, stood above an *anruth*.

Donennach was not so outwardly impressed. Instead his eyes narrowed slightly.

'So? You are Fidelma of Cashel? Sister Fidelma? Your reputation is known throughout the lands of the Uí Fidgente.'

Fidelma returned his scrutiny with a grim smile.

'Yes; I have been in the land of the Uí Fidgente – once. I was invited . . . to a poisoning there.'

She made no further elaboration, knowing that Donennach knew well enough the details of the story.

'My sister is right,' intervened Colgú, coming back to the original point. 'Any charge that my hand is behind this evil act is false!'

Eadulf decided to take a hand again for he was worried about the wounds of the two men.

'This is no time to discuss the matter. Both of you need your wounds properly tended before infection sets in. Let us leave this discussion until a more appropriate time.'

Colgú bit his lip to control a spasm of pain in his arm. 'Is it agreed, Donennach?' he asked.

'It is agreed.'

'I will take matters in hand, brother,' Fidelma said firmly, 'while Eadulf attends to you.'

Gionga took a step forward, the annoyance showing on his face, but before he could speak Donennach raised a hand.

'You may stay with Sister Fidelma, Gionga,' he instructed softly, 'and help her with this matter.'

There seemed an unnecessary emphasis on the word 'help'. Gionga bowed his head and stepped back.

The bearers carrying the litter lifted the Prince of the Uí Fidgente and followed Colgú, helped by Donndubháin, up the steep path towards the royal palace. Eadulf was fussing at Colgú's side.

Fidelma stood for a moment, hands folded demurely in front of her. Her bright eyes held a flickering fire which anyone who knew her would realise indicated a dangerous mood. Outwardly her features were composed.

'Well, Gionga?' she asked quietly.

Gionga shifted his weight from one leg to another and looked uncomfortable. 'Well?' he challenged in turn.

'Shall we let the corpses of these two men be taken to our apothecary? We can examine them later and in better circumstances.'

'Why not examine them now?' demanded the Uí Fidgente warrior, a trifle truculently, but he was cognizant of her rank and appeared to realise that he must keep his arrogance in check.

'Because now I want you to show me where and how you came on them and why you had to slay them instead of taking them captive that we might question their motives.'

Her tone was even and there was not trace of a rebuke in it. However, Gionga grew red in the face and seemed inclined to refuse. Then he shrugged. He turned and signalled to two of his men to come forward.

Someone called to them and Donndubháin came trotting back down the hill. He looked worried.

'Colgú suggested that I might be of more help here,' he explained, his facial expression attempting to imply that Colgú was not happy to leave his sister in the company of the Uí Fidgente warrior. 'Capa and Eadulf are attending him.'

Fidelma smiled appreciatively. 'Excellent. Gionga's men are taking these bodies to the Conchobar's apothecary. Have you a man to guide them?'

Donndubháin called to a passing warrior.

'Escort the men of the Uí Fidgente with these bodies to . . .' He raised his eyebrows interrogatively to Fidelma.

'The apothecary of Brother Conchobar. Tell Conchobar to await my instructions. I wish to examine the bodies myself.'

The warrior saluted and motioned to the Uí Fidgente warriors, carrying the two bodies, to follow him.

'Now, we will start from the spot where Colgú and Donennach were shot,' Fidelma declared.

Gionga said nothing but he and Donndubháin followed Fidelma back to the square. The townsfolk of Cashel had not yet dispersed and many were huddled in groups whispering among themselves. Some cast furtive looks at the Uí Fidgente warrior. Fidelma could sense the dislike in their eyes. Generations of war and raiding were not going to be wiped from their memory as quickly as she had previously thought.

They reached the spot where the arrows had struck both Colgú and Donennach. Gionga pointed across the market square to a cluster of buildings on the far side.

'When the first arrow struck, I looked round to see where it had come from. I saw a figure on the roof of that building there.'

The building he indicated was fifty metres away on the far side of the market square. It had a flat roof.

'It was as I saw him discharging a second arrow that I shouted but it was too late to warn Donennach.'

'I see,' mused Fidelma. 'That was when you spurred your horse across towards the building?'

'It was. A couple of my warriors came close after me. By the time we reached the building, the archer had jumped down, still with his bow in his hand. There was another man there with a sword. I cut them both down before they could use their weapons against us.'

Fidelma turned to Donndubháin.

'As I recall, you followed close behind, cousin. Does this accord with what you saw?'

The heir-apparent shrugged. 'More or less.'

'That is an imprecise answer,' remarked Fidelma quietly.

'What I mean to say was that I saw the archer jump down and join his companion but I did not see them raise their weapons. They seemed to stand waiting for the warriors to come up to them.'

Gionga snorted in disgust.

'You mean, for us to come closer so that they could be sure of their targets?' he sneered.

Fidelma began to walk towards the building without comment.

'Let us see what we might find there.'

Donndubháin glanced at her, not understanding.

'What would we find there? The assassins were both killed and the bodies removed. What can you find?'

Fidelma did not bother to answer him.

The building which Gionga and Donndubháin had identified was a low, single-storey building with a flat roof. It was a wooden structure. It looked more like a stable with two large doors at the front and a small side door. Fidelma, who had been born and spent her early years in Cashel, tried hard to remember what the building was. It was not a stable so far as she could recall but some sort of store house.

She halted and examined it with a careful gaze.

The doors and windows were shut up and there were no signs of life.

'Donndubháin, do you know what building this is?'

The *tanist* tugged thoughtfully at his lower lip.

'It is one of the store houses of Samradán the merchant. I think he uses it for wheat storage.'

'Where is Samradán?'

Her cousin shrugged indifferently.

Fidelma tapped her foot impatiently.

'Make it your task to find him and bring him to me.'

'Now?' asked Donndubháin, startled.

'Now,' affirmed Fidelma.

The heir-apparent of Cashel left to find the merchant, for even a Prince had to obey a *dálaigh* of the courts, aside from the fact that Fidelma was sister to the King. Fidelma walked around the wooden building, examining it. There was a small side door. She tried it and found it was locked. In fact, everything appeared shuttered and secured although, at the back of the building, she noticed a ladder leaning against the wall which had given access to the roof.

'This was where I saw the assassins,' Gionga pointed out.

Fidelma glanced at him quickly. 'Yet you could not have seen this from where you were crossing towards the front of the building.'

'No. I saw only the archer, the man holding his bow. He stood on the roof and then he disappeared towards the back of it. I rode alongside the building just as the two men, one with the bow, the other with a drawn sword, emerged from behind the building.'

'And at what spot did you strike them down?'

Gionga gestured with his hand.

The pools of blood had not dried up on the ground. They were sited at the back of the building but in view of anyone approaching from the square.

Fidelma climbed the ladder onto the flat roof. Towards the front of the roof, behind a small wooden parapet, lay two arrows. They had not been hastily discarded for they were placed carefully. Perhaps the bowman had put them there ready to enable him to shoot several times with rapidity. Fidelma picked them up and examined the markings on them. She compared them with the arrow tucked into her corded belt, the one Eadulf had taken from Colgú's arm. Her mouth compressed grimly. She recognised the markings on them.

Gionga had joined her and was gazing at her moodily. 'What have you found?'

'Just arrows,' Fidelma said quickly.

'Fidelma!'

Fidelma peered over the parapet to where Donndubháin was standing below.

'Have you found Samradán?'

'I am told he is not in Cashel today. He is at Imleach trading goods with the abbey there.'

'Presumably this Samradán does not live here?'

Donndubháin gestured with his arm. 'From the roof where you are you might see his house. It is the sixth house along the main street there. I know the man and have traded with him.' His hand went absently to the silver brooch at his shoulder. 'I am sure he cannot be involved in this matter.'

Fidelma glanced along the street to the house which the *tanist* had indicated.

'Well, it does not need answers from him to see what happened,' Gionga cut in. 'The assassins saw that this flat roof offered a strategic point from which to shoot at Donennach. They realised it was a store house; found a ladder and climbed up to await the arrival of my Prince. They thought they could get away in the confusion.'

He turned to look at the land at the back of the building.

'They could easily have escaped into the copse behind. Why–' his face lightened – 'I will wager that is where we will find their horses tethered, waiting.'

He made to leave as if to prove his suggestion.

'One moment.' Fidelma stayed him with a quiet command.

She was examining the distance between the roof and the spot where Colgú and Donennach had been struck Her eyes narrowed.

'Well, I will tell you one thing about our archer,' she said grimly.

Gionga frowned but did not say anything.

'He was not a good archer.'

'Why so?' asked the Uí Fidgente warrior, reluctantly.

'Because from this point and distance it would have been hard to have missed his target twice in succession. He could well have missed the first time but certainly not the second time when the target was stationary.'

She stood up and, taking the arrows with her, she went down the ladder with Gionga following. Her cousin was waiting for them at the bottom.

'Did you hear Gionga's suggestion about horses?' she asked.

'I did,' Donndubháin affirmed non-committally. Fidelma received the impression that he did not think much of Gionga's ideas.

They moved towards the small copse of trees. There was no sign of any horses tethered.

'Perhaps they had another accomplice?' Gionga hazarded, trying to hide his disappointment. 'He saw his companions struck down and fled, taking the horses with him.'

'Perhaps,' agreed Fidelma, her eyes examining the track on the far side of the copse. There were too many signs of horses and wagons there to draw any firm conclusions.

Gionga stood scowling about him as if hoping to see the horses suddenly emerge from thin air.

'What now?' asked Donndubháin, hiding his satisfaction that the Uí Fidgente warrior had been proved wrong.

'Now,' sighed Fidelma, 'we will go to Brother Conchobar's apothecary and examine the bodies of these assassins.'

The elderly Brother Conchobar was waiting for them at the door. He stood aside as Fidelma approached with Donndubháin and Gionga behind her.

'I was expecting you, Fidelma.' He grimaced wryly. 'And didn't I warn you that no good would come of this day?'

Overhearing this, Gionga snapped: 'What do you mean by that, you old goat? Are you saying that you had prior warning of this deed?'

Donndubháin reached out and put a warning hand on Gionga's arm, for the warrior had seized the old man roughly by his shoulder.

'Leave him alone. He is an old man and a faithful servant of Cashel,' he said sharply.

'He does not deserve to be treated thus,' added Fidelma. 'He saw evil in the patterns of the stars, that is all.'

Gionga dropped his hand in disgust. 'An astrologer?' He exploded a small breath against half-open lips in an expression matching the sneer in his voice.

The old monk readjusted his crumpled clothing with grave dignity.

'Have the two bodies been brought safely to you?' asked Fidelma.

'I have removed their clothing and laid them on the table but, as you instructed, I have not touched either of them.'

'When we are finished, if we have not identified them, you may wash the bodies and wrap them in shrouds but where you will measure their graves I know not.'

'There is always a space somewhere in the earth even for sinners,' replied Conchobar, gravely. 'However, the days of their lamentation will not be long.'

Among the people of Éireann, the funeral obsequies often included twelve days and nights of mourning and weeping over the body which were called *laithi na caoinnti* – the days of lamentation – before which the bodies were laid in their graves.

Inside the apothecary there stood a large broad plank table which was more than adequate to take the two bodies of the slain men. Indeed, this was not the first time that the table was used by Conchobar for laying out bodies as he was often called upon to perform the duties of mortician. The corpses lay side by side, naked except, for modesty's sake, where the old monk had lain a strip of linen to mask their genitalia.

Fidelma went to stand at the foot of the table, her hands folded before her; her eyes were narrowed slightly and they missed nothing.

The first thing that she noticed, almost in grotesque amusement, was that one man was tall, thin and balding although his fair hair was worn long at the back as if to compensate for this fact, while the second man was short, of ample girth with a mass of curly, unruly greying hair. Side by side, their physical differences were almost comical. Only the fact that they were cadavers, the wounds of Gionga's sword marking how they met their deaths, turned the comical into the grotesque.

'Which of these two was the archer?' Fidelma asked softly.

'The bald one,' answered Gionga at once. 'The other was the accomplice.'

'Where are the weapons that they carried?'

It was Conchobar who retrieved the bow and quiver, which contained a few arrows, and a sword from a corner of the room.

'The warriors who carried the corpses here brought these things with the bodies,' the old monk explained.

Fidelma gestured for the old man to lay the weapons aside. 'I will examine them in a moment . . .'

'One moment!' Gionga ignored her. 'Bring the quiver of arrows here.'

Brother Conchobar glanced at Fidelma but she made no protest. She knew what Gionga had spotted on the roof of the warehouse and she realised that it was wise not to delay the point he was inevitably going to make. The apothecary held out the quiver to Gionga. The tall warrior selected an arrow at random and drew it out, holding it out before their gaze.

'What would you say is the provenance of this arrow, *tanist* of Cashel?' Gionga asked with a feigned expression of innocence.

Donndubháin took the arrow and began to examine it carefully.

'You know well enough, Gionga,' interrupted Fidelma, for she was also versed in such matters.

'I do?'

Donndubháin looked unhappy.

'The flights bear the markings of our cousin's people, the Eóghanacht of Cnoc Áine.'

'Exactly,' sighed Gionga softly. 'All the arrows in the assassin's quiver bear the markings of the fletchers of Cnoc Áine.'

'Has that some meaning? After all–' Fidelma turned innocent eyes on the warrior – 'arrows are easily acquired.' She drew out a small knife from her *marsupium*. 'This knife was made in Rome. I bought it when I was on a pilgrimage there. It does not make me a Roman.'

Gionga flushed in annoyance and rammed the arrow back in the quiver.

'Do not try to be clever, sister of Colgú. The provenance of the arrows is clear. And will be borne in mind when I report to my Prince.'

Donndubháin flushed at the direct insult to his cousin. 'There is only one *dálaigh* among us, Gionga, and she will make the report,' he snapped.

Gionga merely showed his teeth in a sneer.

Fidelma ignored him and took the quiver and examined it. Apart from the markings on the flights of the arrows there was no other means of identifying it from a hundred and one other such quivers. She gestured for Conchobar to show her the bow. It was of good, sturdy workmanship and with no other distinguishing marks. Then she turned to the sword. It was of poor quality, rusting around its joints and not even sharpened. The handle was strangely ornamented with the carved teeth of animals. Fidelma had seen the style of sword before – it was called a *claideb dét* and, so far as she knew, only one area in Éireann produced such decoration on their swords. She tried to recall where it was but could not.

'There, Gionga,' she said, at last, 'we have examined these weapons. Are you satisfied that we have done so?'

'In that we can now identify the origin of the arrows – yes!' replied the warrior.

The door opened abruptly and Brother Eadulf entered the apothecary. He halted apologetically on the threshold.

'I heard that you were about to examine the bodies,' he said, a trifle breathlessly. He had obviously been hurrying.

Fidelma turned to him anxiously. 'How is my brother . . . and Prince Donennach?' she demanded.

'Comfortable. There is no danger but they will be sore and irritable for a few days. Do not worry, their wounds are tended and they are being nursed in good hands.'

Fidelma relaxed and smiled. 'Then you are just in time, Eadulf. I may need your eyes.'

Gionga glowered in annoyance. 'This foreigner has no business here,' he protested.

'This *foreigner*,' Fidelma replied in measured tones, 'is the guest of my brother and has been trained in the physician's art at Tuaim Brecain. He has probably kept your Prince out of harm's way by his medical skills. Also, we may need his expert eye in the observation of these bodies.'

Gionga clenched his jaw in an expression of disapproval but made no further protest.

'Come forward, Eadulf, and tell me what you see,' Fidelma invited.

Eadulf moved to the table. 'Two men, one short, one tall. The tall one . . .' Eadulf bent carefully over the body, examining it minutely. 'The tall one died from a single wound. By the look of it, it was a sword thrust into the heart.'

Gionga chuckled sarcastically. 'I could have told you that for mine was the hand that did it.'

Eadulf ignored him. 'The second man, the short one, died from three blows. He had his back turned to his assailant when they were delivered. There is a cut in the neck that is a dire wound. A stab under the shoulder-blade which I do not think was mortal but the back of his skull has been smashed in, perhaps with the hilt of a sword. I would say that this man was running away when he was cut down by someone who was in a position above him. Perhaps someone on horseback.'

Fidelma allowed her penetrating gaze to linger on the Uí Fidgente warrior. The silence was an accusation. Gionga thrust out his chin defensively.

'It matters not how your enemy is slain, so long as he is rendered a threat no longer.'

'I thought that you said this man threatened you with his sword?' Fidelma asked quietly.

'At first,' snapped Gionga. 'Then when I cut down his companion he turned and ran.'

'And you could not capture him?' Fidelma's voice was sharp. 'You had to kill him, in spite of the fact that he could have given us invaluable information about this deed?'

Gionga shuffled his feet. 'Such considerations do not enter one's mind in the act of combat. The man was a menace and I eliminated that threat.'

'A threat!' repeated Fidelma softly. 'He looks like an elderly man and his age and corpulence would have combined to make it easy for a young warrior, such as yourself, to disarm him. Anyway, I would remember this, Gionga of the Uí Fidgente: when a *dálaigh* asks you a question, it is the truth that they seek, not a lie to justify an action.'

Gionga stared back aggressively but did not say anything.

When Fidelma returned her attention to the cadavers, she found Eadulf bending over the head of the shorter corpse. There was an expression of amazement on his face.

'What is it?' she demanded.

Eadulf did not say anything but merely beckoned her to his side.

Gionga and Donndubháin followed curiously.

Eadulf had lifted the head slightly so that they could see the crown. There was a lot of dried blood on it where Gionga had smashed the back of the skull with the blow from his sword hilt.

Fidelma's eyes widened.

'What is it?' demanded Gionga. 'I see nothing except the wound I made. I freely admit that I made it. So what?'

Fidelma spoke very quietly. 'What Brother Eadulf is pointing out, Gionga, is that you will see there is a difference in the growth of the hair on this man's crown to the hair surrounding the crown. As you will see, the hair surrounding the crown is thick and curly. There is a circle on the crown in which the hair is barely more than half an inch to an inch in length.'

Gionga still could not understand what it meant.

Realisation reached Donndubháin first. 'Does this mean that the man was in holy orders until recently?'

'What?' Gionga was startled. He peered forward as if to verify the fact that he had missed.

'The *corona spina* of the Roman following,' observed Eadulf who wore the same tonsure.

'Are you saying that this man was a foreigner?' demanded Gionga of Eadulf.

Fidelma closed her eyes momentarily. 'There are plenty of religious within the five kingdoms who have forsaken the tonsure of St John for the tonsure of St Peter,' she explained. 'The tonsure tells us nothing more than the fact that he is . . . or was . . . a member of the religious.'

'We know also that he wore his tonsure until about two weeks ago. I would say that it has taken that long for the hair to grow thus,' Eadulf added.

'Two weeks?' queried Fidelma.

Eadulf nodded confirmation.

They stood back while Eadulf continued his examination, peering carefully at the body. He pointed to the left forearm. 'Have you all observed this strange tattoo?'

They bent forward to examine it.

'It is a bird of some sort,' offered Donndubháin.

'*Clamhán*,' asserted Fidelma.

'A what?' frowned Eadulf.

'It is a hawk of sorts,' she explained.

'Well, I have never seen its like,' asserted Gionga.

'No,' Fidelma agreed. 'You are not likely to unless you travel to the northern lands.'

'And you have, I suppose?' the warrior jeered.

'Yes. I have seen it in Ulaidh and in the kingdom of Dál Riada when I was on my way to the great council called by Oswy of Northumbria.'

'Ah!' Eadulf was triumphant. 'I recognise it now. In Latin it is called *buteo*, a buzzard. An odd bird for a religieux to have emblazoned on his forearm.'

He continued with his examination, paying special attention to the hands and feet.

'This man is no religieux turned warrior, nor warrior turned religieux,' he announced. 'The hands and feet are soft and not calloused. Indeed, examine his right hand, Fidelma, especially between the first and second fingers.'

Fidelma reached forward and picked up the flaccid, cold hand. She tried not to shiver as a reaction to the repulsive touch of the soft flesh which seemed pliable as to be almost boneless.

She glanced quickly at Eadulf, her eyebrows raised, before replacing the hand.

'What is it now?' demanded Gionga, resentful that he was not able to understand.

'There are ink stains on the fingers,' Eadulf replied to the question. 'It means that our erstwhile monk was a *scriptor*. A strange person to become an assassin.'

Gionga was querulous. 'Well, it was the other man who was the archer and he wore the emblem of the élite bodyguard of the King of Cashel and his weapons were arrows manufactured by the people of Cnoc Áine, a territory ruled by the cousin of Colgú.'

Fidelma did not bother to comment on his statement. 'And so we will turn to the archer himself. What can you tell us of this man, Eadulf?'

Eadulf spent some time examining the tall man's body before he stood back and addressed them.

'The man is well muscled, his hands are used to work, although they are well groomed. They do not carry the dirt of a farmer or labourer. The feet are also hardened and the body is tanned but carries two scars, old scars which have healed. See here, one is near the ribs on the left and the other is on the left upper arm. The man has fought in battles. Furthermore, he is a professional bowman.'

At that last statement, Gionga burst into derisive laughter. 'Just because you have heard me say that he was a bowman, Saxon, you need not seek to impress us with your powers as if you were some sorcerer.'

Eadulf was unperturbed. 'I report only what I see.'

Fidelma smiled gravely. 'Perhaps you will explain it for Gionga as he does not understand your reasoning.'

Eadulf smiled patiently.

'Come here.' He beckoned to the Uí Fidgente warrior. 'Firstly, we look at his left hand in which he holds his bow. Look at the calluses on the fingers. They are not to be found on the right hand. This hand is used to holding a sturdy piece of wood. Now look at the right hand and see the smaller calluses on the tips of the first finger and thumb where this hand repeatedly holds the end of the shaft of an arrow. Return your gaze to the inner forearm of the left hand where you see some ancient burn marks. There, the string of the bow has sometimes vibrated against the flesh. It happens when a bowman is trying to release arrows in quick succession and is not always able to line up the bow with precision.'

Gionga tried not to sound impressed. 'Very well, Saxon. I grant you that there is a logic to your tricks. Nevertheless, I could have told you that he was a bowman for I cut him down with the bow in his hand after he had tried to kill my Prince.'

'*And* tried to kill the King of Muman,' added Donndubháin. 'You keep neglecting that point.'

'Turn to the assassin's clothes.' Gionga was peevish. 'Explain the emblem of the Golden Chain, which is the élite bodyguard of your cousin.'

The old monk Conchobar had placed the clothing on a second table with the weapons for them to examine.

Fidelma picked up the cross on the chain of gold which was the symbol of the ancient order associated with the Eóghanacht Kings of Cashel. There were no distinguishing marks on it. It was similar to the cross and chain that she herself wore around her neck in token of her brother's gratitude for her services to the kingdom.

'Donndubháin, you have been close to your father, King Cathal, who was King of Cashel before my brother. You have personally known the bodyguard of the kings as well as any. Do you recognise the body of this tall archer?'

'No,' averred her cousin. 'I have never seen him before in the company of the bodyguards, Fidelma.'

Fidelma held out the emblem to him. 'Have you ever seen this before . . . I mean, this specific emblem?'

'It is like every emblem worn by members of the Order of the Golden Chain, cousin. You know it for you also wear one. It is impossible to tell one from the other.'

Gionga was sceptical. 'Well, you would say that, wouldn't you? You would hardly admit that one of your bodyguard was an assassin.'

Donndubháin whirled angrily and clapped a hand to his sword hilt as if to draw it in anger but Fidelma held up her hand.

'Stop! Whether you believe it or not, Gionga, this man is not recognised as a member of the Order of the Golden Chain. I do not recognise him nor does my cousin. On that you have our solemn oaths.'

'I would expect you to say no less,' replied Gionga, the disbelief in his voice not dissipated one iota.

'Maybe the cross was carried deliberately to mislead you,' offered Eadulf.

Gionga started to laugh offensively. 'You mean that the assassin meant to be killed so we could find his emblem and be misled?' he sneered.

Fidelma saw the chagrined expression on the face of her Saxon friend and came to his defence.

'It could be that the assassin meant to drop it where we would find it,' she said, though she did not really feel convinced. She hastily turned to the piles of clothes and began to examine them.

'Coarse materials. There is nothing that identifies their origin. These clothes could come from anywhere. Two leather purses. A few coins in each of them but of no great value. Our assassins seem to have been poor. And . . .'

She stopped and her searching fingers encountered something in the purse which Brother Conchobar had identified as belonging to the elderly, rotund man. Slowly she drew it out.

It was a crucifix, three inches in length on a long chain. Both crucifix and chain were exquisitely wrought in sparking silver. Within the four arms of the crucifix were set four precious stones with a larger stone set in its centre. They were emeralds. It was not a cross of native Irish workmanship, that was easy to see, for it was plainer, less intricate than the designs turned out by Irish silversmiths.

Eadulf was staring over her shoulder.

'That is a cross that no ordinary member of a religious community would be wearing,' he observed.

'Nor even a priest. This is the cross of a bishop, at least,' observed Fidelma with some awe. 'Perhaps even more valuable than an ordinary bishop's cross.'

Chapter Five

Colgú was resting in a carved, tall backed chair, stretching his long limbs before a fire in the great hearth. His right arm was bound in white linen but he was looking much more comfortable than when Fidelma had last seen him.

'How is the wound, brother?' she greeted, as she entered his private chamber followed by Brother Eadulf.

'It does not hurt a bit, thanks to the healing powers of our Saxon friend,' Colgú said with a smile. He was still a trifle pale. He gestured for them to be seated in the chairs opposite him. 'What is the news of Donennach's wound?'

The question was directed at Eadulf.

'More of a flesh wound than anything else,' he replied. 'The arrow embedded itself into the fleshy part of Donennach's thigh but did not strike muscle. He may feel discomfort for a day or two but nothing more.'

'At least the wound will not cause a blemish,' chuckled Colgú, in good spirits.

'Yes, that is so,' Eadulf confirmed but there was bewilderment in his tone. 'Why is that a matter of concern?'

'You are the lawyer in the family, Fidelma,' Colgú smiled. 'You explain to our friend.'

Fidelma shifted slightly towards Eadulf.

'A king is expected to have a perfect body under our laws, Eadulf. He must be free of disability or blemish.'

'Is a king really excluded from kingship if he receives a blemish while king?' Eadulf asked, astounded.

'I know only of the case of Congal Cáech, King of Ulaidh who also ruled as High King for a while. He was blinded in an eye by a bee sting and because of that he was dismissed from the kingship of Tara,' Fidelma responded.

'Though it did not cause him to lose the kingship of his own province,' Colgú pointed out, 'and he was King of Ulaidh until he was killed in battle.'

'When was this?' asked Eadulf.

'He was killed at Magh Rath in the year my sister here was born,' smiled Colgú. 'Anyway, what have you discovered, Fidelma? Who is responsible for this attack on Donennach and myself?'

Fidelma's features became grave and she sat still for a while, placing her hands loosely in her lap.

'The situation is not good,' she began. Then she paused a moment before continuing. 'We have here an attempt at assassination. Under law it is the serious crime of *duinetháide* which merits twice the normal penalty from the culprits.'

'Twice the normal penalty?' intervened Eadulf, puzzled.

'An unlawful killing, as you know, is punishable by the loss of rights and the payment of compensation of fixed sums to the family of the person killed. *Duinetháide*, which literally means person theft, as in the assassination of a prince, is regarded as a more serious offence.'

Colgú leant forward, a little impatiently. 'We know the nature of the crime, Fidelma, but why do you say that the situation is not good? The criminals are dead – slain by Gionga of the Uí Fidgente. It is a matter of identifying them and seeing if there are others involved in this crime.'

Fidelma sighed deeply and gave a shake of her head. 'As you know, one of the slain men was wearing the emblem of the Order of the Golden Chain, the emblem of the nobiliary order of the Kings of Cashel.'

Colgú raised a hand impatiently. 'True, but has he been identified? I knew him not nor, I understand, does Donndubháin. I also asked Capa, the captain of the guard, to go to view the body at Conchobar's apothecary. He reports that he, also, did not know this man. It surely follows that he is not one of our select band of warriors.'

'It is true that no one appears to recognise him,' sighed Fidelma. 'However, the arrows that he was using bear the distinct markings of the Eóghanacht of Cnoc Áine.'

Colgú's features had grown long. 'Are you saying that the assassins were men serving our cousin Finguine, the Prince of Cnoc Áine?'

'I am saying that one carried arrows made by a fletcher of Cnoc Áine for the flights bear the marks of that area. Eadulf and I examined the body carefully. There is nothing else which identifies him other than the emblem of the Golden Chain and his arrows. A *dálaigh* could argue that was circumstantial evidence enough to lay claim to his origin. Gionga is already claiming some conspiracy by Cashel to lure the Prince of the Uí Fidgente here and slay him.'

'That is nonsense!' Colgú said angrily. 'He cannot be serious. I was struck by the arrows of the same assassins.'

'This is true enough,' agreed Fidelma. 'But Gionga turns it to his advantage by arguing that you were not seriously hurt . . .'

'Seriously enough,' intervened Eadulf. 'And more seriously than the Prince of the Uí Fidgente.'

'But not so seriously that it prevents Gionga from whispering that the arrow that hit my brother was a decoy; a decoy to make it look as if it were an attack on both men whereas the real victim was intended to be Donennach. He says that had he not been quick in his actions, the assassins would have shot again and disappeared and we would never have known that they were men of Cashel.'

'I have never heard such a fantasy in all my life,' muttered Colgú, leaning back in his chair, for he had unconsciously bent forward due to the tension of his anger and his wound began to throb again. The anger on his face suddenly dissolved into a gloom. 'What do you think, Fidelma? You have had experience in such matters. How can we prevent Gionga's false accusations?'

'If Gionga can substantiate his charge that these assassins are in the pay of Cashel then you, my brother, are responsible in law and you must pay the compensation. You would lose the kingdom. I am afraid that the onus is on us to disprove Gionga's claim as he has the evidence of the emblem and the provenance of the arrows. We must provide counter-evidence to negate the claim.'

There was a long silence.

'If I am found responsible, you know that Cashel will never have peace with the Uí Fidgente,' sighed the young King. 'You must help me, Fidelma. How can we refute these allegations?'

'We can only refute the charges of Gionga by finding evidence that does so,' Fidelma repeated. 'We must find proof as to who these assassins really were. Does the archer have the right to wear the Order of the Golden Chain? Why would he have worn it on such a venture? Why, if they tried to escape without being indentified, as Gionga claims, did the archer carefully leave two of his arrows on the roof which could easily be identified as to their origin?'

'Perhaps he merely left in a hurry?' ventured Eadulf. 'Remember, after he fired, he must have seen Gionga riding across the square and it was then he fled from the roof.'

Fidelma looked at him almost pityingly. 'The man, as you rightly said, was a professional archer. He would not panic in that manner but would keep his weapons by him. I think that he meant us to find those arrows.' Another thought suddenly struck her. 'But if he were such a professional archer, why did he not strike his targets?'

She stood up in her agitation, closing her eyes as if to recall the scene.

'Colgú suddenly halted his horse and bent forward to greet me. Had he not done so he would have been killed. The mystery is why the archer missed with his second shot when Donennach was a sitting target?'

'I suppose even a well-trained professional may have a bad day,' offered Eadulf.

Colgú leant forward eagerly to Fidelma.

'Are you suggesting that the Uí Fidgente had a hand in this matter? That they engineered this to blame Cashel so that there would be a continuance of the war?'

'Before you blame the Uí Fidgente,' Eadulf pointed out, 'don't forget that it was Gionga who cut down the assassins. He would hardly have done so if they were his own people serving him in some plot.'

'What I am saying is that there are many things that need to be explored before we come to a decision,' Fidelma said. 'We also discovered that this archer's companion was a former religieux. He had once worn the tonsure of St Peter but had let his hair grow in these last few weeks. Furthermore, his hands showed ink stains which demonstrated that he was a *scriptor*. And, finally, he was carrying this . . .'

She took out the ornate silver crucifix and held it out to her brother.

Colgú took it and examined it with a frown.

'This is a fine piece of work, Fidelma. It is very valuable. I doubt it was made in this kingdom. The designs are wrong.' He frowned suddenly. 'Yet I swear that I have seen this before. But where?'

Fidelma was interested. 'Try to remember, brother. And also answer why would a former brother of the Faith turn assassin and be carrying such a valuable piece?'

Colgú examined his sister's features thoughtfully.

'Do you believe that there are hidden depths to this matter?'

'I do. There is something that is not right,' she replied. 'There is no easy solution from the information we have at hand.'

There was a knocking on the door and it opened at Colgú's invitation.

Donndubháin entered and spoke without waiting to be invited to do so by Colgú. It was his right. He did not look happy.

'The Prince of the Uí Fidgente is demanding an audience with you. His captain Gionga has persuaded him that Cashel is guilty of some plot to assassinate him.'

Colgú uttered an expressive oath. 'Can we delay him? We have not yet reached a conclusion on this matter.'

Donndubháin shook his head. 'The prince is awaiting you in the Great Hall as we speak. I dare not even rebuke him on his manners for he is in a bad mood.'

Protocol laid down that even a Prince should await an invitation before entering the Great Hall of Cashel which was where the King received official visitors and guests. Protocol also demanded that guests wait in the anterooms before being invited to an audience with the King.

The King rose carefully, taking care not to exert pressure on his arm. He could forgive the emotional stress that drove the thoughts of protocol from the mind of his wounded guest.

'Then we had better go to see what it is that the Prince of the Uí Fidgente demands,' he said with resignation. 'Come; you, too, Eadulf. I may have need of your stout Saxon arm.'

When they entered the hall, the Prince of the Uí Fidgente was already seated. There was a sweat on his face and his posture looked restless. Certainly the wound, flesh wound or not, was making him uncomfortable. Behind him stood a grim-faced Gionga. There was no one else in the hall except Capa of the King's bodyguard standing behind the throne.

Donennach started to rise but Colgú, who was not overly punctilious, waved him back into his seat, while he went to his chair of office and sat down, resting his arm carefully. Fidelma took a chair on the left-hand side while Donndubháin sat to the King's right. Eadulf took a standing position near to Capa.

'Well now, Donennach, how may I serve you?'

'I came here as your guest, Colgú,' the Prince began. 'I came here with the desire that we of the Uí Fidgente might form a lasting peace with the Eóghanacht of Cashel.'

He paused. Colgú waited politely. There was nothing to be said for this was a mere statement of fact.

'The attack on me . . .' Donennach hesitated, 'on both of us,' he corrected, 'raises certain questions.'

'Be assured that they are questions to which we are urgently seeking answers,' intervened Fidelma softly.

'I would assume as much,' snapped Donennach. 'But Gionga here informs me of things which I find disconcerting. He tells me that the assassins, whom he slew, are men of Cnoc Áine, the land ruled by your cousin, Finguine. Therefore, they are men over whom you have responsibility, Colgú of Cashel. I saw for myself the body of one of these assassins bearing the insignia of your own military élite.'

'You have doubtless heard the saying, Donennach, *fronti nulla fides*?' asked Fidelma quietly.

Donennach scowled at her. 'What are you trying to tell me?' he sneered.

'No reliance can be placed on appearance. It is easy to pin a badge on a person just as it is easy to put a coat on a person. The coat or the badge does not really tell you who the person is but only who the person wishes us to believe that they are,' replied Fidelma calmly.

Donennach's eyes narrowed. 'Perhaps you will leave it to the King, your brother, to explain the meaning of that defence?'

'Defence implies an accusation,' Colgú rebuked mildly. 'We should not be interested in throwing accusations at one another but in getting to the truth.'

Donennach waved a hand indifferently. 'So you accept that you have an explanation to make to me?'

'We accept,' replied Colgú carefully, 'that one of the two men killed by Gionga bore the insignia of an order of Cashel. But that does not identify him as being a man in my service. As my sister has told you, it is easy to place something on a man to mislead people.'

Donennach suddenly looked uncomfortable and glanced to Gionga.

'How do I know that this is not an attempt by Cashel to destroy the Uí Fidgente?' he demanded.

At that Donndubháin exploded in anger. He sprang from his seat, hand going to the place where his sword sheath would have been. But it was a rule never to go armed into a king's great hall.

'This is an affront to Cashel!' he cried. 'The Uí Fidgente should be made to swallow his words!'

Gionga had moved forward in front of his Prince, his hand also searching for the non-existent sword.

Colgú held up a hand to stay his *tanist*.

'Calm yourself, Donndubháin,' he ordered. 'Donennach, order your man back. No hurt will come to you while you are in Cashel. I swear this by the Holy Cross.'

Donndubháin sunk back to his chair while Gionga, at a swift gesture from Donennach's hand, retired to his position behind his Prince.

There was an icy silence

Colgú's gaze had never left the face of the Prince of the Uí Fidgente. 'You say that you do not know whether what occurred was an attempt by Cashel to destroy you? Can I be as assured that this was not some Uí Fidgente plot against my life?' he said evenly.

'A plot by me? Here in Cashel? I was nearly killed by the assassin's arrow.' Donennach's voice was developing a tetchiness.

'Instead of hurling accusations at one another, we should be working together to discover the identity of the culprits,' Colgú repeated, trying to curb his annoyance with his guest.

Donennach gave a bark of derisive laughter.

Fidelma rose abruptly and went to stand between the two men, palms held out to each in symbolic gesture.

At this a silence descended, for a *dálaigh* could command silence even from kings in such a fashion.

'There is a dispute here,' she said quietly. 'But the disputants lack sufficient facts to argue logically and in depth for their respective cases. This matter must go to arbitration. We must resolve the mystery of what has happened here and identify who was responsible. Do you agree?'

She glanced at Donennach.

The Prince's lips became a thin line as he stared back at her. Then he relaxed and shrugged. 'All I want is that the facts be examined.'

Fidelma turned to her brother and raised her eyebrows in interrogation.

'An arbitration is agreed. How shall it be done?'

'The law text called the *Bretha Crólige* states the terms,' replied Fidelma. 'There will be three judges. A judge from Cashel, a judge from the Uí Fidgente and a judge from without the kingdom. I would suggest a judge from Laighin as being of sufficient distance to sit without bias. The judges shall be assembled here as the law prescribes in nine days. The facts will be placed before them and we shall all abide by their judgement.'

Donennach looked at Gionga before he turned back to examine Fidelma suspiciously. 'Will you be the judge from Cashel?' he gibed. 'You are the King's sister and should not sit in his judgement.'

'If you imply that my view of law is biased then I deny it. However, I shall not be the judge from Cashel. There are others more qualified than I. I would request that the Brehon Dathal be asked to sit. But, with the King's permission, I will engage to gather the evidence on behalf of Cashel and be its advocate just as you, Donennach, are free to nominate a *dálaigh* to gather evidence that supports your contentions.'

The Prince of the Uí Fidgente sat in thought, clearly suspecting some trap.

'Nine days it is then. The court will sit on the feastday of the Blessed Matthew. I will send for my *dálaigh* and judge. You may appoint your sister as your advocate, Colgú, if you so wish.'

Colgú smiled briefly at Fidelma. 'It will be as my sister has said. She is the advocate of Cashel.'

'So be it,' Donennach agreed then added, thoughtfully, 'but which judge from Laighin shall be our outside arbitrator?'

'Do you have someone in mind?' asked Colgú.

'The Brehon Rumann,' Donennach replied immediately. 'Rumann of Fearna.'

Colgú did not know of the man. 'Have you heard of this judge named Rumann, Fidelma?' he inquired.

'Yes; I have heard of his reputation. I have no objections to his being asked to sit as our third and chief judge.'

Donennach rose from his seat, helped by Gionga.

'That is good. As for our judge, I appoint the Brehon Fachtna. He is already in Cashel for he travels in my retinue. Our *dálaigh* will be Solam and we shall send for him and expect the fullest cooperation when he arrives to present our case.'

'You shall be assured of it,' replied Colgú coldly. 'You may expect nothing less than our cooperation to get to the bottom of this matter. We will have our scribes draw up the protocol for the proceedings. We will sign it and so ensure everyone is gathered on the appointed day.'

When the Prince of the Uí Fidgente had gone, Colgú sat back, clearly troubled. 'I know the suggestion was correct, Fidelma, but, as you pointed out earlier, the evidence is against Cashel.'

Donndubháin shook his head. 'A bad move, cousin.'

Fidelma smiled thinly. 'You doubt my abilities as an advocate?'

'Not your abilities, Fidelma,' interposed Colgú. 'But an advocate is usually only as good as the evidence that is available. Do you know this advocate of the Uí Fidgente . . . what was his name?'

'Solam. I have heard of him. He is said to be effective although given to an uneasy temperament.'

'How will you defend Cashel?' demanded Donndubháin.

'I know that this was not some attempt to assassinate Donennach by Cashel. There remain three alternatives.'

'Only three?' demanded Donndubháin moodily.

'Only three that makes sense. Firstly, it could be counter-claimed that the Uí Fidgente were plotting against Cashel; that this was an elaborate hoax to lay blame on us. Secondly, it could be argued that the assassins were part of a blood feud; that they acted on their own account seeking vengeance against Colgú or Donennach. Thirdly, it might be contended that the assassins acted on their own account merely to destroy the peace now being negotiated between the Uí Fidgente and Cashel.'

'Do you favour any one of these, Fidelma?' asked Colgú.

'I have an open mind though I would say the first possibility was unlikely.'

'The possibility that the Uí Fidgente are behind would-be assassins? Why so? Because Donennach was shot also?' Colgú queried.

'Because, for all that I dislike Donennach, he accepted arbitration and nominated the Brehon Rumann of Fearna easily enough. I know Rumann and his reputation. He is a fair man and not given to bribery. If this were some plot, I would expect the Uí Fidgente might want to weight the odds more in their favour for much will depend on the decision of this third independent judge.'

Colgú turned to Donndubháin. 'You had best devise the protocol and I shall sign it with Donennach. Then we must send emissaries to Rumann at Fearna, also Solam of the Uí Fidgente.'

When Donndubháin had departed to fulfil his task, Colgú turned anxiously to Fidelma. 'I still do not like this, Fidelma. The onus is still on us to refute the Uí Fidgente's accusations.'

Fidelma was not reassuring. 'Then, as your *dálaigh*, my brother, I will have to start finding something with which we can refute the accusations.'

'But we have all the evidence there is . . . unless you can find a sorcerer to resurrect the assassins.'

Eadulf, not used to such humour, genuflected swiftly. Neither Colgú nor Fidelma took any notice of him.

'No, brother. I mean to start where our only real clue allows us to start.'

Her brother frowned. 'Where?'

'In the country of our cousin, Finguine of Cnoc Áine, where else? Perhaps I can discover who made those arrows. If I can do that, perhaps I can discover the identity of the archer.'

'You have only nine days.'

'I am aware of it,' agreed Fidelma.

Colgú's face suddenly brightened. 'You can seek the hospitality of Abbot Ségdae of Imleach, for he is an expert on ecclesiastical art. He might be able to provide you with information about the crucifix. I am sure it is familiar but I can't think where I have seen it before.'

Fidelma had already thought of the idea but instead of confessing as much she smiled and nodded.

'However,' she replied, 'while I can take one of the arrows as a sample, I cannot take the crucifix, which must remain here as evidence for Donennach's *dálaigh*. If I take it, I will be accused of interfering with the evidence. I will get old Conchobar, who is a rare draughtsman, to make me a sketch of it.'

'Excellent. Perhaps there is a small ray of hope in this confusion after all?' cried Colgú. 'When will you start for Imleach?'

'Old Conchobar willing, I can start within the hour.'

Eadulf coughed discreetly.

Fidelma hid a smile. 'I would hope, of course, that Brother Eadulf will see his way clear to accompany me to Imleach.'

Colgú turned to Eadulf. 'Could we persuade you . . . ?' He let the question hang in the air without finishing.

'I will do my best to render every assistance that I can,' Eadulf offered solemnly.

'Then it is arranged.' Colgú gave a quick smile to his sister. 'My best horses are at your disposal to hasten your journey.'

'How far is it to Imleach?' asked Eadulf anxiously, wondering if he had let himself in for a lengthy journey.

'Twenty-one miles or so, but the road is straight. We can be there before this evening,' Fidelma assured him.

'Then the sooner you get Brother Conchobar to make the sketch of the crucifix, the sooner you can set out.' Colgú reached out with his good hand and took one of his sister's hands in his. 'No need for me to say, be careful, Fidelma,' he said gravely. 'Whoever does not hesitate to stop at the death of Kings will not stop at the death of a King's sister. These are dangerous times.'

Fidelma squeezed her brother's hand reassuringly.

'I will take care, brother. But your advice must be heeded by your own self. What has failed once might be tried again. So until we know who is behind this deed, make sure that you keep a wary eye upon the company you keep. I feel that there is danger here, brother. Here in the very corridors of our palace of Cashel.'

Chapter Six

Fidelma met her cousin Donndubháin while on her way to the stables to arrange for the horses for the journey to Imleach. Normally, a religieux below the rank of bishop or abbot would not be expected to travel by horse but Fidelma held rank, not only as the sister of the King but in her own right as a *dálaigh*. The heir-apparent to the throne of Muman was holding a sheaf of papers as he crossed the courtyard.

He grinned at his cousin and held them up. 'The protocol as Colgú has instructed,' he explained. 'I am sure this is a waste of this paper.'

Paper was still scarce, an eastern invention, only a few centuries old, which was so costly that few of the Kings of Éireann bothered to import it. Good vellum was usually preferred as a symbol of their status.

Fidelma was serious. 'I doubt it is wasted, cousin,' she said.

'Do you want to read through it? You have a better legal mind than I do.'

'You are the *tanist*, cousin. I am sure things are in order. Anyway, I must be off. We have only nine days to discover the truth.'

'Time enough,' Donndubháin was encouraging. 'I know you, Fidelma. You have a great gift of sifting sand and coming up with the single grain you seek.'

'You think too highly of my capabilities.'

Donndubháin was two years younger than Fidelma but they had played together in Cashel as youngsters until the time had arrived when Fidelma had been sent away for her schooling.

Since their childhood together Fidelma had only seen Donndubháin a few times before she had returned to Cashel last year after her brother had become King and her cousin had been appointed heir-apparent. She knew he was a quiet, conscientious support for her brother. He might make light of the protocol but she knew that he had the mind of a good lawyer and there would be nothing wrong with the texts.

Donndubháin suddenly glanced around as if to ensure they were alone.

'Sometimes,' he said abruptly, with lowered voice, 'I do not think your brother takes his position seriously enough.'

'How do you mean?'

'He accepts the word of people too easily. Without questioning. He is honourable and therefore he believes everyone is honourable. He is too trusting. Look as this business with the Uí Fidgente. He trusts Donennach too readily.'

'Oh?' Fidelma was curious. 'And you do not?'

'I cannot afford to. What if Colgú is too trusting and this is a plot by Prince Donennach to assassinate Colgú? Someone has to be prepared to protect your brother and Cashel.'

Fidelma admitted to herself that she had been thinking as much. She remembered that only nine months before the Uí Fidgente had attempted to overthrow Cashel. The blood at Cnoc Áine was hardly dried and this change of heart, this willingness to make peace, was so abrupt, so sudden, that she could share her cousin's suspicions.

'With you as *tanist*, cousin, my brother need not fear,' she assured him.

Donndubháin remained worried. 'I wish that you would let me send a company of warriors with you,' he said.

'I refused my brother on this matter,' Fidelma replied firmly, 'and so shall refuse you. Eadulf and myself have made more dangerous journeys.'

Donndubháin frowned for a moment and then his face broadened into a smile. 'You are right, of course. Our Saxon friend is a good support in times of danger. He has served Cashel well since he has been here. But he is no warrior. He is slow when you might need a swift sword arm.'

Fidelma found herself flushing as she felt that she should defend Eadulf. She was, at the same time, annoyed by her reaction.

'Eadulf is a good man. A slow-footed hound often has good qualities,' she added, indulging in an old proverb.

'That is true. But beware of that Uí Fidgente, Gionga. I do not like him. Something about him makes me suspicious.'

'You are not the only one, cousin,' smiled Fidelma. 'Have no fear. I shall be careful.'

'If you see our cousin, Finguine of Cnoc Áine, give him my salutations.'

'That I shall do.' Fidelma was about to move on to the stables when she turned back. 'Did you say that the merchant, Samradán, was trading at Imleach abbey?'

Donndubháin's eyebrows gathered.

'Yes. He frequently trades there. But the assassins would have chosen the roof of his warehouse at random. He could not be involved in this matter.'

'I think you said that before. You have had business with him?'

'That is so. I have bought a few items in silver from him.' He touched his silver brooch. 'Why?'

'I do not know the man. Is he a native of the town?'

'He has lived here for several years. Exactly how long, I do not know. Nor do I know where he came from.'

'It is of no consequence,' remarked Fidelma. 'As you say, he cannot be involved in this matter. Now I must be on my way. We shall all meet here in nine days' time.'

Donndubháin held up his papers and smiled.

'Your brother will be safeguarded until your return. I promise. Go safely, cousin, and come back swiftly.'

The clouds that had so dominated the sky earlier that day had broken up. Now they drifted lazily and high like the fleece of grazing sheep, fluffy against the azure background with the afternoon sun occasionally breaking through to warm the pastures. There was still a faint breeze but the air was pleasant enough and not uncomfortable.

Fidelma and Eadulf had reached a fork in the River Suir, about four miles west of Cashel, where a wooden bridge spanned the fast-flowing waters, crossing a small island in the middle on which stood a minute rath which served as a fortification to protect the approaches to Cashel in times of war. Now it was not used for no enemy host had come close enough to threaten the capital of the Eóghanacht for many years. On either side of the bridge, along the river bank, woodlands stretched for some way. The roadway across the bridge was, so far as Eadulf knew, the only main road westward out of Cashel, joining roads leading north and south on the far side of the river.

Fidelma, riding her white mare from her brother's stables, just in front of Eadulf, halted at the centre of the bridge. Eadulf drew rein on his sorrel colt, frowning.

'What is it?' he demanded.

Fidelma had noticed that there was movement in the rath itself. Then from the shadows of the timbers at the end of the bridge, where it joined the island, two archers appeared with drawn bows. The arrows were strung and pointing in their direction. A third warrior, whose shield carried the insignia of a rampant boar, his sword casually held in his right hand, came forward a pace to halt between the archers. He was careful not to obstruct the bowmen's aim.

Fidelma's eyes narrowed as she observed them.

'Stay alert, Eadulf,' she said quietly. 'That warrior appears to be bearing the insignia of the Uí Fidgente.'

She nudged her horse forward a few paces.

'Halt!' called the central warrior, raising his sword. 'Come no further!'

'Who gives orders on this bridge within sight of the King of Cashel's palace?' she demanded in annoyance.

The warrior laughed sourly. 'One who wishes to stop people from crossing it, Sister,' came the sarcastic riposte.

'Know you that I am a *dálaigh* and you have no authority to refuse to let me pass,' she called in annoyance.

The man's posture did not change. 'I know well enough who you are, sister of Colgú. And I know your Saxon puppy of a companion there.'

'Then, if you know that, you must also know that you have to clear the way, Uí Fidgente, for you have no right to block any public highway in this kingdom.'

The warrior gestured to the archers behind him. 'They give me the right.'

'And who gives you your orders?'

'My lord, Gionga, captain of the bodyguard of Prince Donennach. No one passes this bridge until the time of the hearing at Cashel. Those are the orders I have been given from my lord in order to prevent any further conspiracies against the Prince of the Uí Fidgente.'

Fidelma's eyes widened slightly. Her mind worked rapidly. So Gionga had posted a guard to stop her going to Imleach? The bridge guarded the only quick route across the river on the road to Imleach. How had Gionga known of her journey and why did he feel that he should prevent it? What did he fear that she could discover?

'The bridge is closed to you,' replied the warrior without volunteering further information. 'Now be gone back to Cashel.'

'My brother's guard will soon unblock this barrier,' she retorted.

The warrior made a careful pantomime of looking in both directions. 'I do not see your brother's guard,' he jeered.

Fidelma had not only scrutinised the archers and their commander carefully but noted the fact that there seemed to be more than a dozen other Uí Fidgente warriors encamped within the rath. There was no point in arguing further with them.

She turned her mare carefully on the bridge and walked it back to Eadulf, the shod hooves of the horse echoing like a drumbeat on the wooden planking.

'Follow me,' she instructed quietly. 'Did you hear all that passed between me and the Uí Fidgente warrior?'

Eadulf asserted that he had, obeying her instructions without question. He felt a tingling sensation in his back as he exposed it to the aim of the archers with their taut bows, ready to strike.

'This seems to confirm that there is an Uí Fidgente plot,' he whispered, after they had moved out of range. 'Gionga must have been desperate to attempt to prevent us going to Cnoc Áine to search for evidence. This is all the proof we need of his culpability.'

'That is what makes me worried. Surely Gionga would realise that it would not take long for Cashel's warriors to be alerted and ride here to disperse these men? The logical deduction would be that the Uí Fidgente have admitted their guilt by this action.'

'Well, they have succeeded in one thing, that is that we cannot reach Imleach tonight. It is four miles back to Cashel.'

'We will be there tonight.' Fidelma's voice was firm and confident. 'When we pass the bend of the road ahead, out of sight of the men on the bridge, you will observe a track on the right-hand side leading south. Turn along it.'

'South? I thought this was the only bridge spanning this river for miles?'

Fidelma chuckled. 'It is.'

'Then what . . . ?'

'Quickly, here is the track.'

To call it a track was to do it honour. It was no more than a small pathway along which a horse went with difficulty, brushing against bushes and trees on either side. It plunged blindly into a great strip of dark woodland that ran along the river bank.

'What now?' called Eadulf, as he urged his young horse forward through the dark verdure.

'This leads south through the forests on the river banks. About half a mile further on the forest will give way to open marshy land. I'll take over the lead then, for we will walk our horses through the reeds and marshland. From that point, in another half-mile, we should come to a ford across the river which not many people know of. It is called Atha Asail, the ford of the ass. It is a treacherous crossing but we will make it. We will not be delayed long on our journey.'

'Are you sure this is the best plan?' wailed Eadulf, thinking of the turbulent waters of the rushing river. Although he had found himself in countless dangerous situations, he was not one to go out in search of danger. He did not believe the Saxon proverb that danger and delight grew from the same stalk. Eadulf once found his philosophy in the writing of Lucretius: that it was pleasurable, when the winds disturbed the waves of some great sea, to gaze out from the security of the land upon the dangers of another.

'I used to cross the Ass's Ford when I was a child. There is no danger in it for one who is careful,' Fidelma assured him. 'If you need to exercise your mind, why not consider how Gionga could have found out that we were going to Imleach?'

Eadulf frowned. The point had not even occurred to him. 'Maybe he overheard us discussing it with your brother? Or again, maybe he overheard our discussion with old Brother Conchobar when you asked him to draw a copy of the crucifix? Maybe he simply saw us saddling our horses and made a clever guess?'

Fidelma made a disapproving sound with her tongue against her teeth. 'You are of little help in this matter,' she chided, 'for all you do is give articulations to questions that I have already asked. I need answers. I have already answered your last question in the negative for how would he have had time to send his men to meet us at the bridge, or, if they were already there, to send someone to warn them of our coming. He knew where we were going some time before we set out.'

'Then you need a prophet to answer you,' mumbled Eadulf, irritated because of the discomfit of the road through the snatching briars and branches of the woodland and because of his anxiety of the crossing of the rapid river ahead. 'You should have consulted that old magician friend of yours, Brother Conchobar.'

Fidelma pouted. 'Why do you call him a magician?'

Eadulf groaned as a briar scratched across his ankle. 'Because he practices divination from the stars, doesn't he? How can he claim to be a Christian and do that?'

'Are the two things in conflict?' mused Fidelma.

Eadulf found his irritability increasing. 'How can you say otherwise?'

'Making maps of the stars and deciphering their meaning is an ancient tradition in this land.'

'The New Faith should have replaced such pagan traditions. It is forbidden. Doesn't the Book of *Isaiah* say:

> '"Let your astrologers, your star-gazers who foretell
> your future month by month,
> persist, and save you!
>
> But look, they are gone like chaff;
> fire burns them up;
> they cannot snatch themselves from the flames;
> there is no glowing coal to warm them,
> no fire for them to sit by.
>
> So much for your magicians . . ."'

Fidelma smiled softly. She always had a tendency to smile when

Eadulf began to argue theology for, by his adherence to the new teachings of Rome, he and she found many points of difference in their attitudes to the Faith. Fidelma was a woman of her own culture.

'You quote from the ancient texts of the Judaic Faith,' she pointed out.

'Of which Our Lord came as a Messiah,' snapped Eadulf waspishly.

'Exactly so. He came as a Messiah, as a Saviour, to show them a new path to understanding God. Who, according to *Matthew*, were the first to arrive in Jerusalem after the birth of the Christ?'

'Who?' Eadulf shook his head, wondering what point she was making.

'Astrologers from the east, seeking the Saviour for they had seen his coming in a map of the heavens. And didn't King Herod try to persuade them to betray that knowledge? Astrologers were the first to arrive in Bethlehem and worship the Saviour and offer him gold, frankincense and myrrh. Had astrology been cursed by God, would astrologers have been the first allowed to greet Him on Earth?'

Eadulf flushed irritably. Fidelma always had a good counter-argument when he tried to assert anything that she disagreed with.

'Well, *Deuteronomy* is clear,' he went on stubbornly. 'Nor must you raise your eyes to the heavens and look up to the sun, moon, and the stars, all the host of heaven, and be led on to bow down to them and worship them . . .'

'. . . the Lord your God created them for the guidance of the various peoples under the heavens,' Fidelma added emphatically. 'I trust, Eadulf, you were going to deliver the *entire* verse from *Deuteronomy*? Anyway, astrologers do not worship or bow down to the sun, moon and stars, but use them as guides. Our astrologers argue that we can no more alter the course of our stars than we can change our features and the colour of our hair and eyes. Yet we have free will to do as we please with the things that we are given.'

Eadulf sighed deeply. He was already tiring of the argument. He wished that he had not raised it. Fidelma always thrived on disputations, even to the point of becoming the Devil's Advocate.

'It is against the teachings . . .' he began.

'Show me one clear reference in the holy texts forbidding Christians not to take notice of the ancient science, apart from some obscure references . . .'

'*Jeremiah*,' returned Eadulf, remembering suddenly.

'"Listen, Israel, to this word that the Lord has
spoken against you:
'Do not fall into the ways of the nations;
do not be awed by signs in the heavens;
it is the nations who go in awe of these . . ."'

'What Israel did before the coming of the Messiah is a matter for Israel. But we are of the nations and *Jeremiah* admits, at least, there are signs in the heavens, although we are not awed by them but merely interpret them and attempt to understand them. And if there are signs in the heavens, who put them there? Wouldn't it be blasphemy to claim that they were put there by another hand than God's?'

Eadulf's face was red with mortification. He felt himself about to explode with anger. He didn't. Instead, he suddenly started to chuckle. 'Why do I think that I can win an argument with a lawyer?' he remarked shaking his head ruefully.

Fidelma hesitated a moment and then finally joined in his mirth. '*Castigat ridendo mores*,' she said softly, resorting to one of her favourite quotations. It corrects customs by laughing at them.

They broke out of the woods abruptly onto a broad field of reeds. As their horses emerged from the woodland a group of small birds rose in a body making a twanging 'ping-ping' call-note. They gathered in a flock and swept low over the reeds, searching out the danger, before they settled back among tall feathery-headed reed grass with its dark purple flowered heads and rough-edged leaves.

'Reedlings,' Fidelma explained unnecessarily. 'Our horses disturbed them.'

Eadulf could hear the rushing of the river a short distance away.

'Can the warriors see us from the bridge?' he asked for although some of the reeds stretched as tall as ten feet in height, there was a lot of low growth around the path, which he saw meandering through it to the open river. But along the banks was no more than reed canary-grass, of a shorter and smaller variety.

'No. There is a slight bend in the river which hides us. Besides, the warriors will believe that we have gone back to Cashel to get my brother's warriors.'

She nudged her mare forward and around Eadulf to take the lead.

'Keep close behind me and do not deviate from the track. The grassland may look firm but it is marsh and some people have been known to be sucked under into the muddy depths.'

Eadulf found himself unable to suppress a shudder as he glanced around.

Fidelma pulled a face at his pale features.

'To be alive at all involves risks and dangers so cheer up,' she advised brightly, before she set off confidently enough, her horse picking its way through the tall waving reeds which looked so wild and dramatic against the skyline. Eadulf realised that the marshland was a whole jumble of growths and what he had thought was an entire plain of reeds was in fact intermixed with fen sedge, spike-rush and wilting bulrushes which were long past their flowering period. The whole growth created a curious green, varying brown and yellow surrounding.

The reedlings now and then took wing but only in small individual groups from the nests among the reeds. Their tiny tawny bodies, even the males with black markings, were hard to spot.

Eadulf became increasingly aware of the rushing waters and realised that the river was crossing a series of shallows and the noise that he was hearing was the movement of the waters over the stony bottom, hitting rocks and objects in mid-stream.

Fidelma guided her mare carefully along the pathway. Eadulf, even in his saddle, could feel the springy surface beneath the hooves of his colt and he prayed that the horse would not stumble from the path and precipitate him into the dark mire on either side. The young horse had been chosen for him by Fidelma, who was an excellent judge of horseflesh. She had chosen the colt not because of its youth but because it was one of the most docile beasts in her brother's stable and she knew that Eadulf was not the most expert of horsemen.

They emerged from the waving reeds onto a lush, green embankment, whose turf was still exceptionally springy. Before them was the broad stretch of the River Suir.

Eadulf regarded the fast-flowing water, bubbling with yellow froth over and around the stony surface, with disquiet.

'How deep is it?'

Fidelma gave him a smile of encouragement. 'It will come up to the chest of your horse. Give the animal a free rein and do not try to guide it. The colt has good sense. It will pick its own way through the shallows. I will go first.'

Without another word, she nudged her mare into the waters. The animal was nervous at first, shaking its head and rolling its eyes. Then it began to move forward, placing its feet carefully, stumbling once or twice but recovering. By the time it was in mid-stream, the frothing waters had reached its chest and were swirling over Fidelma's lower legs.

She turned in the saddle and waved Eadulf to come forward.

Eadulf looked at the wild, surging, white water and was almost paralysed with anxiety. He was aware of Fidelma waving urgently at him to start the crossing and he found his hands trembling. He did not want to cross that violent fluctuating deluge. He was aware of Fidelma's eyes upon him and he did not have courage enough to admit his cowardice.

Chapter Seven

Uttering up a prayer, Eadulf urged his sorrel into the waters and in his nervousness he made the horse respond too quickly. The hind legs slipped in the mud and Eadulf thought he was going to be thrown. He clung on for dear life and the colt, snorting and panting, managed to recover and find the rocky shallow. Eadulf let his reins go limp and simply sat with closed eyes, trying to imagine himself safely across.

Now and then the horse jolted him in the saddle as it struggled to find firm footing. Then the icy cold waters of the river were lapping at his feet and then his lower legs up to his knees. Suddenly, turbulent water swept over him at waist level, causing him to gasp with the shock of it. He clutched tightly at the saddle pommel. Then the horse rose above the water level again and he dared open his eyes to find himself only a few yards from the far bank. Fidelma was already there, sitting slightly forward in her saddle, awaiting him.

With a surge of energy, the animal scrambled up the bank and came to a halt beside her.

Eadulf was enough of a horseman to reach forward and pat the animal's neck in gratitude.

'*Deo gratias*,' he intoned in relief.

'We'd best put some distance between ourselves and this place,' Fidelma advised. 'The sooner we reach Imleach, the better.'

'How about a moment to dry ourselves? I am soaked from the waist down,' protested Eadulf.

'Don't bother, we might have to go swimming again. There is a smaller stream to cross, the Fidhaghta. And if the Uí Fidgente have left more warriors at the Well of Ara, which is the main ford across the river, we might be in trouble again.'

Eadulf groaned loudly.

'How far is the Well of Ara?'

'No more than seven miles. We will be there shortly.'

She turned and moved off into the surrounding woodland, heading directly westward. Without turning to see whether Eadulf was following she called over her shoulder: 'The path broadens here and we can canter for a while.'

She pressed her heels into the side of her mount and the powerful white mare surged forward in response. So eager was its stride that Fidelma had to shorten her rein to ensure the horse stayed at a steady canter.

Eadulf followed close behind, bobbing up and down in his saddle, his sodden clothing making him feel more miserable and uncomfortable than he had felt in his life.

It seemed an eternity before they came to a small rise where the road dipped towards another substantial river which bent almost at a right angle at a point where there was a cluster of buildings along its banks. The river seemed to flow from west to east and then turn directly south.

'That is the Well of Ara.' Fidelma smiled in satisfaction. 'That is the crossing point and Imleach lies some miles further on. We can follow the north bank of the river for a while. I can't see any of Gionga's warriors there, though.'

Eadulf sniffed in his discomfiture. 'There are buildings there and smoke. Can't we rest and dry out?'

Fidelma glanced up at the sky. 'We will not have long. We must be at Imleach before dark. However, if there are no warriors of the Uí Fidgente warriors hanging around, there is a tavern at the crossing where you may change or dry your clothes.'

Without more ado she led the way down the hill towards the group of buildings that straddled both sides of the water. Here the water crossed shallows but nowhere as dangerous nor turbulent as the crossing of the Suir.

A couple of boys were sitting on the river bank, casting a line into the waters. Fidelma approached just as one was lifting a wild, brown trout which he brought triumphantly to the bank.

'A good catch,' called Fidelma appreciatively as she halted her horse.

The boy, no more than eleven, smiled indifferently. 'I have made better, Sister,' he replied solemnly, in deference to her habit.

'I don't doubt it,' she replied. 'Tell me, do you live here?'

'Here, where else?' replied the child in a worldly manner.

'Are there strangers in your village?'

'There were strangers last night. The Prince of the Uí Fidgente, so my father says. He and his men. But they left this morning when the great King from Cashel arrived to meet them.'

'But there are no strangers left in the village now?'

'No. They all went to Cashel.'

'Good. We are obliged to you.'

Fidelma turned her mare and moved on towards the river, waving

Eadulf forward. The waters barely came up to the fetlocks of the horses as they crossed the waters of the Ara and reached the far bank. It was not difficult to spot the tavern for it lay exactly by the ford with its swinging sign outside the door.

Thankfully, Eadulf slid from the saddle and hitched the reins to a convenient post. He removed his saddle bag in which he had a change of dry clothing, hoping to find time to change into something warmer.

As he was doing so, the door of the tavern opened and an elderly man came out.

'Greetings, travellers, you are most . . .' The man stopped short as his eyes fell on Fidelma. A smile of welcome broke over his features and he hurried forward to help her from her horse.

'It is good to see you, lady. Why, it was only this morning that your brother was here to . . .'

'To meet with Donennach of the Uí Fidgente,' rejoined Fidelma, recognising the man with a friendly smile. 'I know, good Aona. It is a long time since I have seen you.'

The man beamed in pleasure that she had remembered his name. 'I have not seen you since you were celebrating the attainment of the age of choice. Why, that must have been twelve years or more ago.'

'It was a long time ago, Aona.'

'Long, indeed, and yet you recall my name.'

'You were ever a loyal follower of my family. It would be a bad member of the Eóghanacht who did not remember the name of Aona, one-time captain of the guard of Cashel. I heard that you had decided to retire to run a wayside tavern. I had not realised it was this one.'

'You . . .' He suddenly glanced at Eadulf and took in his clothing and Roman tonsure in one swift glance. 'You and your Saxon companion are most welcome to my hospitality.'

'I need to change my clothes and dry myself,' Eadulf muttered, almost in a voice of complaint.

'Did you fall from your horse into the river, then?' asked Aona.

'No I did not,' Eadulf snapped. He did not bother to explain further.

'There is a fire inside,' Aona advised. 'Come in; come in both of you.' He pushed open the door and stood aside to usher them in.

'Alas, we cannot stay long. I need to get to Imleach before nightfall,' Fidelma told him as she followed Eadulf inside.

Eadulf made a straight line to the roaring fire, where flames ate hungrily at a pile of glowing logs.

'You will stay for a meal, surely?'

Eadulf was just about to say they would but Fidelma shook her head firmly. 'There is no time. We will stay here long enough to warm ourselves with a drink and for Brother Eadulf to change his sodden garments and then be off.'

Aona's features mirrored his disappointment.

Fidelma reached out a hand and touched his arm. 'Let us hope that our journey will return us here quickly and then we will do justice to your hospitality. But this is a matter of some urgency, of importance to the safety of the kingdom, and not a matter of mere whim.'

Aona had served most of his younger life in the bodyguard of the Kings of Cashel and he grew erect. 'If the kingdom is in danger, lady, tell me how best I may serve it?'

Fidelma turned to where Eadulf was uncomfortably standing, with steam rising from his wet garments, in front of the fire.

'Have you a room where Brother Eadulf might change his clothes?'

Aona pointed to a side door across the main tavern room.

'In there, Brother. Bring out your wet clothes and we will dry them before the fire.'

'Time is important,' Fidelma added, as if to excuse her peremptoriness.

When Eadulf had disappeared, taking his saddle bag with him, and Aona had filled two mugs with *corma*, Fidelma sat in a chair and held the hem of her own garment to the fire.

'How did the Uí Fidgente behave while they were waiting for my brother?' she asked the innkeeper.

Aona frowned. 'Behave?'

'Yes. Were they friendly or truculent and ill-mannered? What?'

'They behaved well enough, I suppose. Why do you ask?'

'You heard no rumours among them of any discontent? Received no feelings that some conspiracy was afoot among them?'

The old innkeeper shook his head negatively, handing Fidelma one of the mugs of the potent ale.

She sipped at it absently, then asked, 'And all the members of Donennach's entourage went with him to Cashel? They met with no one else here?'

'No one that I saw. What does this mean?'

'There was an assassination attempt against my brother and Donennach as soon as they reached Cashel.'

The old man started. He looked alarmed. 'Was the King . . . was he badly hurt?'

'Flesh wounds,' Fidelma assured him. 'The wounds were bad enough but they will soon heal. However, some warriors of the Uí Fidgente have accused Cashel of deception and have claimed, in spite of his wound, that my brother is behind this attack.'

Eadulf entered in dry clothes, and bearing his sodden garment over his arm.

The innkeeper automatically took it from him and hung it on a pole in front of the fire. 'It will be dry shortly,' he told Eadulf before handing him the second mug of ale that he had poured. Then he turned back to Fidelma. 'The Uí Fidgente must be mad to make such an accusation . . . unless it be part of their plan.'

Eadulf drained his ale in one swallow and then started to cough as the effects of the fiery liquid were felt.

Aona gave him a sad smile. 'My *corma* is not to be taken like water, Saxon,' he rebuked. 'Perhaps you would like water to ease the effects?'

Eadulf nodded, gasping slightly.

Aona filled the mug with water from a jug and Eadulf drained it immediately, gasping for breath.

Fidelma ignored her companion and sat staring into the fire, as if deep in thought. Then she looked up at the old man.

'Are you sure, Aona, that you observed nothing out of the ordinary, nothing strange?'

'Nothing at all, lady. You have my word on it,' the old warrior assured her. 'Donennach and his entourage arrived here last evening. The Prince of the Uí Fidgente and his personal aides slept in the inn. His warriors encamped in the fields by the river bank. They were well behaved. Then this morning, your brother arrived and they all set off together towards Cashel. That is all I know.'

'They were not followed by anyone? A tall man, an archer, nor a short, rotund man?'

Aona shook his head emphatically. 'I saw no such people, lady.'

'Very well, Aona. But keep a careful watch these next few days. I do not trust the Uí Fidgente.'

'And if I see anything?'

'Do you know Capa?'

Aona chuckled humorously. 'I taught that youngster all he knew. He was but a slip of a youth when he came to join the bodyguard of the King of Cashel. He had no more idea of warfare than . . .'

Fidelma gently interrupted his memories. 'Your pupil is captain of the King's bodyguard as you once were, Aona. If you have news of any movement on the part of the Uí Fidgente, then send a message to Capa at Cashel. Do you understand?'

Aona nodded emphatically. 'That I do, lady. What else can I do for you?'

Eadulf coughed politely. 'Perhaps more of that brew you call *corma*. This time I shall treat it with respect.'

Aona turned away to pour more of the beverage from a wooden cask into Eadulf's mug. When he turned back he was frowning as if something had occurred to him.

'Is something wrong, Aona?' Fidelma was quick to notice his expression.

The elderly innkeeper scratched the side of his nose. 'I was trying to recall something. You asked about a tall man; an archer, and a shorter man, his companion?'

Fidelma leant forward eagerly. 'You did see them? You could not very well miss them if they were together. Side by side, they looked so incongruous.'

'I saw them,' confirmed the innkeeper.

Fidelma's expression was one of triumph. 'You did? Yet when I asked you first, you said that you were sure they were not here.'

Aona shook his head. 'That was because you asked me whether they were here with the Uí Fidgente within the last twenty-four hours. I saw such a pair a week ago.'

'A week ago?' intervened Eadulf in disappointment. 'Then they may not be our pair of villains.'

'Can you describe the men?' pressed Fidelma.

Aona rubbed his jaw with his left hand as if the process would aid his thoughts. 'I can tell you that the round, shorter man was like him.' He jerked his thumb to Eadulf.

Eadulf's mouth opened and an expression of indignation crossed his features. 'What are you implying?' he demanded. 'That I am short and fat? Why . . .'

Fidelma impatiently raised a hand to silence him.

'You should explain, Aona,' she said quietly. 'As my companion is neither short nor fat, you have posed a question. How, then, is he like the man you claim to be built in such a fashion?'

Aona grimaced. 'I did not mean that he looked like the Saxon, either in stature or features. No, I meant that the man was a religieux and that he wore his hair cut in that similar fashion which is unlike the tonsure of our Irish monks. I noticed it most particularly.'

Fidelma's eyes narrowed.

'You mean that he wore a tonsure on the crown of his head cut in the same fashion as my companion?'

'Have I not said as much?' protested the innkeeper. 'Why I noticed it so particularly, and found it curious, was because it was no longer clean-shaven but as if he had started to grow his hair to cover the tonsure.'

'What else can you describe about this short man?'

'That he was short and of ample girth; that his hair was grey and curly otherwise. He was of middle age and although he did not wear the clothes of the religious, he certainly had the manner of one.'

Eadulf glanced to Fidelma. 'That sounds like our assassin.' He turned back to the innkeeper. 'And what of his companion?'

Aona thought a moment. 'I think the other man was fair-haired. The hair was long at the back. I cannot be sure. He wore a cap and was dressed in a leather jerkin. He carried a quiver and bow and by that token I thought he was a professional bowman.'

Fidelma sighed in satisfaction. 'Near enough, I think. And you say that these two were in this very inn a week ago?'

'So far as I can remember. The only other thing that makes me clearly remember the pair was the discrepancies in their build. Just as you have pointed out.'

'You do not recall from whence they came nor where they went.'

'Not I,' replied the innkeeper.

Eadulf's face fell. 'That means we know no more than we did before.'

Fidelma pursed her lips in disappointment.

The door suddenly opened and the boy whom Fidelma had spoken to about his fishing entered.

Aona gestured to the child. 'My grandson, Adag, might be able to help you further. He served them while I tended their horses.'

Before she could raise a question, Aona had turned to his grandson. 'Adag, do you remember the sport you made of the two fellows who were in the inn two weeks ago?'

The boy placed his fishing line and basket on the table and glanced nervously at Fidelma and Eadulf. He said nothing.

'Come on, Adag, you are not in trouble. You must remember that you had such fun because one was tall and lean and the other short and fat and together they made a funny pair?'

The boy inclined his head almost reluctantly.

'Can you tell us anything about them, Adag?' pressed Fidelma. 'Apart from their appearance that is.'

'Only that one was fat and the other a bowman.'

'Well, that we know. But what else?'

Adag shrugged indifferently. 'Nothing else. I served them while my grandfather attended to their horses.'

'So they came on horseback?' Eadulf pointed triumphantly. He turned to Fidelma. 'Unusual, for the monk to travel on a horse.'

The child stared at him curiously. 'Why so, when you and the Sister here travel on horseback?'

'That is because . . .' Eadulf was about to respond when Adag's grandfather interrupted.

'You have to learn, boy, that some religious do not have to abide by the general rule against riding on horses if they are of a certain rank. I will tell you more, later. Now reply to the lady's questions.'

Adag shrugged. 'I remember that the fat one handed the bowman a leather purse while they drank together. That is all.'

'Nothing else?'

'Nothing, save the fat one was a stranger.'

'A foreigner?'

'No. A man of Éireann but not from the south, I think. I could tell by his accent. The bowman was from the south lands. I know that. But not the monk.'

'You did not hear what they spoke about?'

The boy shook his head.

'Did anyone see from which direction they came?'

'No. But the fat one did arrive first,' offered Aona.

'Ah? They did not arrive together?'

'No.' This time it was Aona who spoke. 'I remember now. The fat one arrived first and his horse needed attention. There was only myself and grandson here. So I went out to see to the horse while Adag served the monk with a meal. It was then that the bowman arrived. I did not see from what direction for I was in the stable.'

'And could you tell nothing from their horses?' Fidelma pressed.

Aona was shaking his head and then his eyes lit up. 'The bowman's mount was scarred. It was a war horse. Chestnut coloured. Past its prime. I saw several healed wounds on it. The saddle spoke of a warrior's steed. He had a spare quiver attached to the saddle. Apart from that, he carried all his weapons with him. I recall that the fat one's horse was in good fettle and his harness and saddle were of good quality. They were of the quality one expects a merchant to use. But that is all I remember.'

Fidelma stood up. From her *marsupium* she took a coin and gave it to Aona.

'I think your clothes are dry now, Eadulf,' she said firmly.

Aona was thanking Fidelma even as Eadulf took his dried clothes from the pole and folded them into his saddle bag.

'Shall I look out for these two strangers, then, lady?' Aona asked. 'Are these the people I must tell Capa about?'

Fidelma smiled wryly. 'If you see these two strangers, Aona, I would seek out a priest rather than Capa. They were killed this morning after they tried to assassinate my brother and Prince Donennach.'

She raised a hand in farewell and turned for the door, followed by Eadulf.

Once mounted, she saw Aona and his grandson, Adag, standing at the door, watching them.

'Be vigilant!' she called, turning her horse from the inn yard and along the road to Imleach.

They rode on in silence for a while. The path took them along the north bank of the Ara with the sky darkening perceptibly. To the south of them, the long wooded ridge of Slievenamuck stood framed against the light southern sky while, before them, the tip of the lowering sun was hovering above the western horizon. The road was easy and fairly straight, running across high ground away from the lowlands around Ara's Well. To the north of them, some miles away, there rose yet another range of hills. When Eadulf inquired what they were called, Fidelma told him that they were the Slieve Felim mountains, a rough and inhospitable country beyond which lay the lands of the Uí Fidgente.

For the most part they rode in silence because Eadulf could see Fidelma's brow creased in thought and in such circumstances, he knew it was ill-advised to interrupt her. She was doubtless turning the information they had been given over in her mind.

They had travelled about eight miles when Fidelma suddenly raised her head and became aware of her surroundings.

'Ah, not far now. We are almost there,' she announced with satisfaction.

Almost at once they emerged from the wooded track to an open hilly area. Eadulf needed no prompting to identify the great stone-walled building as being the abbey of St Ailbe. It dominated the little township which stretched before it, although there was a distance between the abbey walls and the edge of the main buildings of the town. Eadulf was aware that both abbey and town were surrounded by stretches of grazing land, edged with forests of yew-trees; yet they were trees of the Irish variety with their curved needles that marked them from the yew-trees with which he was familiar in his own land. The trees were tall and round-headed, some of them, curiously, seeming to grow out of many trunks, twisted and ancient.

'This is Imleach Iubhair . . .' Fidelma sighed. 'The Borderland of Yew-Trees'. This is the land that my cousin, Finguine of Cnoc Áine rules over.'

The township was quiet. It was much smaller than Cashel and to call it a township seemed to be a compliment. But Fidelma knew that the abbey and its church had helped to develop a thriving market there. The area seemed deserted and she presumed everyone would be at their evening meal. Vespers had come and gone.

The market place appeared to be the square directly in front of the gates of the abbey. The far side of the square was formed by the collection of houses which made up the town. Only one or two other buildings gave a cursory marking to the closer sides of the square so even to call it a square was not to be entirely accurate. It was slightly too large. In the centre stood a massive yew tree which surely stood over seventy feet high, a venerable twisted sculpture of dark brown wood and green curved needles. It dominated even the great grey walls of the abbey.

'Now that is a tree worthy of respect,' Eadulf breathed as he halted his horse before it and gazed up.

Fidelma turned in her saddle and smiled at her companion. 'What makes you say that, Eadulf? Do you know about this tree?'

'Know about it? No. I merely remark on its size and age.'

'That is the sacred totem of the Eóghanacht. Remember, I told you about it in Cashel?'

'A totem! That is a silly pagan idea.'

'What else is a crucifix but a totem? Each clan, each family, have what we call a sacred Tree of Life. This is our sacred. When a new king of the Eóghanacht is installed, he has to come here and take his oath under the great yew.'

'The tree must certainly be centuries old.'

'Over a thousand years,' Fidelma remarked complacently. 'It is said that it was planted by the hand of Eber Fionn, son of Milesius, from whom the Eóghanacht descend.'

Aware of the darkness closing in, and hearing the distant howl of wolves and the bark and the whine of watch-dogs about to be released for the night, they continued towards the gates of the abbey.

Fidelma halted her mare and reached forward in order to tug at the bell chain which hung beside the gates. There was a dull clanging sound of a bell from the interior.

A wooden panel slid noisily back behind a metal grille in one of the gates. A voice called: 'Who rings the bell of this abbey at this hour?'

'Fidelma of Cashel wishes entrance.'

Almost at once there seemed a flurry of activity behind the door. The panel slid back with a thud. Bolts were noisily withdrawn, their metal squeaking on metal. Then the tall wooden gates of the abbey were slowly pulled back.

Before Fidelma or Eadulf could move forward, a tall, white-haired figure came running forward from the gates.

Eadulf had seen Abbot Ségdae a few times before. The prelate he had seen at Cashel was a tall, dignified man; a man of quiet authority. But the man who came running forward to greet them was wild-haired and appeared distracted. His usually serene, hawk-like features were haggard. He halted by Fidelma's saddle, gazing up almost in the position of a worshipper at a shrine seeking solace.

'Thank God! You are the answer to our prayers, Fidelma! God be thanked that you have come!'

Chapter Eight

Brother Eadulf stretched himself luxuriously in his chair before the glowing fire in the private chamber of the Abbot of Imleach. He still felt sore and uncomfortable. Eadulf did not like arduous journeys and even though the trip from Cashel to Imleach had been comparatively short it had certainly not been easy. He sipped with relish at the goblet of mulled red wine which the Abbot Ségdae had provided. Eadulf sniffed the aromatic odours of the wine in appreciation. Whoever bought the wine for the abbey had good taste.

Facing him, on the opposite side of the large stone fireplace, sat Fidelma. Unlike Eadulf, she had not touched her wine but was sitting slightly forward in her chair, hands in her lap, the wine on a table by her side. She was gazing towards the dancing sparks on the burning logs as if deep in meditation. The elderly abbot had seated himself between them, directly in front of the fire.

'I prayed for a miracle, Fidelma, and then I was told you were at the abbey gates.'

Fidelma raised herself from her thoughts.

'I sympathise with your predicament, Ségdae,' she said at last. It was the first comment she had made since Abbot Ségdae had explained to her and Eadulf about the disappearance of the Relics of St Ailbe with their keeper, Brother Mochta. Although she had never seen the Relics herself it was impossible to be unaware of their significance. 'But my first priority must be to resolve the matter of culpability for the assassination attempt at Cashel. There are only nine days in which to do so.'

Abbot Ségdae's features were elongated in an expression of consternation. Fidelma had explained how matters stood at Cashel already. There was no formality between the abbot and the sister of the King. Ségdae had served her father in the office of a priest and had known Fidelma since she was a baby.

'So you have told me. But, Fidelma, you know, as well as I do, that the loss of the Holy Relics of St Ailbe will strike fear into all our people. Their disappearance portends the destruction of the kingdom of Muman. We have enemies enough to take advantage of this disaster.'

'Those enemies have already attempted to slay my brother and the Prince of the Uí Fidgente. As soon as I have dealt with that, I promise, Ségdae, that I shall give my mind to solving this matter. I am aware, perhaps more than most people, just how significant the Holy Relics of Ailbe are.'

It was then that Eadulf leant forward, putting down his goblet.

'You do not suppose that the two events are somehow connected?' he asked reflectively.

Fidelma glanced at him in momentary surprise.

Now and again Eadulf had the ability of stating the obvious when others had overlooked it.

'A connection between the loss of the Holy Relics and the assassination attempt on my brother . . . ?' The corners of her mouth turned down in a grimace. She considered the matter. It was true, as the abbot had said, that the people of Muman believed that the Holy Relics of Ailbe acted as a shield for the well-being of the kingdom. Their loss would cause alarm and despondency. Could the attempted assassination be a mere coincidence? 'There might be a connection,' she conceded. 'How better to overturn a kingdom than first to dispirit its people and assassinate its King?'

'And remember that one of the assassins was a former religieux,' Eadulf reminded her. 'He might have knowledge of the meaning of the relics.'

Abbot Ségdae started for it was the first he knew of this fact.

'Are you saying that a member of the Faith took up a weapon against his king? How can such a thing be? That a man of the cloth would take up the weapon of a murderer . . . It is unthinkable!' Words seemed to fail him.

Eadulf gestured dispassionately. 'It is not the first time that such a thing has been known.'

'Not in Muman,' Ségdae responded emphatically. 'Who was this son of Satan?'

'He was doubtless a stranger to the kingdom,' Fidelma replied, sipping her wine for the first time. 'Aona, the innkeeper at the Well of Ara, said he spoke with a northern accent.'

Eadulf supported her. 'I think that we are safe in assuming that the man was from the north. Even that strange tattoo of a bird on his forearm has been identified as one that only appears off the north-east coast and is not known here in the south. So this religieux is not a man from this area.'

The Abbot Ségdae had suddenly frozen in his chair. His face had paled considerably. There was a curiously pinched look on his features. He was regarding Fidelma with an expression approaching horror. He made several attempts to speak before his dry throat allowed him to articulate the words.

'Did you say this assassin carried the tattoo of a bird on his forearm? That he spoke with a northern accent?'

Fidelma affirmed it, wondering what was wrong with the old abbot.

'Would you describe the assassin?' Ségdae asked, a strange tension in his voice.

'Rotund features, short, with a mass of curly greying hair. A fleshy individual of perhaps two score and ten years of age. The tattoo was on his left arm. The bird was a species of hawk . . . it is known as a buzzard.'

Abbot Ségdae suddenly collapsed forward, hands to his head, moaning.

Fidelma rose and took an uncertain step towards the crumpled old man.

'What is it?' she demanded. 'Are you ill?'

It was some moments before the abbot regained his composure.

'The person whom you are describing is Brother Mochta, the Keeper of the Holy Relics. The one who has disappeared from our abbey.'

There was a silence for several long moments.

'Are you sure?' asked Eadulf, feeling foolish as he said it, for the description left one in no doubt. There could surely not be two people sharing such a likeness.

Ségdae expelled the air from his lungs in an almost violent hiss. 'Mochta was originally from the Clan Brasil in Ulaidh,' he began.

'A northern kingdom,' Fidelma interjected for Eadulf's benefit.

'He had that same distinctive tattoo on his left forearm.'

Fidelma was silent for a moment as she considered the matter.

'Then our mystery merely deepens, Ségdae,' observed Fidelma at last. Ignoring their puzzled looks, she went on. 'When did you last see this Brother Mochta?'

'I saw him last evening at Vespers.'

Vespers was the sixth canonical hour of the breviary of the Church, sung by the religious when Vesper the evening star rose in the sky.

'Did he often leave the abbey?' Fidelma pressed.

Ségdae shook his head. 'To my knowledge, he hardly ever left the abbey since he came here to be our *scriptor* ten years ago.'

Eadulf raised his eyebrows and glanced meaningfully at Fidelma. 'Did you say that he was your *scriptor*?' he asked quickly.

Ségdae made an affirmative gesture. 'He came here to work on our *Annals* and then became Keeper of the Holy Relics.'

'Surely, in view of the value and significance of these relics,' Eadulf began, 'it was strange to appoint a man from another kingdom as their keeper?'

'Brother Mochta was a pious and conscientious man who fulfilled his religious duties well and without thought of any particularism. He was devoted to this abbey and to his adopted land.'

'Until now,' Eadulf observed quietly.

'He has been with us ten years, six of which were as Keeper of the Relics. Are you claiming that he stole the Relics and went to Cashel last night to kill King Colgú? It is impossible to believe.'

'Yet if he was as you describe, even to the tattoo of the buzzard on his left forearm, then his body lies dead in Cashel, cut down while trying to flee from the scene of the assassination,' replied Eadulf.

Abbot Ségdae hunched his shoulders in anguish. 'But how is his bloodied and disorderly cell to be explained? Brother Madagan, my steward, and I immediately thought that Mochta had been attacked and wounded by whoever stole the Relics.'

Fidelma looked thoughtful. 'That is a mystery that we must solve. In the mean time, it appears that we have a name to one of our dead assassins in Cashel.'

'But an even greater mystery than before,' sighed Eadulf. 'If this Brother Mochta stole the relics and—'

Fidelma interrupted him, reaching into her *marsupium*, the small leather purse at her waist, and holding out a piece of paper to the abbot. 'I want you to see if you can identify this, Ségdae.' On the paper was the sketch of the crucifix which she had asked Brother Conchobar to make. She flattened the paper so that the abbot could see it.

The abbot reached for it in excitement.

'What does this mean?' he demanded as he gazed on the drawing.

'Do you recognise it?' prompted Fidelma.

'Of course.'

'Then tell us what it is.'

'It is one of the sacred Relics of Ailbe. He was ordained Bishop in Rome, so the story goes. It was said the Bishop of Rome, Zosimus the Greek, presented him with this crucifix made by the finest craftsmen of Constantinople. It is of silver with five great emeralds. Who made this sketch and why?'

Carefully, Fidelma refolded the sketch and replaced it in her *marsupium*. 'The cross was found on the body of the rotund assassin after he was slain by Gionga, the captain of the guard of the Uí Fidgente.'

Eadulf slapped his thigh with satisfaction. 'Well, here is a mystery solved. Your Brother Mochta stole the Relics and then went to assassinate Colgú and Donennach.'

'Is the crucifix still safe?' Ségdae asked anxiously.

'It is being held at Cashel as evidence for the hearing.'

Abbot Ségdae sighed deeply. 'Then at least one item of the Holy Relics is safe. But where are the rest? Did you find them?'

'No.'

'Then where are they?' The abbot almost wailed in despair.

'That we have to discover,' asserted Fidelma. She drained her goblet and rose purposely. 'Let me examine the chamber of Mochta. I presume that you have not disturbed it since your examination this morning?'

The abbot shook his head.

'All remains as we found it,' he replied, also rising. 'But I am still shocked and bewildered that such a man as Brother Mochta could have done this deed. He was such a quiet man, not given to speaking out even on his own behalf.'

'*Atlissima quaeque flumina minimo sono labi*,' intoned Eadulf.

Fidelma wrinkled her nose. 'Perhaps that is true. The deepest rivers flow with the least sound. Usually, however, they leave some mark of their passage and that we must discover. Take us to Brother Mochta's cell, Ségdae.'

Abbot Ségdae took up a lamp and led them from the room. As they passed down the corridors they could hear a faint noise rising from a distance.

'The brothers are at their *clais-cetul*,' explained Abbot Ségdae as he saw Eadulf pause and listen.

It was a new phrase to Eadulf.

'They sing in a choir,' explained Ségdae. 'The term means the harmonies of the voice. Here we sing the Psalms in the manner of the Gauls, who are our cousins, rather than in the manner of the Roman *classis*.'

Eadulf became aware of a strange acoustical effect in this corner of the abbey. The voices of the chanting religious carried clearly from the chapel on the far side of the cloisters. He could even hear the words distinctly.

Regem, regum, rogamus
in nostris sermonibus,
anacht Nóe a luchtlach
Diluui temporibus . . .

'We beseech in both our languages,' translated Fidelma reflectively, 'the King of Kings who protected Noah with his crew in the days of the Flood . . .'

'I have not heard the like before,' Eadulf admitted. 'This joining of Latin and Irish in a verse is quite strange.'

'It is one of the songs of Colmán moccu Cluasaif, the lector of Cork. He composed it two years ago when we were under threat from the terrible Yellow Plague,' explained Ségdae.

They stood listening for a moment, for there was something hypnotic about the rising and falling of the chanting voices.

'It is based, I think, on the prayer in the Breviary for the Commendation of the Soul,' Fidelma hazarded.

'That is exactly what it is, Fidelma,' Ségdae confirmed with appreciation. 'It is good to see you are not neglecting your religious studies in spite of your growing reputation as a *dálaigh*.'

'Which brings us back to why we are here, Ségdae,' Fidelma added seriously.

The abbot continued to lead the way along the dark corridors of the abbey. Torches gave a shadowy, dancing light from their metal burners along the stone walls.

Darkness had fallen now and apart from the pungent smell of the torches and their deceptive lighting, the abbey was shrouded in darkness.

'Perhaps it would have been wise to wait until morning,' muttered Eadulf, glancing around. 'I do not think we will be able to observe much in this light.'

'Perhaps,' agreed Fidelma. 'It is true that artificial light can be treacherous but I want to have a cursory examination for the longer things are left the more likely they are to fall into disarray.'

They fell silent as they continued along the echoing corridors of the abbey and across the cloisters.

'The wind is from the south-west again,' muttered the abbot as the torches nearby flickered violently. He halted in front of a door and bent to open it, then stood aside, holding the lamp for them to enter.

Once inside the light fell across the disordered chamber.

'It is exactly as Brother Madagan and I found it this morning. By the way–' Ségdae turned apologetically to Eadulf – 'I was going to suggest that you share his chamber tonight for we seem to be overcrowded in our guests' hostel. It is only for this night, mind you. We have a band of pilgrims passing through on their way to the coast to take ship for the holy shrine of St James of the Field of the Stars.'

'I have no objection to sharing a chamber with Brother Madagan,' Eadulf replied.

'Good. Tomorrow night our guests' hostel will be relatively empty again.'

'And am I to share a room this night?' asked Fidelma absently as she examined the chamber.

'No; I have set aside a special room for you, Fidelma,' Ségdae assured her.

Fidelma glanced around the chaos in the lamplight. She disliked to admit it, but Eadulf had been absolutely right. There was little to be seen by artificial light in the room. Important items could be lost among the shadows. She sighed and turned.

'Perhaps it is best to examine this room in the light of the morning.' She did not look at Eadulf as she admitted it.

'Very well,' agreed the abbot. 'I shall secure it again so that nothing is disturbed.'

'Tell me,' she said, as Ségdae was bending to lock the room again after they had emerged back into the corridor, 'you mentioned that there were pilgrims filling your guests' quarters. Do you have any other travellers staying here?'

'The pilgrims, yes.'

'No other travellers?'

'No. Oh . . . unless you count Samradán, the merchant. You must know him. He is from Cashel.'

'I do not know him, although I am told that he is known to my cousin, Donndubháin. What can you tell me of him?'

'Little enough,' shrugged the abbot. 'He trades frequently with the abbey, that is all. I think he has been doing so for the last two years or so. I know he is from Cashel. He comes here often with his wagons of goods and stays as our guest while we negotiate barter.'

Fidelma nodded thoughtfully. 'Wagons, you say? Who drives them?'

'He has three companions but they prefer to stay in the inn in the township outside the abbey.' He sniffed in disapproval. 'Not the best of places for it has no good reputation. It is not a lawful inn for it has no licence from the local *bó-aire*, the magistrate. I have had to intervene once or twice with the innkeeper, a lewd woman named Cred, concerning her morals . . .'

Fidelma interrupted. She was not interested in the morals of the woman, Cred. 'How long has Samradán been with you on this trip?'

Ségdae stroked the side of his nose as if it helped the process of his memory. 'You seem very interested in this Samradán? Is he suspected of anything?'

Fidelma made a negative gesture with her hand. 'No. I was just interested. I thought I knew most people who dwelt in Cashel, or of them, but Samradán I do not know. How long did you say he has been staying in the abbey?'

'A few days. No, more like a week to be precise. You will meet him at the morning meal, no doubt. Perhaps he will inform you of those things you need to know. And now, should I show you to your quarters for the night?'

Eadulf smiled, happy at the thought. 'A good suggestion, lord abbot. I am exhausted. It has been a long day filled with incident.'

'Once you have refreshed yourselves,' went on the abbot, 'you will doubtless want to join the brethren for the midnight services.'

He did not notice the woebegone expression on the face of the Saxon as he conducted them along a corridor and across a cloistered courtyard.

'This is our *domus hospitale*,' he said, indicating a door. 'Our guests' hostel,' he added as he knocked once.

A figure appeared in the doorway. A short shadowy figure whose silhouette clearly identified the sex of the person.

'This is our *domina*, Sister Scothnat.'

Eadulf had not realised until that moment that the Abbey of Imleach was a *conhospitae*, a mixed house in which religious of both sexes lived and worked together. Such 'double-houses' were rare among his own people but he knew that both the Britons and the Irish religious foundations were based on such cohabitation.

'This is Sister Fidelma, Scothnat.'

Sister Scothnat bobbed nervously for she knew that Fidelma was the sister of the King.

'I have your room prepared, lady,' she announced breathlessly. 'As soon as the abbot informed me that you had arrived, I prepared it.'

Fidelma held out a hand and touched Sister Scothnat lightly on the arm. Usually, among her fellow religious, she made no distinction of her relationship with the King of Muman. Only when she needed that extra authority did she make the point.

'My name is Fidelma. We are, after all, Sisters of the Faith, Scothnat.' She turned to Ségdae and Eadulf. 'Until the midnight service, then. *Dominus vobiscum*.'

'*Dominus tecum*,' responded Ségdae solemnly.

The abbot conducted Eadulf across the cloistered courtyard once again into a corridor on the far side where they found a tall religieux who greeted them.

'Madagan,' saluted the abbot. 'Excellent. We were coming in search of you. This is Brother Eadulf. Because of the pilgrims in the *domus hospitale* this night, I have suggested that he share your chamber as you have a spare bed there.'

Brother Madagan cast a searching glance over Eadulf, as if assessing him. His eyes were cold and when he smiled there was no warmth in the expression.

'You are most welcome, Brother.'

'Good.' The word on Ségdae's lips seemed to be at odds with his unhappy tone. 'Then, Brother Eadulf, I shall see you at the midnight service.' With a distracted expression, the abbot disappeared.

'I am the steward of the abbey,' Madagan announced confidingly, as he drew Eadulf towards a door in the corridor. 'My chamber is larger than most so I think you will find it comfortable.'

He threw open the door of a chamber which contained two small cots, one table and chair. A candle stood on the table. The whole was exceptionally neat with nothing else on the table by the candle except a small leather-covered book. Another table stood behind the door on which was a bowl, a jug of water, and some drying cloths.

Brother Madagan pointed to one of the two cots in the small cell. 'That will be your bed, Brother . . . sorry, I cannot pronounce your Saxon name. It is hard to my poor ears.'

'Ah'dolf,' pronounced Eadulf patiently.

'Does it have any meaning?'

'It means "noble wolf",' explained Eadulf with some degree of pride.

Brother Madagan rubbed his chin pensively. 'I wonder how that should be translated into our language? Perhaps, Conrí – king of wolves?'

Eadulf sniffed deprecatingly. 'A person's name does not need to be translated. It is what it is.'

'Perhaps so,' admitted the steward of the abbey. 'May I say that you speak our language well?'

Eadulf sat himself on the bed and gently tested it. 'I have studied at Durrow and Tuaim Brecain.'

Madagan looked surprised. 'Yet you still wear the tonsure of a stranger?'

'I wear the tonsure of St Peter,' corrected Eadulf firmly, 'cut in memory of the crown of thorns of Our Saviour.'

'But it is not the tonsure that we of the five kingdoms wear nor that which the Britons nor the men of Alba nor Armorica wear.'

'It is the tonsure of all those who follow the Rule of Rome.'

Brother Madagan pursed his lips sourly. 'You are proud of your tonsure, noble wolf of the Saxons,' he observed.

'I would not wear it otherwise.'

'Of course not. It is merely that it is outlandish to the eyes of the brothers here.'

Eadulf was about to make an end to the conversation when he

suddenly paused as a thought struck him. 'Yet you must have seen it often enough before,' he commented slowly.

Brother Madagan was pouring some water into a bowl to wash his hands. He glanced round at Eadulf and shook his head. 'The tonsure of St Peter? I can't say I have. I have not wandered far from Imleach for I was born near here on the slopes of Cnoc Loinge, just to the south. They call it the hill of the ship because that is the shape of it.'

'If you have not seen this tonsure before, how would you describe Brother Mochta's tonsure?' demanded Eadulf.

Brother Madagan shrugged in bewilderment. 'How would I describe it?' he repeated slowly. 'I have no understanding of your meaning.'

Eadulf almost stamped his foot in irritation. 'If my tonsure seems so strange to you, surely the fact that Brother Mochta wore the same tonsure, until he started growing his hair recently, should have been a matter of some comment?'

Brother Madagan was totally confused. 'But Brother Mochta did not wear a tonsure like the one you wear, Brother Noble Wolf.'

Eadulf controlled his exasperation, and explained, 'But Brother Mochta wore the tonsure of St Peter until a few weeks ago.'

'You are mistaken, Noble Wolf. Brother Mochta wore the tonsure of St John which we all wear here, the head shaven back to a line from ear to ear, so that the crown of thorns may be seen when we gaze upon the face of the brother.'

Eadulf sat down abruptly on his cot. It was his turn to be totally bewildered.

'Let me get this clear in my mind, Brother Madagan. Are you telling me that Brother Mochta did not wear a tonsure similar to that which I am wearing?'

'Assuredly not.' Brother Madagan was emphatic.

'Nor was he growing his hair to cover it?'

'Even more assuredly. At least this was so when I saw him at Vespers last evening. He wore the tonsure of St John.'

Eadulf sat staring at him for a moment or two as he realised what the man was saying.

Whoever the slain monk was at Cashel, and in spite of the description, even down to the tattoo mark, it could not be Brother Mochta of Imleach. It could not. But how was such a thing possible?

Chapter Nine

Fidelma regarded Eadulf across the refectory table, at which they were breaking their fast the next morning, with a slight smile.

'You seem alarmed by this mystery of Brother Mochta,' she observed, as she tore a piece of bread from the loaf before her.

Eadulf's eyes rounded in perplexity. 'Are you not alarmed? This borders on the miraculous. How can it be the same man?'

'Alarmed? Not I. Didn't the Roman Tacitus say that the unknown always passes for the miraculous? Well, once the matter ceases to be unknown it ceases to be miraculous.'

'Are you saying that there must be some logical explanation for this mystery?'

Fidelma looked at him in a reproach. 'Isn't there always?'

'Well, I do not see it,' Eadulf replied, thrusting out his chin. 'It smacks of sorcery to me.'

'Sorcery!' Fidelma was scornful. 'We have sorted out such mysteries before and found not one that was beyond our resources. Remember, Eadulf, *vincit qui patitur*.'

Eadulf bowed his head to hide his exasperation. 'One might prevail through patience but we have never had a mystery as confounding.' He glanced up and saw Brother Madagan approaching. He lowered his voice. 'Here is the Brother who raised the alarm when Mochta went missing. It is the steward of the abbey, Brother Madagan.'

The tall monk approached them with a smile.

'A fine morning,' he said, seating himself and addressing himself to Fidelma. 'I am the *rechtaire* of the abbey. Madagan is my name. I have heard much about you, Fidelma of Cashel.'

Fidelma returned the man's scrutiny and found herself disliking him though she could not put her finger on why. He was pleasant-featured enough, a little angular, a little gaunt, but there was nothing in his face that gave her outward revulsion. His manner too was friendly. She put it down to some chemical reaction which she could not explain.

'Good morning, Brother Madagan.' She inclined her head politely. 'I am told that you were the one who discovered that the Holy Relics were missing?'

'Indeed, I did.'

'In what circumstances did you do so?'

'It being the feastday of Ailbe, I rose early, for on that day . . .'

'I know the order of the feast,' Fidelma interrupted quickly.

Brother Madagan blinked.

It was then that Fidelma realised what it was that made her suspicious of the man. When he blinked his eyelids came down, heavy and deliberately, pausing for a fraction of a second before returning. It was as if he had hooded those eyes. The action bore a curious resemblance to the hooded blink of a hawk. She realised that they were cold in spite of the mask of friendship. There was a personality behind that face which was kept hidden to all but the keenest inspection.

'Very well,' he continued. 'There was much to do here in preparation . . .'

'Tell me how you discovered that the Holy Relics were missing.'

This time Brother Madagan did not seem perturbed at her sharp interruption.

'I went to the chapel where the Holy Relics were kept,' he replied calmly.

'Yet you were not the Keeper of the Holy Relics of Ailbe. Why did you go there?' Her voice was even but the question probing.

'Because that night it was my duty to act as warden – to keep the watch. The duties involve making the rounds of the abbey to ensure all is secure.'

'I presume you found that all was secure?'

'It was at first . . .'

'Until you came to the chapel?'

'Yes. It was then I noticed that the reliquary was missing from the recess where it is kept.'

'At what time was this?'

'An hour or so before dawn.'

'When had the reliquary last been seen in its proper position?'

'At Vespers. We all saw the reliquary. Brother Mochta was also there.'

Eadulf coughed discreetly before interposing: 'What exactly did this reliquary contain?'

Brother Madagan made a small gesture with his hand as if to encompass the contents. 'The Relics of our beloved Ailbe.'

'No, I do not mean that. What did these relics consist of? We know one of them was his crucifix which he had brought from Rome.'

'Ah, I see.' Brother Madagan sat back thoughtfully. 'As well as the crucifix there was his bishop's ring, his knife, a book of Ailbe's

Law written in his own hand and his sandals. Oh, and there was his chalice, of course.'

'Was it usual for people to know what is in the reliquary?' asked Eadulf suddenly. 'In many churches where the relics of the saints are kept, the reliquary is sealed so that none may gaze on the artifacts.'

Brother Madagan smiled quickly. 'It was quite usual in this case, Noble Wolf of the Saxons,' he replied jocularly. 'The contents were shown each year during the feastday ceremony and were carried from the chapel to his holy well, where there is a blessing, and from there to the stone which marks his grave.'

'In temporal wealth, they were not of great value, apart from the crucifix?' pressed Eadulf.

'The crucifix and ring were worth a great fortune,' replied Madagan. 'The ring was of gold set with a gemstone called *smaragdus* – a curious green stone mined in Egypt and said to have been worked into a finger ring by the Chaldeans. The ring was a gift of Zozimus to Ailbe. So, too, was the crucifix. That was worked in silver but also contained this gemstone *smaragdus*.'

'*Smaragdus*?' mused Fidelma. 'A dark green stone?'

'You have seen such stones?' asked Madagan. 'They also embellished Ailbe's crucifix.'

'Oh yes. They are called emeralds.'

'So the temporal value was great?' persisted Eadulf.

'Great enough but such value was of no significance compared with the symbolic value those Relics have to our abbey and to the kingdom of Muman.'

'I have already informed Brother Eadulf of that significance,' Fidelma affirmed.

Brother Madagan bowed his head. 'Then you will understand, Noble Wolf, that the recovering of the reliquary and the Holy Relics are necessary for the well-being of this kingdom. Our people are much given to symbolic belief. They firmly accept that if the Relics are lost then harm will come to the kingdom which they will be unable to prevent.'

'Was the chalice of great value?' asked Eadulf.

'It was also worked in silver and set with semi-precious stones. Yes, it was of great temporal value also.'

'Who knows about their disappearance within the abbey?' Fidelma asked.

'Alas, we have not been able to keep it a secret from those who dwell in this abbey. After all, yesterday was the day when they should have been displayed to the brethren. While the abbot has attempted to prevent the news spreading outside the abbey walls, it will not be long before it does. The pilgrims leave here this morning en route to the coast. They will doubtless speak of it. Then there is the merchant from Cashel and his assistants. They will also talk. I believe that within the week it will be broadcast throughout the kingdom, perhaps even to the other kingdoms of Éireann. It will mark a time of danger for our people.'

Fidelma knew well the implications. She knew that there were many envious people who would like to see the overthrow of the Eóghanacht of Cashel. Especially, she had to admit, Donennach of the Uí Fidgente. He would not be unhappy if the kingdom fell. If people were alarmed by the disappearance of the Relics and so dismayed that they surrendered to the fates and had no will to defend themselves, then Cashel might expect attacks from without and subversion from within. She suddenly felt the weight of responsibility on her shoulders. If she did not solve this mystery, and solve it soon, it could lead to disaster for Cashel.

'So, having found that the reliquary was missing, what did you do then?' she asked.

'I went straightaway to rouse the abbot,' Brother Madagan replied.

'You went straightaway to rouse Abbot Ségdae? Why?'

Brother Madagan looked at her with incomprehension at the question. 'Why?' he repeated.

'Yes. Why didn't you go to rouse Brother Mochta? He was Keeper of the Relics, after all?'

'Ah! I see. Such considerations appear logical in retrospect. The abbot asked me the same question. I confess that in the shock of my discovery, logic had no relevance. I thought that the abbot should be the first to be informed.'

'Very well. Then what happened?'

'The abbot suggested that we inform Brother Mochta. We went to his chamber together to find that he had disappeared, leaving turmoil behind him. There were bloodstains in the room.'

Fidelma rose with an abruptness, surprising both Brother Madagan and Brother Eadulf.

'Thank you, Brother. We will go to Brother Mochta's chamber and examine it,' she announced.

Brother Madagan rose as well. 'The abbot has asked me to conduct you there,' he said. He had brought the key to Brother Mochta's chamber and he led the way keeping up a constant chatter by pointing out sites of interest in the abbey. Both Fidelma and Eadulf later agreed they had felt that the chatter appeared feigned for their benefit.

Fidelma stood on the threshold of Brother Mochta's chamber, once again regarding the disorder with her keen eyes picking out the details.

The room was in total disarray. She noticed that items of clothing were discarded on the floor. The straw mattress had been dragged half off the tiny wooden cot that provided the bed. There was, she saw, a stub of unlit candle toppled in a small pool of its own grease on the floor with its wooden holder nearby. There were even a few personal toilet items scattered here and there. There was a table by the bedside which, oddly, had not been knocked askew and on which was a solitary object. The end half of an arrow. Her eyes dwelt on the flight and its markings with immediate recognition. There were also some writing materials scattered in a corner and some pieces of vellum.

Brother Madagan was peering over her shoulder. 'There, Sister, on the mattress. You may see the bloodstain which the Father Abbot and I noticed.'

'I see it,' replied Fidelma shortly. She made no move towards it. Then she turned to Brother Madagan.

'Tell me, the chambers either side of this one . . . are they occupied?'

Brother Madagan nodded. 'They are, but the brothers who sleep there have gone to the fields to gather herbs. One of them is our apothecary and mortician and the other is his assistant.'

'So, are you saying that at the time that Brother Mochta apparently disappeared from this room, the chambers on either side were occupied?'

'That is so.'

'And no disturbance was reported to you or to the abbot?' Her eyes flickered around the turmoil of the room.

'Just so.'

Fidelma was silent for a moment and then said: 'We need not keep you longer from your duties, Brother Madagan. Where can we find you when we are finished here?'

Brother Madagan tried to hide his disappointment at being so summarily dismissed. 'In the refectory. We shall be bidding farewell to the pilgrims this morning.'

'Very well. We will join you there shortly.'

Eadulf watched Brother Madagan disappear along the corridor before turning with a look of inquiry to Fidelma. She ignored him and turned back into the chamber. She stood in silence awhile and Eadulf knew better than to interrupt her thoughts. After awhile she moved inside the door, standing to one side.

'Eadulf, come and take my place. Do not enter the room but stand there on the threshold and tell me your impressions.'

Puzzled, Eadulf went to stand on the threshold of the door with

Fidelma at his side. He let his gaze wander over the disordered room. That the room was in a chaotic state was obvious.

'From the look of it, Mochta was forced from his chamber, having put up a fierce struggle.'

Fidelma inclined her head in approval. 'From the look of the room,' she repeated in a soft tone. 'Yet no disturbance was reported by the occupants in the adjoining chambers.'

Eadulf glanced at her quickly, picking up the emphasis. 'You mean that this scene has been . . .' he struggled for the word. 'That it has been purposefully arranged?'

'I think so. Look at the way everything is cast around the room. Look at the mattress and clothes taken from the bed. It all indicates a fierce struggle which must logically have taken place sometime after Vespers and an hour or so before dawn. If such a struggle, as represented here, really took place, the noise would have disturbed even the deepest sleeper on either side. Yet no one reported being disturbed.'

'We should make sure by asking the occupants of the adjoining chambers,' Eadulf said.

Fidelma smiled. 'My mentor, the Brehon Morann, said, "He who knows nothing doubts nothing". Well done, Eadulf. We must indeed check to see what they say. But I am working on the probability that they were not disturbed by any noise in this room. And a reasonable probability is the only certainty we have at this time.'

Eadulf gestured helplessly. 'So are we saying that Brother Mochta arranged this scene? But why?'

'Perhaps someone else arranged it. We cannot form a conclusion as yet.'

'If it were true that the slain monk at Cashel was Brother Mochta, then it might make some sense. But Brother Madagan insists that Mochta wore your Irish tonsure and not the tonsure of Rome. Hair cannot grow or be changed in a day. Besides, the innkeeper at the Well of Ara said hair was growing to disguise the tonsure when he stayed there a week ago.'

'True enough. But do you have an explanation for the accuracy of the description of the body at Cashel and that of Brother Mochta? A description which fits even down to the tattoo on his arm.' Fidelma's eyes twinkled a moment. 'That is also a certainty. We can be absolutely certain only about things we do not understand.'

Eadulf raised his eyes to the ceiling. 'A saying of the Brehon Morann no doubt?' he asked sarcastically.

Fidelma ignored him as she looked round the room.

'I believe that whoever did this, whether it was Brother Mochta or some other person, arranged these things carefully. Look at the way the mattress is positioned so that anyone who was not blind would see the bloodstain. Now a mattress, in a struggle, might well fall that way but it does seem contrived. And in a struggle, why would the clothes from that cupboard be taken out and strewn around the room?'

Eadulf began to realise the detail which her examination of the room had picked up.

'Did you notice the arrow on the bedside table?' Fidelma asked him.

Eadulf gave an inward groan.

He had noticed it but only as part of the debris of the room. Now that he focused on it, he realised the significance of the markings on the flight. It was the same type of arrow which had been carried by the archer during the assassination attempt; the same style of arrow which Fidelma was carrying and which had been identified as being made by the fletchers of Cnoc Áine.

'I see it,' he answered shortly.

'And what do you make of it?'

'Make of it? It is the shaft of an arrow which has been snapped in two. The end half of the shaft with the flight has fallen on the table.'

'*Fallen*?' Fidelma's voice raised a little in disbelief. 'It is laying there so clearly exposed that it seems to have been placed there for anyone to see. If it had been broken in some struggle, where is the other half?'

Eadulf's eyes fell to the floor, searching. He examined the room carefully and saw nothing of it. 'What does it mean?'

'You know as much as I do,' Fidelma replied indifferently. 'If the room has been carefully arranged for us . . . well, arranged for whoever was meant to gaze on it . . . what message is it supposed to give?'

Eadulf stood and folded his arms, gazing around before delivering his answer. 'Brother Mochta has disappeared. The room is supposed to make people think that he has been removed from his chamber in a violent struggle. The bloodstain on the mattress and the disorder point to this. Then there is a broken arrow on the bedside table . . . ah, that might signify that the arrow was broken when an assailant plunged it into the body of Mochta. The piece with the arrow head was left in Mochta while the end of the arrow with the flight was broken and tossed onto the table.' He glanced at Fidelma for her approval.

'Excellently done, Eadulf. That is precisely the message we have been asked to believe. Yet as the scene was so carefully prepared we must look behind this message for the real significance of this chamber.'

For the first time she entered it and began to examine it foot by foot. Then she picked up the broken arrow and placed it in her *marsupium*.

'I do not think it will tell us much until we have garnered more facts.'

She then examined the writing materials in the corner and the pieces of vellum.

'Brother Mochta wrote a fair hand. He seems to have been writing a *Life of Ailbe*.' She began to read from one of the pieces of vellum: '"He was called by Christ to his repose in the hundredth year of his life, as recorded in the *Annals of Imleach* which were began in that year of Our Lord 522."' She paused. 'The rest appears to be missing. But here is another fragment.' She read again: '"The repose of Ailbe has been distorted by the scribes of the north for they do not wish to acknowledge his appearance in Muman before Patrick of Armagh."'

'Do these writings have significance?' queried Eadulf.

'Perhaps,' she replied, rolling the pieces of vellum up before placing them in her *marsupium*. Then she glanced around again. 'I do not think this chamber will reveal any more secrets to us. Let us go.'

She locked the room after they left, for Brother Madagan had left the key in the door. They returned to the refectory. Outside, a dozen or more male and female religious had gathered, wrapped in long cloaks, carrying bundles and each holding a pilgrim's staff. Abbot Ségdae was there in front of them, standing with raised right hand, his thumb and third finger pressed against one another so that the first, second and fourth finger were raised to symbolise the Holy Trinity in the Irish fashion.

He delivered the Blessing in Greek, that being considered the language of the Holy Gospels.

Then the pilgrims, two by two, shouldered their bundles and set out towards the open abbey gates. Their voices rose in a joyful chant as they did so.

Cantemus in mni die
concinentes uarie,
conclamantes Deo dignum
hymnum sanctae Mariae

'Let us sing each day, chanting together in varied harmonies, declaiming to a God a worthy hymn for holy Mary,' muttered Eadulf, translating the words.

Soon the singing column of pilgrims had passed through the abbey gates, continuing their pilgrimage, their voices receding beyond the walls.

As they stood watching a burly man approached them. He was of average height, well muscled, solidly built with unexceptional grey-brown hair. He wore a leather jerkin over his workmanlike clothes and carried a short sword at his belt. His eyes were bright and keen. His features were ruddy and a little too fleshy to retain the handsomeness he might have enjoyed in his youth. He had the air of acquired wealth about him; acquired because he wore his wealth ostentatiously. He was bejewelled, which seemed at odds with his choice of clothing. Someone to whom such richness came naturally would not have been so tasteless with their wealth. Fidelma suppressed a smile. She suddenly had a vision of this pretentious character wearing a sign around his neck with the legend: '*Lucri bonus est odor* – sweet is the smell of money'. She wondered where the line came from and then remembered it was from Juvenal's *Satires*. Well, she was sure that the man would not object to the motto.

'Are you the Lady Fidelma?' the man asked, his bright eyes narrowing slightly as he examined her.

Fidelma inclined her head in greeting. 'I am Fidelma of Cashel,' she replied.

'I have heard that you have been asking after me. My name is Samradán of Cashel.'

Fidelma met the gaze of his pale, bright eyes and held it. It was the Cashel merchant that let his gaze dart away first.

'If there is anything I can help you with?' Samradán shifted his weight uncomfortably.

Fidelma suddenly smiled disarmingly. 'Did you know Brother Mochta?'

The merchant shook his head. 'The monk who has vanished? Everyone is talking about it here at the abbey. No, I did not know him. I traded only with Brother Madagan as the steward of the abbey and, of course, with the abbot himself. I never met Brother Mochta, at least the name never registered with me if I encountered him in the abbey.'

'You keep a warehouse at Cashel?'

The merchant nodded warily. 'By the market square, lady. My house is in the town as well.'

'An assassination attempt on my brother, the King, and the Prince of the Uí Fidgente, was launched from the roof of your warehouse yesterday morning.'

The merchant paled slightly. 'I have been here in Imleach for several days. I knew nothing of this. Besides, anyone can climb onto the roof of my warehouse. It is a flat roof and easily accessible.'

'I do not accuse you of anything, Samradán,' chided Fidelma. 'But it was best that you should know this fact, though.'

The merchant nodded hurriedly. 'Of course . . . I thought . . .'

'Do you trade among the people of Cnoc Áine?'

'No. Only to the abbey.'

'That seems to limit your business,' smiled Fidelma. 'You must do a lot of trade here within the abbey to visit so often and stay so long.'

Samradán looked at her uncertainly.

'I mean that I trade only with the abbey in this area. I also trade with the abbeys at Cill Dalua, north of here, and south at Lios Mhór. I have in recent months even traded as far north as the abbey at Armagh. That was an arduous journey. But I have made it twice in the last two months.'

'What sort of goods do you trade in?'

'We barter corn and barley for wool mainly. Around Cill Dalua are first-class tanners and workers in leather. So we buy jackets, leather bottles, shoes and other items and trade to the south.'

'How fascinating. Do you trade in metal work?'

Samradán was dismissive. 'Carrying metal objects is a tiresome business for our horses. It weights our wagons and we have to move slowly. There are enough good smiths and forges throughout the country.'

'So you would not deal in metals like silver? There are some silver mines and other workings of precious metals to the south of here.'

Samradán shook his head vehemently. 'Be one's trade good or bad, it is experience that makes one an adept at it,' he replied, quoting an old proverb. 'I stick to the trade I know. I know nothing of silver.'

'You are right,' agreed Fidelma pleasantly. 'A trade not properly learned can be an enemy to its success. I understand that you have not dwelt at Cashel very long?'

'Only these last three years,' countered Samradán.

'Then, before you came to Cashel, where did you conduct your business from?'

Was there a shiftiness in the merchant's eyes now? 'I was in the land of the Corco Baiscinn.'

'Is that where you come from?' pressed Fidelma.

Samradán raised his chin in an automatic gesture of defiance. 'It is.' His confirmation was a challenge but Fidelma said nothing further.

After the silence continued, the merchant cleared his throat noisily, as if attracting attention. 'Is that all?'

Fidelma smiled again as if it had already been made clear and the man had not understood.

'Why, of course. But when you return to Cashel, you might be questioned about this terrible event. You may say that you have spoken with me. However, your testimony may be wanted by the Brehons in Cashel.'

Samradán looked startled. 'Why should I be questioned?' he demanded.

'For the reason I told you . . . the assassins used your warehouse. No one accuses you of anything but it is obvious that you would be questioned because of that fact. Tell them what you told me. That you have no knowledge of the matter.'

The merchant looked uncomfortable. 'I do not plan to return to Cashel for a few days yet, lady,' he muttered. 'I am going to the country of the Arada Cliach to trade first. I mean to start early tomorrow morning.'

'Then I wish you a good journey.' Fidelma turned and motioned Eadulf to follow her.

'What was that about?' he asked, when they were out of earshot.

Fidelma looked at him in mild rebuke. 'No more than it appeared to be,' she replied. 'I just wanted to check who this Samradán was.'

'And are you satisfied that he is no more than he seems to be?'

'No.'

Eadulf was disconcerted by the enigmatic response.

Fidelma caught his questioning glance. 'Samradán may well be what he claims to be but he admits he is of the Corco Baiscinn.'

'I do not know these people,' Eadulf returned. 'Is there some significance here?'

'They are one of the people over whom the Uí Fidgente hold lordship. They also claim to be descendants of Cas.'

'Then he might well be part of some conspiracy?' suggested Eadulf.

'I do not trust him,' Fidelma returned. 'However, if he were part of some conspiracy I doubt whether it is connected with the Uí Fidgente. He would not have readily admitted that he was of the Corco Baiscinn. Yet it is better to be suspicious about people than not to be.'

Eadulf said nothing.

They found Brother Madagan at the gates of the abbey, speaking with the abbot.

'Have you come to any conclusions?' asked Abbot Ségdae eagerly.

'It is far too early for conclusions,' Fidelma replied, handing the key of Brother Mochta's chamber back to Brother Madagan. 'As soon as I have something positive, I will let you know.'

Abbot Ségdae appeared anxious still. 'I suppose I was hoping for a miracle. But at least, of the Holy Relics, Ailbe's crucifix is safely recovered.'

Fidelma laid a reassuring hand on the old man's arm. She wished she could do something further to enhearten this old friend and supporter of her family.

'Do not worry unduly, Ségdae. If the matter is capable of resolution, we will resolve it.'

'Is there anything else that I can do for you before I return to my other duties?' Brother Madagan inquired.

'Thank you, but not at this time. Brother Eadulf and I are going to the township and may not be back for a while.' She hesitated. 'Oh, you mentioned that the adjoining chambers to Mochta are occupied. Where might their occupants be found?'

Brother Madagan suddenly glanced across Fidelma's shoulder through the open gates of the abbey. 'You are in luck, for the two brothers are coming towards the abbey gates now.'

Fidelma and Eadulf turned and saw two religious approaching the gates, one pushing a wheelbarrow full of herbs and other plants which they had obviously been gathering that morning.

As Fidelma and Eadulf walked towards the gates of the abbey to intercept the two religious, Eadulf said quietly, 'Wouldn't it have been a kindness to report on our conclusions so far?'

Fidelma arched an eyebrow. 'Our conclusions? I did not think that we had any conclusions.'

Eadulf made a gesture with his hand as if to express his confusion. 'I thought that we agreed that Brother Mochta disarrayed his room on purpose to mislead people?'

Fidelma glared at him in reproof. 'What we discovered remains between ourselves until we can put some logic to it. What is the point of revealing our knowledge, which might then get back to the conspirators – whoever they may be – so that they can hide their tracks? We will say no more of this until the time is right.'

She turned and hailed the two men. 'Good morning, Brothers. I am Fidelma of Cashel.'

Their greeting showed that they had both heard of her. News of her arrival at the abbey must have spread quickly.

'I am told that you sleep in the chambers situated on either side of Brother Mochta's room.'

The elder of the two religious was only a little older than Fidelma while the younger was no more than a teenager, fresh-faced and fair-haired. He seemed hardly beyond the 'age of choice'. They exchanged nervous glances.

'Is there news of Brother Mochta?' the younger one asked. 'The news of his disappearance and the Holy Relics is all around the abbey.'

'There is no news, Brother . . . ?'

'I am called Daig and this is Brother Bardán who is the apothecary and mortician of our abbey.' The youth said this with an air of pride as one introducing a more worthy person than himself. He went on eagerly: 'The entire abbey has been talking of your arrival, lady.'

'Sister,' corrected Fidelma gently.

'How may we help you?' interrupted the elder Brother in a less eager fashion than his companion.

'You know that Brother Mochta disappeared from his chamber sometime after Vespers and sometime before dawn on the feastday of Ailbe?'

'We know as much,' agreed Brother Bardán. His tone was curt and he seemed to regard Fidelma with a suspicious look. He was a swarthy young man, his hair the colour of a raven's feathers, with a blue sheen on its blackness. His dark eyes seemed to move quickly, nervously, here and there as if in search of hidden enemies. Although clean-shaven, the shadow of a beard coloured his lower features darkly, contrasting with the fairness of his cheeks.

'Were you sleeping in your chambers that night? I mean, the night when Mochta disappeared.'

'We were.'

'You heard nothing during the night?'

'I sleep soundly, Sister,' replied Brother Bardán. 'I doubt whether anything would awaken me. I heard nothing.'

'Well, I was disturbed,' Brother Daig announced.

Fidelma turned towards him. It was not a reply that she had expected. Out of the corner of her eye she noticed Brother Bardán's expression crease in anger as he glanced at his companion. His mouth opened and she wondered, for a second, if he was going to rebuke the boy. But he did not.

'Did you report this disturbance?' she demanded.

'Oh, it was not that sort of disturbance,' the young boy replied.

'Then what sort was it?'

'I am a light sleeper and I do remember being awakened in the night by a door being shut. I think the wind must have caught it for no Brother shuts his door in such a fashion. It banged shut.'

'What happened then?' asked Fidelma.

'Nothing,' admitted Brother Daig. 'I turned over and went back to sleep.'

Fidelma was disappointed. 'You could not tell which door had banged shut?' she pressed the young man.

'No. But I know this . . . I've heard that there was supposed to have been a fight in Mochta's room about this time. I say that it is impossible.'

'Yes?' Fidelma encouraged the young man.

'Well, had there been such a fight, then it is obvious that I would have heard it. I would have awakened. Apart from the banging of the door, nothing else disturbed me during that night.'

Brother Bardán smiled sceptically. 'Come, Daig . . . young people are known to sleep through great tempests. How can you be so positive that nothing untoward took place in Mochta's chambers that night? From what we have been told, the evidence shows the opposite.'

'I would have awakened had there been such a fight,' Daig replied indignantly. 'As it was, I was awakened by a slamming door.'

'Well, I admit that I heard nothing.' Bardán was dismissive.

Fidelma thanked them both and left them at the abbey gates, followed by Eadulf. After a short distance, crossing the square towards the township, she glanced quickly back over her shoulder. She was intrigued to see Brother Bardán, standing where they had left him, apparently arguing with the younger monk. It seemed that Bardán was telling the youth off in no uncertain terms.

'Well,' said Eadulf, unaware of the argument as he strode on, 'doesn't that prove your point? There was no struggle in Brother Mochta's room.'

Fidelma turned back to catch up with Eadulf.

'But where does that take us?' mused Fidelma as she continued to walk with him, passing the great yew-tree in the square.

'I don't understand,' Eadulf responded.

'It would only take us somewhere if we knew for certain that Brother Mochta was the same man who was killed in Cashel. But, according to Madagan and the others here, we are describing exactly the same man, yet there is one point of difference that cannot possibly be reconciled.'

Eadulf made a groaning sound and spread his hands eloquently. 'I know. The tonsure. I have tried many times to see if I can come up with a reasonable explanation for it. I cannot. Brother Mochta was last seen here less than forty-eight hours ago with his head shaved in the manner of the tonsure of St John. The man we thought was Mochta was found in Cashel twenty-four hours ago with the signs of a tonsure of St Peter on his head but with his hair also showing signs of a few weeks of growth on his pate. How can these things be squared?'

'You have overlooked another point,' Fidelma observed.

'What is that?'

'Aona saw this same man with the same tonsure a week ago at the Well of Ara. Ségdae told us that Mochta hardly ever left the abbey. That is another point against the body of the man at Cashel being Mochta.'

Eadulf shook his head in annoyance.

'I cannot fathom any reasonable explanation for it.'

'Now do you see that it is a fruitless exercise to tell Abbot Ségdae of our suspicions? Until we have some answers they must remain suspicions and not conclusions.'

Eadulf was contrite.

They crossed the square to the beginning of the group of houses, barns and other buildings which comprised the township of Imleach. The urban complex had grown up during the last century in the shadow of the abbey and its cathedral seat. Before then it had simply been the gathering place around the sacred tree of the Eóghanacht where kings came to take their oath and be installed in office. The abbey had attracted tradesmen, builders and others so that a township of several hundred people had grown up opposite the abbey walls.

Fidelma paused at the edge of the buildings and gazed round.

'Where are we going now?' Eadulf asked.

'To find a blacksmith, of course,' she replied shortly. 'Where else?'

Chapter Ten

There was no need to ask directions to the smithy's forge for the heavy breath of the bellows and the ring of iron on iron could clearly be heard as Fidelma and Eadulf came to the group of houses which were spaced along a main street within sight of the abbey gates. The forge was stone built with the furnace constructed on large flags. In one of the flagstones there was a small hole through which a pipe directed the air-current from the bellows into the fire.

The wheezy breath of the smith's apparatus was supplied by an impressive four chamber air pump. Eadulf had heard that such a large bellows existed but had never seen one. He had also heard that it gave a more uniform blast to the furnace than the normal two chamber device. It was obviously much harder to work for they saw the smith, sweating at the fire, assisted by a sturdy bellows blower whose job was to raise and depress end chambers by standing on two short boards and raising one foot at a time in the manner of someone walking slowly and deliberately. The faster he walked the quicker the bellows worked.

The smith was a well built, muscular man in his thirties, wearing leather trousers but no shirt with only a buckskin apron to protect him from the sparks. He was holding a red-hot piece of iron in a *tennchair*, a pair of tongs. In the other hand he wielded his hammer and turning to a large anvil he smote the iron with a thunderous noise before turning to a water trough called a *telchuma* and plunging the iron in.

The smith saw them approaching and paused, spitting into the hot coals of his forge so that there was a momentary sizzling sound.

'Suibne, get me more wood charcoal,' he ordered his assistant without taking his eyes off them.

The bellows pumper jumped down from the boards and disappeared into a shed.

The smith drew the back of his hand across his face, wiping away the sweat, as they halted before him.

'What can I do for you?' he asked, examining them each in turn. 'Do you seek me out as a smith or do you seek me out as *bó-aire* of this community?'

The *bó-aire* was a local magistrate, a chieftain without land whose wealth had been initially judged by the number of cows he owned, hence he was called a 'cow chief'. Small communities, such as a township, were usually ruled by a *bó-aire* who owed his allegiance to a greater chieftain.

'I am Fidelma of Cashel,' Fidelma introduced herself. She was more formal with the man once she heard that he held rank. 'What is your name?'

The smith straightened perceptibly. Who had not heard of the King's sister? The chieftain to whom he owed allegiance was Fidelma's own cousin, Finguine of Cnoc Áine.

'I am called Nion, lady.'

Fidelma drew out the arrows from her *marsupium*. The one from the assassin's quiver and the other, broken one she had taken from Mochta's chamber.

'Tell me what you make of these, Nion,' she asked without explanation.

The smith wiped his hands on his apron and took the arrows from her hands and, holding them up, examined them carefully.

'I am no fletcher, although I have made arrow heads before now. These are of competent workmanship. The head on this one is made of bronze and constructed, as you see, with a hollow *cro* . . .'

'A what?' demanded Eadulf, leaning forward.

'A socket. See there where the wood of the shaft is inserted? These are especially fine for you see that the head is fixed by a tiny metal rivet.'

'And where would you guess they were made?' pressed Fidelma.

'No need to guess,' replied the smith with a smile. 'See the flight? That bears the symbol of a fletcher of Cnoc Áine and you are in that territory, as you must know, lady.'

Fidelma smiled thinly. 'And would you be able to point to such a craftsman, Nion?'

The smith gave an unexpected roar of laughter. 'See my neighbour there . . .' he said, pointing to a carpentry shop nearby. 'He makes the shafts and constructs the flights, while I make the heads and fix them in place. This arrow is one of a batch I made not above a week ago. I recognise the metalworking. Why do you ask, lady?' he added, returning the arrows to her.

His assistant returned and emptied a bag of charcoal on the furnace fire, poking it with an iron rod.

'I would like to know something about the man to whom you sold these arrows.'

At once the smith's eyes narrowed suspiciously. 'Why?'

'If you have nothing to hide, Nion, you will tell me. Remember that you are answering the questions of a *dálaigh* and I hold you to your position as magistrate of this town.'

Nion stared at her as if trying to gauge her intentions and then shrugged. 'Then as *bó-aire* to *dálaigh*, I will answer. I do not know the man. I merely called him the *Saigteóir* because he looked and acted like a professional archer. He came to my forge more than a week ago and wanted me to produce two dozen arrows. He paid me well for the task. He collected them a few days later and that is all I know.'

Eadulf was disappointed but Fidelma did not give up.

'Sometimes memories have to be teased out,' she observed. 'You say the man looked like a professional archer. Describe him.'

After some hesitation Nion the smith described the bowman whom Gionga had slain. It was a good description and there was no doubting the identification of the man.

'You spoke to him. How did he sound?'

The smith rubbed his jaw and then his eyes brightened. 'He spoke roughly, like any professional soldier but he was not of the warrior caste; not a man born into the nobility of the craft of arms.'

'Did you not ask what he was doing here?' intervened Eadulf.

'No. Nor would I ask him. Better not to ask a warrior why he wants weapons unless he wants to volunteer such information.'

'I can understand that,' agreed Fidelma. 'So he volunteered no information?'

The smith shook his head.

'Did he have any companion with him?'

'No.'

'You seem certain of that. Did he ride a horse?'

'Oh yes. He rode a chestnut mare. I noticed that for the beast's rear shoes needed fixing. One had been struck loose by a stone. I sorted out that problem at once.'

'Could you tell anything from the horse?' Fidelma knew well enough that a professional smith should tell in what style a horse was shod, sometimes even to identifying the geographical location of the smith who did the work.

'That it was last shoed in the north was obvious,' the smith replied at once. 'I have seen that style before and know it is used by the smiths of Clan Brasil. I could also tell that the animal had seen its best years. It was not the sort of animal that a warrior of status would ride, though it was a war horse.'

'So what else did you discern?'

'Nothing. What business was it of mine?'

'You are the *bó-aire*,' Fidelma pointed out. 'It is your responsibility to be aware of what takes place in your territory. These arrows that you sold to this archer were used in an attempted assassination on my brother, the King, and the Prince of the Uí Fidgente. Have you not heard?'

Nion stared at her without speaking. It was obvious that the news shocked him.

'I had no hand in this affair, lady,' he said anxiously. 'I merely made the arrows and sold them. I did not know who the man was . . .'

Fidelma raised her hand to quiet his outburst.

'I tell you this only to show that sometimes these matters can be your business, magistrate of Imleach. Bearing this in mind, is there anything else that you should tell me about this archer?'

There was no doubt that Nion was trying his best to think now, and he raised one hand to the back of his head to rub it as an aid to the process.

'I can add nothing further, lady. But, of course, if he were a stranger in the area, then this archer must have stayed a few days within this vicinity in order to wait for the arrows. Perhaps the inn where he stayed might have further knowledge?'

'Where would that inn be?'

Nion gestured eloquently. 'Assuming that he did not seek shelter in the abbey itself, there is only Cred's inn down the street at the far end of the town. It has a reputation and is not licensed by me. That is the abbot's wish, incidentally. He has tried to close it down on moral grounds. But it is the only inn within the town. I think this archer must have stayed there. If he did not, then there is no further help that I can offer.'

Fidelma thanked the smith and left him standing, hands on his hips, feet splayed apart, regarding her with a suspicious look as she walked away with Eadulf.

'If the archer had had his horse shod by a smith in the territory of Clan Brasil,' volunteered Eadulf reflectively, 'then perhaps he knew Brother Mochta? Didn't the abbot say he came from Clan Brasil?'

'Well spotted, Eadulf. But though Mochta came from Clan Brasil and the archer's horse was shod there, we have been told that the archer's accent does not place him as a native from those northern lands.'

Fidelma was silent a minute as she considered the matter. 'We still have to place Brother Mochta in a relationship with this archer, if, indeed, we can square this mystery of the tonsure.'

Eadulf groaned softly in despair. 'These links are so obvious but they fall on that one mystery of the tonsure.'

They had been proceeding along the main street to the far end of the township. There was a complex of small buildings standing apart from the others. Fidelma paused.

'This looks like Cred's tavern.' She gazed back down the street. 'Well, it is sufficiently out of the way here for the archer to have stayed without the smith necessarily knowing if he came from here or not.'

'You mean that you suspected the *bó-aire* of lying?'

'Not really,' Fidelma replied. 'But it is wise to be as precise as possible and double-check all the facts. Let us go in and speak with this Cred who seems so disapproved of in this community.'

Fidelma started forward but Eadulf held her back a moment, pointing up at the tavern sign. It was a muscular smith, swinging his hammer on an anvil.

'Isn't that a coincidence?' he asked.

'Not really,' smiled Fidelma. 'Creidne Cred was the divine artificer of the ancient gods of Ireland who worked in bronze, brass and gold. He was the one who made hilts for swords, rivets for spears and bosses and rims for shields during the war between the pagan gods and their enemies.'

'Then one more thing, before we pass in. I heard both the abbot and the *bó-aire* say that this place was not licensed. What does that mean?'

'It would appear to be a tavern which also brews its own ales but it is not a lawful one, what we call *dligtech*.'

'Then surely the *bó-aire*, as the local law officer, can close it down?'

Fidelma shook her head with a smile. 'It does not mean that this tavern is contrary to law but merely that the law takes no cognisance of it. What this means is, if a question of dispute arises, the person going into an unlawful tavern must be made aware of it for he has no legal grounds for taking action.'

'I am not sure that I understand,' replied Eadulf.

'A lawful tavern keeper must pass three strict tests regarding the quality of the drink he serves. If he serves bad ale he can be challenged under law. In an unlawful house, if a person complains about the quality of the ale, then he cannot demand recompense under the law. Now, enough, let's find this Cred.'

She passed into the tavern. The room seemed deserted except for two men in a corner drinking ale. They were roughly dressed, bearded men, who had the appearance of labourers. They glanced at Fidelma and Eadulf indifferently and carried on with their drinking and their soft-toned conversation.

There was a movement behind a curtained doorway which caused them to turn and the curtain swung back to reveal a woman of ample proportions. She had obviously seen better days. She came forward eagerly but her face fell when she saw the nature of their apparel.

'The abbey has better accommodation for the religious,' she began uncompromisingly. 'You will find this place a little too crude for the likes of the well bred and pious people.'

One of the two men chuckled wheezily in appreciation at what he considered was the woman's wit.

'We do not seek accommodation,' Eadulf replied immediately and with a stern voice. 'We seek some information.'

The woman sniffed and folded her flabby arms across her generous bosom. 'Why seek information here?'

'Because we believe that you can supply it,' replied Eadulf uncompromisingly.

'Information comes expensive, especially to a foreign cleric,' the woman replied, hearing Eadulf's accent. Her eyes examined him speculatively as if wondering how much he carried with him.

'Then you will provide the information to me,' Fidelma said quietly.

The woman's eyes narrowed as they swung round on her.

Fidelma and Eadulf were aware that the two men had stopped their muttered conversation over their drinks and had turned to examine them without disguising the curiosity on their faces.

'Perhaps I do not want to provide any information, even if I have it.' The woman was implacable.

'Perhaps,' smiled Fidelma gently. 'But withholding evidence from a *dálaigh* can be a serious matter.'

The woman's eyes narrowed further. The corners of her mouth turned down. There was a tension in the room and the two men returned to their drinks but from their attitudes they remained acutely aware of the conversation of their hostess.

'Where is the *dálaigh* who demands evidence of me?' sneered the buxom woman.

'I am here,' Fidelma announced softly. 'And I presume that you are Cred, the owner of this unlicensed inn?'

The woman let her arms drop to her side. Various expressions chased one another across her face as if she couldn't make up her mind whether Fidelma was in earnest or not.

The woman flushed in annoyance. 'I am the tavern keeper, Cred. I keep a good, respectable inn, licensed or not.'

'That is a matter between you and your *bó-aire*. I need information. About a week ago there was a man passing through this township. He had the appearance of a professional archer and could not be mistaken for anything else. He rode a chestnut mare with a loose shoe and so had business at the smith's forge.'

Fidelma was aware that the two men had not resumed their conversation and were listening intently to what she was saying. Out of the corner of her eye, she saw a third man enter the room from the back of the inn. She did not turn to examine him closely because she was too intent on gazing directly into the face of the hostess of the inn so that she could gauge her reactions. Yet she was aware that the third man had halted and was staring across the room towards them.

The woman, Cred, still stared defiantly back at Fidelma. 'How do I know that you are a *dálaigh*?' she countered. 'I do not have to answer questions from any slip of a girl – religieuse or not.'

Fidelma reached under her habit and took out a cross on a golden chain. Its symbolism was well known throughout Muman. The Order of the Golden Chain was a venerable Muman nobiliary fraternity that had sprung from membership of the ancient élite warrior guards of the Kings of Cashel. The honour was in the personal presentation of the Eóghanacht kings. Fidelma's brother had bestowed the honour on her because of her services to the kingdom. Cred's eyes bulged a little as she recognised it.

'Who are you?' she asked, but in gentler, more complaisant tones.

'I am . . .' she began.

'Fidelma of Cashel!' The words came from the third man in a hushed breath.

The fat woman's jaw sagged.

Fidelma allowed herself to glance at the man. He was dressed as the other two men, in rough working clothes. His weatherbeaten features spoke of an outdoor life. He jerked his head in a curious obeisance towards her.

'I am from Cashel, too, lady. I work for . . .'

Fidelma's thoughts had moved rapidly. 'For Samradán the merchant? You three men are his drivers?'

The man was nodding eagerly. 'That is so, lady.' He turned to the hostess and added quickly: 'Fidelma of Cashel is not only a *dálaigh* but sister of the King.'

Cred reluctantly bowed her head. 'Forgive me, lady. I thought . . .'

'You thought that you would help me by answering my questions,' Fidelma cut in sharply, with a dismissive nod towards the man who had identified her. He moved to join his companions in their hurried, whispered conversation, casting surreptitious glances in her direction.

'I . . . yes . . . Yes. The *Saigteóir*, we called him. He stayed two or three nights a week ago. A tall man with fair hair. He spoke with a terse accent and invited no questions. He carried a long bow and no other weapon.'

The woman's words came out in a rush.

'I see. Did you gather anything else about him?'

Cred shook her head almost violently. 'As I say, he was a man not given to talk,' she said. 'His words were chosen with care and no more than would convey his wants which were as few as his words.'

'He had business at the smith's?'

'Even as you said. His horse had a loose shoe and I think he bought arrows from the smith as well, for when he arrived he had few arrows in his quiver but when he left here his quiver was full.'

'You have a keen eye, Cred,' Fidelma commented.

'One has to have a keen eye in this business, lady. Guests can come and go leaving the innkeeper without payment. One has to be careful.'

'He paid his dues?'

'Oh yes. He seemed to have enough money. In fact, he had plenty of gold and silver coins with him.'

'Did he visit anywhere else? The abbey for example?' queried Eadulf.

The woman grunted wheezily. It was meant as a chuckle. 'He was not the type to haunt abbeys or churches. No. He had the look of death on him.'

'What do you mean?' demanded Eadulf. 'The look of death? Was he ill?'

Cred looked at him as if he were a simpleton. 'Some go to battle because there is no other choice,' she deigned to explain. 'Others go and find they have an affinity for death and destruction and so roam the country selling their warrior skills to whoever will pay them to pursue the one thing they have grown to like – the inflicting of death and destruction on others. They become death itself. The *Saigteóir* had the pale hue of death on him. He was without emotion, without a soul.'

To their surprise the fat innkeeper genuflected.

'I feel that in such men, their souls are already dead and they follow the blood and carnage merely waiting for their time to come.'

'So he did not spend any time at the abbey?' insisted Eadulf. 'If not there, where else? If he were here two or three days, where else? This town is not so large that he would not be noticed.'

'He did not spend much time in the town,' the woman replied.

'You sound certain,' Fidelma observed.

'Certain for the very reason that you have already stated. He ate here in the evening and slept here at night. But he left just after dawn and did not come back until the late afternoon. One of my neighbours saw him riding in the hills just to the south after his horse had been re-shod.'

'What's there? A farm? A tavern?'

The woman shrugged. 'Nothing. Perhaps he was merely hunting.'

'And in the days he was here he never spoke his name or mentioned anything about himself?'

'And none dared asked him,' confirmed the woman.

Fidelma suppressed a sigh of frustration that she had learnt so little. 'I am obliged to you, Cred.'

'Has he broken the law? What has he done?' she asked eagerly. 'Innkeepers like a fine tale to tell of those who have slept under their roofs.'

Fidelma regarded her for a moment and then said quietly: 'He has achieved what you thought he was waiting to achieve.'

The innkeeper looked puzzled.

It was Eadulf who explained in a quiet tone. 'He has achieved the death which you said that he was waiting for.'

Fidelma turned to the three drivers who were now trying to avoid her gaze. 'A pleasant journey to you on the road to the land of the Arada Cliach.'

The man who had identified her frowned. 'What makes you think we are going there, lady?'

'Samradán told me.'

The three exchanged glances and then their spokesman forced a nervous smile. 'Just so, lady. A pleasant journey to you.'

They left the inn of the 'artificer of the gods' and walked slowly back down the street in the direction of the abbey.

'Well,' observed Eadulf, 'we have not learnt anything of significance about this archer. In fact, we do not appear to have learnt anything of significance at all.'

He was surprised when Fidelma reached out a hand to his elbow and propelled him to a corner of a building away from the main road.

'On the contrary, I think we have learnt a great deal,' she replied after she had glanced up the street behind them. 'We will wait here a moment.'

Eadulf was astonished at her behaviour.

Fidelma took pity on him. 'We have learnt that he was a professional archer but not of the warrior caste. So he was no noble. We have learnt he had had his horse shod in Clan Brasil. We have learnt where he obtained his arrows. We have learnt that he had a chestnut mare. We have learnt that he seemed to have plenty of money.

We have learnt that he spent a few days riding in the hills south of here.'

Eadulf mentally ticked off the points. 'But that is little enough. We more or less knew this much when we left Cashel?'

Fidelma raised her eyes to the heavens and gestured as if in despair. 'Think, Eadulf! There are three important things that we have learnt about this archer. Two of those things raise important questions which we must resolve.'

'You mean, where did he go to in the southern hills?'

'That stands investigation, yes. But what else have we learnt?'

Eadulf hit his forehead with his clenched fist. 'Of course! Where is his chestnut mare? He was without a horse when he was killed.'

Fidelma smiled and suppressed an exasperated sigh. 'You are the most inconsistent person I know. Sometimes you point to the most obvious point that we have all overlooked. Other times you overlook the obvious which everyone else has accepted. You really are frustrating, Eadulf. Yes, I mean the matter of the archer's mare. Where is it? It seems that there was another accomplice waiting with the horses of both assassins. This accomplice rode off with the horses to hide them once he knew that the archer and his friend had been killed by Gionga.'

'Which means there is still a third assassin in Cashel?'

'Perhaps more. How many are in this plot? And what of the other point we have learnt?' pressed Fidelma.

Eadulf thought hard but could not identify any other point. Fidelma was patient.

'The archer and his friend had hardly any money on them when they were killed. Cred, the innkeeper, tells us that the archer was not lacking in money. Where did he keep it?' she suggested at last.

Eadulf pursed his lips, annoyed with himself for missing the obvious. 'There is another question,' he said. 'Why are we waiting here?'

Fidelma smiled mysteriously and put her head around the corner of the building again to glance up the street. 'The answer is on its way.'

At that moment, one of the drivers from Cred's tavern, the one from Cashel who had recognised her, came hurrying along the street, gazing about him as if looking for something.

'A person can signal with his eyes as well as his hands and mouth,' Fidelma muttered to Eadulf.

The driver came abreast of them and Fidelma coughed. He gave a startled glance in their direction. Then, without acknowledging them, he dropped to one knee and began to fiddle with his boot.

'Pretend that you are not talking with me,' he whispered sibilantly, his eyes on his boot. 'There are eyes and ears everywhere.'

'What do you want with us,' asked Fidelma, turning her head as if she were still talking to Eadulf.

'I cannot discuss that here. Do you know the Well at Gurteen, the little tilled field?'

'No.'

'It is less than a mile north-east from this point. You proceed along a pathway towards the yew woods and come to a field bordered by a dry-stone wall. The well is just beyond the wall. You cannot miss it.'

'We can find it.'

'Be there at dusk and we shall speak. Tell no one about this meeting. It is dangerous for all of us.'

Then the driver rose and ambled off as if he had simply been adjusting his boot.

Eadulf exchanged a glance with Fidelma.

'A trap?' suggested Eadulf.

'But why would the driver want to lure us into a trap?'

'He and his friends might think we know more than we actually do,' Eadulf suggested.

Fidelma considered this for a moment, head to one side, pondering. 'No, I don't think so. His fear of being seen talking with us was genuine enough.'

'Well, I think it is dangerous to go . . . and at dusk no less. It is a trap for the fox.'

Fidelma grinned. 'The fox never found a better messenger than myself,' she replied.

Eadulf groaned in impatience at another of Fidelma's axioms.

'Don't you have another proverb in this land – do not show your teeth until you can bite?' he demanded sarcastically.

Fidelma chuckled. 'Well said, Eadulf. You are learning. But tonight at dusk we shall be at the Well at Gurteen.'

Chapter Eleven

Dusk was approaching when Fidelma and Eadulf left the abbey. Making sure that they were not observed, they began to follow the directions that Samradán's driver had given them to the Well of Gurteen. As the day had been warm and the approaching night was clearly going to be cold, there was a faint ground mist already beginning to rise from the fields around them. There was no movement for there was no wind, not even an evening breeze to rustle the trees or bushes.

They had decided to walk from the abbey rather than ride for Fidelma believed it would draw less attention to their excursion. Eadulf had brought a stout staff with him, a discarded pilgrim's staff which he had found in the abbey. It was wise to have some means of protection when being late abroad. At night wolf packs roamed the countryside and it was not unknown for them to attack lonely wayfarers. In some areas they were so numerous, dwelling in the woods and fastness that, if pressed by hunger, they could present a formidable danger to whole communities let alone those who dwelt on the isolated farmsteads.

Even as they walked along the track, a lonely howl rent the air not too far away. Eadulf clenched his staff more tightly and glanced quickly in the direction of the wailing, siren-like sound.

'Now I understand why the Irish word for a collection of wolves is *glademain*,' he observed, his eyes anxious. The word was derived from *glaid* meaning 'cry'; hence, a cry of wolves.

'They have a strange, bewitching call,' Fidelma admitted. 'Sometimes people have been so beguiled by it as to forget the dangers. They are the only really dangerous animal in the country. Many of the nobles have annual hunts to keep down their numbers.'

A dog began to bark in answer to the howling of the wolf.

'Now that's another danger,' Fidelma observed. 'It is custom and law that watch-dogs on farms are tied up early in the morning but set free at cow-stalling to protect the farmsteads. Sometimes they can be just as vicious in their attack as that "son of the country" you hear calling.'

Eadulf was about to say something when the eerie call of the wolf came again. He waited until the cry died away.

'I have heard a wolf called many things but "son of the country" – why that?' He shivered slightly.

'I can think of four names for the animal as well as the collective name. To call it *mac-tíre*, "son of the country", is just an allusion to the fact that it haunts the wild woods and fastnesses.'

She suddenly halted and gestured for him to also stand still.

'Up ahead,' she said quietly. 'There is the tilled field which I think Samradán's driver alluded to. The well must be nearby.'

The twilight, coupled with the ground mist, had not yet obscured the field. In fact, the mist had not risen more than a few feet. It swirled around their lower legs as if they were wading through white, shallow water. Eadulf followed the direction of her outstretched arm and saw in the gloom a rectangular enclosure which was clearly outlined by surrounding trees.

'That must be it,' he agreed, pointing to a corner where he could just make out a large, curving bough. It was obviously man-hewn, and rose from the misty ground to a height of nine feet or more. At the end of this they could see a rope from which a wooden bucket was suspended.

Fidelma led the way again, climbing on the low stone wall into the field and proceeding across the damp, ploughed soil towards the well.

'No one seems to be here yet,' grunted Eadulf as he looked about him in the semi-gloom.

Almost as he spoke there was a movement on the other side of the small stone wall which surrounded the well head; it was a wall made of piled boulders of varying sizes placed there without mortar.

'Who's there?' demanded Fidelma.

There was a wheezy cough and the voice of Samradán's driver greeted them.

They moved around the well head and found the man seated with his back to the low wall. His legs were placed straight out in front of him and his arms were loose at his side. They could not discern his features in the shadows.

'I . . . I was hoping that you would come soon,' the man said, raising his head to them.

Fidelma gazed down at him with a frown. 'Is there something the matter?' she asked, wondering why he did not rise.

'I have not long,' the man broke in impatiently. 'Do not speak but listen to what I say.'

Fidelma and Eadulf exchanged a glance expressing their perplexity.

Nearby came the plaintive wail of a wolf once more. This time it was joined by several others so that the sounds seemed to rise all around them.

'Speak, then,' Fidelma invited, seating herself on top of the small wall. 'What do you want with us?'

Eadulf continued to stand, his hands on his staff, gazing anxiously into the growing dusk. 'A fine place to set for a meeting,' he muttered. 'Wouldn't it be better to leave here and seek some more protective spot?'

The man still had not risen and he ignored Eadulf. 'Sister Fidelma . . . I am of Cashel. Let that suffice, for my name will mean nothing to you. Cred did not tell you the whole truth.'

'I don't doubt it,' Fidelma greeted the statement in even tones. 'We all shape truth to fit our perception of it.'

'She lied in what she admitted to you,' the driver insisted. 'I saw the man she calls the archer meet with other people at the tavern. She knew it and lied.'

'Why would she do that?'

'Listen to me first. The archer met with a Brother of the faith. I saw this Brother enter the inn. He did so when Cred was in the inn. She did not think that I observed him for I was taking a nap by the fire after my meal. The archer's entry had disturbed me and I was about to bestir myself when I saw the religieux enter. He was nervous so I decided to pretend that I was still asleep and watched from under lowered lids.'

'Who was he? Did you recognise the man?'

'No. But I felt it strange for a religieux to have entered a tavern the like of which Cred ran, if you know what I mean.'

'So you saw a religieux enter. Was he a rotund, moon-faced Brother?' asked Fidlelma.

The driver nodded.

'With greying, curly hair which had once been cut into the tonsure of Rome?' added Eadulf. 'A tonsure like mine?'

'No,' the man shook his head. 'He wore the tonsure of an Irish brother. What you call the tonsure of St John. But he was, as you say, a rotund, moon-faced brother.'

'When was this?'

'Less than a week ago. I cannot be precise.'

'Did you see the monk leave the inn?'

'Some time later. I had gone to the blacksmith's by then. One of the wagons had a broken axle and the smith was mending it. While I was there I saw the very same Brother hurrying by towards the abbey.'

'Brother Mochta?' queried Eadulf, more to Fidelma than to the driver.

'The name means nothing to me,' the man insisted.

'How do you know that he met with the archer? He could have been visiting someone else in the tavern.'

'Apart from myself and the other two drivers, only the archer was staying at the tavern. When the Brother came in, he said something to Cred who replied, "He is waiting for you above the stair". Who else could be waiting for him but the archer?'

'Very well,' agreed Fidelma. 'I cannot flaw your logic. So the Brother from the abbey met with the archer.'

'There is another thing which confirms that this religieux came in search of the archer.'

'What?'

'Several days later he came again to the inn, this time in broad daylight and with another member of his community. The Brother asked Cred where the archer was. He was not there, so this religieux and his companion left.'

'Did you see this religieux or his companion again?'

'No. But there is something else and something more important. I saw the archer meet another man later on the same night that the religieux paid his first visit to the inn. I was disturbed in my sleep and I heard voices below my window in the courtyard of the tavern. Curious, I peered out. There were two men there, one of them holding a horse. They were engaged in conversation. They were standing underneath the tavern light.'

One of the duties, enforced by law on all tavern keepers, was that a light had to be kept burning during the night to guide travellers to the hostel, whether it was situated in the countryside or in the town.

The driver suddenly coughed, a racking cough. Then he recovered himself. 'One of the men was, of course, the archer.'

'The other?' pressed Eadulf eagerly. 'Did you recognise the other man?'

'No. He had a cloak and hood over him. I can tell you this. He was a man of rich apparel. His cloak was of wool, edged with fur. There was little else that I could see but it was the horse with its saddle and bridle which really showed a richness few people could afford. Anyway, I tried to listen to their conversation. I could tell but little. The archer was very respectful of the man in the cloak. Then . . .'

The driver hesitated and started coughing again. Fidelma and Eadulf waited patiently until he had regained his composure.

'Then the fine lord said, well . . . I think it was an old proverb. *Ríoghacht gan duadh, ní dual go bhfagthar.*'

'No kingdom is to be obtained without trouble,' repeated Fidelma softly. 'It is, indeed, an old proverb meaning that without pain you do not gain anything.'

The driver was coughing again.

'It is a bad cough for you to be seated on the damp ground with,' chided Eadulf.

The driver went on as if he had not heard him. 'The archer responded. He said, "I will not be found wanting, *rígdomna*." His exact words.'

Fidelma started forward, her body suddenly tense. '*Rígdomna*? Are you sure that he used that form of address?'

'He did so, Sister,' replied the driver.

Eadulf looked at Fidelma in the deep gloom which had now descended over the field. 'That word is a title for a prince, isn't it?'

The term meant literally 'king material' and was an official term of an address to the son of a king.

The driver was coughing again.

'What is the matter with you?' demanded Fidelma, beginning to wonder at the man's condition.

The driver gasped for breath. 'I think that I will have to ask you to help me back to the town, for I fear I cannot make it by myself.'

He started to move and then began to cough again. Abruptly he gave a curious whining cry and fell forward onto his side.

Eadulf dropped his staff and knelt down in the darkness, for dusk and mist had combined so swiftly as to obscure all details from their sight. He reached for the man's head and felt along the neck for a pulse. He found it fluttering and then it stopped.

'What is it?' asked Fidelma impatiently.

Eadulf stared up, unable to see her features. 'He is dead.'

Fidelma gave a sharp intake of breath. 'Dead? How can that be?'

Eadulf felt a still-warm and wet substance at the corner of the man's mouth.

'He has been coughing blood,' he said in surprise. 'We would have noticed it had it been light.'

'But the man did not look ill earlier. He did not appear to be the sort to cough blood.'

Eadulf bent forward and tried to bring the body back into an upright seated position. His left hand was trying to act as a brace for the back of the man when he felt the same warm, sticky substance over the man's back. There was a tear in the man's shirt and Eadulf's fingers touched the ragged, torn flesh.

'Oh, *dabit deus his quoque finem*!' he muttered in the dark.

'What is it?' Fidelma was frustrated as it was too gloomy now to see exactly what Eadulf was doing.

'The man has been stabbed in the back. He lay here talking with us all the while he was mortally wounded. God knows how he survived. He has been stabbed in the back . . .' Eadulf paused. 'The very movement he made to get up must have ruptured his wound further and caused his death. Maybe he would have lived had he not moved. I don't know.'

Fidelma remained silent for a moment.

'He should have spoken up before,' she said eventually, articulating a brutal realism. 'We cannot help him now.'

Eadulf reached for the well bucket which was full of the water and cleaned the blood from his hands.

'Shall I carry his body back to the inn?' he asked. 'We should tell Samradán.'

Fidelma shook her head in the gloom before realising that it was too dark for Eadulf to see the negative gesture.

'No. If we announce our involvement with this man we might be prevented from following up the information he has given us.'

'How so? The man was stabbed in the back. Murdered. He was on his way to meet with us. When he arranged the meeting this afternoon he feared to be seen talking with us. Whom did he fear? Whoever it was must have killed him to prevent him passing on information.'

'We do not know that for certain. But I am inclined to agree. If he was killed to prevent him telling us what he knew then it would be wiser to let whoever killed him believe that he was unable to speak with us. We must keep quiet about this. He will be found tomorrow when someone comes to the well. We will work on the assumption that he was killed to keep him silent, and we should pretend he kept that silence.'

'I do not like it,' confessed Eadulf. 'It seems an unChristian thing to do, simply to go away and leave him thus.'

'He will not mind and, as we are in pursuit of justice, neither will God. It might be an advantage in tracking his killers for if they are connected with our assassin friends then we have learnt something important which gives us a small advantage.'

She knelt down beside the body and uttered a short blessing before standing up.

'*Sic itur ad astra*,' muttered Eadulf sarcastically. Thus one goes to the stars.

Eadulf was suddenly aware of the continued howling of the wolves which seemed to have grown closer while they had been talking at the well. He picked up his staff, which he had let fall when he had examined the body, and turned to Fidelma.

'We'd best start back.'

Fidelma was in agreement. She, too, had noticed the growing nearness of the sound of the wolves.

They went back across the field and climbed over the short stone wall which bordered the field and onto the track. The moon was up now, a bright mid-September moon. It seemed no longer dark. There were a few clouds in the sky but they did not obscure the pale white brightness. The gloom and mist had only hung in the field around the well, encouraged by the dampness. Here on the track the darkness had been dissipated and the pallid light cast shadows across the lane as they hurried towards the distant lights of the township.

The rising cry of the wolves caused an involuntary shudder, not for the first time, to tingle its way down Eadulf's back.

He cast a nervous glance around. 'They sound as if they are pretty near,' he muttered.

'We will be all right,' Fidelma replied confidently. 'Wolves don't attack adult humans unless they are starving.'

'Who's to say that these beasts aren't starving?' Eadulf grunted.

If the truth were known, Fidelma was thinking the same thought.

Eadulf was not sure that he had seen it, so quickly did the shape flit across his gaze. It appeared to be a large dark shadow which moved swiftly across the path about twenty yards ahead. Some instinct caused him to halt.

'What is it?' whispered Fidelma, seeing his shoulders suddenly tense. She stood still by his side, peering forward.

'I am not sure . . .' began Eadulf.

The soft growling caused their limbs to feel as if they had suddenly been frozen.

The shadow moved again, a long low, muscular shape and suddenly the pale moonlight reflected on two round pinpoints which seemed to twinkle like points of fire. The growling sound increased.

'Get behind me, Fidelma,' hissed Eadulf, raising his staff protectively before him.

The beast took a step nearer, all the while continuing its deep growling sound.

'I can't see if it is a wolf or just a watch-dog from a farm,' Fidelma whispered, squinting into the darkness.

'Either way, it is a threat,' replied Eadulf.

Abruptly, with no warning at all, the great animal launched itself forward. Had Eadulf not been possessed of quick reflexes it would have been at his throat. Even as the animal was springing from the ground, Eadulf swung his staff and met the creature halfway with a blow, more out of luck than a sound aim, that contacted with its muzzle. He had put what force he could muster into the stroke. With a yelp of pain the animal was knocked to the ground and, whining, it trotted back a few yards. Then it halted, its whimper turning into a snarl of defiance.

When Fidelma spoke, Eadulf heard fear in her voice for the first time since he had known her.

'It's no dog, Eadulf. It's a wolf.'

Eadulf had not taken his eyes from the beast which began to move slowly back and forth before them, continuing to growl, as if watching them for some weak spot. It started to make short little runs up and down but did not approach them. The red, luminescent eyes were constantly fixed on Eadulf as he turned, keeping the staff held before him at all times.

'We cannot keep this up all night,' he muttered.

'There is nowhere to go,' replied Fidelma.

'There is a tree a few yards down there . . . if I keep the animal at bay, perhaps you could make it . . . scramble up into the branches . . . ?'

'And what would you do?' she protested. 'You would not be able to reach the tree before the beast reached you.'

'What alternative do we have?' replied Eadulf, fear giving him an irascible tone. 'Shall we both be caught here and savaged by the animal? I will try to turn the beast out of the path so that you can slip by it. That will give you a clear field to run. When I call to you . . . run! Don't look back and make sure you climb as high as you can.'

There was such determination in his voice that Fidelma realised it was pointless to protest. In any case, logically, Eadulf was correct. They had no other choice.

Eadulf made a few lunges at the growling wolf which caused it to start back in surprise at his audacity. Then it seemed that its fiery eyes narrowed and it showed its great slobbering fangs again. It had turned a little. Eadulf lunged again.

There came a single eerie wail from nearby. The howl sent shivers through them both. It echoed from the direction of the field that they had just left.

The attacking wolf stood and lifted its head to the moonlight, which fell with its soft white rays on the upturned muzzle of the animal. From some point deep down in the throat there rose a sound, faint at first, then welling in strength and volume until the jaws parted and the most unearthly shrill howl rent the air. Never had Eadulf heard anything like it. Once, twice and a third time the cry shattered the evening stillness around them. As the cry subsided, the wolf seemed to pause and listen.

Sure enough, from the field, came an answering cry, an awesome wailing sound.

Without further ado, not even so much as a glance in Eadulf's direction, the attacking wolf turned and loped over the stone boundary wall and away towards the field behind them.

Eadulf found himself still transfixed and the sweat was pouring from his brow. His staff was slippery in the palms of his hands.

It was Fidelma who moved first.

'Come on, lest there be others of those creatures nearby. Let's get to the safety of the township.'

When Eadulf did not move, she reached forward and tugged him by the sleeve.

He tried to collect his wits, turned and hurried after her in a rapid trot, now and then casting nervous glances across his shoulders.

'But they are heading for the field where we left the . . .'

'Of course!' snapped Fidelma. 'Why do you think the wolf abandoned its attack against us? Its mate–' her voice trembled slightly – 'had found the carcass; found more easy prey than us. That was the meaning of those terrible cries between them. In death that poor man has saved us. *Deo gratias*!'

A feeling of nausea welled up in him as Eadulf realised what gruesome meal must now be being enjoyed by the well. Yet they could have been that meal. Fidelma could have been . . . He began to mutter, '*Agnus Dei* . . . O Lamb of God . . .' It was the prayer in the office for the burial of the dead.

'Save your breath,' Fidelma interrupted irritably. 'Honour the man's sacrifice by being worthy of it and reaching safety.'

Eadulf fell silent, hurt by Fidelma's curtness. He was, after all, more concerned with her safety than his own. However, he had realised, for the first time since he had known her, that she, too, could be inspired by fear.

They did not speak again until they had reached the edge of the township and went along the main street, quickly passing the glowing lamp of the tavern of Cred. There were a few people on the street but no one seemed to notice them until they came to the blacksmith's forge.

In spite of the lateness of the hour, the smith was seated near to a glowing brazier which stood by his anvil. He was polishing a metal sword blade. He glanced up and recognised them.

'I would have a care about being abroad after dark, lady,' he greeted.

Fidelma halted before him. She had entirely recovered her composure now and returned his gaze evenly. 'Why so?'

The smith cocked his head to one side in a listening attitude. 'Have you not heard them, lady?'

In the stillness of the evening the sounds of the baying wolves came faintly to their ears.

'Yes, we've heard them.' Her voice was tight.

The smith nodded slowly. He did not cease in his polishing. 'I have never known them nearer to the township,' he observed. 'I would hurry back to the abbey, if I were you.'

He bent to his task as if engrossed. Then he raised his head again. 'I think, as *bó-aire* of the township, I shall have to call a hunt tomorrow to flush these brutes out from their lairs.'

It was not unusual for a local chieftain, or even a prince or the King himself, to organise a wolf hunt in order to keep the numbers of the savage beasts at an acceptable level. Yet it seemed to Eadulf that there was some other meaning behind the man's words. He wondered whether he was right or whether he was hearing things which were not there due to the emotion of the evening's events.

Fidelma left the smith without another word and began to walk towards the tall, dark walls of the abbey, along the path by the great yew-tree. Eadulf hurried after her. Once out of earshot, he articulated his thoughts.

'Do you think that he had some hidden meaning in his words?'

'I do not know. Perhaps not. At this stage I think we should be prepared for anything.'

'What is our next course of action?'

'I think that should be obvious now.'

Eadulf pondered for a moment or two.

'Cred, I suppose? We must question her again.'

Fidelma's voice was approving in the gloom. 'Excellent. Yes, we must go and have another word with Cred because if Samradán's driver was correct, that innkeeper knows more of this than she has told us.'

'Well, I think the solution is clear.'

Eadulf sounded so positive that Fidelma was surprised.

'You have solved our puzzle already, Eadulf?' There was a faint sarcasm in her voice which he did not detect. 'That is clever of you.'

'Well, you heard what the driver said. The archer was receiving instructions from a prince. Are there so many princes who are enemies of Cashel?'

'Many,' she replied dryly. 'Though I do confess that the Uí Fidgente did spring to mind. But we cannot accuse Donennach merely on the fact that the driver heard the archer address a man as *rígdomna*. Many princes would like to see the Eóghanacht fall from power. The greatest enemy of the Eóghanacht are the Uí Néill, particularly Mael Dúin of the northern Uí Néill, the King of Ailech. Their enmity goes back to the time of the ancestor of the Gaels Míle Easpain. His sons Eber and Eremon fought over the division of Éireann. Eber was killed by the followers of his brother Eremon. It is from Eremon that the Uí Néill claim their descent.'

Eadulf was impatient. 'This I know. And the Eóghanacht of the south claim their descent from Eber. But do you really think that Cashel is threatened by the Uí Néill of the north?'

'That which grows in the bone is hard to drive out of the flesh,' observed Fidelma as they came to the gate of the abbey and paused.

'I don't understand,' protested Eadulf.

'The Uí Néill have spent over a millennium hating the Eóghanacht and envying them their kingdom.'

The monk in attendance at the gate was Brother Daig, the fresh-faced youth they had seen earlier. He seemed happy to see them.

'Thanks be to God that you are safely returned. I have been listening to the cries of the wolves in the hills these last two hours or more. It is not an evening to be without shelter.'

He drew the gate shut behind them.

'We have heard them as well,' Eadulf observed dryly.

'You should be aware that there are many wolves in the woods and fields around here,' Brother Daig went on good-naturedly. 'They can be very dangerous.'

Eadulf was just about to rejoin that he was all too well aware of it when he caught Fidelma's warning glance.

'You are most considerate, Brother,' she said. 'We will have a care the next time we venture abroad at dusk.'

'There is cold food in the refectory, Sister, if you have not eaten,' the young monk continued. 'As the hour is late I am afraid that you have missed the hot food.'

'It is of no consequence. Brother Eadulf and I will go to the refectory. Thank you for being so solicitous. It is most appreciated.'

As they continued towards the refectory Eadulf whispered: 'Should we not go to question Cred after our meal?'

'As Brother Daig has said, the hour is late. Cred will keep until tomorrow. As soon as I have eaten I intend to go to bed and rest. It has been an exhausting day. We can start that task directly after breakfast.'

Chapter Twelve

It was the sound of war horns that awoke Fidelma only moments before Sister Scothnat, the *domina* of the guests' hostel bust into her chamber, crying in a loud and fearful voice.

'Rise and prepare to defend yourself, lady, we are under attack.'

Fidelma sprung up in a moment of panic, now fully aware of the blaring horns and distant cries and screams. She started from her bed and struggled in the shadows to light a candle. The flickering light revealed Sister Scothnat standing at her chamber door, wringing her hands and weeping distractedly.

Fidelma moved to her, seizing the woman by both arms. 'Pull yourself together, Sister!' she said sharply. 'Tell me what is happening? Who is attacking us?'

Scothnat paused in her distraction, cowed by the sharpness in Fidelma's tone. Then she began to softly sob again. 'The abbey, the abbey is under attack!'

'But who is attacking it?'

She saw that Sister Scothnat was too overcome with fear to answer her question.

Fidelma turned and hauled on her clothing. It was still dark outside her chamber window and she had no idea what time it was although she felt it could not be long before dawn.

Hurrying out of the chamber, she left Scothnat still sobbing behind her. She almost collided with a dark, muscular figure, hurrying in the opposite direction. Even in the gloom she recognised Eadulf.

'I was coming to find you.' His voice was anxious. 'The abbey is being attacked by warriors.'

'Do you know anything more?' she asked.

'Nothing. I was aroused only moments ago by Brother Madagan. He has gone to ensure the gates are secured but I believe the abbey has little defence except its walls and the gates.'

Suddenly the abbey's great bell began to toll, the sound increasing in volume as the hands which tugged the bell-rope grew more frenzied with each chime. The sound was more a frantic peal for help than a solemn warning.

'Let us see what we can discover,' cried Fidelma above the din, heading down the corridor towards the main gate.

Eadulf followed, protesting, 'The other women have been led to a place of safety within the abbey vaults.'

Fidelma did not bother to respond. She moved quickly and Eadulf was hard pressed to keep up with her. They hurried down the dark cloisters, through which several panicking brethren ran hither and thither, distracted and with no coordination.

Fidelma became aware of the increasing sounds of war horns and the screams and cries of fighting from beyond the great walls of the abbey. They passed into the main courtyard. There they could see a group of young, more sturdy monks, trying to secure the wooden bars on the great central gate. Directing them was the *rechtaire*, the steward of the abbey, Brother Madagan.

Fidelma hailed him as they came up.

'What is happening? Who are the attackers?'

Brother Madagan paused from directing his fellows.

'Strange warriors, that's all we know. So far they have not attacked the abbey directly. They seem more intent on sacking the township.'

'Where is the abbot?'

Brother Madagan pointed to a small square-built watch-tower which rose by the gate to a height of three storeys.

'Forgive me, Sister–' Brother Madagan turned away – 'I must continue to see to our security.'

Fidelma was already making for the tower, with Eadulf at her heels.

Inside the tower a stairway led to each of the storeys. It was large enough for only one person to ascend at a time. Fidelma did not pause but raced upwards with Eadulf behind her.

The lower floors were empty but they found Abbot Ségdae on the top of the tower, standing behind what, if the place had been built with a martial purpose, would have been battlements. A wall surrounded the roof, rising to chest height. From this vantage point, one could see all around the abbey.

Abbot Ségdae was not alone. Next to him stood the burly figure of the merchant Samradán. Ségdae was standing behind the wall's protection and gazing across the square towards the township beyond. His shoulders were hunched, his hands were two balled fists, held at his sides and his head thrust forward as he watched the scene grimly. Samradán seemed equally transfixed by the spectacle. Neither man acknowledged Fidelma nor Eadulf as they climbed onto the roof.

Fidelma and Eadulf had already become aware of an unearthly red glow, a strange yellow-red flickering light bathing the front of the abbey. Its curious colour of menace reflected off the low clouds which hung above them. It was obvious that many buildings in the township were already in flames. The screams and cries plus the protesting whinny of frightened horses filled the night air. There was a lot of movement beyond the abbey walls. Men on horseback, some brandishing flaming brands, others with swords, were riding to and fro across the square and moving through the streets among buildings. It was clear that it was the unprotected buildings of the town that were suffering the first onslaught. Now that her eyes had grown accustomed to the curious twilight, the gloom of the night, lit by the fires of burning buildings and movement of flaming torches, Fidelma could see something else. Here and there on the ground were dark mounds which were obviously bodies. Worse still, she saw people, singly or in small groups, running for their lives, being pursued by the mounted warriors. Now and then there came a scream as the flashing swords found a victim.

Fidelma turned grimly to Abbot Ségdae.

'Are there no means of protecting Imleach?' she demanded.

The abbot seemed too shocked to answer at first. He suddenly looked a frail old man. Fidelma shook him roughly by the arm.

'Ségdae, innocent people are being cut down. Are there no warriors near here whom we can call upon?'

Almost reluctantly the hawk-faced abbot turned. His expression was dazed as he tried to focus on Fidelma.

'The nearest are the warriors commanded by your cousin, the Prince of Cnoc Áine.'

'Is there any way we can contact him?'

Abbot Ségdae raised a hand as if to indicate the bell-tower on the far side of the abbey. The frantic tolling of the bell was continuing. 'That is our only means.'

Samradán was looking on the scene as one hypnotised; his face was ghastly. Fidelma had rarely seen such naked fear on a man's face before. Even in that situation, a thought came to her mind. What was it that Vergil has written? Fear betrays unworthy souls. Why had that come to her mind? There was, so she believed, nothing uglier than fear on the face of a man.

The burly merchant now turned to the abbot. 'Do you think that they will breach the walls of the abbey?' His voice held more than anxiety in it.

'This is no fortress, Samradán,' the abbot replied grimly. 'Our gates were not built to keep out armies.'

'I demand protection! I am only a merchant. I have done no harm

. . . I am not a warrior to defend . . .' His voice rose in sheer panic. It seemed to raise Abbot Ségdae from his lethargy.

'Then get down to the vaults below the chapel with the women!' he snapped. 'Leave us to defend ourselves . . . and you!'

The merchant almost cowered away from him.

Fidelma gave an expression of disgust. She turned to Eadulf. 'Take Samradán to the vaults and then ask Brother Madagan to come here,' she said. Command suddenly came easily to her. She was of the Eóghanacht of Cashel and these were her people.

Eadulf pulled the trembling merchant roughly away from the scene of death and destruction on which they gazed.

Fidelma stood by Abbot Ségdae regarding the scene with growing anger.

She could make out the smith's forge erupting in sheets of flame. Several of the buildings were already destroyed. She turned her gaze to the shadowy figures of the horsemen, hoping she could make some identification of them but there was little to see in the darkness beyond men in war helmets, some with flashing shirts of chainmail. But there were no identifying badges on them.

She heard a scuffling sound on the stairs and Brother Madagan came breathlessly onto the roof.

He glanced grimly towards the burning town.

'They have gone for the easy option first,' he observed once more. 'Once they have finished sacking the undefended township then they will make an onslaught on the abbey.'

Abbot Ségdae suddenly gave a cry and fell backwards onto the floor. They turned to look at him in surprise. There was an ugly, bloody wound on his forehead. Fidelma glanced round, puzzled for the moment. She had heard the sound of something striking stone. She bent and picked up a small pebble.

'A slingshot,' she observed. 'Best keep away from the walls.'

Brother Madagan was already kneeling by the abbot.

'I'll send for Brother Bardán, the apothecary. The missile has struck his forehead. He is unconscious.'

Fidelma moved carefully to the wall, keeping low down so that it afforded her shelter. The missile must have been delivered by a passing horseman and the shot had been a lucky one. It did not seem part of a concerted attack on the abbey as yet. The raiders were still riding backwards and forwards through the township.

'When they do attack us, the walls will not keep out the warriors for long,' muttered Brother Madagan, following her gaze and apparently reading her thoughts.

Fidelma gestured towards the abbey's bell-tower; the bell was still pealing.

'Will that bring any help?'

'It may but there is little counting on it.'

'Then it is true that there are no warriors nearer here than Cnoc Áine who would come to our protection?'

'No. We can only hope that Finguine at Cnoc Áine is alerted.'

'Six miles away,' reflected Fidelma, thinking of the distance between Imleach and her cousin's fortress. 'Will they hear the tolling of the bell?'

Brother Madagan grimaced. 'While we may not count on it, there is a good possibility. It is a still night and the sound of our bell can carry.'

'But we may not count on it,' echoed Fidelma bitterly. She turned and gazed again on the scene of destruction. 'Have we no way of knowing who these people are? Why would they attack the abbey?'

'I have no idea. In the entire history of our community no one has ever attacked this sacred spot.' He suddenly paused and a troubled look crossed his features.

'What?' demanded Fidelma.

Brother Madagan avoided her gaze. 'The legend. Perhaps it is true?'

For a moment Fidelma did not understand him and then she remembered.

'The disappearance of the Ailbe's Relics! Superstition. That is all.'

'Yet the coincidence is great. The Holy Relics have disappeared. It is said if they leave this spot, then Muman will fall. They have done so and now the abbey is about to be destroyed!'

Fired by her own apprehension Fidelma became angry.

'Foolish man! The abbey is not destroyed yet and will not be if we put our minds to defending it.'

Eadulf came hurrying back. He glanced at the prone body of the abbot in horror. 'Is he . . . ?'

'No,' Brother Madagan replied. 'Ségdae has been struck by a missile. Can you find someone to fetch our apothecary, Brother Bardán?'

Eadulf turned back down the stairway. Almost at once he was back. 'A young Brother has gone for the apothecary.'

Fidelma glanced grimly at him. 'And how is Samradán?'

'The merchant is being comforted by Sister Scothnat.' Eadulf suddenly glanced across the wall towards the square in front of the abbey. 'Look!'

They followed his outstretched hand with their eyes.

A band of half a dozen men had dismounted from their horses near the great yew-tree which grew before the abbey walls. They all bore axes and began to systematically hack at the ancient tree. They worked in coordination as if the matter had been carefully planned and was no mere whim of vandalism.

Eadulf frowned, perplexed.

'What is going on?' he demanded in bewilderment. 'In the middle of a raid, they are stopping to cut down a tree?'

'God protect us!' cried Brother Madagan. His voice was almost a despairing wail. 'Can't you see? They are cutting down the sacred yew-tree.'

'Better that than they cut down people,' observed Eadulf in black humour, still not understanding the significance of the raiders' actions.

'Remember what I told you,' Fidelma spoke sharply. Even she had a sudden pale cast to her features. 'This is the sacred tree symbol of our people said to have been planted by the hand of Eber Fionn himself, the son of Milesius, progenitor of the Eóghanacht of Cashel. It is an ancient belief among our people, Eadulf, that the tree is the symbol of our well-being. If the tree flourishes, we flourish. If it is destroyed . . .'

She did not finish.

Eadulf received the statement in silence. Once again he was confounded by the curious mysticism of this land that he had grown to love. On the one hand the country was more Christian than any of the Saxon kingdoms he knew of. On the other it was far more pagan than most Christian lands he knew. And Fidelma, the most rational and analytical of people was actually troubled by the fact that someone was cutting down the great yew-tree. Eadulf began to realise the true significance of that symbolism. He had always thought that in pagan times the trees had been worshipped. He now realised that this was but a special veneration for trees as symbolic of the oldest living things in the world. Living! What was happening through the destruction of this symbol, which was called 'The Tree of Life', was much more than an insult to the Eóghanacht dynasty of Cashel. It was a means of dispiriting them and their people.

There were many things he felt he ought to say but then considered it wiser to say nothing.

They could just hear, in spite of the tolling of the great bell, the axes of the attackers biting into the ancient wood with a rhythmic sound that seemed at odds with the din of destruction and death.

Brother Bardán, the apothecary, came up onto the roof followed by young Brother Daig, his assistant. Bardán immediately knelt by the abbot and examined his wound.

'He has been struck a nasty blow but it is not life threatening,' the apothecary commented after a cursory examination. 'Brother Daig will help me carry him to his chamber.' He glanced up at Brother Madagan. 'What are our chances, Brother?'

'Not good. They are not attacking the abbey as yet but they are cutting down the great yew.'

Brother Bardán gave a sharp intake of his breath and genuflected as he looked over the wall to confirm the truth of what Brother Madagan had said. For a moment he stood mesmerised by the sight beyond. The sound of axes being swung was clear now. The apothecary shook his head in dismay.

'So that is why they are not attacking the abbey directly,' he observed softly. 'They do not have to.'

'Oh, for a few good archers,' Fidelma cried in frustration.

Brother Daig looked momentarily shocked. 'Lady, we are of the Faith,' he protested.

'That does not mean that we should let ourselves be destroyed.'

'But Christ taught . . .'

Fidelma made a typical gesture of impatience, a cutting motion of her hand. 'Do not preach to me of poverty of spirit as a virtue, Brother. When men are poor in spirit then the proud and haughty oppress them. Let us be true in spirit and determined to resist oppression. Only then do we not court further oppression. I say again, a good archer might save this day.'

'There are no such weapons in the abbey,' Brother Bardán commented, 'let alone men to use them.' He turned back to the unconscious abbot. 'Come on, Daig, we must see to the abbot's welfare.'

They lifted the elderly abbot between them and carried him down the stairs.

For some time Fidelma, Eadulf and Brother Madagan stood in frustration watching the attackers hacking at the old tree. It was impossible for Eadulf to entirely empathise with the angry impotency shared by Fidelma and Madagan as they stood watching its destruction. He could intellectualise about its meaning but to actually feel the alarm and trepidation that the act was causing, was still beyond him.

His eyes suddenly caught sight of a movement and Eadulf pointed across the square.

'Look! Someone is running towards the gates of the abbey. A woman!'

A shadow had detached itself from the burning buildings and was running and stumbling forward in an obvious attempt to gain the protection of the abbey gates.

'The gates are closed,' Brother Madagan cried. 'We must go down and open them for the poor creature.'

With one more quick glance at the scene below and realising that she could do no more from that vantage point, Fidelma turned and followed Brother Madagan and Eadulf to the courtyard.

At the gate they found Brother Daig who had apparently just returned after helping the abbot back to his chamber.

'Get the gate open,' shouted Brother Madagan as they hurried up. 'There is a woman trying to enter!'

The young man hesitated with an alarmed expression. 'But that might let the attackers in,' he protested.

Eadulf simply pushed the young man aside and began to tug on the wooden bolts.

Brother Madagan joined him.

Together, they drew back the great wooden bars which secured the gates, much to the consternation of several of the other brethren who gathered behind Brother Daig. They appeared uncertain what to do. Eadulf and Madagan pulled the main gates inwards.

The running woman was a dozen paces away from the gates. Eadulf had a feeling that she seemed familiar. He moved forward to shout words of encouragement to her but, to his dismay, he saw that a mounted raider had began to pursue the woman and was about to overtake her.

Brother Madagan ran forward through the gates and was holding his crucifix before him as if it would turn back the approaching warrior just by the sight of it.

'*Templi insulaeque!*' he cried. '*Sanctuarium!* Sanctuary! Sanctuary!'

He had managed to insert himself between the woman and the approaching rider whose sword was upraised, the blade flashing against the light of the fires across the square.

The warrior's sword arm swung back and Brother Madagan half spun, a splash of red across his forehead. Then he fell face down on the ground. Eadulf reached forward to pull the woman to safety but the attacker reached her first. His sword swung again and she gave a shriek as it smashed into the back of her head. The momentum still carried her forward and she stumbled into the abbey courtyard.

The forward motion of the charging horse of the pursuer also carried the warrior forward through the gates, the horse clattering into the paved courtyard. What happened next took place so quickly that no one had time to draw breath before it was over.

The momentum of the horse had knocked the wounded woman

aside so that she spun forward, crashing against a wall, and fell onto the ground. Eadulf himself only had time to turn sideways to avoid being knocked down by the horse. As he swung round, some instinct had caused him to grab the leg of the rider and heave with all his might. The rider, already precariously balanced by the effort of his swinging sword arm, came unseated and, as Eadulf fell, he was dragged down from his saddle. The man fell hard but on top of Eadulf, driving the breath from him so that Eadulf lay stunned and unable to move.

The warrior was a professional. His fall cushioned by Eadulf, he half rolled over and sprung to his feet, coming up in a fighting crouch, sword in hand, ready to face any attack.

He was stocky but well-muscled. Thus much could be seen of him but he was clad in black dyed linen with an iron coat of chainmail, the *luirech iairn*, over a corselet made of bull-hide leather. From the knee down his legs were protected by leather *asáin* studded in brass; the leather encasing the lower legs was tied firmly. He bore a helmet of polished brass with a small visor over his eyes so that the only feature that could be seen in the flickering light of the courtyard's brand torches was a thin red slit of a cruel mouth.

His shield was still on his horse which had clattered to a halt on the paved courtyard a short distance away, blowing and snorting from its strenuous run.

The warrior crouched, the sword, which he now held in both hands, swinging round to ascertain what dangers lurked around him. He momentarily relaxed when he saw only half a dozen clearly frightened religious huddling behind the gates and a solitary female religieuse who stood facing him.

The man straightened up and bellowed with laughter before raising his sword in a threatening gesture at the religious. They cowered back, causing him even more merriment. Then he realised that the female religieuse stood unmoved, regarding him, hands folded demurely in front of her. He relaxed in her tall, well-proportioned figure and pleasantly attractive features.

'Who are you, warrior?' Fidelma demanded.

The man blinked at the quiet authority in her voice. Then he smirked.

'A man, a man compared with these eunuchs which you have surrounded yourself with, woman. Come with me and let me show you what a man can do.'

Fidelma's eyes had flickered anxiously to Eadulf, who was still lying winded. Beyond the gate, Brother Madagan was probably dead. The woman also lay crumpled and inert. She let her eyes return to the warrior with open scorn.

'You have already shown me what you can do,' replied Fidelma in a quiet tone, without a hint of fear. 'You have the murders of a Brother of the Faith and a defenceless woman on your hands. That makes you no man at all but something I scrape off the heel of my shoe with a stick after I have walked through a bog land.'

Her tone was so even that the warrior still stood smirking some moments after she had spoken. It took him a while to realise just what she had said.

He drew his thin mouth into an expression of rage.

'You can come with me or die now!'

He made a threatening gesture with his sword.

One of the Brothers, it was the youthful Brother Daig, his face red with mortification at his earlier moment of cowardice, came forward as if to protect her. He did not even have time to speak but his movement caused the warrior to turn, sinking the metal point of his sword into Daig's chest. The young man gave a grunt of pain and dropped to his knees, the blood gushing over his habit. He stared down at the wound as if he could not believe his eyes.

'You are brave against unarmed boys and women,' snapped Fidelma, who took a step forward but was halted as the point of the sword swung towards her. 'Have you a name? Or are you ashamed of it?'

The warrior gasped at her audacity.

'My name is not for the likes of you, wench. Do not think that because you are a woman you can insult me with impunity!'

Fidelma glanced down to where young Daig was trying to staunch the blood from his wound, his hand pressed over it.

'You have already proved your branch of courage. As I am also unarmed, doubtless you will feel brave enough to show how despicable you really are.'

Brother Daig look up painfully. There were tears in his eyes. He glanced towards the group of frightened brethren and tried several times to speak before succeeding. 'The gate, Brothers . . . the gate must be shut before others of this man's tribe enter the abbey.'

Indeed, it was something that Fidelma had just realised. The longer the gate stood open, eventually other attackers would notice it and enter the abbey. Then there would be nothing to prevent them from the wholesale slaughter of the community.

'Do not try it, wench,' grunted the warrior as he saw her anxious glance towards the gate. 'You will be dead before you reach it. My comrades will be here in a few moments.'

Brother Daig gave a groan of pain as he tried to move forward. 'He is only one man, Brothers. He cannot kill you all. Shut the gate and disarm him!'

The warrior gave a hiss of anger and the steel of his sword struck the young Brother full in the neck.

Brother Daig fell backwards. There was no need to check whether he was dead or not. That much was obvious.

It was now that Eadulf finally began to recover his wind. He took several deep breaths and began to scramble to his feet, only to find himself pinned by the point of the raider's sword.

'The gate!' cried Fidelma determinedly to the cowering religious. 'Your Brother's dying command must be accomplished!'

'Move and this one dies,' snapped the warrior, pricking Eadulf's shoulder with his sword.

'Do it!' cried Eadulf loudly, anger overcoming his personal fear.

The warrior's gaze was distracted momentarily as he glanced to the religious to see if they were obeying Eadulf. It was a moment that Eadulf had hoped would come. He suddenly rolled away from the reach of the warrior's sword point, diving towards the gate.

The warrior turned back to him, sword raised, but it was too late.

With a scream of rage he hurled himself forward as Eadulf began to push against the gate. Suddenly Fidelma was in his way. He turned his sword to strike her. Then he was flying through the air, he knew not how.

Only Eadulf, out of the corner of his eye, saw Fidelma spring forward. His heart lurched as he saw her but somewhere, dim in his memory, he recognised the stance she had taken with her body. He had seen her perform the feat a few times now. The first time had been in Rome. She was poised as if to take the blow from the descending sword on her unprotected head. Then it seemed as if she merely reached forward, caught the arm of the man and heaved her assailant into the air, over her hip, and sent him cannoning into the stone wall of the abbey wall. There was a strange thudding sound and, without even a grunt, the warrior fell to the ground, unconscious.

Fidelma had once told Eadulf that in ancient Ireland there had been a class of learned men who taught the time-honoured philosophies of her people. They journeyed far and wide and did not believe in carrying arms to defend themselves because they did not believe in killing people. But they had to protect themselves from attacks by thieves and bandits on the highways. Thus they were forced to develop a technique called *troid-sciathaigid* – battle through defence. Defence without the use of weapons. It was a method taught to many religious missionaries before they left Éireann and went into strange lands to preach the word of the new Faith.

'Come on! Help Brother Eadulf!' cried Fidelma. 'Get those gates closed.'

She rushed forward herself to help but suddenly seemed to change her mind and ran on through the gates. Brother Madagan's body lay only ten feet beyond.

'Help me Eadulf, quickly!' she called.

Realising what she intended, he went after her. They grabbed Brother Madagan unceremoniously between them, lifting him by the shoulders of his clothes and dragged him back within the gates just as the Brothers had recovered sufficiently to help swing the gates closed. They paused inside as the bolts were pushed home.

Fidelma was soon active again.

'Bind that warrior!' she cried to the Brothers who now stood about in shameful consternation that they had not acted before. 'Disarm and bind him so he does no further harm.'

She glanced down at Brother Madagan. Eadulf was by his side, examining him.

'He's still alive,' he announced with satisfaction. 'The wound is not bad at all. So far as I can see, he only received the flat of the sword on his skull. The blood on his forehead is from a slight nick from the sword's edge. He should recover consciousness soon.'

Fidelma glanced anxiously at Eadulf for there was blood on his habit where the warrior had pricked him with his sword point. 'And yourself?' she asked quickly.

Eadulf grinned and automatically raised a hand to his shoulder. 'I have survived worse things. It was no more than a needle prick. The weight of the man was far worse when he fell on me. I might be stiff for a while.'

Fidelma was already moving to the crumpled body of the woman who was still stretched on the cobbles.

'It is the innkeeper!' Fidelma had recognised Cred under the bloodstained mask of her face. 'By the Faith!' she cried, 'I think she still breathes.'

She bent and held up the woman's head.

Eadulf looked quickly at the wound and then at Fidelma. He shook his head slowly. The injury placed the woman beyond any temporal help.

At that moment, Cred's eyes opened. There was fear in them.

'Hush!' Fidelma spoke gently. 'You are among friends.'

Cred groaned and rolled her eyes. She had difficulty in speaking. 'I . . . I know . . . more . . .' she gasped.

Eadulf turned to where one of the Brothers was waiting. 'Fetch water!' he snapped.

The man hurried off immediately.

'Rest,' Fidelma told Cred. 'We will take care of you. Lie still.'

'Enemies . . .' gasped Cred. 'I heard the archer speak. Enemies . . . the enemy is in Cashel. The Prince . . .'

Her head lolled back, though her eyes remained wide open.

Eadulf genuflected. He had seen enough death to know that there was an end to the tavern keeper's life.

Fidelma stayed still a moment, frowning.

The monk who had been sent for the water returned with it and so Eadulf rose and set about reviving Brother Madagan. The steward of the abbey came round slowly.

Eadulf turned to the group of young brethren now standing like sheep awaiting someone's orders.

'Does Brother Madagan have an assistant?' he demanded. 'Is there an assistant steward of the abbey?'

There was a muttering and shuffling of feet.

'It would have been Brother Mochta,' offered one young man. 'I wouldn't know now.'

'Well, until we find out, I shall take charge,' Eadulf announced. 'I want one of you to assist Brother Madagan to his chamber. He has had a nasty blow on the head. Get the apothecary. I want volunteers to take the bodies of Cred and Brother Daig to the mortuary and have this blood cleansed from the flagstones.'

'Leave it to me, Brother Saxon,' said one of the monks. 'But what shall I do with the warrior?'

Eadulf turned towards the raider.

The man was now securely trussed up but had recovered consciousness. He was lying with his back against the wall secured by his feet, his hands tied behind his back. He was testing his bonds but ceased as Eadulf approached him.

'You will wish that you had killed me, Brother,' he snarled between clenched teeth.

'You might wish that I had, my vicious friend,' returned Eadulf grimly. 'I would think your murderous friends out there will not think much of you, allowing yourself to be disarmed and captured by a woman. Indeed, an unarmed woman of the Faith who knocked you unconscious. What an epitaph for a warrior such as yourself. *Aut viam inveniam aut faciam*, eh? Victory or death is the warrior's motto. But you managed to achieve neither.'

The warrior screwed up his mouth and tried to spit at Eadulf.

Eadulf smiled broadly and turned back to the helpful young monk who was waiting his orders.

'Leave our valiant warrior where he has fallen, Brother . . . ?'

'Brother Tomar.'

'Well, Brother Tomar, leave him there and get on with the other tasks first.'

Eadulf went across to Fidelma, who was still standing by Cred's body, looking down thoughtfully.

'Do you know, I believe that Cred was not running to the abbey to seek shelter,' she said, raising her eyes to his. 'I think she might have been running here to see me.' She sighed, then said: 'Did the warrior tell you anything?'

'Nothing. He has not identified himself.'

'Well, plenty of time to question him later.'

Fidelma turned for the watch-tower. 'Let us see what is happening out there first. If these warriors are going to attack the abbey, they appear to be delaying it. I find that puzzling. It is nearly dawn now.'

They returned to the roof of the tower and gazed out across the square towards the town. The buildings were still on fire but the blaze was not so intense as it had been earlier. Columns of black smoke were arising. What caught Fidelma's attention immediately was the sight of the remains of the great yew-tree. Part of the trunk had been cut through and then ropes had obviously been fastened to it for it had been pulled over, causing a splintering. The severed tree had then been set alight.

Fidelma closed her eyes in anguish.

'Never in over sixteen centuries since Eber Fion set up the yew as symbol of our fortunes has this ever happened,' she said softly.

She frowned suddenly. She realised from the movements around the town that groups of raiders were reorganising themselves.

Fidelma also realised that the bell of the abbey was still clanging frantically. Indeed, it had never ceased. It was strange how she could have grown so used to the noise that she had not even noticed its continuing clamour.

'Let that noise be stopped,' she instructed Eadulf. 'If no one has heard it by now and come to our aid, no one will.'

'If I can find that young Brother Tomar he can see to it.'

He was about to go down the stairs when Fidelma stayed him.

'Wait! There is a movement in the woods to the south. I think the raiders are gathering for their attack on the abbey at last!'

Eadulf came forward and followed her directions.

'We will have no form of defence. If they can cut down that yew and destroy it in so short a time, then their axe-men would be able to break through the oak gates of the abbey within minutes.'

Fidelma reluctantly had to admit that Eadulf was right. 'We might be able to negotiate with them,' she said, but without conviction.

Eadulf said nothing but let his gaze sweep across the burning township and the remnants of the great yew-tree. With dawn casting its grey light across the hills they could see bodies scattered in profusion.

The youthful Brother Tomar came hurrying up the steps to join them.

'I have done everything that you have asked, Brother Saxon,' he told Eadulf. 'Brother Madagan has recovered consciousness but is weak. Abbot Ségdae has also recovered and is trying to organise the brethren to face our enemies with more discipline.' He glanced rather shame-faced at Fidelma. 'We did not acquit ourselves well at the gate when the warrior came, Sister. For that I must apologise.'

Fidelma was forgiving. 'You are Brothers of the Faith and not warriors. There is no blame on you.'

She was still peering anxiously southward where she had detected the movement of a body of horsemen.

Brother Tomar followed her gaze.

'Are they massing to attack the abbey?' he whispered anxiously.

'I fear so.'

'I'd better warn the others.'

Fidelma gestured negatively. 'To what purpose? There is no way to defend the abbey.'

'But there might be a way of evacuating the Sisters of our order, at least. I have heard the abbot once speak of a secret passageway that leads into the nearby hills.'

'A passageway? Then go; speak with Abbot Ségdae at once. If we can evacuate some of the members of the abbey before these barbarians break in . . .'

Brother Tomar had already left before she had finished speaking. Eadulf now touched Fidelma on the arm and pointed silently. She followed his gesture and saw, at the north end of the burning town, a band of attackers riding away in the opposite direction to the oncoming column of horsemen.

'Some of the attackers are leaving,' he observed with curiosity. 'Why?'

Fidelma turned from the column of disappearing attackers to look southwards again. The movement of horses she had seen in the dim early light had been revealed more fully as the tip of the sun broke across the top of the eastern hills, flooding the forest area with light. A body of twenty or thirty horsemen had emerged. She could see a fluttering banner among them.

It was a royal stag on a blue background.

'That's a Eóghanacht banner!' she gasped.

The horsemen were galloping across the plain towards the abbey.

Fidelma turned to Eadulf. There was relief suddenly on her face. 'I believe that they are men from Cnoc Áine,' she said, excitement in her voice. 'They must have come in answer to the tolling of the abbey bell.'

'It would make sense as to why the attackers are leaving so hurriedly.'

'Let us go down and tell the others.'

At the foot of the tower they found Brother Tomar and Abbot Ségdae. He looked slightly strained and pale and there was a bluish lump on his forehead but he seemed in control again. A trumpet note was echoing in the air as the column of horsemen approached the abbey. Abbot Ségdae recognised it. Fidelma did not have to explain.

'*Deo gratias!*' breathed the abbot thankfully. 'We are saved! Quick, Brother Tomar, open the gates. The men of Cnoc Áine have arrived to give us aid.'

As the abbey gate swung open, the column of horsemen came to a halt in front of them. They were led by a young, good-looking, dark-haired warrior, richly clad and equipped for battle. He was evenly featured, with curly close-cropped red hair and dark eyes. He wore a blue woollen cloak fixed at the shoulder with a silver brooch. It was quite distinctive, wrought in the shape of a solar symbol with semi-precious garnets on each of the three radiating arms.

His eyes fell on Fidelma as she emerged through the gates, with the others, to greet them. His features split into a broad smile.

'*Lamh laidir abú!*' he cried, raising a clenched fist in greeting.

Eadulf had been long enough in Muman to recognise the battle cry of the Eóghanacht. A strong hand to victory!

'You are welcome, cousin Finguine,' Fidelma replied, also raising her clenched fist in greeting.

The young man leapt from his horse and embraced his cousin. Then he stood back and gazed around in dismay.

'But I have arrived late rather than early,' he said in disappointment. 'Thank God that He has cast His mantel of protection over you, cousin.'

'The raiders left riding towards the north only minutes ago,' Eadulf offered.

'We saw them,' the Prince of Cnoc Áine nodded, glancing at him and observing his Saxon accent and tonsure. 'My *tanist* and half of my men have already started in pursuit. Who were they? Uí Fidgente?'

Fidelma had to admit that it was a logical assumption. It was in this very area, indeed, at Finguine's very capital at Cnoc Áine, that the last great battle had been fought with the Uí Fidgente scarcely a year before.

'It is hard to say, but the Prince of the Uí Fidgente is at Cashel, supposedly engaged in peace talks with my brother.'

'So I have heard,' observed Finguine dryly. His expression conveyed how much he distrusted such an event. But now he turned to the Abbot Ségdae, noting his bruise. 'Are you badly hurt, Father Abbot?'

Ségdae shook his head as he greeted the youthful Prince. 'A bruise, that's all.'

'Has harm come to any other of the brethren? Are you all well?'

'The most harm has been done to the township,' replied the abbot, his face still anguished. 'We have suffered one Brother killed and one bruised, like myself. But there must be many dead in the township. And, look . . .'

Finguine followed his gaze as did everyone else.

'The sacred yew-tree of our race – destroyed!' cried Finguine, his voice a cross between horror and rage. 'There will be much blood to pay for this. This is an insult to all Eóghanacht. It will mean war.'

'But war between whom?' Fidelma posed the question without humour. 'Firstly, we must identify those responsible.'

'Uí Fidgente,' snapped Finguine. 'They are the only people who will benefit from this.'

'It is an assumption only,' Fidelma pointed out. 'Never act before you know for sure.'

'Well, we have captured one of the raiders,' Eadulf reminded them. 'Let us question him and make him tell us who he takes his orders from.'

Finguine appeared surprised at the news. 'You have actually captured one, Saxon?' He sounded impressed.

'Well, Fidelma did the capturing,' Eadulf corrected disarmingly.

Finguine turned to his cousin with a grin. 'I should have known that you had a hand in it. Well, where is he? Let's us see what we can get out of the cur.'

They walked back into the courtyard of the abbey, after Finguine had issued orders to his men to fan out through the township and see what they could do to help the injured and to quench the fires.

'He is trussed up over here,' Eadulf said, leading the way to where they had left the surly warrior.

The man was lying where they had left him, his back against the abbey wall, hands tied behind him, his legs outstretched before him, still tied at the ankles. His head was slumped forward a little on his chest.

'Come on, man,' cried Eadulf, moving forward. 'Rouse yourself. It is time to answer a few questions.'

He bent and touched the warrior lightly on the shoulder.

Without a sound the warrior rolled over on his side.

Finguine dropped to his knee and placed his hand on the pulse in the man's neck.

'By the crown of Corc of Cashel! Someone has revenged themselves on this man. He's dead.'

With an exclamation of surprise, Fidelma moved forward to her cousin's side.

There was blood on the man's chest. Someone had stabbed him through the heart.

Chapter Thirteen

Night had made the raid seem more destructive than it had been in reality. There were a score of dead from the town and a further dozen or so were wounded or injured. Only half a dozen buildings had been burnt down. A few more buildings were damaged, though not beyond repair. Even so, the effect on such a small community as Imleach was devastating. Among the main buildings destroyed was the smith's forge, a warehouse and the inn that had belonged to Cred.

Abbot Ségdae and Brother Madagan, wearing their bandaged foreheads like insignia of distinction, had turned lauds into a short service of thanksgiving for the safe delivery of the abbey. Even the burly Samradán was there, looking somewhat shame-faced and irritable. Fidelma and Eadulf set off with her cousin, the Prince of Cnoc Áine, to walk to the town in order to assess the damage for themselves.

Little was said about the great yew-tree whose wood still smouldered in front of the abbey. Its destruction was beyond mourning.

The first person they saw as they walked across the square was Nion the smith, the *bó-aire*. Nion was leaning heavily on a stick and his leg had been bandaged. He wore a long woollen cloak wrapped around him against the morning chill. It was fastened at the shoulder by a silver brooch in the design of a solar symbol with three red garnets, similar to the one Finguine wore. He was staring morosely at the remains of his forge while his assistant, Suibne, was picking through the rubble. As they approached, they could smell the acrid stench of burnt wood mingling with other odours which they could not begin to identify, all rising together to make the atmosphere corrosive and caustic in their lungs.

Nion did not glance up as they approached.

'It is good to see you alive, Nion,' Finguine greeted him. He seemed to know the smith of old.

Nion looked up, recognising the Prince of Cnoc Áine, and bent his head slightly forward in acknowledgement.

'My lord, thank God that you came in time. We might all have been slain and the whole town destroyed.'

'Alas, I did not arrive in time enough to spare your loss, Nion,' replied the Prince of Cnoc Áine, looking grimly over the ruins of the forge.

'I will survive, I suppose. There are others of our township who will not. We shall see what we can recover from the ashes.'

Finguine shook his head sadly. 'It will take a while to restore your forge,' he observed. 'A pity. It was only the other day that I thought to prevail on your craftsmanship and commission you to make me another of these silver brooches.' He fingered the brooch on his cloak absently. Then he noticed Nion's injury. 'Were you badly wounded?'

'Bad enough,' Nion replied. 'And I shall not be earning a living as a smith for a while yet.'

'Were you here when the raid began?' Fidelma intervened for the first time.

'I was.'

'Can you describe exactly what happened?'

'Little to tell, lady,' he said ruefully. 'I was awakened by the clamour of the attack. I was asleep at the back of my forge. I ran out and saw upwards of a score of men riding through the streets. Cred's tavern was already in flames. People were running hither and thither. I could not recognise who the attackers were; just that they were intent on burning the town. So I grabbed a sword from those I had been sharpening. I had my duty as *bó-aire*. I ran out, determined to save my forge and the town but – the cowards! – I was struck from behind. As I fell, another attacker speared me in the leg. Then the flames were eating at the forge. My assistant, Suibne, dragged me away and we took shelter.' He glanced, embarrassed, at Finguine. 'Although I am *bó-aire*, and it is my task to protect my people, I am not expected to commit suicide. There were no warriors here and none who could help me drive off the attack.'

'You did not recognise the attackers? You do not know who they were or where they were from?' pressed Finguine.

'They rode from the north and returned to the north.' The smith spat on the floor. 'There is little need to ask who they were.'

'But you do not know who they were for certain?' insisted Fidelma.

'Who else could they be but Dal gCais? Who else but the murdering Uí Fidgente would make such an attack on Imleach and destroy the great yew?'

'But you do not know for sure?' she stressed once again.

The smith's eyes narrowed in unconcealed anger. 'Next time I meet an Uí Fidgente I will not need proof before I slaughter him. If I am wrong, I am prepared to go to hell just for the pleasure of taking one Uí Fidgente with me! Look what they have done to my township.' He flung out his arm expressively to the smouldering ruins.

Finguine turned with a serious look to his cousin. 'It is true that most of the people feel like this, cousin. Indeed, who else can it be but the Uí Fidgente?'

Fidelma drew him and Eadulf out of earshot of Nion, away from the forge.

'This is precisely what I need to find out,' she said. 'If it is the Uí Fidgente, so be it. But we must be sure. Donennach of the Uí Fidgente stays currently in Cashel to conduct a treaty with my brother. He and my brother were wounded in an attempted assassination. In a few days there will be a hearing in which we must prove Uí Fidgente duplicity or be held up before all the five kingdoms of Éireann as the aggressors. I do not want theories, I need proof of their involvement.'

Finguine was sympathetic. 'It was a pity someone took vengeance on your captive. We might have been able to learn something from him.'

'I wonder if vengeance *was* the motive to stab him in the heart and dispatch him so quickly and silently?' Fidelma said the words absently as if pondering the matter.

Finguine and Eadulf regarded her with surprise.

'I am not sure what you are implying?' the Prince of Cnoc Áine said hesitantly.

'My implication is simple enough,' she responded.

'Do you think that he was murdered to prevent him revealing the identity of the attackers?' Eadulf had more quickly understood the implication of what she had said.

Fidelma's expression told him that he was correct.

Eadulf's mind worked quickly. 'But that would mean . . . surely, that would mean that a member of the abbey was working hand in glove with the raiders?'

Fidelma shook her head at his tone of incredulity.

'Or someone in the abbey,' she corrected. 'Is that so difficult to believe? Every strand of this mystery leads to this abbey.'

Eadulf raised a hand and tugged at his ear thoughtfully.

'I am casting my mind back. We left the warrior trussed up and went into the tower. Was he still alive when we came down, having heard the approach of Finguine? I cannot vouch for it.'

'Nor I,' confirmed Fidelma. 'Was he killed when we were in the tower or was he killed when we opened the gate and came out to greet Finguine?'

'Well, if he had been killed when we were in the tower, there were several brethren still in the courtyard by the gates. There were those involved in removing the bodies of Cred and Brother Daig to the mortuary and in helping Brother Madagan to his chamber.'

Fidelma was reflective.

'When we returned to open the gates, Brother Tomar was there with the Abbot Ségdae. There were a couple of other Brothers standing nearby. We hurriedly opened the gate and came out to greet Finguine. Someone could easily have stabbed the man during that time.'

'There was certainly time to kill him and any one of the brethren could have been responsible.' Eadulf sighed.

'That does not help me much, cousin, to identify the raiders,' interrupted Finguine. 'A dead man can't tell tales.'

Fidelma looked at her cousin for a moment and then smiled knowingly. 'Sometimes a dead man can reveal much,' she replied solemnly. 'As the dead warrior is the only evidence we have of the raiders, I think we should go and examine him and his belongings. There might be a clue on him.'

They were turning back to the abbey when one of Finguine's men, who had been examining the fallen yew-tree, came hurrying across and whispered urgently to the Prince. Finguine turned to them with a smile of triumph.

'I think that we have the confirmation we need to apportion blame,' he announced with satisfaction. 'Come.'

They followed the man to the yew-tree. He stood aside and pointed to part of the unburnt wood, to something engraved on the fallen trunk. It was a symbol, a crude carving of a boar.

'The emblem of the Prince of the Uí Fidgente.' Finguine did not have to explain.

Fidelma regarded it for a moment.

'It is interesting that, during what was a stealthy night attack, someone went to great pains to let us know who the attackers were,' she mused.

At that moment a clear note on a trumpet sounded.

It was Finguine's men returning, those whom he had sent to chase the raiders.

They came riding into the township, their horses dusty and tired. Their leader saw Finguine and rode over, halting and sliding from his mount. Even as his feet touched the ground he was shaking his head in disgust.

'Nothing,' he growled angrily. 'We lost them.'

Finguine frowned in displeasure. 'Lost them? How?'

'They crossed a river and we lost their tracks.'

'Which way were they going when you lost contact with them?' asked the Prince of Cnoc Áine.

'North, veering towards the mountains, I would say. But we lost their tracks in the Dead River. They could have turned in any direction from there. I believe that they continued north.'

'Didn't you scour the north bank to find out where they left the river?' demanded Finguine.

'We rode a mile or so in both directions in order to pick up their tracks but we were unable to do so. There was a lot of stony ground there.' The man sounded bitter at his Prince's rebuke.

'I did not mean to criticise your ability,' Finguine assured him. 'Go, get some food and rest.'

The warrior was turning back to his men when his eyes fell on the shattered ancient yew-tree.

'This is a bad sign, Finguine. It is an evil augury,' he stated quietly.

The Prince of Cnoc Áine's mouth was a thin line. 'The only thing that this means is that those who did it will be brought to justice,' he snapped.

'Just a moment,' Fidelma called after the warrior as he began to lead his horse away. 'What makes you think that they continued in a northerly direction from the Dead River?'

The man glanced back. He hesitated and then shrugged. 'Why would you ride as if the Devil were on your tail, directly north, and then turn aside at the river in a different direction? They were obviously in a hurry to get back to the safety of their own territory.'

'Perhaps they rode for the river knowing that it might be a good place to lose any pursuers?' Eadulf posed the question for Fidelma.

The warrior regarded him with a sour look. 'I won't preach a sermon, Brother, if you do not lead warriors in battle. I still say they were heading north.'

'Then perhaps you should have gone north as well?' replied Fidelma blandly.

The warrior was about to respond when Finguine signalled him to leave.

'He is a good man, cousin,' Finguine said, defensively. 'It is bad manners to question a warrior's decision.'

'I still think that he made the wrong decision. If he thought they were going north he should have followed his intuition.' Fidelma glanced towards the fallen yew-tree. 'Everywhere I turn in this matter I am left with supposition, with guesses. I want more than a carving on a tree. Anyone can carve such a well-known symbol.'

Finguine looked surprised. 'You mean that you will ignore this evidence?'

'No. I never ignore evidence. But such evidence as this needs to be considered more carefully than simply reacting to it. I want something more than a drawing which might have been left purposely to make us believe it was a boastful acclamation of the raiders.'

'Perhaps we should examine the body of the warrior next?' ventured Eadulf after a moment. 'As you have said, it might give us some clues as to his identity.'

They left Finguine continuing to examine the damage in the township and went back to the abbey. Eadulf suddenly asked: 'You don't suppose all these things are coincidences, do you?'

'Not connected?' Fidelma considered the proposition seriously.

'Coincidences do happen.'

'The reason why we started out on this journey to Imleach was because of the attempted assassination in Cashel. That brought us to the abbey. When we arrived here, we found that Brother Mochta, Keeper of the Holy Relics of Ailbe, had vanished with those relics and that one of the relics had been carried by one of the assassins and that person is thought to be Mochta, except we have the contradictory evidence of the tonsure. The attack on the abbey and the township and the destruction of the sacred yew of the Eóghanacht might be coincidence but it seems unlikely.'

'I do not see the connection,' protested Eadulf, who did not notice the slight smile playing around the corners of Fidelma's mouth.

'Let us consider the connections then,' Fidelma said. 'The finding of the relic on the assassin. The fact that the assassin was a religieux and that his description fits that of Brother Mochta even down to the tattoo of a particular bird on his forearm. These are facts, *not* coincidences.'

'How do you deal with the mystery of the tonsure?' Eadulf asked irritatingly. They had halted in the cloistered courtyard of the abbey.

'What of the fact that the other assassin, the one called the archer, *Saigteóir*, was known to have spent a few days here in Imleach? He bought his arrows from Nion the smith here. Why was Samradán's driver killed when he was revealing that the archer also met Brother Mochta here and another man whom he addressed as '*rígdomna*', the title of a prince. These are facts.'

'True. But I will give you another fact which does not make sense,' Eadulf offered. 'There is the fact that the timescale does not really coincide. That makes no sense. How could this Brother Mochta be seen in Imleach at Vespers wearing a tonsure of St John and less than twelve hours later be in Cashel with the remnants of a Roman tonsure over which he had been growing hair for several weeks?'

Fidelma waved the objection aside. 'What of the fact that the Cashel merchant, Samradán, whose warehouse was the point from which the assassination attempt was launched, is here in Imleach? It was his driver who told us about the archer for which he paid with his life. Is that a coincidence?'

'Perhaps. I don't know. We must have a further word with Samradán.'

Fidelma smiled. 'On that point I agree with you.'

'I still believe that we might be putting facts together which are unconnected,' Eadulf persisted.

Fidelma restrained a chuckle. She enjoyed it when Eadulf summarised matters for it helped in her consideration of the facts. Often she used him as devil's advocate to sort out her own ideas but she could not tell Eadulf that.

'I think that we can be certain of one thing,' Eadulf summed up. 'That is I believe that Nion, the smith, is right. I know little of these people you call the Uí Fidgente but everyone seems agreed that their hand is behind this attack. They can't all be wrong.'

'Eadulf, if I did not have to present proof but only suspicion to a court, I do not doubt that we would have all the Uí Fidgente convicted within the hour. But that is not how our laws work. Proof is what is needed and proof we must obtain or declare the Uí Fidgente to be innocent.'

Brother Tomar was crossing through the courtyard at that moment.

'Do you know where the merchant Samradán is?' called Fidelma.

Brother Tomar shook his head quickly. He was, so she had found out, the stableman at the abbey. He was a rough-mannered country youth who preferred the company of his animals than the company of people.

'He has left the abbey.'

Brother Tomar was about to move on when Fidelma stayed him. 'Left?' she asked. 'To go to the township?'

'No. He left with his wagons.'

'Did his drivers escape unhurt? I thought I saw Cred's tavern burnt to the ground.'

Brother Tomar responded in a morose tone. 'So I understand from one of the drivers. It seems that only two of the drivers escaped from that carnage for Samradán arrived here with three drivers and he has left with two of them. The two wagons came to the abbey, each driven by one man, and Samradán joined them. They set off on the road north.'

'North,' muttered Fidelma.

'Samradán did tell you that he was going north,' Eadulf reminded her.

'So he did,' Fidelma agreed slowly. 'North.'

Brother Tomar waited hesitantly. 'That is correct, Sister. I heard him instruct his drivers to head for the ford on the Dead River.'

Fidelma thanked the stableman and she and Eadulf continued their way in search of the apothecary.

It turned out that Brother Bardán was alone in the mortuary room of the abbey when they entered. The apothecary and mortician was putting the finishing touches to the winding sheet of his late friend, the young Brother Daig. His eyes were red and there were tearstains on his cheeks.

He glanced up with an angry look. 'What do you seek here?' he asked in an irritable tone.

'Calm yourself, Brother.' Fidelma spoke in a pacifying voice. 'I realise that you were close to poor young Daig. We are not here to intrude on your grief but we must examine the body of the raider.'

Brother Bardán gestured in annoyance to the far side of the chamber.

'The body lies on the table in that corner. I will not prepare it for burial. It deserves no decent Christian service.'

'You are within your rights,' Fidelma agreed, unruffled, for the apothecary was aggressive as if he expected her to argue. 'Where is the body of Cred? Is it also here?'

'Her body was already prepared and taken by her relatives to the cemetery of the township. I am told there are many people slain in the attack who must be buried this day.'

Fidelma turned to where the body of the dead warrior lay and motioned Eadulf to join her.

The arms and legs of the man had not even been unbound. His helmet still covered his head and the visor was still drawn over the upper features.

With a click of her tongue to indicate her displeasure, Fidelma reached forward and removed the helmet. The man was in his early thirties. His features were coarse and, in life, were doubtless made hard by the life he led. There was the pale mark of an old sword wound on his forehead. He had a bulbous nose and the grossness of his features inclined her to think that he had been given to an abundance of drink and food.

'Untie his hands and feet, Eadulf.'

Eadulf did as she instructed while she stood staring down, hoping there was something that might identify the man. Now that she could view him in a more relaxed state, her first impression was confirmed that he had the appearance of a professional warrior. Yet his chainmail shirt was old and there were areas of rust eating into the links in patches.

She helped Eadulf remove the belt from which his weapons had hung. Then they removed his mail shirt and leather jerkin. Underneath it, he wore a black dyed linen shirt and kilt. There was nothing to identify who he was nor where he had come from.

She observed that whoever had killed him had slipped a dagger through a joint of the mail shirt and under the ribcage. It would have been a swift and instantaneous death. Eadulf, on her instructions, set to work to remove the shirt and undergarments.

There were no identifying marks on the body, just a number of old scars from wounds which confirmed that the man had spent his life as a professional warrior.

'And not a good warrior at that,' responded Fidelma when Eadulf commented on the fact.

'How do you know?'

'He has been wounded too many times. If you want the better warrior, look for the man who inflicted those wounds not the one who received them.'

Eadulf accepted this wisdom in silence.

'Surely it is strange that he does not carry a purse?' Fidelma pointed out after a while.

Eadulf drew his brows together as he tried to understand the point she was making.

'Ah.' His face lightened. 'You mean that if he were a professional warrior, a mercenary, he would want payment for his services?'

'Precisely. So where would he put his purse?'

'He would leave it at home.'

'And if he were far from home, what then?'

Eadulf shrugged, unable to answer.

'He might leave it somewhere meaning to return and pick it up after the raid. That is a dangerous practice. No; most professionals tend to carry their wealth with them.' Her face suddenly brightened. 'Maybe he had saddle bags. I had almost forgotten that we have his horse here as well.'

She looked across to where Brother Bardán was finishing his task. 'What do you mean to do with the body of this man?'

'Let it rot, for all I care,' returned the apothecary in an uncompromising tone.

'It will rot, surely,' Fidelma agreed. 'But a decision has to be made whether you want to let it rot here or elsewhere.'

Brother Bardán sighed. 'It will not be buried within the abbey grounds among our brethren, next to . . .' He half gestured towards the body of Brother Daig. 'I will send for Nion, the *bó-aire*, and ask him to remove the body to the town burial ground.'

'Very well.' Fidelma turned back to Eadulf and said quietly, 'We will go to the stables and examine the warrior's horse and harness.'

Eadulf picked up the man's sword as they were about to leave.

'Have you examined the sword?' he asked.

She shook her head and reached for it. It was about thirty-five inches in length, the blade nearest the point splayed out in almost a leaf shape before narrowing down to the hilt. The hilt was riveted on. There were six rivets.

'This is no poor man's sword,' Eadulf said, with a frown. 'I am sure that I have seen a similar style of sword just recently.'

'You have,' she replied with irony. 'It is the same style as the one carried by our assassin. Remember? This is a *claideb dét*.'

'A sword of teeth?' translated Eadulf literally. 'I thought it was made of metal like any other.'

Fidelma smiled patiently and pointed to the handle. 'The hilt is ornamented with the carved teeth of animals. As I recall, there is only one territory in Éireann's five kingdoms where the smiths indulge in such embellishment. If only I could recall where. It is such a distinctive ornamentation.'

'You mean that it might indicate where this man came from?'

'Not necessarily,' she replied. 'It will only tell us where the sword was manufactured. But, speaking of coincidences as we were, surely it is not coincidence that both the assassin and this raider carried such a distinctive weapon?'

Eadulf considered the point and nodded assent. 'What did you say it was called – *claideb dét*?' he asked, examining the weapon with a new regard.

'*Macheram belluinis ornatam dolatis dentibus*,' she explained in Latin. 'A sword ornamented with the carved teeth of animals. Hang onto it, Eadulf. It may well be important.'

She made a final examination of the body and the clothing.

'No,' she finally said, 'there is little here by way of identification. All we know is that this man is no amateur but whether he was a professional in the service of some prince or whether he was just an outlaw raiding the country in search of booty, it is impossible to say. Most of what he is wearing can come from any corner of the five kingdoms with . . .'

'With the exception of his sword,' Eadulf interrupted.

'With the exception of his sword,' echoed Fidelma. 'But that is of no use to me unless I can remember what people it was who specialised in decorating their sword hilts in such a fashion.'

She turned to the door of the mortuary, glancing at Brother Bardán. 'I have finished with the body of the raider.'

The apothecary nodded curtly. 'Do not worry. It will be disposed of.'

Outside Eadulf grimaced disapprovingly. 'I see that Brother Bardán does not take the Faith's teaching of forgiving one's enemies too seriously. "Be you kind to one another, tender-hearted, forgiving one another, even as God for Christ's sake has forgiven you." Perhaps he should be reminded of the text?'

'*Ephesians*, chapter four,' Fidelma identified the quotation. 'I rather think that Brother Bardán is one of those who prefer to hand his enemies over to God's forgiveness and show none himself. But then he is a man with all the frailty of men. Daig meant a lot to him.'

Eadulf suddenly realised what she meant and said no more.

As they passed back through the cloisters they found Abbot Ségdae sitting in the shade, his head sunk on his shoulders. He was still wearing his bandage and was sniffing at a small bunch of herbs.

He glanced up as they approached and smiled weakly. Then he gestured with the bunch of herbs.

'Brother Bardán says the aroma of these will help with my head-ache.'

'Is your wound healing, Ségdae?' asked Fidelma solicitously. She was fond of the old abbot who had been such a close friend to her family over the decades.

'I am told that the bruise looks bad but the slingshot fortunately, did not break the skin. I have a lump and a bad headache. That is all.'

'You must take care of yourself, Ségdae.'

The abbot smiled weakly. 'I am an old man, Fidelma. Perhaps I should make way for a younger one here. It will be recorded by the annalists that during my years as Comarb of Ailbe I allowed his Holy Relics to be stolen, that I allowed the sacred yew-tree of Imleach to be cut down. In short, that I allowed the Eóghanacht to be disgraced.'

'You must not think of resigning office,' Fidelma protested. She had always thought of Ségdae as one of the permanent factors of the kingdom.

'A younger man might not have been so stupid to stand on the tower as I did and allow himself to be felled by a slingshot,' replied Ségdae ruefully.

'Ségdae, if you were a captain of warriors, then I would tell you immediately to stand aside,' Fidelma told him candidly. 'But you are a captain of souls. It is not your task to organise a defence against attack. You are here to act as counsel and guide and be a father to your community. All acts of bravery must be judged by comparisons. Sometimes it is an act of bravery merely to live.'

The abbot, who, in Eadulf's eyes, seemed to have aged greatly since their arrival at the abbey, shook his head.

'Make no excuses for me, Fidelma. I should have acted as the need arose. I failed my community. I have failed the people of Muman.'

'You are a harsh judge of your own actions, Ségdae. Your community needs your wisdom more than ever. Not battle wisdom but the practical wisdom that you are renowned for. Make no hasty decisions.'

The old man sighed and raised the bouquet of herbs to his face.

Fidelma made a motion with her head to indicate to Eadulf that they should leave him to his contemplation.

They found Brother Tomar at the abbey barns where their own horses were stabled. He was cleaning out the stalls.

The stableman looked surprised at being disturbed twice by them in a short space of time.

'Did you forget something, Sister?' he asked.

Fidelma came straight to the point.

'The horse of the raider who was killed. Is it here in the stables?'

Brother Tomar pointed to one of the stalls.

'I have taken great care of it, Sister. I have rubbed it down and fed it. The horse is not to blame for the faults of the master.'

Fidelma and Eadulf went to the stall. Fidelma was a good judge of horses and had ridden almost before she had learnt to walk. Her keen eye ran over the bay filly. She noticed a scar on its left shoulder and some sores from the rubbing of the bit and harness. Clearly the warrior had not been a good horseman or else he would have taken better care of the young mare. The scar confirmed that the horse had been in conflict. However, it was not a recent wound.

Fidelma entered the stall and examined the hooves, one by one. The animal stood docilely enough for a horse can sense when a human knows what they are doing and means them no harm.

'Anything of interest?' asked Eadulf after a while.

Fidelma shook her head with a sigh.

'The beast is well shod, that's for sure. There is nothing that indicates where it was shod or, indeed, from where it has come.'

'We might ask Nion if he can identify the shoeing,' suggested Eadulf.

Fidelma came out of the stall and examined the harness hanging nearby.

'I presume this was the harness that belonged with this horse, Brother Tomar?' she called.

The stableman was still sweeping among the stalls. He glanced across. 'Yes. That saddle there belongs with it as well.'

The bridle was of the usual single-rein type called a *srían*, whose rein was attached to a nose-band not at the side but at the top, and came to the hand of the rider over the animal's forehead, between the eyes and ears, held in its place by a loop or ring in the face-band which ran across the horse's forehead and formed part of the bridle.

The saddle was a simple leather one which was strapped on top of an *ech-dillat*, a horse cloth, of a type that many warriors affected. Fidelma immediately noticed that a leather saddle bag was attached to the saddle by leather thongs.

With a soft grunt of satisfaction, she bent forward, picked it up and opened it. To her surprise it was empty. There was not even a change of clothing in the bag. It was obvious that whatever had been inside had been removed.

'Brother Tomar,' she called, 'did you unsaddle the young mare?'

Brother Tomar ambled over, broom in hand, curiosity on his features. 'I did.'

'Was there anything in this saddle bag when you did so?'

'I think so, though I did not look. It was heavy right enough. I put it there and did not touch it.'

Fidelma stood staring at the empty bag, deep in thought as she examined the possibilities.

'Has anyone else been around the stable since you put the horse in here?' she finally asked Brother Tomar.

The young stableman rubbed his chin reflectively.

'Many people,' he finally replied. 'The Prince Finguine and some of his men. Many of the brethren have been here for various things.'

'What do you mean?'

'This is a short route to one of our store houses. Many brethren went to the town to see what they could do to help and have come here to get supplies to take there to assist those who were in need.'

Fidelma pursed her lips in frustration.

'So if this saddle bag contained anything then, any one of many people could have examined it and removed things from it?'

'Why would they wish to do so?'

'Why, indeed?' Fidelma said softly, more to Eadulf than the stableman.

Eadulf set his jaw. 'I see. The same person who stabbed the raider while we were not looking probably took his personal possessions? Once more we are prevented from identifying . . .'

He paused when he saw Fidelma frowning at him.

Brother Tomar was gazing at him in curiosity.

'A bad day,' the stableman said finally.

'It will get better,' Eadulf assured him.

'I doubt it, Brother Saxon,' the man replied. 'There is too much blood shed for this spot ever to be purified again. Perhaps Imleach has been cursed. But vengeance is understandable. Many in this community were angered by the senseless death of poor Brother Daig.'

'Time has a way of purifying places where senseless slaughter has been made,' Fidelma asserted. 'No place is cursed unless it be in people's minds.'

She took Eadulf by the elbow and, with a nod to the stableman, she guided her companion outside. Then she turned to Eadulf with an excited expression.

'We have been overlooking the obvious about the killing of the warrior.'

'What have we overlooked?' Eadulf demanded.

'That Brother Bardán was especially close to the young Brother. Vengeance is a word that Brother Tomar used. I think we should ascertain where Brother Bardán was when the warrior was killed.'

Chapter Fourteen

There was no sign of Brother Bardán when they returned to the mortuary of the abbey. The room was deserted. Only the body of Brother Daig lay wrapped in its linen burial shroud on the table. There was also no sign of the body of the warrior. They left the apothecary's and almost immediately encountered Sister Scothnat, looking rather pale and shaken after the events of the previous night.

Fidelma made enquiries about the whereabouts of Brother Bardán. Sister Scothnat did not know but thought that he might have gone to see Nion, the smith. She added that Brother Daig was to be interred in the abbey grounds that evening at sunset, according to custom, when a requiem, called the *écnairc*, would be sung over his grave.

'What now?' asked Eadulf as he followed Fidelma towards the gates of the abbey once more.

'We will go in search of Brother Bardán.'

As they crossed the square towards the township, Fidelma noticed several of Finguine's warriors resting from their exertions, sprawled around a fire near the old yew-tree. They passed by the smouldering ruins that had been Nion's forge and looked up and down the main street.

There was more activity in the township than there had been earlier that morning. They could hear some noise not far off and turned a corner of a building to find out where it was coming from. It appeared that some of Finguine's men were helping the surviving menfolk in digging a large grave in a field behind some of the buildings which, it seemed, had already been used as a burial ground before. A line of bodies, each in its linen grave clothes, lay to one side, ready for the excavation to be completed. A small group of womenfolk stood round the bodies uttering the usual cries of lamentation and clapping their hands in the traditional manner to express their sorrow.

Elsewhere, other men, women and children were toiling among the wreckage of the buildings that had been destroyed. Apart from the frenzied activity, there had been little change in the scene since they had been there a short time before.

'I don't see Brother Bardán anywhere,' Eadulf observed.

'He is probably somewhere about,' Fidelma assured him as they passed back to the wreckage of Nion's forge and looked down the street towards the blackened shell of Cred's inn. 'We'll try along the street here; there seems to be a crowd of people up at the far end.'

They had not gone far when it became obvious that the people Fidelma referred to were converging on a figure who had just ridden into the end of the street. It was then they realised that the noise of the people were actually screams and shouts of anger and abuse. Even as they looked on in surprise, the foremost members of the crowd were reaching forth their hands and clawing at the man, dragging him from the ass which he was riding. He gave a shrill cry, waving his hands desperately in the air, before he disappeared under the surrounding people.

Fidelma started to run forward in alarm. As she did so, Finguine and a couple of his men appeared from a building in the street. Fidelma saw behind them the figure of Brother Bardán but more urgent things now demanded her attention.

'What is it?' cried Finguine as she rushed by with Eadulf in her train.

'Bring your men, quickly!' she flung over her shoulder.

They reached the edge of the crowd who were screaming abuse at the figure in their midst. The man had managed to regain his feet but was being pulled and punched and ill-treated. There was blood on his face.

'Stop it! Stop it, I say!' cried Fidelma, as she attempted to push her way through.

Finguine and his men caught up with her and followed her example, without asking questions, pushing people out of the way to get to the victim, shouting at them to stand back. Recognising the figure of the Prince of Cnoc Áine and two of his warriors, the crowd hesitated and then fell back a step or two.

Fidelma managed to reached the thin figure of the man who had been accosted.

He was slightly built, with greying hair. His clothes, which were now ripped and stained with blood and dirt, were of good quality. His cloak was trimmed with fox fur. A gold chain of office hung around his neck. He had a curious bird-like, jerking motion of his head. The neck was scrawny and the adam's apple was prominent, bobbing in his agitation. Fidelma couldn't make up her mind whether he reminded her of a bird or a ferret. Both creatures seemed to bear similarities to the man. The thought crossed Fidelma's mind in a fraction of a second before she remembered the viciousness with which the people had attacked him.

Observing that the man was not too badly hurt, she glared at the people and held up her hand for silence. They continued to circle them, still yelling abuse. The hate and anger showed in their faces; yes, and fear as well.

'What is the meaning of this?'

It was actually Finguine whose powerful voice finally quelled their outcry.

'An Uí Fidgente!' cried one man. 'Look at him! Come to gloat over the death and destruction that his fellows have visited upon us.'

Fidelma glanced at the small, pale-faced man, whose blood-splattered face held an expression torn between fear and anger.

'Who are you?' she asked. 'Are you of the Uí Fidgente?'

The little man drew himself up. His head barely reached her shoulder.

'I am . . .' he began.

The people interrupted with a collective howl of rage as they interpreted this as confirmation.

'Wait!' snapped Finguine. 'Let the man speak. Besides, as you can see, he is no warrior. Warriors attacked you last night, not strangers riding on asses. Now speak, man, and explain who you are and what you are doing here.'

Still looking agitated, the little man decided to address himself to Fidelma.

'It is true that I am of the Uí Fidgente but I am no warrior. What does this man say, that you were attacked by Uí Fidgente warriors? I'll not believe it.'

'As the Prince of Cnoc Áine says,' pointed out Fidelma softly, 'we were attacked last night.'

The man made to reply but his words were lost in new cries for vengeance.

Nion, the smith, had pushed his way forward, leaning heavily on a stick.

'See? He admits that he is an Uí Fidgente. Let us kill him.'

The little man looked nervous and thrust out his chin, his anger overcoming his fear. 'What hospitality is this, that you set on innocent wayfarers? Is there no respect for law in this place?'

'Law!' sneered Nion. He waved his hands to the smouldering buildings. 'Did the Uí Fidgente who did this thing care anything about law? Come and count the bodies at our graveyard and then tell us how you of the Uí Fidgente admire law.'

The little man looked bewildered. 'I know nothing of this. Furthermore, I would demand proof of your accusations.'

'Proof, is it?' cried another man in the crowd, supporting Nion. 'We'll show you the proof of a rope and a tree.'

Finguine's sword was abruptly in his hand. 'No one harms this man. The rule of law still runs in the territory of the Prince of Cnoc Áine.'

Fidelma shot a grateful glance at her cousin.

'Be about your tasks,' she instructed. 'This man is in the custody of the Prince of Cnoc Áine and if he bears any responsibility for what has happened to you, then he will be heard before the courts.'

There was an angry muttering but with Finguine and his men standing there, each with drawn sword, the crowd reluctantly began to dispel.

The little man was wiping the blood from a scratch on his cheek. He was beginning to recover his courage and his pale face was suffused with a flush of anger.

'Animals! I have never been greeted like this before. Compensation is due me, if you are Prince of Cnoc Áine.'

This last sentence was addressed to Finguine who had turned to him and was sheathing his sword.

'I am Finguine,' he affirmed shortly. 'Who are you?'

'I am Solam of the Uí Fidgente.'

Fidelma's eyes widened slightly. 'Are you Solam the *dálaigh*?'

The little man smiled thinly. 'That is precisely who I am, Sister . . . ?'

'I am Fidelma of Cashel.'

Solam managed to contain his surprise very well.

'Ah!' It was an exclamation which appeared to mean many things. 'I should have known that you would be here, Fidelma.'

'And what are you doing here?' demanded Finguine.

The little man pursed his lips and gestured towards Fidelma. 'She will know.'

'He is doubtless on his way to Cashel for the hearing,' Fidelma responded. 'Prince Donennach of the Uí Fidgente said he would be sending for Solam to represent him before the Brehons of Cashel, Fearna and the Uí Fidgente.'

Eadulf had caught hold of the *dálaigh*'s ass and led it forward.

'I need to bathe and recover from this greeting,' Solam announced irritably. 'Is there no inn here?'

'Your friends burnt it down and killed the innkeeper,' one of Finguine's men sneered.

The little man's eyes flashed. 'Have a care about further accusing the Uí Fidgente. I have heard also that we are under suspicion by some of attempting to assassinate the King of Muman!'

Fidelma regarded him with equal seriousness, then said, 'These burning buildings did not ignite spontaneously, Solam. The great yew symbol of our land did not chop itself down. Nor did those whose bodies are about to be consigned to a mass grave, slaughter themselves. Do you want to go and look carefully at them?'

Solam grimaced in repugnance. 'The Uí Fidgente are not responsible for the actions of outlaws and renegades. Where is your proof that we did this thing?'

It was Finguine who replied. 'Come with me,' he ordered grimly, giving Solam no other choice.

He led the way towards the newly dug grave where the women were still crying and clapping their hands in the lamentation of sorrow. Some of his warriors were still digging a grave. They paused as Finguine came up with the Uí Fidgente lawyer leading his ass and with the two warriors on either side of him. Fidelma and Eadulf brought up the rear.

Finguine walked to one body laid slightly apart from the others and not wrapped in the traditional linen shroud, but covered instead by an old horse blanket. The Prince tipped the edge of the blanket aside with the point of his sword. His gaze did not leave the face of Solam.

Under the horse blanket lay the corpse of the raider who had been slain.

'Do you recognise him?'

Solam examined the corpse carefully and then shook his head.

'You either speak the truth or you are a good liar,' observed Finguine bluntly.

He returned the blanket to cover the face of the body, still using the tip of his sword. 'I would advise you to continue your journey to Cashel immediately.'

Solam was proving to be a highly strung, impulsive little man whose excitable temper showed in his irritation. However, it also seemed that he had the quality of stubbornness.

'Preposterous! I entered this township, was attacked, injured, accused unjustly and then, in need of hospitality – mine by right of law – am told to ride on. You are truly making my case strong when I plead at Cashel.'

Fidelma decided to take a hand.

'Without proof of Uí Fidgente involvement in the raid, Solam does have a point, cousin,' she ventured. 'We cannot prove who the raiders were. Solam, therefore, is entitled to seek and receive hospitality and rest here on his journey to Cashel.'

Solam raised his chin defiantly. 'I am glad that there is someone with sense in this land,' he observed bitingly.

Fidelma's cousin expressed his dissatisfaction with a long, irritable sigh. 'Very well. Solam may seek hospitality but since these raiders destroyed the only inn in the township, I cannot suggest where he might receive it.'

'At the abbey, of course,' Solam replied.

'You are not a religieuse.'

'That does not matter. The rules of hospitality are there for everyone,' interposed Fidelma. 'Go to the abbey, Solam, and you will receive hospitality.'

Solam smiled, a little smugly, and turned to the abbey. Then he frowned and turned back, his stubbornness tempered by reality.

'You don't expect me to walk through the township again without protection, do you?' he asked almost peevishly.

Fidelma looked at Finguine. She did not say anything but her cousin read the message in her expression.

The Prince of Cnoc Áine signalled to one of his warriors. 'Escort the *dálaigh* safely across to the abbey gates then you may return to me.'

The man frowned and seemed about to protest but, seeing his Prince's expression, shrugged.

When Solam had gone, Finguine turned to Fidelma with a shake of his head. 'I hope you know what you are doing,' he warned. 'The longer that this man Solam stays here, the more his danger will increase. There are many who have lost relatives here.'

'But if the Uí Fidgente are not responsible . . . ?' Fidelma posed the question.

'You really think that Solam arrived here this morning by chance?'

'We have no reason to suppose otherwise . . . at the moment,' she replied.

'I think we do. Why would someone who set out on a journey from the country of the Uí Fidgente to Cashel arrive here, in Imleach? We are far south of the road that leads from their lands towards Cashel.'

Fidelma smiled briefly. 'Of that I am aware. But cunning is superior to strength. If Solam came here to enact some treachery let us observe what he does and where he leads us. That way we may set a snare for the wolf.'

'Better to hold the wolf by the ears than let him loose among the sheep,' Finguine countered.

'We will not let him loose; just hold him on a long leash and see where he wants to go. Do not worry; I, too, do not believe he came here by chance.'

Finguine opened his mouth but Fidelma had already begun to walk away.

Eadulf was perplexed as he hurried after her.

'I cannot make anything out of this. If the Uí Fidgente were the raiders last night, why would this man Solam come riding into the township this morning?'

'Speculation without knowledge is pointless,' Fidelma replied shortly.

They returned to the main street.

'Now where did we see Brother Bardán?'

Eadulf silently rebuked himself. In the excitement of Solam's arrival he had forgotten the reason they had come to the township.

'I did not see him,' he replied.

Fidelma shook her head in mock-admonishment.

'My cousin and two of his men came out of a house. Did you not see Brother Bardán behind them?'

Apologetically, Eadulf shook his head.

'You didn't see him?'

'I saw the house where your cousin was,' replied Eadulf. 'It was that one, across the street there.'

Fidelma and Eadulf walked across to it. It was a single-storey house of stone which seemed completely untouched by the raid. Its thatched roof was still intact while the roofs of the buildings on either side had not been so lucky. On one side the thatch was scorched and on the other an area was totally burnt away. This house had been lucky.

Fidelma went to the door and struck it with her fist.

There was no response for a moment. Then they heard a shuffling sound.

The door opened and Nion, the smith and *bó-aire* of the township, stood there. He still wore the long cloak with the small silver solar brooch with three red garnets. He frowned at Fidelma.

'What can I do for you, lady?'

His bandaged leg caused him to balance awkwardly against the door jamb, holding onto it with one hand.

Fidelma offered him a friendly smile. 'You can sit down and take the weight off your wound, Nion. Then we will speak.'

Reluctantly, Nion found himself backed into his house by Fidelma. Eadulf followed her in and closed the door behind him. Nion hobbled to a stool and sat down, staring up at Fidelma with a puzzled look.

'Is this your house?' she asked, gazing round.

Inside, there was a single chamber with a great fire at one end. A ladder gave access to a loft where the sleeping quarters were.

'Yes. The forge is where I work.'

'I thought you said that you slept at the back of the forge?' Eadulf asked suspiciously.

'I said I was sleeping at the forge when the attack took place. If I am working late, then I sometimes do so. This house is my right as *bó-aire*.'

Eadulf could not fault his response.

'That is certainly so. And, as this is untouched while your forge is destroyed, it is certainly a lucky thing that you have the two houses. You do not have to have the indignity of having nowhere to sleep while your forge is being rebuilt.'

Nion made an expressive cutting motion with his hand. 'You did not come here to congratulate me on my house, lady. Why are you here?'

'I could not help noticing as I passed earlier, that my cousin and his warriors were here.'

'Surely,' the answer came back immediately. 'Your cousin came to consult with me. I am, after all, the *bó-aire*.'

'That is fair enough.' She paused. 'What was Brother Bardán doing here then? Did he need to consult you . . . as *bó-aire*, of course?'

Nion did not even blink at the sharpness in her tone.

'Of course,' he affirmed.

'I see. Is it a matter of confidentiality if I inquire about the subject of his visit?'

'No.' Nion shook his head. 'Though I can't think why you are interested. Bardán came here to ask me if I would be prepared to bury the body of the raider who was killed last night. I gave permission for it to be buried near the graves of our people. That is all.'

It did seem plausible. Yet there was something troubling Fidelma.

'Where is Brother Bardán now?'

Nion spread a hand around the room in a gesture which invited her to search.

'I have no idea where he is. He left here when that sly Uí Fidgente lawyer arrived to check the damage which his kinfolk had done.'

'You did not see which way Brother Bardán went when he left your house?' Fidelma pressed him.

'No. If you recall, I followed you to see what the furore was about.'

'You arrived after most other people,' observed Eadulf, clearly irritated by the smith's evasive attitude.

Nion pointed to his injured leg. 'I cannot exactly hurry,' he said sarcastically.

Eadulf flushed.

'My comrade did not mean to be insensitive.' Fidelma smiled apologetically. 'However, you cannot even hazard a guess as to where Brother Bardán might have gone?'

'No. He's probably at the cemetery . . .'

'We've just comes from there,' Eadulf said.

'Then try at the abbey.'

Fidelma moved towards the door and halted, turning back to the smith.

'While Solam is here, treat him with the respect due to any visiting *dálaigh*. We have no proof that he is other than what he is. If any harm comes to him, the culprit is answerable to the law.'

When Nion made no reply, she lifted the latch and Eadulf followed her out into the street.

Outside they paused.

'You sounded as if you suspected him of something?' Eadulf reproached her.

'Did I?' she mused but said no more.

They walked in silence back to the abbey. Eadulf said nothing further for it seemed that Fidelma had sunk deep in thought and he felt it wiser not to interrupt her.

By the time they returned to the abbey its bell was tolling for the midday Angelus.

Fidelma and Eadulf exchanged no words as they went into the chapel. It was an automatic decision, made separately, to join the other worshippers. The psalm chanting was led by the Abbot Ségdae, who seemed to have recovered something of his old spirit. His voice rang out above the chanting of his congregation.

'*Oculi omnium in Te aspiciunt et in Te sperant!*'

The words stuck in Fidelma's mind. She lowered her head and translated to herself: 'The eyes of all things look to you and hope in you.' It was as if Ségdae were reminding her of her responsibilities. Yet, for the first time in her life, she felt utterly confused. Usually, during the investigations she had undertaken, there was a single path to pursue. Now she found several paths and several mysteries that did not necessarily appear connected. But were they? She was not even sure.

She scarcely noticed the rest of service until the final psalm was sung and the congregation began shuffling towards the refectory for the *etar-suth*, or middle meal, of the day. As was the custom, all shoes and sandals were removed at the entrance to the refectory. She was hardly aware of removing her footwear, entering and sitting at one of the long, wooden dining tables. She was vaguely aware of Abbot Ségdae intoning the *gratias* in Latin then a soft murmur arose as the community began its meal.

As with most midday meals, it was a light meal of bread, cheese and fruits, with ale or water served, depending on taste. Fidelma ate mechanically, her mind still turning over the questions that vexed her mind.

Eventually she became aware of someone addressing her.

She glanced up and found it was the steward of the abbey, Brother Madagan, still wearing his bandage around his head and looking slightly pale but otherwise in good spirits. She realised that the refectory was almost empty now except for a few people, one of whom was Eadulf, who had been sitting by her side awaiting her to rouse from her thoughts. Brother Madagan slid onto a bench on the opposite side of the table.

'I wanted to thank you and Brother Eadulf here for dragging me inside during the attack,' Brother Madagan said. 'I do not remember much between the time I was struck and coming to in the courtyard. It was Brother Tomar who told me what had happened. That poor misguided woman, Cred, struck down and poor young Brother Daig killed. You both risked your lives to save me.'

'How is your wound, Brother, is it better?' asked Fidelma, with a deprecating gesture. She found that, in spite of the steward's effort to be friendly, there was nothing which endeared him to her. She still did not like him. The eyes were still cold and Fidelma felt that there was some merciless quality in the man.

'Thanks be,' acknowledged Brother Madagan. 'The warrior luckily struck me on the skull with the flat of his sword. My head was pounding like the hammer of a smith on his anvil for a while. There is a lump the size of a *camán* ball.'

The *camán* ball, called a *liathróid*, was about four inches in diameter, made of some light, elastic material, such as woollen yarn, wound round and round and covered with leather. It was used in the game of hurley.

'We thought that you had been killed for sure,' Eadulf said.

'The unGodly are not so easily victorious,' Brother Madagan intoned piously. Yet there was a cold note of hatred in his voice.

'Yet they inflicted much death and destruction,' pointed out Fidelma.

Madagan's eyes were like ice.

'So Sister Scothnat has told me. Alas, I should not have tried to stop the raider by a plea to religious sanctuary. He could not have understood the term. Steel was all he understood.'

'So you were regaining consciousness when you were dragged through the gates?' asked Fidelma.

'Yes. Though my mind is hazy and I think I was more unconscious than conscious. I remember feeling thankful when the abbey gates were banged shut. Then I do not remember much until I heard cheering. Sister Scothnat tells me that this was when your cousin, the Prince of Cnoc Áine, arrived and drove the raiders away.'

Fidelma looked thoughtful for a moment.

'Do you remember being carried to your cell?' she asked.

Madagan nodded slightly. He winced as the action caused the obvious ache to his cracked skull to worsen momentarily.

'Do you remember anything beforehand?'

The steward considered for a moment. 'Such as?'

'You say that you remember being dragged into the courtyard?'

'I do. I remember hearing some lamentation from the brethren over poor young Brother Daig. Indeed, he was no more than seventeen years.'

'There was also the captured raider who lay trussed up nearby.'

Brother Madagan's eyes flickered with momentary fire.

'Sister Scothnat told me that he had been captured but not killed. Had I known then what I know now, I doubt not that I would have risen and killed him myself.' Fidelma felt the intensity in his voice. He hesitated and relaxed. 'You condemn me for the thought? A Brother of the Faith should not give voice to such natural feelings of hate and anger? Yet Daig was such a gentle soul and would have harmed no one. He had no violence in him and yet that animal struck him down. I will not pray for his soul, Sister Fidelma.'

There was a brief silence.

'I will not ask you to,' Fidelma replied gravely. 'What I will ask you to do is cast your mind back to that time, Brother Madagan. Do you remember being carried back to your chamber?'

Brother Madagan rubbed his chin.

'Vaguely. The apothecary came to check on each of us, I think. He bent over me. I was still trying to recover consciousness. He saw that I had received a blow on the head but not an open wound and told two young brothers to help me to my room and bathe and bind my head.'

'The apothecary?' Eadulf leant forward eagerly.

'Brother Bardán. We have no other apothecary here.'

'Then what happened?'

'I was carried to my cell as he instructed.'

'Had he examined the others before you? Or did he examine you first?' Fidelma asked.

'As I recall – remember that I was only partially conscious – I think he examined Brother Daig first. He was quite moved by the fact that the boy was dead. They were close. It was only when Brother Tomar insisted that he must look to the living that he came to me. While he did so, two of the Brothers were removing the body of Cred and another two removing that of Brother Daig.' He grimaced without humour. 'I think that the last thing I remember was hearing the whining merchant arguing with Brother Bardán.'

'The merchant? Do you mean Samradán?' asked Fidelma hastily. 'Was he in the courtyard at that time? Surely he was hiding in the chapel vaults with the women of the community?'

'No. I remember he was definitely in the courtyard and arguing with Brother Bardán. He was demanding something. Protection, I think. I recall now that Brother Bardán shouted to him that he should fend for himself because people lay dead and dying. I am afraid the merchant is a selfish man.'

'Fend for himself for people lay dead and dying? Were those Bardán's words?'

'Yes. You have stirred my memory, Fidelma.'

'So you were the last to be removed from the courtyard?'

'With the exception of the raider,' agreed Brother Madagan.

'Well, it is good to see that you are recovering, Brother Madagan.' Fidelma rose from her place, and Brother Madagan followed her example hesitantly.

'Sister Scothnat says that the attack was carried out by the Uí Fidgente. Is that true?'

'We do not know,' corrected Fidelma. 'It is only suspicion that lays the blame on them.'

Brother Madagan sighed.

'We have to be suspicious of our enemies. It is our only defence against betrayal and treachery.'

'Suspicion is the mother of suspicion, Brother Madagan,' replied Fidelma. 'If you let suspicion into your heart you will allow all trust to exit from it.'

'You may be right,' Brother Madagan said. 'However, we may place our trust in God . . . but we should ensure our horse is tethered safely at night. I only ask because an Uí Fidgente has arrived here. I do not like him. He says he is a *dálaigh*.'

'I know. He is what he says he is, Brother Madagan. His name is Solam and he proceeds to Cashel to plead the case of his Prince before the Brehons there. I am to plead against him.'

'Is it so?' Brother Madagan seemed about to say something else and then he smiled and left them almost abruptly.

Eadulf glanced at Fidelma.

'Brother Bardán and Samradán were both in the courtyard with that warrior. My wager would be on Brother Bardán. I think he is our main suspect. The motive is obviously vengeance for the death of his friend, Brother Daig.'

Fidelma considered the matter for a moment.

'Perhaps. There is a doubt in my mind. It could well be that the warrior was killed in order that he did not reveal who sent him and his comrades. Also, you are quite forgetting the disappearance of the contents of the warrior's saddle bags from the stable. Why would Brother Bardán remove the contents of the saddle bags if he had killed the warrior merely out of vengeance?'

Eadulf groaned. He had indeed forgotten the very reason why they had set out to look for Brother Bardán in the first place.

'We'd better find Brother Bardán,' he said. 'I did not see him at either the service or the meal.'

He was surprised when Fidelma replied: 'We do not have to question him at the moment. We know where he was at the time when the warrior was stabbed. We know he had the time and opportunity. But I am not satisfied how it links up with everything else that has happened here. Are you sure that Brother Bardán did not come in for the meal?'

'I didn't see him.'

'We shall keep an eye on him without alarming him.'

'There has been no word about the discovery of the remains of Samradán's driver,' Eadulf added with an involuntary shiver.

Fidelma wrinkled her nose distastefully.

'Sometimes those taken by wolves are never found. I will say a prayer for the repose of that poor man's soul.'

They entered the cloisters and were about to cross the courtyard towards the guests' hostel when Eadulf suddenly pulled Fidelma back into the shadows.

She opened her mouth to protest but was silenced by a finger placed to Eadulf's lips. The Saxon monk jerked his head in the direction of the cloistered passage on the far side of the courtyard.

She looked across.

There was the small, pale-faced figure of Solam, the *dálaigh* of the Uí Fidgente. He was talking animatedly and waving his arms. He seemed excited. She was not sure to whom he was talking for the other figure stood behind one of the columns of the cloisters. That it was a religieux was obvious from what little she could see of the figure's habit.

'Our lawyer friend seems rather agitated,' muttered Eadulf.

'I wonder why?' mused Fidelma. 'Can we get near without being seen?'

'I doubt it.'

'Let's try anyway.'

They began to walk slowly and as quietly as they could along the cloistered corridor along one side of the courtyard before turning down the other. They could hear Solam's voice raised slightly but could not make out what he was saying.

Then his voice stopped, as if in mid-flow.

'I think we have been seen,' muttered Eadulf.

'Walk on as if you are not aware of them,' instructed Fidelma softly. She increased her pace slightly.

By the time they came to the corner, with a view along the far corridor, the two figures had vanished. Solam had obviously entered one of the nearby doorways which gave access to the guests' hostel. Of the other figure they could hear the slapping of leather sandals on the flagged stones as the wearer hurried away. Eadulf ran forward and peered through the stone arches across the courtyard. A door banged on the far side.

At that moment, Abbot Ségdae appeared through another side door. He halted when he saw Eadulf standing there, a little breathless from the exertion of his sudden run.

'I heard a door slamming,' the abbot announced with disapproval in his voice.

Eadulf's expression was bland. 'Yes. I think a Brother left the courtyard hurriedly on the far side.'

'Shame on him. Even in a hurry a member of the abbey is taught not to slam a door and disturb God's peace in this holy place.'

Fidelma came up, overhearing the abbot's remarks.

'Sometimes the desire to fulfil a task quickly makes one forget one's etiquette, Ségdae,' she murmured.

'If I discover the culprit, he will be given penance enough to remember the lesson,' the abbot muttered irritably and strode off.

Fidelma turned to Eadulf with a meditative look.

'Wasn't it young Brother Daig who said that he was awakened in the night by a slamming door? I thought it was unusual for a member of a community to slam a door. Perhaps the same person has slammed a door on both occasions? A pity we do not know who it was.'

Eadulf smiled conceitedly.

'But we do.'

Fidelma almost swallowed in surprise.

'You recognised the person? Then tell me!' she gasped impatiently.

'The man half turned in the open doorway as he was closing it. The light was full on him as he was framed there. It was Brother Bardán.'

Chapter Fifteen

Eadulf had been dispatched to gather what information he could on Brother Bardán's background from Abbot Ségdae with strict instructions to tell the abbot that nothing should be said that might alert Bardán that he was being investigated. Fidelma herself went in search of the highly strung *dálaigh* of the Uí Fidgente.

She found him, at last, in the *tech screpta*, the library of the abbey. Imleach was possessed of one of the great libraries in the kingdom for there were well over two hundred manuscript books housed there. Most of the books were not kept on shelves but in leather satchels, hung on pegs or racks round the wall. Each satchel contained one manuscript volume. But one section of the library contained some elaborately wrought and beautifully ornamented leather-bound volumes embellished with silver plating. A few of these were contained in small cases called *labor-chomet*, or book holders, which were made of metal in order to preserve works of great value. The 'Confession of Patrick', the earliest 'Annals of Imleach' and a 'Life of Ailbe' were amongst them.

Imleach had in its library an area in which scribes worked and studied. When Fidelma entered there were several members of the community bent over their tasks of copying books. The copying was being done on long, thin, smooth, rectangular boards on which vellum was stretched. The vellum was variously made from the skins of sheep, goats or calves. The scribes used ink made from carbon kept in cows' horns and the work was done with pens made from the quills of geese, swans or even crows.

She noted that a few of the scribes were reading from the *flesc filidh*, or poet's rods, staves and wands made from yew or apple tree on which Ogham, the ancient form of Irish writing, was carved.

Fidelma paused a moment to take in the atmosphere of the large room which comprised the abbey's library. She always felt pleasure at being in a library; it gave her a sense of being in touch with both past and future at the same time for here was the knowledge of the past being transmitted through the present to the scribes of the future. She experienced a sense of childlike wonder whenever she entered any library, but Imleach was regarded as one of the greatest in the kingdom.

She spotted Solam almost at once, apart from the scribes, seated at a reading table in a corner of the library. She walked quietly across to his table.

'I see that you are rested and not ill-affected by your experience, Solam.' Her tone was slightly ironic as she seated herself in front of him.

He glanced up in apparent irritation at being interrupted.

'It is a matter of luck that I was not injured, Sister,' he replied, also speaking softly so as not to disturb the others in the library. 'I will still register my complaint to the Chief Brehon of the five kingdoms. Do not think that you will be able to persuade me otherwise.'

He thrust out his chin defiantly.

'I would not dream of doing so,' Fidelma returned gravely. 'However, as a *dálaigh* of some reputation . . .' she paused pointedly,' I know that you will take into account the nervousness of the people in view of what happened last night.'

Solam was not mollified. 'It does not mitigate the fact that, having identified myself, those people tried to kill me.'

'But you were not killed,' pointed out Fidelma. 'However, I would not dream of preventing you from registering your complaint.'

Solam sniffed deprecatingly. 'I shall do so.'

'Of course, compensation in settlement to your complaint is only given if it can be justified. That is, if the people had no valid cause to fear you. If they did not genuinely believe that they had been attacked by the Uí Fidgente, then, of course, there would be no cause for their anger to be raised against you. However, if they did believe they had been attacked . . .'

She waved her hand to dismiss the matter and smiled.

'You do not have to instruct me in law,' snapped Solam, his voice rising so that a number of scribes looked up. A stentorian voice from the chief librarian, seated at his central desk, hissed a command for silence.

'How well do you know Brother Bardán?' Fidelma continued innocently.

The little man looked at her disdainfully.

'Do you think it proper that we, as opposing counsels, should be discussing any matters affecting the hearing at Cashel?'

Fidelma felt her temper stirring but kept it in check.

'I was not aware that we were doing so,' she replied, trying to soften the icy tinge to her voice. 'Though from what you tell me you have been informed of all the details of the case so it matters not if we talk in general terms.'

'As a *dálaigh*, it is my task to question who I please. My Prince, Donennach, sent a messenger instructing me to proceed to Cashel and the messenger had a copy of the protocol drawn up by Donndubháin, the *tanist* of Cashel. Therefore, I set out immediately.'

Fidelma smiled quickly. 'I suppose that the messenger from Cashel told you that I had come to Imleach, which is why you came here?'

Solam flushed.

'I came here . . .' he began, and then he realised the path he had been drawn along.

'The road from Luimneach to Cashel runs north of here. So I deduced that you thought it wise to come here first. Is that so?'

The little man's eyes narrowed.

'You are a very clever lady, Fidelma,' he said icily. 'I have heard of your reputation.'

'That is gratifying.' She paused, allowing the silence to press the question.

'As a *dálaigh*,' Solam explained, 'it was my duty to see if you had been able to identify the crucifix. I understand that you have. It was the crucifix of Ailbe who founded this abbey; a crucifix which has disappeared from the chapel where it has been kept for the last century or more.'

Fidelma tried to hide her surprise that Solam had been able to gather the information so quickly.

The *dálaigh* was sitting back with a self-satisfied look.

'I did not know that Brother Bardán was such a loquacious man,' she said quietly.

Solam did not attempt to deny his information had come from the apothecary. 'He is certainly more helpful than many here.'

'You do your reputation justice, Solam,' Fidelma replied.

'You will find that I now have proof that this assassination plot was not inspired by the Uí Fidgente as you have claimed it to be.'

'You have been misinformed, Solam,' countered Fidelma. 'I have never claimed anything. You mention the duties of a *dálaigh*. It is also my duty to gather the facts and present them to the Brehons. Other people have made claims, not I. I shall continue to seek the truth until I am satisfied that I have found it.'

'I think that the truth will be found much closer to Cashel than you think,' the Uí Fidgente lawyer replied. He suddenly leant forward across the table, thrusting his face towards her in an unblinking stare. He kept his voice in an even monotone, scarcely above a whisper. 'I believe that your brother plots to destroy the Uí Fidgente. I believe that he means to complete the victory he gained at Cnoc Áine last year when our king, Eóganán, was slain. How better to find justification to annihilate us than to claim that our Prince Donennach was involved in a plot to assassinate him out of vengeance? If he can persuade people to believe that story, then he will gain their support to destroy the Uí Fidgente. Well, I shall reveal the truth – and the truth is that it is Colgú, your brother, who is behind this plot!'

Solam sat back in defiance and folded his arms.

Fidelma was quiet for a moment or two and then she allowed a small smile to crease the corner of her mouth. She shook her head sadly.

'You have an excellent court-room technique, Solam. Unfortunately, you would do better to keep it for the court room. But remember this, Brehons deal in facts, not in emotional outbursts.'

Solam leapt to his feet. His face was flushed. Fidelma's assessment of his highly strung character was certainly an accurate one. Mentally she noted that his expressive irritability might be a weapon in her hands when arguing her case before the Brehons. For a moment or two, Fidelma thought that Solam's rage was about to explode in verbal anger. Then the little *dálaigh* managed to control himself.

'We shall see,' muttered Solam angrily before he flounced from the library room. One or two of the scribes glanced up from their books, disturbed at his noisy exit.

The chief librarian rose from his seat and came over. There was a look of annoyance on his features.

'The Uí Fidgente did not hand back his book,' he pointed out. The book Solam was looking at was still on the table. 'I presume that he has finished with it?'

Fidelma grimaced at the librarian. 'I should imagine he has.'

The librarian bent to pick up the small, leather-bound volume. Fidelma suddenly stretched out a hand and stayed him.

'One moment . . .'

She turned the book around so that she could read the title. It was a 'Life of Ailbe'. She passed it back to the chief librarian thoughtfully.

Fidelma found Abbot Ségdae still with Eadulf in his private chambers. Both of them looked up with surprise as she entered the room. She came straight to the point.

'How would Brother Bardán know that I had shown you a sketch of a crucifix found on one of the dead assassins in Cashel and that it had been identified as one of the missing Relics of Ailbe?' she demanded without preamble.

The elderly, hawk-faced abbot blinked.

'I did not tell him,' he protested. 'But it is no secret that the Relics and Brother Mochta have vanished, Fidelma.'

'But no one would know that the crucifix had been discovered on the body of the assassin.'

The abbot spread his hands.

'I did not think it was a matter to be made a secret among the senior religieux of this abbey. The Relics are of concern to us. After all, we are the primacy of the kingdom. This is where the Eóghanacht kings come to take their sacred oath by the ancient yew-tree. Why should this matter be a secret?'

'I am not blaming you for anything, Ségdae,' Fidelma assured him. 'So, tell me, who did you mention it to?'

'I told Brother Madagan, he being the steward of the abbey.'

'And Brother Bardán? He was told?'

'The abbey is a close community. New travels quickly. You cannot keep secrets from among the Brothers and Sisters of the Faith.'

Fidelma gave a mental sigh. The abbot was perfectly right in what he said.

Ségdae was clearly worried as he glanced from Fidelma to Eadulf.

'Why do you both mention Brother Bardán?' he asked. 'Brother Eadulf here was also asking about him. Do you suspect him of any conduct unseemly for a member of this abbey?'

'I have told the Father Abbot that we merely want to clarify some points of background,' interposed Eadulf hurriedly.

'That is so, Ségdae,' Fidelma agreed. 'Eadulf has doubtless asked you to use total discretion. You see, in order to get at the truth it is often necessary to ask questions about people in order to verify facts. It contains no slur on their character nor any suspicion of wrongdoing. So we would appreciate it if no mention was made of our questions to Brother Bardán.'

The abbot looked bewildered but indicated his assent. 'I shall not speak about this to anyone.'

'Not even to your steward, Brother Madagan,' insisted Fidelma.

'Not to anyone,' emphasised the abbot. 'I have told Eadulf here that I have every confidence in Brother Bardán. He has been with our community for over ten years, working as our apothecary and mortician.'

'The abbot tells me he was a local man,' Eadulf said. 'That he was a herbalist before he went to the medical school at the monastery of Tír dhá Ghlas. He became an apothecary and mortician and then joined the community here.'

'Had he ever been a warrior?' asked Fidelma.

'Never,' replied the abbot in some surprise. 'What gave you that idea?'

'Just a thought. Do you know if he was a particular friend of Brother Mochta?'

'We are all Brothers and Sisters in this community, Fidelma. Brother Bardán's chamber was next to Brother Mochta's. I do not doubt they would be friends. So was young Daig. Poor child. Brother Bardán had recently asked permission to take Daig into the apothecary and train him to be his assistant.'

'So, as far as you knew, Brother Bardán was not close to the monk who vanished?' insisted Fidelma.

Abbot Ségdae shook his head. 'I would not know. In this community, we are all one under God.'

Fidelma nodded almost absently. 'Very well.' She opened the door. 'Thank you, Ségdae.'

The abbot looked anxious. 'Is there any news of a resolution to this mystery?' he called fretfully.

'I will let you know when I have some news,' replied Fidelma tersely.

Outside, she said to Brother Eadulf: 'Let's go and examine Brother Mochta's room again.'

'Do you have an idea?' Eadulf asked as he followed her along the corridor. She caught the expectation in his voice and had to answer him with a sardonic grunt.

'This is one case, Eadulf, where I am totally at a loss. Whenever I think I see links, they vanish as abruptly as they come. There is nothing here but suspicion. On this evidence I would not even obtain the sympathy of the court. We now have less than a week to gather evidence.'

'But if we cannot get evidence which points to those responsible, neither can the other side get evidence to prove their case,' Eadulf pointed out.

'It does not work like that,' Fidelma told him. 'Prince Donennach was a guest under the protection of my brother when the assassins launched their attack. My brother was responsible for the safety of his guests. He now has to demonstrate that he is not to be held responsible. Prince Donennach does not have to prove that my brother was to blame.'

'I am not sure that I follow that.'

'Only if my brother can show that this was a plot by the Uí Fidgente or some other faction is he absolved from his responsibility.'

'It is a fine point,' observed Eadulf.

'But the fulcrum of the law nevertheless.'

'Well, what can we hope to see in Brother Mochta's room now? We have examined it before.'

They had reached the door of the chamber.

'I do not know what I hope to see,' confessed Fidelma. 'Something. Some path out of this morass.'

The sound of something being dropped caused them both to start and glance at each other. The sound had come from Brother Mochta's chamber.

Fidelma placed a finger against her lips and slowly reached for the handle, her hand closing tightly on it. Then, with a quick jerk, she opened it and flung open the door. As she had guessed, it was not locked.

Finguine, Prince of Cnoc Áine, stared up at them with surprise from a kneeling position on the floor.

After a moment or two of silence, he climbed to his feet and brushed the dust from his knees.

'Fidelma, you gave me a start,' he rebuked.

'No more of a start than you gave us,' Eadulf replied.

'What are you doing here, cousin?' asked Fidelma, looking quickly about the room.

Finguine grimaced awkwardly. 'I heard from the steward of the abbey . . .'

'Brother Madagan?' interposed Eadulf.

'The same. He told me about the disappearance and I asked to see the room. It looks as if there has been a struggle here and the poor Brother was taken off by force. Perhaps he was made to get the Relics from the chapel and then was carried off into the hills. He was probably killed there.'

Fidelma regarded her cousin seriously for a moment. 'Is that your interpretation of events, Finguine?'

'I don't think that you need to have a keen imagination to interpret this,' Finguine said, waving his hand around the room.

'But . . .' began Eadulf and suddenly saw the icy fire in Fidelma's eyes. He snapped his mouth shut almost painfully.

Finguine turned to him questioningly.

'What was that?'

Eadulf grimaced awkwardly. 'I just meant that appearances can sometimes be misleading. I . . . er . . . well, what you say does seem to be a logical interpretation.'

Finguine turned back to Fidelma. 'There, you see? I am afraid that we might be looking for a body rather than Brother Mochta alive. Once the thieves had the Holy Relics in their grasp what need would they have of Brother Mochta?'

'Then why take him in the first place?' Fidelma could not help the response.

'Perhaps to prevent him raising the alarm?'

'They could have left him trussed up in his chamber,' suggested Eadulf.

'True. But he might have been found earlier than they would wish and so they decided to take him with them. Then the community would spend time searching and allow the thieves time to ride away.'

'I think, my cousin, the Prince of Cnoc Áine, has a good point, Eadulf.'

Eadulf stared at Fidelma in bewilderment. She was trying to convey something to him by the slight inflection in her tone. She was obviously warning him not to be free with his opposition to the points being made by Finguine.

'Anyway, cousin,' she went on easily, 'your theory can only be proved one way or the other, if we find Brother Mochta's remains in the hills.'

Finguine drew himself up and his smile was one of painful satisfaction.

'I am afraid that I can now prove that.'

Eadulf's jaw dropped. 'Do you mean that you have found the remains of Brother Mochta?'

'I do.'

They greeted the news with some moments of silence.

'Where were the remains found?' Fidelma asked.

'Come, I will show you,' Finguine replied briskly. 'One of my men found the grisly thing in the fields not far from here. It was being ravaged by wolves. He brought it here in a sack so that it could be identified. We took it to the apothecary.'

'To Brother Bardán?'

'If he is the apothecary, yes, to him.'

'Has he identified the remains?'

'Not yet. While I was waiting, I came to Mochta's chamber to see if the scene fitted with my conception of the event.'

They followed the Prince of Cnoc Áine to the apothecary. Inside one of Finguine's warriors perched moodily on the edge of a table. Brother Bardán himself was bending over something that had been previously wrapped in sacking. It was laid on the table.

Brother Bardán glanced at them as they entered with a bleak expression.

'I am afraid there is no doubt,' he said as if in answer to their unasked question.

'Is it the missing monk?' Finguine wanted the matter clarified.

Brother Bardán nodded morosely. 'This is the forearm of Brother Mochta. It had been severed by wolves. Look at the mark of canine teeth on it.'

Fidelma set her jaw firmly and moved to his side. She looked down. It was a forearm, torn and blooded. It had been severed at the elbow. The hand was still attached to it. It was a left forearm.

'Well, that solves the mystery of where the poor Brother has vanished too,' Finguine announced. 'I think it also proves my point about the theft.'

Fidelma said nothing. She was still staring at the severed forearm. The she turned, wrinkling her nose in distaste.

'Are you sure that you can positively identify this as the remains of Brother Mochta?' she asked.

'There is no doubt of it, as I have said.' The apothecary nodded affirmatively.

'Thank you, Brother.'

'I will send some men to scour the hills where it was found,' Finguine assured the apothecary. 'We might pick up the trail of the thieves but I doubt it.'

'Let me know if anything else is discovered,' she requested her cousin as she signalled to Eadulf to follow her.

'Well,' Eadulf said slowly, once they were on their own, 'that appears to be that. Now we know what happened to Brother Mochta.'

'No we don't,' snapped Fidelma irritably. 'What has just been confirmed is that Brother Bardán is a liar.'

Chapter Sixteen

'Brother Bardán, a liar?' Eadulf's eyebrows shot up expressively. 'How do you deduce that?'

'Brother Bardán identified that arm, positively and without question, as that of Brother Mochta, didn't he?'

'Yes. Are you saying that he lied? That it was not Mochta and the apothecary knew it?'

Fidelma stamped her foot in annoyance. 'Surely you were not misled?'

Eadulf shook his head, frowning. 'How can we be sure it was not Brother Mochta's arm?'

'Which arm was it?'

'The left arm. The left forearm . . . oh!'

Eadulf stopped as the realisation struck him. According to the description of Abbot Ségdae, Mochta's left forearm had carried the tattoo mark – the bird – exactly as it was on the forearm of the body at Cashel. Brother Bardán must have known that the tattoo would have been on that arm.

'So he deliberately lied,' affirmed Fidelma.

'But why? And whose arm was it?' asked Eadulf.

'Doubtless it was the arm of the poor driver of Samradán . . . after the wolves had done with him. But why the lie? Is it to stop us pursuing the missing Brother Mochta further? Can Mochta be the same person as the Cashel assassin? More questions. But, at last, I believe that we are getting somewhere. Come on.'

She hurried off down the corridor and came to a halt back where they had started from, at Brother Mochta's cell door. This time, however, she did not go to that room but, glancing round to ensure they were unobserved, she tried the next door – the door of Brother Bardán's room. It was open, of course, and she pulled Eadulf into the room after her.

'What are we looking for?' whispered the astonished Saxon.

'I am not sure. Just stand by the door and let me know if anyone comes.'

The room was sparsely fitted. A bed, table and a chair; hooks for hanging clothing. There were two spare habits, a woollen cloak for winter, a leather hat to keep off the rain, two extra pairs of sandals, one studded with nails and stained green – shoes that the apothecary doubtless used on his field trips to gather wild herbs. There were two books on the table. Both were on herbal cures. In fact, when she looked closely, she found that the second one was in the process of being written. Most of its pages were untouched and pristine. The early pages were written in an interesting style.

She suddenly recalled something and reaching into her *marsupium* pulled out some of the paper which she had found in Brother Mochta's cell. The notes from the 'Annals of Imleach'. Both were written in the same hand. Had Brother Mochta been helping Brother Bardán write his medical treatise? If so, that showed that the two men were close enough; and close enough for Brother Bardán not to have made a mistake about the identification of the forearm.

There was apparently little else of interest in the room.

Then some instinct made her get to her knees and glance under the wooden cot that served as a bed. There were a couple of dark objects under there. She reached forward. First she pulled out a coiled rope. Then she found a lantern, its wick trimmed and filled with oil. The third item was a *sacullus* of large proportions. It was filled with items of food and a small *amphora* of wine.

Fidelma stared at the *sacullus* and its contents for a moment or two before nodding grimly to herself as if she had expected to find the objects.

She replaced the items carefully before rejoining Eadulf. Without exchanging a word they passed out into the corridor. Eadulf followed Fidelma silently as she walked along the corridor and through a door which led into the cloisters around the courtyard, on the far side of which was the guests' hostel. On the other side was the abbey chapel and on the third side was an entrance which led into a small garden area.

'That is where Brother Bardán grows some of his herbs,' she announced. 'Let's have a look at it.'

Still without speaking, Eadulf followed her across the courtyard and through the arched area into the small herb garden.

'Ah!'

Fidelma went directly to a small wooden door on the far side. It was securely bolted and quickly she pulled back the bolts and opened the door.

'Where does it lead?' Eadulf was moved to break his silence as curiosity got the better of him.

Fidelma stood aside silently.

Eadulf saw that beyond the door was nothing but a pleasant field and a fringe of yew-trees beyond. The door led directly out of the abbey on the side facing away from the township. Fidelma then shut the door and pushed back the bolts. Suddenly she bent forward with a slight gasp. She reached out a finger to touch something on the gatepost.

Eadulf looked at it carefully over her shoulder.

'It looks like dried blood.' he offered. 'What does it mean?'

'It means,' replied Fidelma, straightening up, 'that we shall have to sit up tonight and watch the activities of our friend Brother Bardán. I think I am beginning to see some pattern emerging.'

'Something that you can share with me?' Eadulf felt somewhat peeved by her mysterious attitude.

'In time,' she replied. 'Perhaps we should get some rest before the evening meal. After that, it may be a long night.'

As they came out of the herb garden, she gazed around the cloistered courtyard as if searching for something. Then she indicated a small alcove.

'That is a good position from which to watch. At night it will be in shadows and there is a seat there so that we can make our surveillance of the courtyard in comfort.'

'But what are we watching for?'

'Brother Bardán. Who else?'

The bell was tolling for the last service of the day. Eadulf was hurrying along the corridor to the chapel. Fidelma had decided to take up her self-imposed lookout duty but insisted that Eadulf joined the community so that their absence was not made too obvious. If anyone asked where she was he was to say that she was weary and had retired early. Eadulf was actually pleased to attend the service for he had been feeling guilty about missing so many observances since he had arrived at the abbey.

He joined the line of Brothers entering the chapel stalls. He found a suitable place in a pew in front of the high altar and went down on his knees, hands extended before him in order to commence his prayers. He opened his mouth but the words did not emerge. Instead he swallowed hard.

He had noticed Brother Bardán in a small alcove at the side of the chapel some distance away. Brother Bardán seemed to be talking earnestly, his hand moving to emphasise whatever point he was making. He turned a little to one side to reveal the person with whom he was so animatedly conversing. It was the recognition which caused Eadulf to swallow hard.

It was Fidelma's cousin, Finguine, the Prince of Cnoc Áine. There was nothing suspicious in the mere fact that Brother Bardán was speaking with the Prince of Cnoc Áine but it was the manner in which he was doing so that seemed odd. They were smiling together as if they were sharing some conspiratorial joke.

Brother Bardán must have realised that the service was about to begin because he said something to Finguine, turned, and walked rapidly away along the side aisle of the chapel, his hands folded before him, his head lowered on his chest, in an attitude of meditation.

Finguine hesitated, glanced round as if he wanted to ensure that he was unobserved, and then exited from the abbey chapel through a side door.

Abbot Ségdae began the service.

Eadulf almost cursed. He quickly genuflected in penance. If only he had spotted Brother Bardán and Finguine before he had taken his seat. Now he could not leave the chapel until the service was over. He would have given anything to know what was being discussed.

The rituals of the ceremony passed with interminable slowness. Finally, when he was able to leave the chapel, he went immediately to where Fidelma was sitting in the dark shadows of the alcove in the cloister courtyard. Glancing swiftly round and seeing that there was no one else about, he ducked into the alcove. Hurriedly, he told her what he had seen.

She took it calmly.

'This is the second time that Brother Bardán and Finguine have been in conversation together. Once at Nion's house and now here. Nothing wrong in that but they seem rather conspiratorial. That and Brother Bardán's lie about Mochta makes it a matter of curiosity.'

'What shall we do, then?' asked Eadulf.

Fidelma looked up and smiled in the darkness.

'We shall proceed with our plan. We will remain here and see if my suspicion is justified. I think that Brother Bardán might visit his herb garden before the night has passed.'

'This is ridiculous,' moaned Eadulf, not for the first time. 'He will not come now. It is too late.'

They were still seated in the alcove in the courtyard. It was chilly and Eadulf had long since given up trying to count the hours which must have passed since the midnight bell had tolled and a silence had settled throughout the abbey. Hours must have passed. It must be time for the same bell to announce the hour for lauds? A new day was soon to dawn.

'Quiet. You must have patience,' replied Fidelma.

'But I am tired. I am cold. I want my bed. I want my sleep and . . .'

He was cut short as Fidelma dug him sharply in the ribs.

Someone was coming. They could see the dark shadow passing through the cloisters before it crossed the moon-dappled courtyard. The figure carried a lamp but it was not lit. Fidelma noted with satisfaction the large *sacullus* and rope slung across the back of the figure. The head was thrust forward, as if the person was keeping their eyes on the ground to search for obstacles in the darkness.

Unerringly, the figure headed through the gloom towards the arch which separated the cloistered area from the herb garden and passed through. Fidelma rose immediately, almost dragging Eadulf with her. Together they went cat-like through the cloisters towards the entrance to the herb garden. They arrived just in time to see the figure pausing by the gate which opened on the outside of the abbey. They could hear the gentle scraping of bolts being drawn back. There was a slight whine of the metal hinges as the door opened and then shut.

Fidelma whispered immediately: 'Quickly! We must not lose sight of him.'

Eadulf followed her, protesting in a hoarse whisper. He was not prepared to venture out of the protection of the abbey and was not equipped with his pilgrim's staff. He had grown fond of it since his encounter with the wolf. But he had not thought to bring it on this nocturnal vigil.

'Are you sure that it is Brother Bardán? Do we have to follow outside the abbey? What of the wolves?'

Fidelma did not deign to reply but was already crossing the herb garden with a rapidity that astonished Eadulf for he had to trot to keep up with her. The gate was unbolted and so they passed quickly through into the darkness of the countryside beyond.

The moon was still up, round and almost full, so the light outside the shadows of the abbey was almost twilight rather than the dark of night. There was not a cloud in the sky and the dark blue of the canopy of the sky was dotted with a myriad of twinkling lights. Yet low down on the tips of the eastern hills there was a lightness which presaged the approach of dawn. Fidelma drew Eadulf back into the shadows of the abbey's wall and pointed.

Brother Bardán's figure could clearly be seen now, striding rapidly across the field some distance away. He kept his head forward and was moving at a rapid pace. Fidelma looked vainly for some cover and realised that there was none. Brother Bardán was moving away from any trees or buildings and across a heather-strewn field.

With a sigh, Fidelma motioned Eadulf to follow her and began to hurry after the quickly disappearing figure. Had Brother Bardán glanced round, Fidelma did not doubt that they would have been spotted and she had no good reason to offer why they should be following the apothecary.

After a while it became apparent that Brother Bardán's path was leading him to a dark silhouette of a building in the corner of a large field which stood beyond the fringe of yew-trees. It was a small stone chapel. It stood in darkness and all they could make out was that it was no more than about fifteen feet in height and twenty feet in length, a tiny oratory rather than a chapel. It appeared to be made of stone and the walls seemed to merge into the roof.

Brother Bardán had disappeared into the building.

Fidelma halted and glanced about her in the moonlight.

'If he comes out, he will surely spot us,' Eadulf offered, stating the obvious.

Fidelma pointed to a cluster of trees which stood a short distance away.

'That is our only cover. We will wait behind the trees until he comes out.'

'Do you think Brother Bardán is meeting someone there?' asked Eadulf as they settled in their new shelter.

'Speculation without knowledge is dangerous,' Fidelma replied with one of her favourite axioms. She was fond of repeating it.

'You suspect that he is up to no good.'

'I do not judge him.'

'But you must have some idea what he is about?' protested Eadulf.

'Publilius Syrus wrote that a hasty judgement is a first step to being forced to retract it. We will wait to see what happens.'

Eadulf sighed and settled himself against the trunk of a tree. The ground was growing wet with the approach of the early morning and he tried to find some dried wood to sit on. Fidelma found part of a tree stump on which she took a seat and from were she could view the entrance of the building.

Eadulf leant back and sighed deeply. He closed his eyes.

A moment later, or so it seemed, he opened them and saw to his surprise that he was surrounded by the grey light of dawn. He had that sticky taste in his mouth which indicated that he must have fallen asleep. He yawned, blinking his eyes rapidly. He felt stiff and uncomfortable. He glanced at Fidelma.

She was still sitting on her tree stump, leaning forward slightly, her arms folded on her knee. She glanced at him as he awoke.

'How long . . . ?' His voice was thick in his dry mouth.

'How long have you been asleep? Long enough for the dawn to approach.'

There was no reproach in her voice.

'What has happened?'

Fidelma unfolded her arms and stretched in her sitting position.

'Nothing. Brother Bardán has not reappeared from the building.'

Eadulf looked at the building which was now plainly discernible in the grey light.

It was of a grey stone corbel pattern, large and rectangular. The dry stone work of the masonry was arranged to slope slightly downwards and outwards to throw off the rain. The idea of its dimensions, which they had guessed by the moonlight, had been an accurate one.

'It is a little chapel,' ventured Eadulf.

'That it is,' agreed Fidelma. 'An oratory to pass the time in prayer.'

'And Brother Bardán has not come out? What can he have been doing in there all this time?'

'As you suggested, perhaps he is meeting someone. Have patience.'

Eadulf suppressed a sigh. He felt an uncommon thirst and his stomach was protesting.

'I wish I had brought something to drink or something to eat.'

'Patience,' repeated Fidelma, unperturbed.

Eadulf felt frustrated. 'Patience!' he complained. 'It can be an excuse for timidity of purpose disguised as a virtue.'

Fidelma did not rise to his irritation. She kept silent.

Time passed and soon the sun appeared on the eastern horizon; its first rays were weak and pale, stretching over the plains beyond the mountains. Still there was no sign of Brother Bardán reappearing. The abbey bell began to toll for the first service of the day.

Fidelma stood up purposefully.

'What now?' asked Eadulf, wondering what she had in mind.

'Brother Bardán has not emerged. Now we will go in and see what he is about. I suspect he must have spotted us following him after all. That is why he is still in that chapel there.'

Fidelma moved hurriedly across the heather-strewn field towards the building, Eadulf at her side.

The doorway to the chapel was big enough to admit one person at a time and then only if they crouched as they entered. There were no windows in the building and so it was in complete darkness. Fidelma, entering first, was forced to wait a moment or two for her eyes to adjust to the difference in light. The grey dawn light filtered in through the doorway. Eadulf came in behind her.

They stood just inside the door and stared about in amazement.

The oratory was empty.

Chapter Seventeen

There was nowhere in the interior where anyone could hide. The floor was flagged and there was only a small altar table with a carved wooden cross on it at one end. On either side of where the cross stood were two unlit tallow candles in metal holders; before the cross stood a bowl of flowers, dry and wilting.

The oratory was clearly deserted. Eadulf tried not to look smug as he said: 'He must have sneaked by your gaze.'

Fidelma took the statement seriously.

'The entrance was in full view all the time. He did not come out once he had gone in,' she said firmly as she examined the interior in disbelief.

'The evidence contradicts that.'

Her eyes flashed angrily. 'Unlike you, I did not close my eyes.'

Eadulf allowed himself a smile of superiority but said nothing further.

Fidelma was clearly bewildered. The only explanation she could find was that Brother Bardán had left the oratory by a means other than the door. But there was no other means of exit.

With a sigh she decided to give up the attempt to fathom out the unfathomable.

'Let's go back to the abbey. It does not help to consider this problem on an empty stomach,' Eadulf suggested.

The sun was growing warm now and the dew was rising. A faint mist hung in patches here and there. It did not take them long to return back across the heather fields towards the abbey. The small wooden gate into the herb garden was still open.

Fidelma paused thoughtfully as she glanced down at the bolts.

'Well, that proves one thing.'

Eadulf looked at her questioningly, examining the bolt on the gate and the door itself. 'Have I missed something?'

'The fact that the bolts have not been shot home shows that Brother Bardán has not returned this way.'

'How can you be sure?'

'Because Brother Bardán left by this gate, unlocking it to leave the abbey. Naturally, he could not thrust home the bolts behind him. Had he returned through this gate, however, he would have secured the bolts. Brother Bardán is still out there.' She inclined her head in the direction of the oratory. 'Yet I am at a loss to understand how he gave us the slip.'

Eadulf could think of no rejoinder.

They passed through the herb garden and crossed back through the courtyard and along the cloisters. The abbey was now coming to life.

The grim, hawk-like features of the Abbot Ségdae, appeared before them.

'You did not attend lauds,' he greeted. There was a slight note of rebuke in his voice.

'No,' Fidelma agreed hurriedly. 'We had much to do. Can you tell us where Brother Bardán is? I wanted to have a word with him but he seems to have left the abbey.'

Abbot Ségdae did not appear surprised, explaining, 'His routine is to go early abroad in search of healing herbs. He has probably left already on one of his trips.'

'Then it is quite usual for Brother Bardán to leave the abbey so early?'

'It is.'

Fidelma appeared to change the subject.

'The other day I noticed a little chapel standing a short distance away from the abbey which I had not seen before,' she went on, falling in step with Ségdae as they walked along the corridors of abbey.

Eadulf reluctantly followed behind them. His thoughts were concerned with reaching the refectory and satiating his hunger and thirst.

'Ah, you mean the little sanctuary of the Blessed Ailbe?'

'An old, dry stone corbel oratory?'

'That is the one. It stands in a heather field,' confirmed Ségdae. 'That's curious.'

'What is curious?' asked Eadulf.

'The *dálaigh* of the Uí Fidgente . . . what's his name? Solam? Solam was just asking about the same chapel.'

'Solam?'

Ségdae had apparently not noticed the tension in Fidelma's reaction. 'The place is called Gort na Cille,' he said.

'The "field of the church" seems an appropriate enough name,' Fidelma observed, recovering her composure. 'Why did Solam want to know about it?'

'I do not know. Some people think that cures might be had there if one washes in the water drawn there before dawn,' offered the abbot.

Eadulf, who was thinking of quenching his thirst, groaned. If he had known there was a stream at that spot then he would not be suffering now. He tried to recall where such a stream could have been.

'Drawn from where, Father Abbot?' he asked innocently. 'I do not remember a stream in that field.'

Abbot Ségdae shook his head. 'There is no stream there but simply a well. It is called Tobar na Cille . . . the Church Well. That is because the chapel was built over it. The well is in the oratory itself.'

Fidelma suddenly halted in mid-stride.

'Do you mean that there is a well *under* the flagstones of the chapel?' she asked slowly.

Ségdae regarded her in amusement.

'Oh yes. One of the flagstones is hinged so that it can be opened. It lies behind the altar table.'

They had reached the door of his chambers and several members of the community were waiting to speak with him.

'Do you know where the Uí Fidgente lawyer is now?' asked Fidelma.

'I saw him but fifteen minutes since coming from the morning service. But I do not know where he was going.'

Fidelma's face suddenly showed a curious purpose as she thanked the bemused abbot and hurried away with Eadulf trailing in her wake.

Eadulf groaned at her abrupt change of direction.

'This isn't the way to the refectory, Fidelma,' he protested breathlessly.

She silenced him with a cutting gesture of her hand. 'Don't you see?' she pressed.

He shook his head in bewilderment. 'See what?'

'The mystery of Brother Bardán's disappearance is explained.'

He thought a moment and then saw what she meant.

'Are you telling me that Brother Bardán was hiding from us down a well shaft?'

'Perhaps the well shaft has another purpose. We must go back directly and examine it. What I do not like is that Solam has been asking about that oratory. What does Solam know about it?'

Eadulf suddenly halted. His expression was defiant.

'I will not return . . .' he began. He paused as he caught the glitter in her eyes and continued, 'not before I find some food and drink to take with me.'

Impatiently, Fidelma allowed herself to be hurried to the refectory. The long tables were almost deserted for most of the community had already broken their fast and started their daily routine.

'We might as well take some food with us,' Fidelma suggested. 'There is not much time to be lost. Solam is up to something, I am sure of it.'

Eadulf grabbed a couple of loaves of freshly baked bread, still warm. He added to the bread several pieces of cold meat and some cheese as well as fruit. He found a *sacullus* hanging among several nearby and confiscated it, putting the food in it. Fidelma had found a water container, filled it with water and handed it to him to place in the bag.

'Now let us return to Gort na Cille,' she said when he had indicated that he was ready.

As they passed out of the refectory, Eadulf could not resist the temptation to seize another piece of bread and some meat and thrust it into his mouth, experiencing a pleasing sense of satisfaction as he began to chew on it.

The day had turned quite warm by the time they reached the tiny oratory again. They had once more left the abbey by the side gate through the herb garden and, so far as they were aware, they were not been observed by anyone. By the time they had reached the field in which the tiny oratory stood, Eadulf had devoured a large quantity of his share of the food from the *sacullus*. Fidelma was not hungry and merely contented herself with a drink from the water container they had brought.

The oratory was still deserted and gloomy.

Eadulf lit one of the candles on the altar table to help them identify the flagstone covering the well entrance. It was easy to spot now that they knew what they were looking for. The flag had a small iron ring in it. Eadulf bent forward and heaved. He nearly stumbled backwards for the flag was fixed onto some pivotal device which made it swing upright with little effort.

A large back hole plunged beneath them.

Eadulf held out his candle. It was of little help except to illuminate the first few feet.

'Total darkness,' he muttered. 'There is nowhere that anyone could hide in that blackness.'

'Examine your candle,' Fidelma advised him.

Eadulf did not understand. 'Examine . . . ? What do you mean?'

'Your candle is fluttering and flickering when you hold it out over the well head. What does that mean to you?'

Eadulf regarded the spluttering candle flame in silence. Then he glanced to the doorway. He was beginning to understand what Fidelma was trying to indicate to him.

'There is air rising from the shaft here and you think it indicates that there is something more than water down there?'

Fidelma pointed. 'That fact coupled with another. See, just there . . . a wooden ladder is fixed to the side of the shaft. Now why have a ladder leading down into a well?'

Eadulf peered dubiously downwards. 'It's dark. I'd better go down and look.'

He held out the candle to Fidelma but she shook her head.

'I am lighter than you. We do not know how firm the ladder is.'

Before he could protest, she had swung over the edge and was already starting downwards into the blackness.

'It seems firm enough,' she called up after a few moments.

Eadulf lost sight of her as she disappeared down into the darkness of the pit.

'You will need a candle to see,' he called down.

There was no answer.

'Fidelma!' called Eadulf anxiously.

Her voice came back immediately.

'It's all right. I have found a tunnel. There is some sort of faint light along it.'

'I'm coming down then,' Eadulf replied firmly, swinging the *sacullus* around on his back and, holding the candle firmly in one hand, he began to descend into the well shaft using one hand to grip the outside edge of the ladder.

He had descended some ten feet into the blackness when he saw the opening which Fidelma had discovered. She had already moved from the ladder into the tunnel. She held out her hand for the candle so that Eadulf could more easily negotiate the tunnel entrance. He passed it across.

'There is plenty of space in the tunnel,' she assured him.

Eadulf saw that she was right. It was about three feet in width and five feet in height, so that he had only to bend forward and be cautious of hitting his head on the low, rocky ceiling. The tunnel, judging by its shape, which was almost oval, appeared to meander and its course marked it as a natural cavity formed by the corrosion of water in the limestone. It was very damp and the atmosphere was fetid. Like Fidelma, he realised that further along the tunnel there was a faint light but it did not seem natural.

'What is it?' he whispered.

'I have seen it before. It is a substance which is luminous in the dark, an odd waxy matter which I have seen craftsmen use to make fire from. It is inflammable. I think the Greeks name it after the Morning Star.'

They exchanged no further word as they followed the passage. It was some time before Eadulf heard Fidelma utter a suppressed exclamation as she suddenly found she was able to stand upright. He saw that the passageway had emptied into a moderately sized cave. It was about ten feet in height, rounded and maybe twenty to thirty feet in diameter.

'There's no one here,' Eadulf muttered, stating the obvious, as he examined the emptiness of the cave.

Like the passageway along which they had come, the cave was very wet and there was a small pool in the centre. There was a constant drip, drip of water from the roof striking the pool's surface. The noise echoed and re-echoed and to Eadulf the sound seemed unbearable for any length of time.

'It is not the sort of place anyone would remain,' Fidelma said, appearing to read his thoughts. Then she pointed across the cave. On the far side there were two black holes marking entrances to other tunnels.

'Two entrances. Which one shall we choose?' she asked.

'The right-hand path,' said Eadulf unthinkingly.

Fidelma glanced at him but the light distorted her features so that he could not discern her expression.

'Why choose right?' Her voice was amused.

Eadulf shrugged. 'Why not?'

They crossed the cave floor, which was slippery with lichen and some moss-like growth, and went into the tunnel. It was not long before the narrow passage bulged into a wider chamber. This chamber was dry and dusty. Eadulf felt the dust as he breathed in, feeling its tiny particles coating his mouth and windpipe. He coughed for a few moments.

There was dust and rocks on the floor. Fidelma stood still and held her candle up high to spread the maximum possible light.

'The rock face here has been worked,' Eadulf pointed out. 'What have we come into? Some sort of mine?'

Fidelma was about to make a rejoinder that this fact was obvious but she held back. She was aware of the fault of her waspish tongue. Eadulf did not deserve to be made the object of it so often. It occurred to her that she had been thinking a lot about her relationship with Eadulf of late. She had, particularly this last month, been growing increasingly irritated by his faults. These last nine months they had always been together. They had shared many dangers. Yet she was dissatisfied with the friendship and she could not understand why. She seemed to be constantly watching for his faults and reacting to them. What was the old saying? Reckoning up is an end to friendship?

She tried to bring her mind back to the present.

'The rock here seems to be more granite than limestone. Unusual. Ah, see this, traversing the granite . . . argentite.'

Eadulf frowned and peered over her shoulder.

'Silver? Is this a working silver mine?'

'Someone has certainly been working here – and recently.' She pointed to a broken tool on the floor. The wooden haft of a pick had recently been smashed. Judging from the newness of the splintered wood it was obvious that the handle had not lain on the floor for more than a few days.

Eadulf, in the meantime, had picked up a lump of ore and rubbed it. In the lamplight he could see the veins of white, ductile metal.

'Let us move on,' Fidelma instructed. 'Perhaps we will learn something up ahead.'

Almost at once the chamber narrowed back into a passageway which only one person could proceed along at a time. It grew smaller until they were soon having to crouch as they moved along it. After a while they could hear water gushing.

'There is a light up ahead,' Fidelma called over her shoulder. 'This time it is daylight. We are nearly at the entrance.'

They had to go on hands and knees before, finally, they emerged into a sheltered area filled with the sound of rushing water. One side of the enclosure was fully open to the elements. It was not so much a cave but an open area covered by a large rock overhang. This consisted of a great protruding limestone rock. As they rose to their feet they saw a pool being fed by waters which emanated from the rocks, gushing quite strongly.

'An underground well stream,' Fidelma explained, having to raise her voice above the sound.

They climbed out of the half cave and looked around the countryside. They seemed to have gone in a semi-circle, for the oratory and its well had been to the north of the abbey and now they had emerged on the south side of the ecclesiastical complex. In fact, they were not far from the abbey's southern extremity. Fidelma estimated that they were no more than four hundred yards away. The abbey walls were secluded from view by a copse consisting of lines of tall spruce. Only the towers could be seen rising behind them.

'Would Brother Bardán have come all this way when he could easily have left the abbey and walked across a field or two to come to this spot?' asked Eadulf. 'And for what? Do you think he has some connection with that silver working?'

Fidelma did not answer. It was pointless speculating.

It was Eadulf who caught sight of some object on the ground just beyond the mouth of the opening. He reached for it and held it up.

It was a torn piece of brown woollen cloth. There were fresh bloodstains on it.

'Do you think this belongs to Samradán's driver? Could the wolves have brought it here?'

He suppressed a shudder of revulsion as he conjured the vision of what must have been the fate of the driver's body. Memory of the encounter with the wolves caused him to feel a chill in his spine. He glanced round quickly to see if he could spot the signs of a wolves' lair in the cave entrance.

Fidelma took the piece of woollen cloth from him and examined it. She gave a negative shake of her head. Her expression was grim.

'Samradán's driver was not wearing clothing like that. That is the cloth usually worn by religious.'

She gazed round. The ground here was a gentle slope, inclining downward from the cave mouth. The grass was chewed short by grazing animals. Fidelma pointed to the ground.

'The earth here is soft and muddy underneath. There seems to have been a number of horses here recently and there have been heavy wagons as well. Look at the indentations.'

'How can you be sure that it was recently?' asked Eadulf.

Fidelma simply stamped her foot into the ground. It took him a moment to realise that it was not done out of temper.

'The indentations would not have remained deep for longer than twenty-four hours and . . .' She dropped abruptly to one knee. 'Look at this patch of blood. Not yet dry. We may presume it to be the same as the blood on the cloth.'

Eadulf verified her statement with a nod.

'A few hours old, no longer. That rules out it being the blood of Samradán's driver.'

'Or any of the poor townsfolk who were killed in the raid,' agreed Fidelma. 'It looks like some horsemen, probably those driving wagons, picked up the man wearing religious clothing at this point. There are no footprints, so he obviously went off with them. I doubt if he went willingly.'

'Are we talking about Brother Mochta?'

'Or our apothecary friend who insisted that Brother Mochta was already dead.'

Fidelma examined the ground for some time as if hoping to find the answers to the questions that came into her mind. All she knew for certain was that there were signs of more than one wagon and several horses. Then she realised that the prints of shod horses overlaid the tracks of the wagons. Well-shod horses usually meant warriors for few others would ride in groups and have horses so carefully tended.

'After the wagons were here,' she said slowly, 'there must have been a group of horsemen who came to this place.'

Eadulf rubbed his jaw thoughtfully. 'So our search has come to a dead end?'

'Not necessarily.' Fidelma carefully wrapped the bloodstained cloth and placed it in her *marsupium.* 'I think we should go back into the cave and take the other tunnel to see where it leads before we quit.'

Eadulf was not enthusiastic. 'I was afraid that you were going to say that. But surely it is a waste of time? Whatever happened must have happened here.'

Fidelma shot him one of her mischievous grins.

'Going right is not always right. We will try the left-hand path before returning to the abbey,' she announced firmly before plunging back into the tunnel.

It did not seem long before they were back in the large damp cave again, with its noisome dripping of water into the central pool. They turned into the second tunnel. This was pretty much like the first one they had entered through the small oratory. Their progress along it was more rapid than the one which had led into the silver workings. Eadulf particularly noticed that the floor was beginning to slope upwards as if they were going up a steep incline. The climb was fairly exhausting and by mutual agreement they paused to rest, squatting on the stony floor which was now dry and covered with dust that seemed to be a combination of shale and ground stone.

'How can we be going upwards for so long?' mused Eadulf. 'Surely, we could not have been so deep below the surface?'

'I think this passage is leading into one of the hills surrounding the abbey. There is a tall hill called the Hill of the Cairn nearby.' She suddenly snapped her fingers. 'That's it. I had forgotten. What was it Brother Tomar said when the abbey was under attack? He had heard of a secret passageway leading to the Hill of the Cairn.' She frowned in the effort of remembering. 'That's it. He had heard the Abbot Ségdae speak of it. He thought it might be a way of allowing the women of the community to escape the attackers.'

'This must be the same tunnel then?'

'It seems so. Unless these hills are riddled with such passageways. That is possible, of course. I have heard of several cave complexes within this countryside, many with underground streams and lakes. That is why there is shale here. Shale is ground shell.'

'Are you saying that we are going into the hill?' Eadulf appeared worried. He never liked being underground for lengthy periods. 'We have only a stub of candle to lead us wherever it emerges. If, hopefully, it does emerge into daylight.'

Fidelma glanced down to the flickering light in her hand. It was true that there was only an inch left. In her enthusiasm to follow the tunnel she had forgotten about the light.

'Then we had better continue on as fast as we can,' she replied. 'I've noticed that the strange phosphorescent matter no longer exists in this section of the tunnel.'

The idea of being caught below the ground in total darkness now leant a new speed to their efforts as they continued to move upwards through the tunnel. Its uneven course confirmed Fidelma in her belief that once upon a time this had been an underground stream which must have started at the hill top and moved into the valley to feed the wells, most of which no longer existed or were fed by some other source.

Abruptly the flickering candle blazed brightly for a moment and died. They were plunged into darkness.

Eadulf shivered and stood still. He hoped that his eyes would grow accustomed to the lack of light. They did not. It remained totally dark.

'Eadulf–' it was Fidelma's voice somewhere nearby – 'stretch out your hand.'

He did so. He felt something brush it. A moment later he felt Fidelma's warm clasp.

'Good. We mustn't let go of each other. I am going to move on slowly ahead.'

'How will you see where to go?'

'I will feel with one hand. I can reach to the top of the roof and feel my way forward.'

They moved on, inching their way through the blackness.

'Well, one thing is for sure,' Fidelma's voice echoed cheerfully.

'What is it?'

'We will not be able to return this way . . . not unless we find a lantern at the other end.'

It was a poor attempt to be cheerful and they soon fell back on silence. Once or twice, Fidelma grazed her arm and Eadulf cracked his toes on a rock. Yet slowly they moved forward, still up the incline, inch by inch. Then Fidelma halted.

'What now?' demanded Eadulf.

'Don't you see it?' she whispered in excitement.

Eadulf squinted forward and then he realised what it was.

'A light ahead,' she confirmed. 'Natural light. But there is something else as well.'

They moved forward a little, turning round a bend in the passage. The light became clearer; a grim, grey light filtering along the tunnel. And in the silence they could hear the sound of a crackling fire.

Fidelma put her head close to Eadulf's ear in the gloom. He felt her lips brush against his cheek.

'Not a sound,' she whispered. 'Someone is in the cave ahead of us.'

She began to move forward, almost imperceptibly. After a while, as the light grew stronger and brighter, she halted and disengaged her hand from his. There was no longer any need for they could see each other plainly. In front of them stretched a fair-sized cave with an entrance which seemed blocked by a wooden barrier, over the top of which was an expanse of azure sky. Rays of sunlight filled the cave.

The cave was large and dry except for a small trickling stream that ran to one side of it. A fire was crackling in the centre. There were various items strewn around the cave. Near the fire, stretched on a palliasse, lay the figure of an elderly, rotund man. He was clad in the habit of a religieux. His left arm was bandaged and so was his left foot. A staff, laying near to his hand, obviously served him as a crutch. There was no one else in the cave.

Eadulf and Fidelma stared at the figure in growing amazement.

It was Eadulf who moved into the cave first, causing the figure to start, half raise himself on an elbow, and reach for his staff as if he would defend himself. He paused as his eyes took in Eadulf's religious clothing.

'Who are you?' he cried, his voice cracking with fear.

Eadulf halted with an expression of utter amazement on his features.

Fidelma pushed by Eadulf and fought to find her voice. 'Have no fear, Brother Mochta. I am Fidelma of Cashel.'

The rotund religieux visibly relaxed and, with a sigh, fell back on his palliasse.

Eadulf continued to stare at the recumbent form in fearful astonishment. 'But you are dead!' he blurted.

The round-faced man raised himself again on one elbow. Although there was pain on his face, he was clearly amused.

'I would disagree with you, Brother Saxon,' he replied. His tone was droll. 'But if you can prove it, I will accept your judgement. God's truth, I feel near enough to death not to argue.'

Eadulf moved forward and stared down, examining the man's features carefully.

It was true. There could be no doubt about it. The man lying before him, perched on one elbow, grinning up at him, was the same moon-faced man whom he had last seen dead in the mortuary of Cashel. It was the same man, even to the tattoo of the bird which Eadulf now identified on the injured man's left forearm.

Chapter Eighteen

Fidelma seated herself by the man on the palliasse. She did not seem unduly surprised at the appearance of the moon-faced religieux who had, apparently, last been seen by them dead in the apothecary of Brother Conchobar of Cashel.

'How bad are your wounds, Brother Mochta?' she inquired with some solicitude.

'Painful still but I am told they will heal,' replied the man.

'Told by Brother Bardán, of course?'

The man grimaced in an affirmative gesture.

Eadulf could not take his eyes from the man whose features did not deviate in one jot from the dead assassin, except . . . Eadulf could not quite place it. There was something else, of course. This man still wore the Irish tonsure of St John, his forehead shaved back to a line from ear to ear. But there was another indefinable difference.

'I presume that Brother Bardán has been treating your injuries while you have been hiding here? You trusted no one?'

'It is hard to trust anyone, especially if you have been betrayed by someone whom you have known all your life; flesh and blood that you have grown up with. Once betrayed by your own kin, how can you trust anyone else?'

Fidelma motioned to Eadulf to sit down. Reluctantly, Eadulf did so, still unable to take his eyes from the portly monk.

'You are referring to your twin brother, of course?' Fidelma asked.

'Of course.'

Eadulf's surprise became apparent on his features. 'His twin brother?' He echoed stupidly.

Brother Mochta nodded sadly. 'My twin brother! You do not have to mince words with me, Sister. Brother Bardán told me how he was killed in Cashel. Yes, he was my twin brother, Baoill.'

'I had begun to suspect as much,' Fidelma said with little satisfaction in her voice. 'One person cannot be in two places nor wear two distinctive tonsures. The answer to that conundrum could only be that there must be two people. How can two people look so exactly alike?

It can only be that they are related, siblings, no less. And, even further, it can only be that they are twins.'

Brother Mochta nodded morosely. 'Identical twins,' he agreed. 'How did you find me here? I suppose Bardán told you where I was? We talked about it yesterday, after the attack. He was beginning to be confident that we could trust you. But then he saw you being friendly with the Uí Fidgente lawyer, Solam. Solam has been keen to discover my whereabouts.'

'Is that when Bardán identified some remains as being you?' asked Fidelma.

'I did not like that idea but Bardán felt it was the only way to stop Solam continuing to search for me. To buy us some time to discuss what best we should do.'

'Perhaps you had better tell us in your own words what happened to bring you to this state,' she invited.

Brother Mochta looked at her thoughtfully for a moment. 'Can I trust you?'

'I cannot answer that,' replied Fidelma. 'All I can tell you is that I am Colgú's sister and my loyalty is to Muman. I am a *dálaigh* and took an oath to uphold the law above all things. If that is not sufficient for you to trust me, then I can add nothing further.'

Brother Mochta compressed his lips for a moment in silence as if struggling to make up his mind.

'How much of the story do you know?' he finally asked.

Fidelma shrugged. 'Little enough. I know that you faked your disappearance, taking most of the Holy Relics with you. I presumed that your brother managed to steal one of the items, Ailbe's crucifix, in which struggle you probably received your injury. Not trusting anyone, you hid here and Brother Bardán kept you supplied with food and medicine. Where is he now, by the way?'

Brother Mochta was puzzled.

'Brother Bardán? I have not seen him since last night? Didn't he send you here?'

Fidelma leant forward, eyes narrowed. There was an edge to her voice.

'Are you saying that he has not been here at all this morning?'

The injured monk shook his head. 'I am expecting him sometime for we decided last night that our best course of action was to seek protection, especially after the attack.'

'What manner of protection?'

'Bardán decided to go to the Prince of Cnoc Áine and tell him the story. We knew that Finguine was a friend to the abbey and a loyal cousin to the King. We agreed to lay the matter before him and Finguine could then make the decision as to whether to tell you. When you came, just now, I thought that Finguine or Bardán had sent you . . .' He broke off, looking disturbed. 'How did you find me?' he insisted.

'With luck,' muttered Eadulf, still perplexed by the whole matter.

'Why didn't you confide in me and tell me that you were safe as soon as I came to the abbey?' demanded Fidelma, annoyed that so much time had been lost by the subterfuge.

Brother Mochta gave a tight smile. There was some pain in it and he eased his left leg carefully to take some pressure from his wound.

'We do not know you to trust you, Sister. We did not know who were our friends and who were our enemies.'

'I am the King of Cashel's sister,' Fidelma repeated.

'But a sister who has been a long time away from the kingdom and . . .' Brother Mochta glanced towards Eadulf. 'There is also the matter of keeping company with a cleric of the Roman order.'

Eadulf flushed angrily. 'Is that a disqualification in this land?'

'It is a fact that those who argue for the Rule of Rome are not always friends to those of us who follow the ways of our fathers.'

'Do you or Bardán really suspect that I could betray my brother and this kingdom?' interrupted Fidelma.

'Blood is no cement for unity of purpose,' replied Mochta calmly. 'I have learnt that the hard way.'

'Perhaps you are right. Why not trust Abbot Ségdae who would have been the natural support to turn to in time of crisis!'

'The Father Abbot is an honourable man. He would not have approved of my plan to hide the Holy Relics. He would have maintained them in the chapel, believing them to be safe. But then what? That would practically invite the attack on the abbey. Why do you think that the raiders did not attack the abbey itself? Because they found out that the Holy Relics were not there.'

'You know who the raiders were?' demanded Fidelma.

'I have a good idea.'

'Very well. Let's hear your story from the beginning,' invited Fidelma. 'Your brother, Baoill, was part of a conspiracy to bring down the Royal House of Cashel. How did this come about?'

Brother Mochta lay back and tried to gather his thoughts.

'It is best that I start at the beginning. I was born in the territory of Clan Brasil . . .'

'That we already know,' Eadulf interrupted only to be met with a frown of irritation from Fidelma.

'Go on, Mochta,' she invited.

'I am a northerner, therefore. My brother and I were, as you realise, identical twins. We were so alike that no one could recognise us apart; not even our mother at times. We grew up as wild and rebellious youths. When we were approaching the age of choice, our distracted father paid a wandering tattooist to inscribe an emblem on our forearms so that he might tell us apart. We bribed the tattooist to place exactly the same emblem on both our left forearms. A bird of prey . . .'

'A buzzard,' smiled Fidelma. 'I recognise it. What made you choose that particular bird?'

Mochta grimaced. 'Because it is only found on our wild north-east coast and it was familiar with the tattooist who also came from that area. There was no other reason.'

'I see. Continue.'

'Our father was angry with us when he discovered our prank. In fact, he had been angry with our growing youthful rebelliousness and high spirits for some time. When the time came, and we reached the age of choice, he told us that the choice before us was a simple one. We could choose what to do in life so long as we both left home and persecuted him no more.'

'So you went into the religious life,' Eadulf prompted when the monk paused, reflecting. 'A strange sort of life for such high-spirited youths. Surely there were other occupations more suited?'

'Our high spirits were damped when the door of our father's house shut against us, Brother Saxon. Somehow we both decided to enter the abbey of Armagh, which is in our clan lands where Patrick . . .'

'We know of the history of Armagh,' Fidelma assured him shortly.

'Well, we both trained as *scriptors* there. Then we began to grow apart. My brother decided to follow the Rule of Rome which is encouraged at Armagh. I felt our traditional ways were better and so I rebelled against Armagh and adopted the tonsure of St John. I had a fair reputation for my penmanship and so I bade farewell to my brother and wandered for a while, being welcomed at several abbeys and even at chiefly courts who were in need of a scribe. That is how I eventually arrived in this kingdom and joined the community of Imleach. That was ten years ago.'

'Did you keep in touch with your brother during that time?'

Mochta shook his head. 'Once or twice only. Through him I learnt that our parents had died. We had an older brother who took over their farm. But we had all became strangers to one another.'

'And you saw no more of your brother until recently?'

'That is right. Baoill had, it seems, become a more fanatic adherent of Rome than ever, which is to be understood for Ultán, the Comarb of Patrick, his abbot and bishop of Armagh, is in favour of extending the rule through all the five kingdoms.'

Fidelma made an affirmative gesture. 'I know of Ultán's ambition to unite all the churches in the five kingdoms in the manner of Rome, with one central primacy and rule. It will never work here because it is against our culture.' She paused and was apologetic. 'I take it that you disagreed with your brother's views?'

'Even as you say, Sister. I believe in the traditions of our people and not in these new ideas that spring from foreign places.'

'So how did you come to meet your brother again?'

'As you may know, from being a *scriptor* I had risen to become the Keeper of the Holy Relics of Ailbe. There is no need to tell you what those Relics symbolise in this kingdom?'

'No need at all,' agreed Fidelma gravely.

'Well, a week or two ago, a man came to the abbey and asked to see me. He looked like a professional warrior. Tall, with long fair hair and . . .'

'Armed with a bow?' Eadulf chimed in. 'An archer?'

Mochta nodded. 'Yes. He had the appearance of a professional archer. He told me that he had a message from my brother, Baoill, who wanted to meet me. He stressed that because of certain matters, which he left unexplained, Baoill wanted to meet me alone and in secret. The archer was staying in the inn run by Cred. Intrigued by this approach, I went to Cred's inn. She opened the door and, thankfully, I did not see anyone else. For the Father Abbot frowned on that place. His anger would have been great if he knew that I was visiting anyone there.'

'Go on.'

'Cred told me that the archer was waiting for me in an upstairs room. And so was my brother, Baoill. After we had exchanged greetings, as only two brothers who had not seen each other for a long time could do, we fell to talking politics . . . church politics mostly. It was then that I became aware of his views. Once he knew mine, he suddenly avoided the subject. He was a clever man, that brother of mine.

'He turned the conversation by saying that he had heard that I was one of the scribes working on the 'Annals of Imleach'. I confirmed that I was. He asked me what date had I given to the foundation of Armagh. I told him that its foundation I had accorded to the year of Our Lord Four Hundred and Forty-Four. He then asked, on what date I had placed the repose of Patrick. So I told him the Year of our Lord Four Hundred and Fifty-Two. These dates were not in dispute.

'It was when he started to ask about the dates accorded to St Ailbe and the foundation of Imleach that I saw what he was after. He told me that the northern scribes were placing those dates nearly a hundred years after Patrick.'

'I saw the notes you had made on the subject for the "Annals",' Fidelma said. She drew the vellum out of her *marsupium*. Mochta glanced at it and nodded.

'I stand by what I say. When I told Baoill that it was absurd for Ailbe's dates to be made so much later because he preached the Faith in Muman before Patrick and, indeed, had jointly baptised the King of Muman – your own ancestor Oenghus Nad Froích – with Patrick at Cashel, Baoill began to argue with me again.'

'But what does this bickering about dates mean?' demanded Eadulf, trying to follow but succeeding only in being bewildered.

'I understood from my brother that he was trying to persuade me to record Ailbe as someone who came after Patrick. To state that Ailbe and his followers founded Imleach after Armagh had been established. He even wanted me to assert that Ailbe should not be regarded as patron of Muman and that Cashel be accorded the title "The Rock of Patrick". He wanted my writing to support the claims that Armagh had the historical right to claim to be the primacy of the Faith among all the five kingdoms.'

Fidelma looked grim. 'I know all about the ambition of Ultán of Armagh. He is not the first Comarb of Patrick who has wished for Armagh to be established as the primacy in all five kingdoms and the churches to be brought under the Rule of Rome. To do that he must first ensure that Imleach's claims to be the primacy of Muman are discredited. But, surely, this is not what these events are all about?'

'I scarce know myself, Sister,' confessed Brother Mochta. 'All I know is that my brother turned to the subject once again and this time to the Holy Relics of Ailbe. How clever he was. He played on my vanity. I had told him that there was a date on some of the Relics which would prove the date when Ailbe was made bishop. He said he would believe if he could see the Relics. I told him to come to the abbey but he refused, saying that it was not seemly that my twin brother should be seen at Imleach with the tonsure of Rome. It was a silly excuse but I did not think more of it. Instead, I suggested that he came in secret to the gate which led into Bardán's herb garden one evening and I would show him the Relics. He agreed and said that this would resolve the dispute between Armagh and Imleach.'

Fidelma looked thoughtful. 'It was naïve of you to believe him.'

'He was my brother. Even then I did not suspect his devious mind.'

'So what happened?'

'The following evening, at the appointed time, I went to the chapel and, unobserved, took down the reliquary box. I was about to take it to the assignation when something made me pause. Perhaps I had begun to suspect him, so I decided to take only Ailbe's crucifix as a token of proof, for there is a date inscribed on the back. I brought the crucifix from the reliquary to the gate of the herb garden. There was my brother outside with the archer . . . God forgive Baoill! He snatched the crucifix from my hand and demanded to know where the rest of the Relics were. When he realised that I had not brought them, he became uncontrollable. He struck me so that I fell against the gate and blood poured from a wound.'

'That explains the dried blood on the gatepost,' Eadulf said.

'It was then I realised that my brother's intention had been to steal the Relics all along.'

'Do you think that it was his own plot or had someone put him up to it?' asked Fidelma. 'Ultán of Armagh, for example? The plan to discredit both Ailbe and Imleach seems clear.'

'All I know is that my life was in the balance. I think my brother would have killed me. Then Brother Bardán came along. He had come to gather herbs. He saw the attack and used a staff to beat back my brother and his companion. They had Ailbe's crucifix. As Bardán secured the gate my brother threatened that others would come and take what I would not give.'

'Then surely it implies that your brother, Baoill, and his archer friend were not acting on their own account?'

Brother Mochta inclined his head in agreement.

'That is true. I was in too great a state of shock to take such matters in at that time. Bardán helped me back to my chamber and I told him the story as I knew it. He told me to tell Abbot Ségdae at once that the crucifix of Ailbe had been stolen. I could not bring myself to do so because I wanted to give Baoill time to reflect on his crime and return it. I still could not believe that my own brother had turned into such an evil person.'

'But he did not return it, obviously,' Eadulf pointed out.

'Some days went by. He did not return with it. I decided to go in search of him.'

'Wasn't that dangerous?'

'I asked Brother Bardán to come with me. We went to Cred's inn. There was one of the Cashel merchant's drivers there, looking strangely at me.'

'That was because he had seen you come to the inn several days before,' murmured Eadulf.

'I did not see him.'

'He saw you.'

'Well, Cred came out and I told her that I was looking for the archer and his companion.'

'She said that she knew nothing of a companion . . .'

'Which is true,' asserted Fidelma. 'Your brother, being your twin, could not afford to show himself openly in the township because of his likeness to you. He would be remarked upon. He stayed outside.'

'Cred said that the archer was hunting in the hills,' Brother Mochta continued. 'Bardán and I walked on a bit, rather aimlessly, in case we discovered the archer. Then we returned to the abbey. Bardán usually left the side gate open and we returned towards the herb garden. We were in the stretch of yew-trees before crossing the heather field, not far from the gate, when my brother suddenly appeared. He had, apparently, been waiting for us.

'I demanded the crucifix that he had stolen and he demanded the entire reliquary and its contents. He threatened me. I refused and he laughed and said that he only sought to make things easy. We would not like the next visitors to Imleach.'

'What then?'

'I told him that he was mad. He replied that he had the backing of a powerful prince and that it was Muman that was mad not to bow down to the inevitable. There would be one primacy for all five kingdoms and one power ruler over the whole.'

Fidelma brightened. 'Those were his exact words?'

'Yes. Those were his exact words.'

'I think I see the hand of Mael Dúin, King of Ailech, in this plot. What the Comarbs of Patrick seek for Armagh, the Uí Néill kings seek for their dynasty. They want to turn the High Kingship of Éireann into a strong central kingship, like the emperors of Rome. This mystery is dissolving. Go on, Mochta. What then?'

'We turned in disgust, Bardán and I, and left Baoill to his ranting. We began to walk across the field to the gate . . .'

'We know the spot,' intervened Eadulf.

'We were halfway across the field when there was a whistle in the air and the next thing I felt this pain in my shoulder.' He raised a hand and touched his wound. 'I fell forwards. Bardán later said that he saw the archer, my brother's companion, standing at the edge of the yew-trees and fitting another arrow to his bowstring. Bardán grabbed me and began to half drag and half propel me to the gate. We just made it when the man's second shot caught me in the leg.'

'Did no one in the abbey observe this?'

Mochta shook his head. 'You have seen that area. It is not overlooked by any window nor is it a frequented area. Bardán helped me inside, shot home the bolts, and then helped me to my chamber. Being the apothecary, he was able to remove the arrows, which, thank God, had not penetrated deeply, and dress the wounds.

'It was then we discussed what best we should do. It had become clear that my brother and his friend were part of some conspiracy to discredit Muman as well as Imleach. But why? For what purpose, I do not know. What was of more immediate concern to me was the threat to attack and steal the Relics. I was afraid many of the brethren would be killed in such an event.

'We spent some time talking about this and then we decided that I should disappear with the remaining Holy Relics. Bardán would ensure that on the following day the news that the Relics and I had disappeared was spread. We hoped, by this method, that we would deflect any attack or attempt to steal them from the abbey and the community would therefore be saved from harm.

'No one had seen me come back injured to the abbey. Having had my wounds bound I would go to Vespers and be seen. Then I would return to my chamber. That was an uncomfortable experience for while my wounds were bound, they were painful. I was in considerable distress. However, once the service was over, I returned to my chamber.

'We arranged for Bardán to take the reliquary box from the chapel and bring it to me. We carefully arranged my room, so that it appeared that I had been carried off against my will. Then we took a few items. I had placed one of the arrows with which I had been shot where it could be seen, hoping to provide a clue to my assailant.'

'We saw it,' observed Eadulf.

'Then Bardán conducted me to this spot. Being a local man, the cave was known to him and is infrequently used. He thought I could hide here until Baoill and his friends came into the open. The day afterwards, you arrived at the abbey with news that my brother and his companion had been killed trying to assassinate Colgú and the Prince of the Uí Fidgente. Bardán said it was not so simple as it appeared for whoever was behind this plot was not revealed. This meant that we had to consider our next step; to decide who was safe to trust.'

Fidelma gave a long drawn-out sigh. 'I wish you had trusted me before this.'

'It would have made little difference in diverting the attack on the abbey,' pointed out Brother Mochta.

'Who do you say the attackers were? Warriors from this King of Ailech, supporting Armagh's plan to exert its control here?' pressed Eadulf.

'No, I think they were Uí Fidgente,' replied Brother Mochta. 'There were stories early this year that the Uí Fidgente were seeking some alliance with the Uí Néill kings of the north against Cashel. They have not forgiven Colgú for their defeat at Cnoc Áine and the death of their king. They would join with the Uí Néill and Armagh to see Cashel weakened and defeated. How better to defeat the kingdom than to divide it?'

'You may well be right, Mochta,' agreed Fidelma. She paused as if a thought struck her. 'You are a close friend of Bardán, of course?'

'Yes. Of course.'

'Being a good penman, you helped Bardán in preparing a book on the properties of herbs?'

Brother Mochta was surprised. 'How did you know that?' he demanded.

'It's of no consequence. Don't you think it curious that Bardán has not put in an appearance and–' she glanced through the mouth of the cave towards the sky – 'it must be about midday?'

Brother Mochta frowned. 'It is a worry,' he confessed. 'He was going to see Finguine this morning to tell him our story. That is all I know.'

Fidelma stood up and went to the mouth of the cave. She negotiated some boxes and stared down the hillside. At the foot of the hill, woodland stretched as far as the banks of the River Ara. Fidelma turned back with decision.

'Mochta, you are an important witness for Cashel. We must get you there immediately for you will be better protected by my brother's warriors. You and the reliquary.'

'What about Bardán?' protested Mochta.

'We will see to him later. Right now, do you think you can ride?'

'Not all the way to Cashel,' he protested.

'Then we will take it in easy stages,' she assured him. 'The worst part of the journey is for you to leave this cave with Brother Eadulf here and walk it down the hill towards that wood there.' She turned to Eadulf. 'Let no one see you until I come along with the horses.'

Eadulf was bemused. 'Where are you getting horses from?'

'I will pick up our horses from the abbey.' She pointed to a lamp by Mochta's palliasse. 'If you will lend me that lamp, I will go back through the tunnels and come back as quickly as I can by the track around the bottom of the hill. Do not bring anything other than the reliquary, Mochta. You may also trust Brother Eadulf here with your life. In fact, that is what it amounts to. Understand this clearly, Mochta, every minute you now stay here, in this cave, you are in the most deadly danger.'

Chapter Nineteen

Fidelma entered the side gate into the herb garden. Obviously, Brother Bardán had still not returned this way; the bolts were withdrawn as earlier. She made her way immediately to Abbot Ségdae's chamber and knocked cautiously upon the door. The elderly, hawk-like abbot was seated in his high-backed, carved wooden chair before his fire, his chin resting on his hands, his eyes staring meditatively into the flames. He looked up as she entered with an expression of some hope.

'What news, Fidelma?' he asked.

Fidelma did not like telling lies to the man whom she had known all her life and who was more like an uncle to her than merely a religious adviser.

'Little enough,' she said cautiously.

The abbot's face fell.

'However,' she went on, 'I believe that I will be able to supply all the answers to these matters when the Brehons meet at Cashel in a few days from now.'

Ségdae's face resumed a hopeful look. 'You mean that you can discover the whereabouts of the Holy Relics of Ailbe?'

'That I can guarantee,' she said briskly. 'But I want no one else to know. Say nothing to anyone, not even Brother Madagan.'

The abbot was reluctant to make such a promise.

'It is a matter affecting the morale of the abbey, Fidelma. Surely I can give the community something to hope for?'

Fidelma shook her head. 'There are many dark forces at work here which may mean the downfall of this kingdom. I need your solemn word on this, Ségdae.'

'Then, of course, you shall have it.'

'Brother Eadulf and I are returning to Cashel immediately for there is no more that I can do here. However, I would like you to start your own journey to Cashel tomorrow.'

The abbot looked surprised. 'Why must I come?'

'Have you forgotten the protocol, Ségdae? You are the Comarb of Ailbe, the principal abbot-bishop of Muman. When the court of Cashel is in session over such a serious matter, you, as the King's principal bishop, must sit at his side.'

Ségdae sighed softly. 'I had forgotten about the hearing. The loss of the Relics and the attack on Imleach drove it from my mind. Then there is the matter of Brother Bardán.'

'What about Brother Bardán?' she asked innocently.

'He has not been seen all morning. Do you remember that you asked me where he was? He seems to have vanished . . . just like Brother Mochta.'

Fidelma compressed her lips. 'I do not think the circumstances will be found to be similar. I have a feeling that all will be answered in Cashel.'

'Should I alert your cousin, Finguine? His men are still in the township helping to repair the damage of the raid.'

'You may tell Finguine. If I do not see him as I leave, I shall see him at Cashel at the hearing. It is sad that there has been so much destruction.'

'Well, there are small mercies. It seems Brother Madagan has been able to make a donation of silver coins which will go some way to mending the destruction.' He gestured at a small bag on the table.

'May I?' Fidelma took the bag and dropped a few of the coins onto her palm. She stared at them. 'How did Madagan come into this largesse?' she asked.

'I believe he said something about a relative from the north.' Ségdae barely paused. 'Are you really confident about your ability to find a resolution to these mysteries?' he pressed.

Fidelma replaced the coins and put the purse back on the table.

'You know me better than that, Ségdae. I am never confident until after the event. Remember *Corinthians*, one, chapter ten, verse twelve?'

Fidelma knew that Ségdae had an almost encyclopedic mind when it came to scripture. The abbot answered her smile.

'If you feel sure that you are standing firm, beware!' he quoted. 'You may fall.'

'So, I will not commit myself but I shall say that the probability is that all will be resolved.'

'You have not garnered your reputation for no reason at all,' Ségdae remarked. 'When will you and our Saxon brother leave?'

'I am going to start out at once. Do not worry, Ségdae. All will be well . . . eventually.'

'I shall be in Cashel on the day of the hearing, then.'

'Bring Brother Madagan with you. I might need his testimony.'

'Will you need Brother Bardán, if he can be found?'

'If he can be found,' affirmed Fidelma.

Ségdae rose and offered her his hand. 'Where is our Saxon brother?'

'I shall meet him along the way,' Fidelma replied hastily. 'Farewell, Ségdae. Until we see each other in Cashel.'

She went on to the guests' hostel and bundled her few belongings into her saddle bags. Eadulf had moved into a nearby chamber after the first night, following the departure of the pilgrims. It took her a moment to pack his saddle bag. She remembered to take the pilgrim's staff of which he had become so fond. She was glad that Sister Scothnat was not about for she did not want to go to the trouble of having to explain her intentions again.

She took the bags and made her way to the stables.

Brother Tomar was at work, as usual, feeding the horses there.

'Are you leaving us?' he asked immediately as his eyes fell on the saddle bags.

Fidelma groaned inwardly. 'For a while,' she responded brightly. 'Perhaps you could help me saddle our horses? Mine and the Saxon brother's horse.'

Brother Tomar turned from the grain bag and regarded her, head to one side.

'The horse of the Saxon as well?' he questioned.

'Yes. If you will saddle Brother Eadulf's horse there, I will get mine ready.'

'You are both leaving then?'

'Yes,' she replied patiently.

'Is the mystery of Brother Mochta's disappearance solved?'

'We will know more when the Brehons meet in Cashel in a few days' time,' she replied, taking the bridle and drawing it over her mare's head. She busied herself adjusting the straps and then swinging the saddle onto the patient beast.

Reluctantly, Tomar began to put the bridle on Eadulf's sorrel.

'I heard that the Uí Fidgente lawyer has already gone on to Cashel.'

Fidelma did not want to show too much interest but she was surprised. So that was why she had not seen Solam about that morning.

'Really? I thought that he might be asking some more questions here in Imleach before he went on to Cashel?'

Brother Tomar chuckled sardonically.

'He would have a hard task with all the feeling against the Uí Fidgente. No, he had to seek protection from the Prince of Cnoc Áine even to ride through the territory just now. I saw him riding in the company of Finguine only an hour ago when he left here.'

'Do you mean that Solam is being escorted by Finguine, personally, on the road to Cashel?'

Brother Tomar was chuckling. 'If he went alone, I doubt whether he would have reached Ara's Well. In fact, I think that Finguine might suspect that there will be an attempt to waylay Solam on the Cashel road.'

Fidelma turned to the stableman who had her complete attention. 'Why do you say that?'

'Because when Finguine and Solam left here, saying they were departing for Cashel, they took the road northwards. The road to Cashel is directly east. I believe that Finguine took Solam on a circular route to avoid the main road to Ara's Well and Cashel.'

Fidelma bent her head in thought for a moment and then continued saddling her mare.

'Are you sure that they said that they were going to Cashel?' she asked.

Brother Tomar smirked indulgently. 'Solam told me himself that Cashel was his destination.'

Fidelma did not make any further comment. What Solam told Brother Tomar did not have to be true. What she couldn't understand was why Finguine would have accompanied Solam in person and not left the task to some of his warriors if it was merely a matter of providing safe passage for the Uí Fidgente out of Cnoc Áine territory.

Fidelma finished saddling the horse in silence. She made sure that the saddle bags were firmly tied and that Eadulf's staff was strapped to the saddle. Brother Tomar led Eadulf's horse out of the stall.

'Where is the Saxon?' he asked, looking round.

'I am meeting him in the township,' Fidelma lied swiftly, justifying herself by remembering the proverb *minima de malis* – of evils, the least – choosing between the less desirable alternatives. The most desirable of the alternatives here was not to let Brother Tomar know what she was about.

She led her mare from the stable before mounting and taking the reins of Eadulf's colt in her hand. She bade farewell to Brother Tomar who stood, an interested spectator, at the doors of the stables. She walked the horses across the courtyard and through the gate, glad that only the inquisitive Brother Tomar was there to see her departure. Outside the gate she sent the horses into a canter across the green towards the township. A mixture of the townsfolk and some of Finguine's warriors were still engaged in clearing up the debris of the raid.

At the edge of the town she slowed down, walking the horses by the smith's forge and turning through a side alley, away from prying eyes. She saw Nion, the *bó-aire*, with his assistant Suibne, working at the wreckage of their forge. Nion raised his head to watch her but she pretended not to notice him. She did not like the way he was staring at her. Out of the corner of her eye she saw him say something to his assistant and hurry away. She turned quickly along the main street in the direction of the ruined shell of Cred's inn before turning down a side alley between the buildings towards the surrounding fields. She had plotted her route carefully in her mind as she wanted no prying eyes to follow her.

She rode firstly in a direction away from the edge of the town, away from the Hill of the Cairn, where she was due to meet with Eadulf and Mochta. If anyone from the abbey or township observed her, she thought that they would presume that she would continue in that direction. There was enough open grassland between the town and the skirting woodland through which she planned to ride, and only after she had reached the cover of the trees would she swing in a semi-circle towards the pre-arranged rendezvous.

Indeed, once in the shelter of the woods, along the small woodland track, she nudged her mount into a canter again, with Eadulf's colt following patiently behind. She was not sure if she had been seen. It took a full ten minutes or so before she decided to slow the pace to a walk. Only then did she allow herself a glance behind. She could still see the edge of the township between the trees and shrubbery. From this distance, the township, and the abbey behind it, seemed almost deserted. There was no sign of movement anywhere. Fidelma gave a small sigh of relief. The way should be easy now.

She continued along the track and altered her direction, swinging round in the start of the semi-circle which she had planned would lead her to the Hill of the Cairn. It was cold and dank within the woods. She wondered whether it was here that the wolves had their lairs and she shivered slightly. She did not want to be reminded of the dangers of that night.

She was aware of constant movement within the woods. The passage of its denizens, varying from the stealthy tread of smaller mammals to the crack of twigs that marked the passage of a deer. There was also the cacophony of nesting birds from the higher branches.

She moved as fast as safety allowed through the woods, crossing a shallow stream here and there, before coming on a brief stretch of meadowland. She had almost exited from the woods into the meadow when she became conscious of a new sound rising above the other noises of the forest. It was the sound made by hooves. Shod hooves. They were moving rapidly. Swiftly she turned the horses back into the forest, her eyes searching for thick cover away from the track.

There was a suitable thicket nearby and she slid from the saddle of her horse, gathered the reins of both animals, looping them securely to a branch. Then, keeping low, she edged forward.

Half a dozen horsemen appeared along the side of the woodland and came to a halt near the entrance to the track from which she had been proceeding.

She stared in unbelief at the leading horsemen.

One was the Uí Fidgente *dálaigh*, Solam, and the other was her cousin, Finguine, Prince of Cnoc Áine. The other four men were obviously members of Finguine's warriors.

'Well?' she heard Solam's high-pitched, querulous tones. 'Have we lost the tracks or not?'

She heard her cousin's voice, tight and also irritable. 'Do not concern yourself. I know this country. There is little choice in the places where they can hide. We shall find them.'

Fidelma found herself growing cold.

To whom were they referring? What was Finguine doing with Solam when he claimed to be suspicious of him; when he blamed the Uí Fidgente for the raid against Imleach? Had Finguine been riding only with his men, she would have undoubtedly contacted him and explained all about Brother Mochta. But why was he with Solam?

'Well, the sooner we find this monk – what's his name? – Mochta? – the sooner we shall resolve this business,' snapped Solam. 'The key is the Holy Relics, of that I have no doubt at all.'

Fidelma's eyes rounded.

Her cousin was responding. 'We will try the southern caves first. Then there is a cave on the Hill of the Cairn to the north.'

He raised his hand and motioned the body of horsemen forward.

For a few moments Fidelma remained where she was, trying to make sense of what she had heard.

Then she rose and hurried back to the horses. Whatever it meant, it seemed that her own cousin, the Prince of Cnoc Áine, was searching for Brother Mochta. She wondered if Eadulf had begun to move Mochta down the hill to the safety of the forest cover along the banks of the River Ara. She must not let Finguine and Solam reach the cave on the Hill of the Cairn first. She was thankful that Finguine had suggested going to the southern caves first, wherever they were. It gave her time to reach Mochta and Eadulf before they did.

Pressing her heels into the flanks of her horse, Fidelma set off at a canter across the meadowland, swinging around the edge of the forest towards the hill. She was thinking about Finguine, about

Brother Mochta and his bitter betrayal by his brother. What was it he had said? Unity is not cemented by blood. She skirted the broad base of the hill and came round to the eastern side, where a new tract of forest began to stretch along the valley which eventually led towards the Well of Ara.

As she rode across the shoulder of the hill, she saw the small figures of Eadulf and Mochta on the hill above her. Eadulf was carrying the reliquary under one arm while the other supported Brother Mochta, who had his arm around the Saxon's shoulders and was struggling to keep his footing.

Fidelma gave a cry to attract their attention. The pair halted, then recognised her. They began to struggle downwards again.

Fidelma urged the horses upwards, as far as the steep slope would allow, then waited for them to come to her, dismounting and holding the horses steady. It took a while for Eadulf and Mochta to struggle down the hill to her.

'Phew!' Eadulf gasped as they came up. 'I could do with a rest.'

He was about to ease Brother Mochta into a sitting position when Fidelma shook her head swiftly.

'Not here. We must get to the shelter of the woods down there as soon as possible.'

'Why?' demanded Eadulf, puzzled by her sharpness.

'Because horsemen are coming and they are searching for Brother Mochta and the Holy Relics.'

Brother Mochta blinked. 'Uí Fidgente?' he gasped.

'One of them is,' acknowledged Fidelma. 'Solam.'

Eadulf pursed his lips as he caught her inflection. 'Who are the others?'

'My cousin rides with Solam.'

Eadulf was about to make a further comment when Fidelma swung up on her horse.

'Give me the reliquary,' she instructed. 'I'll carry that. Brother Mochta will have to mount in front of you, Eadulf. That way you can give him support. We can continue this conversation when we are safely away from this exposed place.'

Eadulf did not say anything further. Instead he handed up the reliquary box to Fidelma and then helped Brother Mochta into the saddle of his horse before he scrambled up behind him. Eadulf was no skilful horseman and he did not use the most elegant method of mounting his patient colt. And it was a very ungainly rider who directed the young horse down from the hillside in the wake of Fidelma and trotted towards the cover of the forest through which the river ran. However it sufficed.

Fidelma did not stop immediately once they were under the canopy of the trees but continued on for a while. After a mile or so, they came to a clearing by the banks of the river and it was here that Fidelma slid from the saddle and led her mare to the water. Then she turned to help Eadulf assist Brother Mochta down for a rest.

The monk sank thankfully to the grass.

'Are you claiming that the Prince is part of this conspiracy?' he gasped immediately, while massaging his leg.

'I am not saying anything of the sort,' Fidelma replied quietly. 'I am merely saying that he and Solam, with some of his men, appeared to be searching for you and the Holy Relics. They were searching the caves.'

Eadulf gestured in annoyance. 'But that means he is in league with the Uí Fidgente, with Armagh, with the Uí Néill! Your own cousin has betrayed his King.'

'It means that he and Solam were searching for Brother Mochta,' replied Fidelma waspishly. 'Make no judgements until you have all the facts. Remember my principles?'

Eadulf raised his head defiantly. 'You may not wish to see your cousin guilty of such treason. However, what other interpretation can be put on what you say?'

'There are several interpretations but it is pointless speculating about them. It is the worst thing that can be done, to speculate before you are in full possession of the facts. I have said so many times. To do so means that you will distort those facts in order to fit your theory.'

Eadulf relapsed into an ungracious silence.

Brother Mochta eased his aching limbs, glancing up uneasily at Fidelma. 'So, Sister, what is your plan now?'

Fidelma examined Brother Mochta for a moment before making up her mind.

'I do not think, in your condition, that you will be able to travel much further today. We will see if we can make it to the Well of Ara and rest there. I can trust the innkeeper there. Then, by easy stages, we will go to Cashel.'

They reached Aona's inn at nightfall. At Fidelma's insistence they did not approach it directly but moved around the rear of the inn. It was not yet time for the dogs to be loosed although they could hear a couple of hounds barking at their tethers. As they approached the rear door of the inn, it opened and a voice cried out, demanding to know who it was approaching in such a stealthy fashion.

Fidelma relaxed a little as she recognised Aona's voice.

'It is Fidelma, Aona.'

'My lady?' Aona's voice was puzzled because Fidelma responded so quietly.

The innkeeper came forward to hold the bridle of her horse while she dismounted. Then he turned aside and yelled at the dogs to quiet them. They relapsed into protesting whines.

'Aona, is there anyone else in the inn tonight?' Fidelma asked immediately.

'Yes; a merchant and his drivers. They are at their evening meal.' He screwed up his eyes in the darkness to where Eadulf and Mochta still sat on their horse. 'Is that the Saxon Brother?'

'Listen, Aona, we need rooms for the night. And no one must know that we are here. Do you understand?'

'Yes, lady. It shall be as you ask.'

'Did your guests hear us arrive?'

'I don't think so. They are making so much noise over their meal. The ale has circled well in them.'

'Good. Is there a way we can go to a room without the merchants or anyone else seeing us?' pressed Fidelma.

Aona did not reply for a moment and then he nodded. 'Come directly to the stables with me. There is a spare room above them, which is only used in an emergency if the inn is crowded . . . which it never is. It is crudely equipped . . . but if you want seclusion, then no one would ever come across you there.'

'Excellent,' said Fidelma approvingly.

Aona realised that Brother Mochta was injured as Eadulf tried to help him from the horse. He went forward to assist him. As he did so, Fidelma laid a cautionary hand on his arm.

'No questions, Aona. It is for the safety of the King of Muman. That is all you need to know. Do not let anyone know we are here. Especially do not let any visitors to the inn know.'

'You may rely on me, lady. Lead your horses into the stable. This way.'

He helped Eadulf take Brother Mochta to the stables, while Fidelma led the horses. There were two heavy drays or wagons parked in the yard before the stables. As they were in semi-gloom they had to wait until Aona lit a lamp. He motioned them inside. Fidelma put the horses into separate stalls.

'I will tend to their wants in a minute,' Aona said. 'Let me take you to the room first.'

He helped Brother Mochta ascend a narrow flight of stairs which led to a loft room. It was a plain room with four cots and straw mattresses on them. There were some chairs, a table and little else. The whole place was covered with dust.

'As I said,' he observed apologetically, drawing some sacking over the window, 'it is not really used.'

'It will do for now,' Fidelma assured him.

'Is your companion badly hurt?' Aona inquired, indicating Brother Mochta. 'Should I find a discreet physician?'

'No need,' replied Fidelma. 'My companion has trained in the schools of medicine.'

Aona suddenly held up the lamp, close to Brother Mochta's face. His eyes widened.

'I know you,' he said. 'Yes, you are the very man Sister Fidelma was asking about. But . . .' He suddenly appeared bewildered. 'You were not wearing that tonsure when you stayed here last week. I swear it.'

Brother Mochta suppressed a groan. 'That is because I did not stay here last week, innkeeper.'

'But, I swear . . .'

Fidelma interrupted him with a smile of reassurance. 'It is a long story, Aona.'

The innkeeper was still apologetic. 'No questions, lady. I remember.'

He opened a cupboard and drew out some blankets.

'As I say, this room is used only when the inn is full, which is hardly ever. It is very basic.'

'It is better than sleeping under the heather,' replied Eadulf.

Fidelma took the innkeeper aside to give him instructions.

'Once you have taken care of our horses, we would like something to eat and drink. Can you arrange that without anyone knowing?'

'I will see to it. I must let my grandson, Adag, know. He is a good boy and will not betray you. He is my right hand in helping me with the inn. I have no wife. She was carried off by the Yellow Plague during the same year as my daughter-in-law. My son perished in the wars against the Uí Fidgente. So there are just the two of us left to run this place now.'

'I remember young Adag,' Fidelma assured him. 'By all means tell him. Who else did you say was in the inn at the moment? Some merchants?'

'A merchant and two drivers. Those are their wagons outside the inn. In fact . . .' He paused thoughtfully. 'In fact, you may know the merchant as he is from Cashel.'

Eadulf, overhearing, suddenly leant forward. 'Do you mean Samradán?'

Aona glanced at him in surprise. 'That is the very man.'

'Then do not mention our presence to him.' Fidelma was adamant.

'Is there something I should know about him?' demanded Aona curiously.

'It is just that it is better if he did not know of our presence,' replied Fidelma.

'Has it something to do with the attack on the abbey the other night? I heard all about that.'

'I said, no questions, Aona, and you agreed,' Fidelma rebuked him patiently.

The former warrior looked contrite. 'I beg your forgiveness, lady. It is just that Samradán was talking about the attack.'

'Oh? What was he saying about it?' She pretended to be more concerned in adjusting the sackcloth curtain.

'He described the attack and said that it was the Uí Fidgente. How can they be so treacherous? And all the while their Prince is your brother's guest at Cashel?'

'We do not know for a fact that it was the Uí Fidgente,' she corrected. 'When did Samradán arrive?'

'An hour or two before you did, lady.'

Fidelma was thoughtful and she gazed at Eadulf. 'That means he could not have gone north. That is even more interesting.'

Eadulf could not see why it was interesting at all.

Aona opened his mouth to ask a question and then thought better of it.

'Off with you, Aona,' she instructed. 'We need that refreshment as soon as you can.'

The innkeeper turned down the stairs.

'And, remember,' Fidelma called after him, 'not a word to anyone apart from your grandson.'

'I swear it on the Holy Cross, lady.'

When he had gone, Eadulf settled to examine Mochta's shoulder and leg. Since his days studying medicine, although he was no qualified physician, Eadulf took to the habit of carrying some medicines in his saddle bag.

'Well, the wounds are still healing,' he announced. 'The journey has not worsened it. Brother Bardán did a good job. It is just that the wounds will ache for a bit but they are healing nicely. No need for me to change the dressings at all.'

Brother Mochta forced a smile. 'The journey has worsened my disposition, however, my Saxon friend. I feel as if I have been dragged over a stony stretch of land.'

Fidelma had discovered a stub of candle which she lit from the lamp which Aona had left.

'What is it?' asked Eadulf as she started towards the stairs, carrying it in her hand.

'I am just curious about what Samradán trades in,' she replied. 'I am going to have a look in the wagons.'

Eadulf was disapproving. 'Is that wise?' he asked.

'Curiosity is sometimes a more powerful force than wisdom. Look after Brother Mochta until I return.'

Eadulf shook his head in censure as she disappeared into the stable below.

Aona was not in the stable and the horses had not been unsaddled. Presumably he had gone to give instructions to Adag.

Fidelma went on into the yard. It was now in darkness, except for a lamp which, by law, announced the presence of the inn. The clouds had caused the night to come down rapidly. She made her way to the two heavy wagons. Both were covered in tarpaulins which served to keep the rain off their contents. She sheltered the flickering flame of the candle with her hand and moved round the wagons. Leather thongs kept the tarpaulins secure. She balanced the candle on top of one of the wheels, hoping that no sudden breeze would blow it out, as she undid one of the thongs. Then she heaved the covering aside.

By the light of the candle, she could see a number of tools inside, tools for digging. There were spades and picks and other such implements. She turned to some leather bags nearby. They seemed to be filled with rock of some kind. She reached forward and drew out some of the rocks and examined them. They meant nothing in the candlelight. She replaced them and looked into a second leather bag. There were a number of metal nuggets in it. She drew out one. It reflected and gleamed in her hand.

So Samradán and his men were not merely merchants? She had a feeling that what they were up to was something illegal. The metal was silver. She pursed her lips in disapproval as she replaced it back in the bag.

'What are you doing?'

The voice cut into Fidelma's thoughts and she swung round, her heart beating fast.

A small boy stood there with a lantern in one hand.

Fidelma relaxed visibly as she recognised him.

'Hello, Adag,' she greeted Aona's young grandson. 'Do you remember me?'

The boy nodded slowly.

Fidelma replaced the leather covering and secured the fastener. Then she moved away from the wagon.

'You did not say what you were doing?' The boy insisted.

'No,' agreed Fidelma. 'I did not.'

'You were looking for something.' The boy sniffed in disapproval. 'It is wrong to look through other people's possessions.'

'It is also wrong to steal other people's possessions. I was just examining these wagons to see if everything belonged to the people who drove them. Now your grandfather said you can keep a secret. Can you?'

The boy regarded her with some scorn. 'Of course I can.'

Fidelma looked solemnly at the small boy. 'Your grandfather has told you not to breathe a word about the presence of my companions or myself to anyone. Especially not those men in the inn?'

The boy nodded solemnly. 'You still have not told me what you were looking for in the wagons, Sister.'

Fidelma grew conspiratorial. 'Those men in your grandfather's tavern are robbers. That is why I was looking in their wagons. I was looking for proof. Your grandfather will tell you that I am a *dálaigh* as well as a Sister.'

The child's eyes widened. As Fidelma thought, the boy responded more positively to being allowed into an adult secret than simply being told to mind his own business.

'Do you want me to keep a watch on them, Sister?'

Fidelma was serious. 'I think that you are the best person for the job. But do not let on to them that you suspect them of anything.'

'Of course not,' assured the boy.

'Just watch them and come and tell me when they leave the tavern and in which direction they go. Do it stealthily, without them knowing.'

'Whatever time they leave?'

'Exactly. Whatever time.'

The boy grinned happily. 'I shall not let you down, Sister. Now I must unsaddle your horses. My grandfather is making a meal for you and your friends.'

When Fidelma explained matters to Eadulf and Brother Mochta, Eadulf said: 'Is it wise to involve the boy?'

Brother Mochta was a little fearful and added: 'Are you sure the boy won't betray himself?'

'No.' Fidelma was adamant. 'He's a smart lad. And I do need to know when Samradán and his wagons leave here.'

'What did you mean by telling the boy that they are robbers?' asked Eadulf.

'Because it is the truth,' Fidelma assured him. 'What did I find in the wagons? Tools for digging and bags of rocks. What does that say to you, Eadulf.'

The Saxon shook his head, mystified.

Fidelma was exasperated. 'Rocks . . . ore . . . mining tools!' she exploded the words like the crack of a whip. Eadulf caught on.

'You mean, they were the ones mining the silver in the caves?'

'Exactly. I have heard of metals being mined a little further south of here but I did not know there was a silver vein in these hills until we discovered it. But, whoever the vein belongs to, I am sure it does not belong to Samradán. He is mining illegally, according to the judgements given in the *Senchus Mór*.'

Brother Mochta whistled slightly. 'Has Samradán anything to do with the rest of this puzzle?' he asked.

'That I don't know,' confessed Fidelma. 'Anyway, our first priority now is to eat and then we will see what is to be done. I hope Aona hurries up with that food.'

It was just after dawn that Fidelma was dragged from her sleep by a hand shaking her. She came awake reluctantly, blinking at the eager face of young Adag above her.

'What is it?' she mumbled sleepily.

'The robbers,' hissed the boy. 'They've gone.'

She was still sleepy. 'Robbers?'

The child was impatient. 'The men with the wagons.'

Fidelma was wide awake. 'Oh. When did they go?'

'About ten minutes ago. I awoke only because I heard the sound of their wagons on the stone of the road outside.'

Fidelma gazed across the room to where her two companions were still sleeping peacefully.

'At least you were alert, Adag,' she smiled. 'We did not hear a thing here. Which way have they gone?'

'They went off along the road to Cashel.'

'Good. You have done well, Adag, and . . .' She paused.

There came the sound of horses clattering into the yard outside. 'Could they have come back?' she asked Adag quickly.

Eadulf groaned in his sleep and turned over but did not wake, and at that moment Fidelma realised that the sounds were not those of pack animals nor of wagons being pulled. They were the shod hooves of warriors' horses.

She quickly rose from her palliasse and went to the window, taking care to keep well back, and moved the corner of the sackcloth curtain aside.

Down in the yard were the shadows of seven horsemen. The inn light which had been burning all night, cast a faint and uneven glow. Nevertheless, she caught her breath as she saw the thin, bird-like features of Solam together with her cousin, Finguine. They were accompanied by four warriors. She could not make out the features of the seventh man. There had been only six men when she had last seen Finguine.

'Adag,' she whispered to the boy. 'You'd better go down and see what they want. Answer them truthfully except do not tell them that we are here. On your life. Do you swear it?'

The boy nodded and went off to do as he was bid.

She returned to the window, peering through the chink in the sackcloth curtain. She could hear her cousin, Finguine, saying: 'It is clear they are not here, Solam. It is not worthwhile rousing the innkeeper.'

'Better to make sure than make an assumption which might be false,' replied the Uí Fidgente lawyer.

'Very well.' He turned to one of his men. 'Rouse the innkeeper and . . . no, wait. Someone is coming.'

Adag came out of the stable and Fidelma saw him approach the riders.

'Can I help you, lords?' he asked, his voice piping up proudly.

'Who are you, boy?' she heard Solam demand.

'Adag, son of the innkeeper here.'

Eadulf groaned from his palliasse and Fidelma turned as he sat up.

'What is . . . ?' he began.

She quickly put a finger to her lips.

The movement distracted her from the conversation below. She glanced back through the window and saw the boy pointing in the direction of the Cashel road.

'You've been of great help, boy,' Finguine was saying. 'Here, catch!'

A coin flickered through the air.

Adag caught it deftly.

Finguine dug his heels into his horse and the whole band of them trotted out of the yard and away in the direction of Cashel. It was only then that she caught the features of the seventh rider as he passed momentarily in the light of the inn's lamp. It was Nion, the *bó-aire* of Imleach.

Fidelma drew the curtain back and heaved a sigh.

'What is going on?' demanded Eadulf.

She glanced to where Brother Mochta was still sleeping and then to the stairs for Adag came pounding up with a smile on his face.

'They rode off for Cashel, Sister,' he said breathlessly.

'What did they want?'

'They wanted to know if there was anyone staying in the inn tonight.

I said that there had been some men with wagons who had left on the Cashel road. But I did not say anything about you nor your friends. The horsemen thanked me and rode towards Cashel. They seemed very interested in the wagons.'

Eadulf was looking from the boy to her in bewilderment. Fidelma met his eye.

'The horsemen were Finguine and Solam,' she explained slowly. 'They were accompanied by Nion.'

Chapter Twenty

The journey back to Cashel from the Well of Ara was uneventful. Surprisingly, there were no warriors guarding the bridge across the River Suir at the little fork of Gabhailín where Fidelma and Eadulf had been prevented from crossing some days before. However, when Fidelma thought the matter over, she realised that it would be logical for Gionga to remove his warriors once he learned that Fidelma had reached Imleach.

It was Eadulf who articulated the problem that had been uppermost in Fidelma's thoughts since they had left Aona's inn.

'Is it wise to bring Brother Mochta into Cashel itself?' he asked. 'There might be dangers there for him and it is still a few days before the hearing in front of the Brehons.'

Brother Mochta was feeling somewhat better after his night's rest, with his wounds not paining him so much.

'Surely no harm will come to me among the religious at Cashel?' he asked.

'I would be happier if the presence of yourself and the reliquary in Cashel was not known until the last moment,' Fidelma announced. 'There is an unused back road which will bring us to the edge of the town close to where a friend of mine lives. Mochta can stay with her until the day of the hearing.'

'In the town itself?' Eadulf asked. 'Is that wise?'

He was referring to the fact that in towns the people hardly barred their doors and were always in and out of their neighbours' houses. Towns were usually made up of dwellings of many extended families. There was no fear of strangers.

'Don't worry,' replied Fidelma, 'my friend is one who does not welcome guests.'

'I think that you are going to a lot of trouble for nothing,' Brother Mochta averred. 'Who could harm me at the royal palace of Cashel?'

The corner of Fidelma's mouth turned downward momentarily. 'That is precisely what we have to discover,' she said quietly. 'My brother asked the same question.'

They came to Cashel some time later by the back road which Fidelma had led them along. When they came to the edge of the town, Fidelma left Eadulf and Brother Mochta in the shelter of a small copse, after she'd explained that she would go ahead to prepare the way. It was a matter of minutes before she came back. Brother Mochta looked concerned for she was not carrying the reliquary which she had kept carefully since they had left Imleach. She saw his anxious gaze and assured him that she had left it safely with her friend. She led them to a house on the edge of the town, standing a little apart from the others. It was a medium-sized structure with its own outhouse and barn. Fidelma led them immediately into the barn which served as a stable. Eadulf helped Brother Mochta down from the colt while Fidelma secured the horses.

With Eadulf supporting Brother Mochta, Fidelma preceded them to the house. The door opened and together they helped Brother Mochta inside. Fidelma gave a quick glance round, as if to see whether they had been observed, before closing the door behind them.

Inside stood a woman of short stature. She was in her forties yet maturity had not dimmed the youthfulness of her features and the golden abundance of her hair. She wore a smock-like dress which emphasised a good figure whose hips had not broadened and whose limbs were still shapely.

'This is my friend, Della,' announced Fidelma. 'This is Brother Mochta who will stay with you and this is Brother Eadulf.'

Eadulf smiled appreciatively at the attractive woman.

'Why is it that I have not seen Fidelma's friend at the court of Colgú?' he asked in greeting.

He was immediately aware that he had said something wrong.

'I do not venture out of this house, Brother,' replied the woman called Della. Her voice was solemn but there was an attractive quality to it. 'I am reclusive. People in Cashel respect that.'

Fidelma added, almost sharply, as if to cover some error of courtesy: 'This is why Brother Mochta will be safe here until the day of the hearing.'

'A reclusive?' Eadulf was confused. 'Surely it is hard to be a reclusive in this town?'

'One can be isolated in the midst of many,' replied Della calmly.

'You will look after Brother Mochta, Della?' Fidelma's glance told Eadulf that he had said enough.

Della smiled at her friend. 'You have my word, Fidelma.' She had already helped the injured monk to a seat. Nearby stood the reliquary of St Ailbe, the sight of which caused Brother Mochta to visibly relax.

Fidelma took Eadulf's arm, for he would have stopped and talked more on the principles of solitude, and hurried him to the door.

'We will be back in time for the hearing, Brother Mochta. Take care of those injuries.'

She raised a hand in farewell to the monk and smiled appreciatively at her friend.

Outside, as they mounted their horses once again, Eadulf remarked: 'You have a curious friend there, Fidelma.'

'Della? No, not curious. She is merely a sad woman.'

'I see no need for sadness. She is still attractive and she does not seem to be in want.'

'I tell you this so that you may not refer to it ever again. Della was a woman of secrets.' She used the term *bé-táide*.

'Woman of secrets?' Eadulf frowned, struggling with the euphemism. Then his face lightened. 'Do you mean that she was a prostitute?' He dredged from his memory the word *echlach*.

Fidelma nodded curtly. 'That was why I did not want you to say more in there. It is a sensitive matter.'

They had turned from the side street into the main street through Cashel and passed a tavern on a corner. A shadowy figure was standing outside with a drinking horn in his hand. The man stared at them and then hurried inside. Eadulf pretended not to notice him but once they had ridden past, he turned to Fidelma.

'I have just seen Nion in the doorway of that tavern back there. It is obvious that he has seen us but does not want to be seen himself.'

Fidelma was not perturbed. 'After he paused at Aona's inn this morning, I would have expected him to be in Cashel.'

Eadulf was disappointed by her reaction but interested in returning to the subject of Della.

'How did you become friendly with Della?' he asked.

'I represented her when she was raped,' replied Fidelma calmly.

Eadulf pulled a cynical face. 'A prostitute *raped*?'

Fidelma's face became a mask of irritation. 'Cannot a woman be raped simply because she is a prostitute? At least we have the provision which allows a woman compensation in such circumstances even if she is a *bé-táide*. Half of her honour price is paid.'

Eadulf stirred uncomfortably at the vehemence in her voice. He spoke penitently. 'It is just that I thought that a prostitute was not entitled to such compensation nor did I think that she could acquire a property.'

Fidelma became a little mollified. 'She can inherit property from her parents but, generally, she cannot acquire property through marriage or cohabitation and, if a profit has come through her work in such a union, she has no claim to a share of it.'

Eadulf smiled in satisfaction. 'So I was right?'

'Except that you neglected the fact that a prostitute can renounce her previous way of life and, if so, can be reinstated in society.'

'Is that what happened with Della?'

Fidelma gave an affirmative gesture. 'To a certain extent. She renounced her previous life after the rape. After the case in which I represented her, she withdrew to the house that had been owned by her father. This was a few years ago. Many people, sadly, still treat her with contempt and her means of protection has been to become a recluse.'

'That is no answer,' Eadulf replied. 'You only find in solitude what you take into it.'

Fidelma glanced at him. Now and then Eadulf came out with such pertinent remarks that she knew clearly why she had come to like and almost rely on the Saxon monk. At other times he was clumsy and did not seem sensitive to people and events. He was a man of paradoxes; brilliant and intuitive on the one hand, slow and unheeding on the other. There seemed no continuity in his character. It was so against her own clear, analytical nature and her trenchant temperament.

They relapsed into silence as they rode through Cashel. Many people recognised her and some greeted her with a smile while others stood in groups along the way, watching her in undisguised curiosity and whispering among themselves. They continued up to the gates of the towering royal palace of the Kings.

Capa, the captain of the guard, was at the gate.

'Welcome back, lady,' he greeted, as they rode in. 'The Prince of Cnoc Áine arrived this morning, so we knew you would be arriving sometime late today.'

Fidelma exchanged a look with Eadulf.

Before she could speak, her cousin Donndubháin, the heir-apparent to Colgú, came hurrying out of some nearby buildings, smiling in welcome.

'Fidelma! Thank God that you are safe. We have heard all about the attack on Imleach. Of course, Prince Donennach is denying any Uí Fidgente involvement in it . . . but he would, wouldn't he?'

Fidelma dismounted and was embraced by her cousin. She turned to unstrap her saddle bag while Eadulf followed her example.

'You must have a lot to tell us about the attack on the abbey!' Donndubháin sounded excited. 'When we heard – why, I was hard pressed to prevent your brother leading a guard to Imleach. But–' he glanced around in conspiratorial fashion – 'that would have left

Cashel unguarded and there is Gionga and his Uí Fidgente troop to consider.'

Fidelma turned to Capa and instructed him to ensure that the horses were taken to the stables and cared for. Then she turned back to her cousin.

'Has anything else transpired here that I should know of?'

Donndubháin shook his head. 'We were hoping that you had brought some news that will resolve the mystery.'

Fidelma smiled wanly. 'Things are never simple,' she commented in a tired tone.

'Your brother, the King, wants to see you right away,' her cousin went on. 'Do you mind? Or do you want to refresh yourself from your journey first?'

'I'll see Colgú first.'

'There is no need for Brother Eadulf to accompany you,' Donndubháin said hurriedly, as he led the way.

'I will see you later then,' Fidelma smiled, a trifle apologetically at her companion.

Colgú was waiting for Fidelma in his private chambers. Brother and sister exchanged affectionate greetings and Fidelma immediately asked after her brother's wound.

'Thanks to our Saxon friend, the wound is healing well. See?' He raised his arm above his head and moved it about to show its mobility. 'There is slight discomfiture but no infection and it will be all right soon, just as he promised it would.' He paused then asked: 'Is Brother Eadulf not with you?'

Fidelma glanced to Donndubháin who was standing by the door with a frown.

'I understood that you wanted to see me alone?'

Colgú looked puzzled for the minute.

'Ah, so I did. Very well, Donndubháin. We will join you shortly.' After he had left, Colgú motioned her to a chair. 'Donndubháin has become an ardent believer in the conspiracy theory, that enemies lurk everywhere. I hope Eadulf was not insulted. He is a person whom I can trust.'

Fidelma smiled quickly as she seated herself. 'I think your trust will not be misplaced.'

'What information have you been able to gather at Imleach? We have had the news of the attack. Our cousin, Finguine, the Prince of Cnoc Áine, arrived earlier today. He gave us details.'

'So I understand,' Fidelma replied. 'There is little to add, apparently. Abbot Ségdae and the witnesses from Imleach should be here in the next day or so.'

'Witnesses?' queried Colgú, hopefully.

'I believed that the events at Imleach, the disappearance of the Holy Relics and the attack on the township, are all connected with the attempted assassination. How is the Prince of the Uí Fidgente, by the way? I neglected to ask about his wounds.'

Colgú was sardonic. 'He bears a slight limp. The wound is better but his temper is worse. Otherwise he is in good health and still claiming a plot against us. His bodyguard Gionga hardly ever leaves his side.'

'Did you know that Gionga placed warriors at the bridge over the Suir to prevent me leaving here?'

Her brother looked troubled. 'I found that out afterwards. Gionga, or his Prince, was cunning. Once it was known that you had reached Imleach safely, Prince Donennach came to me and explained that Gionga, through zeal, had placed a guard there to prevent any accomplices of the assassins escaping. Misinterpreting their orders, they tried to prevent you from going to Imleach. Donennach apologised profusely and said he had ordered the warriors to disperse.'

Fidelma chuckled derisively. 'If one believes that . . . ! They had specific orders to prevent *my* going to Imleach. They made that clear enough.'

'But can we prove it? Just as Donndubháin argues his conspiracy theory against the Uí Fidgente, what proof is there? The ninth day will be here soon. I am told that the Brehon Rumann from Fearna, with his entourage, will be here shortly. Perhaps tomorrow. The Brehons Dathal and Fachtna are already come. The nobles of the kingdom are also gathering. Oh, and our cousin Finguine has come escorting Solam, the *dálaigh* for the Uí Fidgente.' Colgú did not disguise his anxiety. 'I am worried, Fidelma. I freely confess it. Do you have a solution to this conundrum yet?'

Fidelma was torn between sounding optimistic and telling her brother the brutal truth.

'I believe that I can see various paths along which the truth may be found but they are paths to be explored only. The short answer is, alas, I do not have the solution as yet.'

'I thought as much, otherwise you would have told me immediately. It seems that we will have to trust that your skills in the court will discover the truth during the hearing.'

Fidelma wished that she could reassure her brother, but instead she asked, 'Is Donennach of the Uí Fidgente still persuaded to go ahead and claim conspiracy against you?'

'So far as I know, Solam is persuaded to argue that I was involved in a plot to kill Donennach. The nobles of Muman have let it be known that they will have none of it. Rightly or wrongly, they believe in me as their King and say that I have done no wrong . . .'

'That is true.'

'But we must be able to prove it. If I and the Eóghanacht are condemned in a court, then I fear the nobles will cry conspiracy, even as Donndubháin is doing! They will take matters into their own hands to punish the Uí Fidgente. Donndubháin has become increasingly incensed at the behaviour of the Uí Fidgente. For him, there is no doubt that it was they who attacked Imleach. I can see a position arising where Donndubháin will lead the nobles in an attack on all the Dál gCais clans. The kingdom could be split by wars. Instead of this peace that I had hoped for, we could enter another cycle of conflict lasting for centuries.'

'The nobles of Muman will obey you, if you order them . . .' Fidelma began but her brother interrupted.

'Already there are threats and mumblings against the Uí Fidgente. It is claimed that the whole affair has been a deliberate attempt to destroy the Eóghanacht and the power of Cashel. What can I answer them about the attack on Imleach . . . ?'

'We do not know yet if the raid on Imleach was inspired by the Uí Fidgente,' insisted Fidelma. 'Brother, you must control the nobles of Muman for if anything happens before the hearing then we will truly stand condemned before the five kingdoms of Éireann.'

Colgú was unhappy. 'All my efforts are being made to that effect, Fidelma. But I fear . . . truly I do . . . I know just how hot-headed some of the younger nobles can be and they might take justice on the points of their swords and ride into the lands of the Uí Fidgente to take revenge for the destruction of the great yew at Imleach.'

'I can only tell you that there is more to this matter than mistrust between the Eóghanacht and the Uí Fidgente, brother. Tell me, as I was away from Cashel at the time, was there ever any dissension between you and Finguine of Cnoc Áine?'

Colgú was slightly bewildered by the question.

'Finguine? Our cousin? Why should there be?'

Fidelma did not feel his questions needed an answer. 'Was there?'

'None as I recall. Why do you ask?'

'When the *derbfhine* of our family met to appoint the *tanist* to his father Cathal Cú cen Máthair, was there dissension between you?'

Cathal had been King of Cashel before Colgú.

'I do not think so.' her brother frowned.

'Cathal had two sons,' she pointed out. 'Finguine, who is now Prince of Cnoc Áine, and Ailill, who is Prince of Glendamnach. Of the two, Finguine was of age to be elected *tanist*; surely he was hurt when he was not chosen to succeed his father as King of Cashel?'

'So were many others of the *derbfhine* who were equally qualified, Fidelma. But that is the law of our kingship succession. It has been so even when our ancestor Eber Fionn settled with the children of the Gael in this land and it will be so while noble Gaelic families survive in this land. Our young brother, Fogartach, might well have been my *tanist* if he had chosen but he prefers to stay away from politics. So when Donndubháin was elected my *tanist*, my heir-apparent, it could be said that many of our cousins were disappointed. Yet the heir is always elected by the *derbfhine* of the family. The *tanist* must be appointed and confirmed by the *derbfhine*.'

Fidelma understood the kingship succession of the kingdoms of Éireann very well. There was no automatic eldest male heir succession as in other lands. Among the children of the Gael, the family of the king formed an electoral college, and a *tanist*, or heir-apparent, was chosen as being the man best fitted for the task of kingship; he could be a son, but equally a brother, uncle or cousin of varying degrees of relationship. While usually a male *tanist* was chosen, it had even been known that a female could be chosen as leader but only for the term of her life, for her offspring could only be regarded as belonging to the clan of their father and not to the people of their mother's father.

'What makes you ask about Finguine?' Colgú was interested.

'I was interested, that's all. Some idea that I had.'

'Well, I can't recall any animosity between Finguine and myself when I was made Cathal's heir-elect although . . .' he paused, as if he had suddenly remembered something.

Fidelma raised her head and looked searchingly at him. 'What?'

'I do recall that there was some quarrel between Finguine and Donndubháin when he was elected my *tanist*. Finguine was favoured to be *tanist* but he seems to have accepted the decision. He was undoubtedly vexed at that time. Though I cannot understand it. Finguine is nearly my age and I plan to live a long life, so that the chances of him ever becoming king, even if he were my heir-elect are slim indeed.' Colgú grinned at his sister: 'I plan to be King of Muman a long time in spite of conspiracies and assassinations.'

'Then,' Fidelma observed quietly, 'I have much work to do, brother, to ensure that this hearing does not go against us.'

She rejoined Eadulf after the midday meal and they took a stroll around the walls of the palace. The wind was blowing strongly from the south and it was chill. They had put on their woollen cloaks and wrapped themselves against the icy fingers of the southerly winds as they paced the battlements.

'Apparently there is quite a lot of excitement in Cashel,' Eadulf remarked as they gazed down on the town below. 'People have been flocking in to attend the hearing from many places. I understand that there is a lot of ill-feeling towards the Uí Fidgente since news of the attack at Imleach and the fate of the yew-tree has been spread about the country.'

Fidelma looked troubled. 'Have you ever played *tomus*?' she asked.

Eadulf shook his head. 'I have never heard of it,' he assured her.

'It's a word that means "seeking out", "weighing matters". It's the name we give to a game here in which we have numerous little wooden pieces which can fit together to form a picture.'

'*Tomus*? No, I've never come across it.'

'No matter. It's just that I feel that I have all the pieces spread out on a table before me. Some of them have already fitted themselves into a pattern. Some are more intriguing and seemed to fit here or to fit there. But what it needs is one more single piece which would suddenly make all the pieces fit and thus the picture will be clearly revealed.'

'Then you feel that you are close to the answer to this mystery?'

Fidelma sighed deeply. 'So close . . . and yet . . .'

'Fidelma!'

They turned at the call and were confronted by Finguine, who came up behind them. He was also dressed for the winds that blew across the Rock of Cashel; his thick, dyed woollen cloak was fastened around his neck by his round silver, solar-symbol brooch with its garnet stones.

'I am glad that you made it back safely. Had I known you were leaving Imleach when you did I would have offered you an escort.'

Fidelma regarded her handsome cousin speculatively, trying to read what lay behind his smiling features.

'I probably would not have made good company with Solam,' she pointed out.

He laughed disarmingly. 'Solam? Had I not escorted that little ferret of a man, then I doubt he would have reached here at all. Have you heard of the anger building up against the Uí Fidgente? The news of the attack at Imleach has been spreading rapidly. The destruction of the sacred yew-tree is something that the people are not going to forgive.'

'So everyone has made up their mind that it was the Uí Fidgente?' queried Fidelma. 'I know that Nion, the *bó-aire* of Imleach, firmly believed it.'

Finguine frowned. 'Nion? Yes, he is sure that there is some conspiracy . . . here in Cashel.'

'Is that why he accompanied you here?' she asked mildly.

'So you have seen Nion in the palace? Yes, that's why he accompanied me here, so that he might testify. When he does, those who stand ready to betray Cashel to the Uí Fidgente will fall.'

Fidelma blinked at the curious inflection in his voice. It was as if Finguine were trying to tell her something by innuendo.

'Do you share Nion's belief?'

'There is no doubt in anyone's mind. As the *dálaigh* of Cashel you will be expected to destroy the Uí Fidgente Prince at the hearing. The eyes of all the nobles of Muman will be upon you. A great restitution will be demanded and that compensation will place the Uí Fidgente for ever in our debt so that they will never rise up again.'

'That sounds dangerously close to seeking punishment rather than retribution,' observed Fidelma.

Finguine's voice was harsh. 'Of course. Let us plant the seeds of destruction among the Uí Fidgente now. For too long they have been an irritant to the Eóghanacht of Muman. If our children are to live in peace, we must ensure that they are so suppressed by our anger that they will never dare raise their eyes again and cast envious looks against Cashel!'

'It is in the epistle to the *Galatians* where it is written "whatsoever a man soweth, that shall he reap",' Fidelma remarked.

'Nonsense!' snapped Finguine. 'Are you saying that you plead for the Uí Fidgente? Remember your duty is to Cashel. Your duty is to your brother!'

Fidelma flushed. 'You do not have to remind me of my duty, Prince of Cnoc Áine,' she replied; her voice was cold.

'Then remember the writing of Euripides, for I know that you are always fond of quoting the ancients. The gods give each his due at the time allotted. Due will be given to the Uí Fidgente and the allotted time draws near.'

The Prince of Cnoc Áine wheeled about and stalked away, his temper clearly getting the better of him.

Eadulf shook his head wonderingly. 'That is a young man with fire in his head,' he observed.

'He will plant thorns and expect to gather roses unless he is dissuaded,' agreed Fidelma seriously.

The winds had eased a little and they came to a sheltered battlement. Leaning on it, they stared down at the town below them. Although it was growing late, the town seemed to be alive; horses, riders, wagons, and people were thronging the streets.

'Like an audience waiting for the drama to commence,' Eadulf observed. 'It's becoming like a market day.'

Fidelma did not reply. She knew that Finguine, her cousin, spoke for many people who were now gathering below. Yet if he were so animated in his anger against the Uí Fidgente, what was he doing with Solam? She could not quite accept the idea that he merely escorted Solam to Cashel out of duty. Why were he and Solam riding in the woods searching for Brother Mochta and the Holy Relics? What did they know about them? No, there was something not right there.

She found her eyes suddenly dwelling on the roof of a warehouse on the far side of the market square. She blinked. The warehouse of Samradán.

'Samradán's warehouse,' mused Fidelma. 'I think part of our answer will be found there.'

'I am not sure that I understand,' Eadulf replied, following her gaze towards the building.

'No matter. Tonight, after dark, we are going to pay a visit to Samradán's warehouse. It is from there that this mystery started. I suddenly feel that it is from there that this mystery will be resolved.'

Chapter Twenty-One

Obediently, Eadulf followed Fidelma into the night, leaving the dark walls of the palace by a small side door away from the main gates to avoid the speculative gaze of the sentinels. Darkness had spread like a shroud over the town of Cashel. Clouds, scudding at hilltop level, obscured the moon.

However, now and then the round white orb of the bright new moon broke through sudden gaps in the clouds, bathing the scene momentarily with its ethereal light, almost as limpid as day. Apart from the twinkling lights from the buildings, they could smell the pungent smoke rising from numerous chimneys, marking the start of the contest to keep the autumnal chill at bay. There seemed little movement in the town. Most of the visitors crowding the streets a few hours before had taken themselves into the inns and taverns but the din of their entertainment was muted. A dog barked here and there and once or twice there came the scream of enraged cats disputing a territory.

Fidelma and Eadulf reached the market square without anyone observing them in the evening gloom.

'That's Samradán's warehouse.' Fidelma pointed unnecessarily, for the events of the attempted assassination were still clear in Eadulf's memory. The warehouse stood on the far side of the square in complete darkness. It appeared deserted.

They crossed the square quickly and Fidelma made immediately for the side door of the building which she had noticed before. It was shut and fastened.

'Is it barred from the inside?' asked Eadulf as Fidelma tried vainly to open it.

'No. I think it is merely locked.'

She used the word *glas*. Irish locksmiths were proficient in the manufacturing of locks, keys and even door chains to secure buildings and rooms. Some of them were very intricate. However, when he was a student at Tuaim Brecain, Eadulf had been taught the art of how to unpick a lock by the insertion of a strand of metal into the *poll-eochrach* or keyhole. He reached into his purse and drew out the small length of wire which he had come to carry and grinned in the darkness.

'Stand aside, then. You need an expert,' he announced, as he bent to the lock.

It took him longer than he expected and he sensed Fidelma's growing impatience. He was just beginning to wish that he had not been so confident when he heard the telltale click that told him that he had been successful.

He reached for the handle and the door swung inwards. Then he clambered to his feet.

Without a word, Fidelma went inside. He followed and closed the door carefully behind them.

The warehouse was in darkness and they could see nothing.

'I have flint and tinder and a stub of candle in my purse,' Eadulf whispered.

'We dare not use a light in case we are observed from outside,' returned Fidelma in the stillness. 'Wait a moment or two until our eyes adjust to this darkness.'

At the same time the moon broke through the clouds again and the gap seemed large enough to allow the light to bathe through the upper open windows of the warehouse, illuminating it. It was a shell of a building. There was no upper floor. Just the flat roof on which the would-be assassins had found shelter. At the back of the warehouse were bales packed high and stalls in which Samradán obviously stabled his dray horses. Taking up most of the space in the warehouse were the two heavy drays, or wagons, which Fidelma and Eadulf had last seen in the yard of Aona's inn.

The coverings on the wagons had been stripped back and she could see that only the tools were still piled in them.

'Samradán appears to have taken the bag of silver and the one of ore,' Fidelma muttered, looking around.

'That's to be expected. He has probably taken it to whoever reduces the ore into the silver.'

Fidelma groaned aloud.

'Are you ill?' asked Eadulf in alarm.

'Ill with stupidity,' sighed Fidelma. 'I had forgotten the process. The ore has to be burnt down in a smith's forge and the silver extracted.'

'Of course.'

'Last night, when I was looking through the wagon and found the sack of ore, some of it was already reduced to silver! It had already been extracted from the ore. Samradán had the services of a good smith before he set out from Imleach to Cashel.'

'When he left Imleach, he must have driven with the mined ore to a smith's,' Eadulf agreed. 'When he told us that he was proceeding north it was to mislead us.'

'So it seems. But why didn't the smith reduce all the ore to silver?'

The moon suddenly went behind a cloud, plunging the warehouse into darkness again.

Fidelma remained still. Eadulf had prompted a point. She smiled in the darkness. She realised that she already knew the answer. The moonlight bathed the interior once again, seeping through the high windows.

'Have you seen enough?' Eadulf asked.

'Wait a moment longer,' instructed Fidelma.

Fidelma moved around the warehouse, examining the odd box here and there before turning eventually to the stable area. By some bales she paused and abruptly dropped to one knee, reaching forward and tugging at something with her hand.

'Eadulf, come here and help me. I think this is a trapdoor to a cellar. Help me draw the bolt.'

Eadulf went to join her. Sure enough he could see the wood trap secured by two iron bolts. He moved them carefully back and swung the door open. Below was nothing but blackness. Not even the pale moonlight could penetrate into the gloom below.

He was about to say something but Fidelma held out a hand to stay him.

Something was moving in the darkness below.

'Is anyone there?' Fidelma called softly.

In the silence they could hear a rustling sound but no one replied.

'We may chance a candle but keep it covered until we see what is below in this cellar,' Fidelma instructed.

Eadulf rummaged in his leather purse and found the stub of candle and worked as rapidly as he could with his flint and tinder. It took several moments before he was able to make a spark ignite the tinder before lighting the candle.

He moved forward, holding the candle carefully, and leant over the edge of the trapdoor.

There were steps leading down to a small stone-walled room which was no higher than a tall man. It was about eight feet by eight feet in its dimensions. There was a straw palliasse in one corner. There was little else except . . . staring up at them with wide eyes above a gag, bound hand and foot, were the unmistakable features of Brother Bardán.

With an exclamation of surprise, Eadulf slipped down the steps followed by Fidelma.

While he held the candle, Fidelma reached for a knife in her *marsupium* and cut at the monk's wrist bonds and then removed his gag. While he breathed deeply, she severed the bonds around his ankles.

'Well now, Brother Bardán, what are you doing here?' she greeted almost jovially.

Brother Bardán was still trying to adjust to being unrestricted in his breathing. He coughed and gasped. Finally he found his voice.

'Samradán! That evil . . .'

He paused and frowned at Fidelma and Eadulf.

'How much do you know?'

'We have seen Brother Mochta and he has told us about your involvement in his . . . er, disappearance. I presume that you were on your way through the secret tunnels to see Brother Mochta when you met up with Samradán?'

Brother Bardán nodded swiftly. 'I was going to fetch Brother Mochta to bring him to the Prince of Cnoc Áine. He had promised to give us protection.'

'So, you had informed my cousin, Finguine, where Brother Mochta and the Holy Relics were?'

'Not exactly. I saw Finguine at the midnight Angelus and told him that I knew where Brother Mochta was hiding with the Holy Relics and the reason why – because he feared for their safety and his own life.'

'Did you mention that he was hiding in a cave?'

'Not the specific cave. I promised Finguine that I would fetch Brother Mochta and bring him to Finguine at a certain place on the following morning.'

'I saw you speaking with Finguine in the abbey chapel that night,' Eadulf recalled.

'What exactly was arranged between you?' asked Fidelma.

'I agreed that Finguine would protect the Relics and escort Mochta to Cashel.'

That explained why she had seen Finguine and his men in the woods but why had he been in the company of Solam?

'Did Finguine say anything to you about letting Solam in on this secret?' she asked.

'Solam? The *dálaigh* of the Uí Fidgente? I did my best to mislead him.'

'You told him about the crucifix.'

'It was nothing he did not know or could not learn.'

'And you falsely identified the severed forearm as being that of Brother Mochta to mislead us?'

'I knew you and Solam were searching for Mochta. We needed time to work out what we should do, Mochta and I. Who could we trust? When I explained matters to Finguine, he understood.'

'And you trusted Finguine rather than I?'

Brother Bardán was self-conscious.

'Do not tax yourself, Bardán. Mochta has told me why you were not forthcoming with me. Silly but I suppose it is understandable. It appears that you trust me now?'

'Samradán and his men said enough to make me believe that we had made a mistake in not trusting you.'

'Samradán! Yes; tell us how you came to be imprisoned here?' Eadulf demanded.

'To fulfil my promise to Finguine, I rose early and was hastening through the tunnel to Brother Mochta, in order to bring him to the rendezvous with Finguine, when I reached a chamber where there are two passages . . .'

'We know it,' interrupted Fidelma. 'Go on.'

For a moment, Brother Bardán looked startled. 'You know it . . . ?' He caught himself. His questions could be answered later. 'Well, when I reached there, I heard a noise in the other tunnel. I remember starting to go towards it. I feared for Mochta's safety and thought he had been discovered . . . then nothing. I think I was hit on the head and knocked unconscious because my head is still very sore.'

'You mentioned Samradán?' pressed Fidelma.

'Yes. I came to, bound and gagged, even as you found me, but I was lying under a tarpaulin in the back of a wagon. It was moving, bumping and rocking along a roadway. I remember hearing Samradán's voice. I know it well enough from the times he had stayed at the abbey.'

'Go on,' urged Eadulf.

'I slipped back into unconsciousness for a while. Then I came to again and, after some time, the wagoners stopped and I would say it was after noonday. They had stopped for food. That was when I heard them heartily cursing you and the Saxon brother for interfering and altering their plans. Then I heard a strange thing.'

'Strange, in what way?' encouraged Fidelma when he paused.

'There came the sound of horses, obviously coming up to where Samradán and his men were halted. I heard Samradán being greeted by name by someone who was obviously the leader of the horsemen. I did not recognise the voice. I can tell you that it was not a man of Muman who spoke. It was tinged with northern accents.

'Well, after the exchange of greetings I heard someone fiddling with the tarpaulin. I lay back with my eyes closed. A hand shook me and I continued to breathe deeply and not respond. A voice said: "He's still unconscious. We can speak freely." Then the tarpaulin was replaced and I could still hear their voices.'

'What was said?'

'Samradán started to bemoan that the attack had destroyed the smith's forge and he would have to find a new means of reducing the ore to silver. I have no idea what he meant. The man to whom he was speaking simply chuckled. He said that it could not be helped. Samradán's illegal activities were no concern of his nor of the Comarb. Samradán protested and said that the *rígdomna* approved of them and that he acted under his protection. The other rejoined that so far as he knew, Samradán was just a messenger between the *rígdomna* and the Comarb.'

Fidelma leant forward eagerly. 'Both men referred to the "*rígdomna*"?'

'Yes. The man said that whatever Samradán was doing, it was no concern of his. He had his orders. He was answerable only to the power of the Comarb . . . At that moment they moved on out of the range of my hearing.'

Fidelma gave a repressed groan of annoyance. 'And you are certain that the title of Comarb was mentioned?' she persisted.

Brother Bardán was not offended by her question but said quietly: 'Do you think that I do not know the significance of that title? There are only two Comarb in all the five kingdoms – the Comarb of Ailbe and the Comarb of Patrick.'

Eadulf whistled softly as he suddenly understood why Fidelma was so tense.

'What happened then?' Fidelma said, after a moment. 'Did you hear more?'

'After a while, I heard the riders leaving. A short time passed and the tarpaulin was flung aside. It was Samradán and I had no time to feign unconsciousness again. Samradán took off the gag and threatened to replace it if I said anything. He then gave me drink and some food and replaced the gag immediately afterwards. Doubtless, he thought I had only just recovered and had not heard the meeting with the horsemen. He replaced the tarpaulin. Time passed and off we went again.

'It was a terrible journey. I sensed rather than felt it was nightfall. Everything was dark. The wagons stopped. I dozed fitfully. There was no movement at all. Now and then I awoke and thought that I heard voices. There was some movement and at one point, I thought I heard your voice, Sister Fidelma.'

Fidelma grimaced bitterly. 'You did. You were stopped in an inn at the Well of Ara and spent the night until dawn. Then Samradán and his wagons came on here. I must have been within a few feet of you last night.'

Brother Bardán regarded her with curiosity.

'What has happened?' he demanded. 'How did you find me?'

'Continue with your story first,' Fidelma urged.

'Well, you were right. When the wagons finally halted, they were within a large store house. I was taken out and placed here, in this cellar-like room and here I have stayed in the dark until you discovered me.'

Fidelma sat back, her mind working rapidly. 'Well, the first thing to do is to get you out of here Brother Bardán and to a place of safety.'

'What danger am I in, Sister?'

'I think you are in considerable danger. Had Samradán mentioned your presence to the raiders, when he spoke to them, you would already be dead. Fortunately, as much as the raiders thought that Samradán's illegal mining was none of their business, Samradán thought the same. He thought that you had merely stumbled on his illegal mining activity. As it is, you are witness to a conspiracy which places you in the gravest of danger. We shall take you to a friend and you must stay there until tomorrow evening.'

'Why tomorrow evening?'

'Because then we will come for you and smuggle you into the palace at Cashel. I do not want anyone to know of your existence here.'

'Samradán will know when he finds me missing.'

'A good point,' Eadulf muttered.

'I have not overlooked it. Once Brother Bardán is lodged safely, we will go and have a word with Samradán.'

'But what of Brother Mochta and the Holy Relics?' protested Bardán. 'What of Finguine's protection? Did Brother Mochta receive it?'

Fidelma shook her head and smiled thinly. 'At the moment, you are under the protection of Cashel and you will find Brother Mochta in the place where we are taking you – together with the Holy Relics.'

They climbed out of the cellar and Eadulf replaced the trapdoor behind them and shot home the bolts. Then he reluctantly blew out the candle. The clouds seemed to be dispersing, however, and the moon, still bright and full, was this time constant. Fidelma led the way through the shadows to the door and they exited behind the warehouse.

With Eadulf helping Brother Bardán, who was not able to walk well, having been tied for so long, Fidelma conducted them as quickly as Bardán's weakness allowed, from the back of the warehouse along the outskirts of the town, trying to avoid bringing themselves to the attention of the guard-dogs whose barking could still be heard not far off.

'Thank God, it is probably a wolf or some other scavenger venturing too near the town limits that has distracted their attention,' whispered Fidelma, as they paused a moment for Brother Bardán to recover from his cramp.

It took them fifteen minutes to reach their destination: the house of the female recluse, Della.

Fidelma knocked quietly on her door, giving her the special signal which she had arranged.

Hardly a moment passed before Della appeared in the doorway. Her face was pale and fearful in the light of the hanging lantern inside the door.

'Fidelma! Thank God you have come!'

'What is it, Della?' asked Fidelma, surprised at the trembling anxiety of her friend.

'It is the man whom you brought here . . . Brother Mochta . . .'

Fidelma led the way into the house and stood facing Della. The woman was trembling almost in hysteria. Something was frightening her.

'What about Brother Mochta? Where is he?'

She suddenly noticed that the room was in chaos.

'He has been taken!' gasped Della.

'Taken?'

'He and that reliquary he was always clasping. He and the box were taken away. There was nothing that I could do.'

Fidelma reached out her hands to grasp the woman's shoulders.

'Get a grip on yourself, Della. You are unharmed anyway. This–' she waved one hand to encompass the chaos – 'can easily be tidied and repaired. But what of Mochta and the reliquary?'

Della caught her breath and steadied herself. 'You left him in my care and he has been taken.'

Fidelma struggled to retain her patience. 'So you say. Taken by whom?'

'By your cousin. By Finguine, Prince of Cnoc Áine.'

Fidelma let her arms drop from Della's shoulders. Her expression was one of dismay.

Brother Bardán's reaction was of relief. 'So you brought Brother Mochta here with the Relics? Well, thank God that Finguine has finally taken him into protection. We can rest easy now.'

Fidelma swung round as if to rebuke him. Instead she hesitated and said quietly: 'Can we?' She turned back to Della. 'Who else came here with Finguine? Was it Finguine who destroyed your possessions?'

'No, a warrior. Finguine did rebuke him and say it was unnecessary. The warrior was the leader of the band who accompanied the Prince of the Uí Fidgente when he rode into Cashel. I recognised him when he rode with Donennach.'

It was Eadulf who exclaimed in disbelief: 'Gionga? Do you mean Gionga, the captain of the bodyguard of Donennach?'

Della shrugged miserably. 'The Uí Fidgente. I do not know his name. All I know is that when Donennach rode into Cashel, that man was in charge of the bodyguard of the Prince.'

Fidelma stood quietly, as if trying to recover her scattered thoughts. 'I think we have a problem,' she said quietly.

Brother Bardán was regarding them in bewilderment. 'I do not understand.'

Fidelma did not respond but looked at Della and smiled tightly. 'I must ask a further favour of you, Della. Eadulf and I must go now. I need you to look after Brother Bardán here until Eadulf or I come for him. This will be tomorrow evening.'

'I can't!' protested Della. 'You see what they have done . . .'

'Lightning does not strike twice in the same place, Della. Now that they have Brother Mochta and the reliquary, no one will think of looking here for Brother Bardán.'

Brother Bardán's face continued to be a mask of confusion. 'I do not understand at all. Why should I hide now? Finguine is protecting Brother Mochta and has the Holy Relics safe.'

Fidelma did not answer him and continued to look at her friend. 'Della, I need you to do this for me.'

The woman gazed into Fidelma's eyes for a moment or two and then sighed. 'Very well. But, like the Brother here, I wish I understood.'

'Understand, both of you, that the well-being of this kingdom of Muman depends on doing exactly as I have told you.'

'Very well.'

Fidelma opened the door and motioned Eadulf to follow her back into the darkness of the night. Della came to the door and forced a smile on her anxious features.

'Solitude is the best society and a short abstinence from solitude urges the sweet return,' she said.

Fidelma returned her smile. She felt sorrow for the woman whose life she knew had been filled with so much unhappiness. She reached out her hand and touched the other's arm.

'We are all of us condemned to solitude, Della,' she said, 'but some of our sheltering walls are merely our own skins and thus there is no door to exit from solitude into life. We are thus condemned to solitude for all our lives.'

They left the house of the reclusive former prostitute and walked back along the night-darkened alleys of the town.

'How did Finguine know where you had hidden Brother Mochta and the reliquary?' demanded Eadulf.

'Remember you told me that you saw Nion in the tavern nearby? The fact that we had ridden out of the side street here was duly reported to Finguine. It would not take much investigation by Finguine to discover that I have one particular friend here and that is Della. He must have put two and two together. He must have realised that I had recovered the reliquary and Brother Mochta after he had failed to find them.'

'Yes, but why take Gionga with him? Finguine claims that he hates the Uí Fidgente. I confess to being as confused as Brother Bardán.'

'Remember that I told you of the game of *tomus*? Well, several more pieces have now come together. Yet I still need that single piece around which all will fit. Samradán will provide that piece. That's where we will go now – to see that greedy merchant.'

'Do you know where Samradán lives?' asked Eadulf.

'Yes. Donndubháin pointed the house out to me when we were examining his warehouse the other week.'

They walked along a back path, away from the main street of the town. After a while, Fidelma halted to indicate a house. It was a rich, two-storey construction of timber. There was no light emanating from the building. They had approached it from the rear. Fidelma was about to move through the backyard to the rear door of the house when there came a rustling sound and then a low whine. Screwing his eyes up in the gloom, Eadulf saw a dark shape on the ground and caught at Fidelma's arm.

'Samradán's guard-dog!' he warned.

Fidelma could see the shape as well. The dog lay by a post and the rustling appeared to be the leather thong, by which it was tethered, moving as it turned. It appeared actually to be sleeping, whimpering as it lay there.

'Some guard-dog,' muttered Eadulf. 'But good for us that it is still tethered and sleeping.'

'It means that we will have to go round to the front of the house,' replied Fidelma.

Eadulf led the way along the side of the building. The dog was not disturbed. But on reaching the corner he stopped abruptly and motioned Fidelma to move back into the shadows.

'There is a horseman outside the house,' he whispered.

Fidelma moved cautiously forward to find a vantage point.

A tall figure sat astride a horse, resting slightly forward in the saddle, examining Samradán's house with some intensity. He was alone.

The moon shone brightly enough. There were almost no shadows at all.

Even in the gloom Fidelma would have recognised her cousin, Finguine, *rígdomna* Cnoc Áine.

Chapter Twenty-Two

Even as Fidelma watched, Finguine straightened in his saddle, as if he had come to a decision, and pulled on the reins of his horse, turning and sending the animal trotting down the main street towards the towering fortress above the town. Fidelma and Eadulf waited until he had gone before they moved out of the shadows.

'Why is Finguine hanging around Samradán's house?' whispered Eadulf. 'He seems to be keeping bad company. First Solam and then Gionga and now the merchant.'

'Let us hope that we can persuade Samradán to answer our questions honestly,' Fidelma rejoined.

Eadulf glanced up at the house.

'The front is in darkness as well. Perhaps he is not here?'

'With his dog still tethered at the back?' She moved forward and some instinct made her try the door of the house first. It was not secured and swung open. She entered cautiously and motioned Eadulf to follow.

They had entered into the single ground-floor room which served as living room, kitchen and store room. A short stairway led to the sleeping quarters. There was a fire glowing in the central hearth and its radiance gave sufficient illumination to the room for Fidelma to see that it was deserted.

'What did I say?' muttered Eadulf. 'He is not here.'

Fidelma cast him an irritable glance. 'Then he can't be far away for the fire has been banked recently. Light a candle from it.'

Eadulf did so. Fidelma was already moving around the room, examining it.

'I can't see what you hope to find here?' muttered Eadulf, his eye nervously on the door. 'And Samradán could come back any moment. What then?'

Fidelma did not reply. Having examined the room, she went to the back door. It was unbolted from the inside. She opened it and looked out. The dog was still lying by the post, stretched out and whining in sleep. It was then Fidelma realised that there was something odd about the animal's behaviour. At night, dogs came alive in Muman for then they were untethered and sent to guard the houses against predators, both human and animal. Why was this animal stretched in sleep, and an unnatural sleep at that, for the sound it made was quite pitiful.

Ignoring Eadulf's protest, she walked quickly to where it was chained and bent down.

Eadulf, coming up behind, determined to persuade her to leave. In his haste he came running out with the candle flickering in one hand.

Fidelma, bending by the dog, ordered him curtly to bring the candle nearer. The beast did not stir. There were flecks of foam around its muzzle.

Fidelma glanced up at her companion. 'This animal has been drugged.' She came to her feet so abruptly that Eadulf started back. 'For what purpose was it drugged?' she demanded. Eadulf was quiet for he deemed it a rhetorical question.

She contemplated the darkened house.

Then she was hurrying back to it with Eadulf following in her wake, wondering what on earth was possessing her.

She paused in the main room which they had just quit and looked swiftly around. Then she muttered something under her breath and headed for the stairway to the floor above.

Eadulf shrugged helplessly as if expressing his perplexity to some unseen audience and followed.

In the sleeping quarters above the stairs Fidelma had come to a halt and was staring at an object stretched on the bed.

Behind her, Eadulf raised his candle high.

Samradán the merchant lay sprawled across the bed. There was blood all over him and the haft of a knife was still buried in his chest. His eyes were open but glazed in death.

'Too late,' muttered Fidelma. 'Someone has decided that Samradán might lead us to the truth.'

'What truth?' demanded Eadulf in desperation.

She infuriated him by not replying. Her thoughts were elsewhere. She bent down and examined the knife. There was nothing to identify it from a hundred similar knives. There were no distinguishing marks on it at all; nothing to point to its ownership. There was nothing she could see to identify the killer.

'Finguine!' Eadulf decided. 'He was leaving when we arrived. He was in league with Solam and Gionga. God! Now I see why you were upset that Finguine had taken Brother Mochta and the reliquary.'

She nodded absently. Then something caught her eye. In falling back, Samradán must have clutched at his assailant's clothing for in his twisted fingers was a piece of cloth, part of a linen shirt. She realised, with all the blood about, the assailant must be splattered with it. She reached forward and levered the cloth from Samradán's fingers, realising that there was something attached to it.

It was a small, silver, solar emblem. A brooch picked out in semi-precious garnets. There were five garnets on each of the radiating arms of the emblem. She quickly placed it in her *marsupium* after showing it to Eadulf.

'It must belong to the murderer,' Eadulf said, stating the obvious.

'You have not seen this before?' queried Fidelma.

'It seems familiar,' agreed Eadulf.

'It is the central piece in our game of *tomus*.' She smiled, before returning to the body to examine it further.

Eadulf's hand suddenly squeezing her shoulder made her start. She glanced round and was about to rebuke him for frightening her when she saw that he had placed a finger to his lips. He motioned with his head towards the stairs.

The sound of someone moving in the room below could clearly be heard.

Fidelma stood up. 'Be ready,' she whispered.

Footsteps could be heard ascending the stairs. They saw the point of a sword appear first and then the head. It was Donndubháin.

The young heir-apparent of Cashel stared at them in surprise.

'What are you up to?' he demanded, recovering from his apparent surprise. He ascended the final stairs, sheathing his sword. 'I thought I heard . . .'

His eyes fell on Samradán's body and widened.

'What happened?'

Fidelma did not reply immediately.

'What are you doing here?' she demanded at last.

'I was riding by. With all the people coming into Cashel for the hearing, I thought that I ought to check the watches around the town. I was in the back alley when I saw a light and noticed the back door was open and I saw figures moving. The dog seemed asleep and wondered whether there was something the matter. So I came in. I was downstairs and I heard a movement above. And here you are.' He glanced dispassionately at Samradan's body. 'Did you kill him?'

'Of course not!' snapped Eadulf. 'We saw Fin—'

'We also saw the dog and the door open,' Fidelma interrupted, lying naturally. 'We have only just arrived ourselves.'

'A robbery?'

Fidelma pointed to a leather purse still tied to Samradán's belt.

Donndubháin leant across and opened it. He drew out a handful of silver coins.

'Not a robbery then,' he mused. 'It can't be something to do with the assassination? What would Samradán have to do with that?'

'There seems to be nothing here to enlighten us,' Fidelma said.

Eadulf was puzzled as to why Fidelma was being so frugal with the facts.

She turned down the stairway to the ground floor.

Eadulf and Donndubháin followed.

'If we can leave this matter in your hands,' Fidelma told him, 'Eadulf and I will return to the palace.'

'I will alert the watch,' the heir-apparent agreed. He went to the back door where he had left his horse and on the threshold paused as if a thought had struck him. 'Have you searched Samradán's stables at the back there? Perhaps it was robbery after all? Something to do with what he kept there?'

'I thought Samradán kept all his trade goods at his warehouse on the market square?' Fidelma said.

'Whether he does or not, I would not know. But there is a stable which belongs to him on the other side of the stream there.'

He pointed towards the dark shadow of a building at the back of the house.

'Then we'd better see if there is anything there that can enlighten us,' Fidelma replied.

Donndubháin took down a lamp and lit it from the fire.

He had left his horse tethered by the back gate of the yard and they passed the still drugged animal lying by its post. There was a small enclosure through which a stream passed, providing water for the house. Beyond it was a dark building, not large at all.

'I didn't know that this barn belonged to Samradán,' Fidelma mused as thcy approached the building. Donndubháin led the way and opened the door for them.

Inside were a couple of stalls. Two horses were stabled inside.

'I didn't know Samradán owned as many horses,' Donndubháin muttered. 'But these are not dray horses . . . they are thoroughbreds.'

Fidelma's gaze had encompassed the stables. There was certainly nothing else in there but the horses and tackle. The pungent smell of leather and the faint odours of hay and barley were almost overpowering to the senses.

Fidelma went to the larger of the two animals, a great chestnut mare. She could see some long-healed scars on one shoulder and flank. Old wounds. The animal had been used as a war horse. She leant forward and patted its muzzle. Then she opened the stalls and went in. The mare stood calmly, allowing her hands to traverse its warm, sweaty coat. She glanced down at its hooves.

'Not the sort of animal a mere merchant might own,' observed Donndubháin.

'A war horse, so it seems,' she agreed. 'But the other animal is not.'

Fidelma turned her attention to the second horse. 'It is a strong and well-bred mare but not a horse for battle. A good riding horse though.'

She patted it and turned back.

She found that Donndubháin was examining a saddle and bridle nearby.

'Look, Fidelma,' he said eagerly, 'this is a warrior's equipment. Look, there is no mistaking it.'

Eadulf had already begun examining the richly equipped saddle. It was well ornamented.

'The Prince is right,' he muttered. 'Here . . .'

Attached to the saddle was a small, long sack. It was the shape of a quiver but not a quiver. It was where a warrior might carry a spare supply of arrows. Eadulf had undone the strings and drawn an arrow out.

'Isn't this . . . ?' he began.

Fidelma took it and examined it. 'Yes. The arrows have Cnoc Áine markings. The same arrows which our assassin friend, the archer, used. They are the same as those made by Nion the smith.'

'And look at this . . .' Donndubháin pointed to a silver emblem among the ornaments on the saddle.

'Why,' Eadulf said excitedly. 'Isn't that a boar which is the emblem of the Prince of the Uí Fidgente?'

'Then we were right!' cried Donndubháin. 'Do you remember that we wondered if the assassins must have come on horseback and tethered them behind the trees at the back of Samradán's warehouse? Didn't we say that a third person must have led the horses away when the assassins were killed. And here they are, showing that Samradán was involved.'

'Yet Samradán had been in Imleach for at least a week at that time,' pointed out Fidelma.

'Well, he could have instructed one of his men to place the horses here. An accomplice.' Her cousin was momentarily crestfallen.

'There is much that needs to be considered,' agreed Fidelma. 'The appearance of these harnesses certainly tends to clarify the puzzle. Is there anything in that saddle bag?'

She pointed to the small leather bag that was attached. Donndubháin undid the straps and opened it. He began to take out some items of clothing.

'There's nothing here but clothes,' Eadulf said, in disappointment.

'There's nothing that tells us anything apart from the Uí Fidgente emblem which says a lot,' observed Donndubháin. 'But that is enough.'

Fidelma reached for the bag and peered into it, feeling with her hand inside before returning it to him.

'So it seems.'

They left the stable and walked slowly back to the gate of the yard. They paused by Donndubháin's horse.

'Well, I will alert the watch about this murder,' Donndubháin said, untying his horse. 'Will you wait here until I raise the guard so that I may accompany you back to the palace?'

'No,' Fidelma replied. 'We will make our own way back. It is not far. Don't worry, we shall be safe, Donndubháin.'

They watched him swing up and ride off into the night and then began to walk slowly back to the house. They passed through it and out into the main street. Isolated figures were still moving here and there, some late-night revellers scurrying back to their own houses from the inns and taverns. No one challenged nor bothered them as they continued towards the tall walls of the palace.

'Well,' ventured Eadulf, 'the horses now prove completely that Samradán was involved. They must have been there since the attempted assassination.'

'No. They have been there less than half an hour,' Fidelma contradicted him with confidence. 'Their coats were still sweaty from the exertion of being led from wherever they were hidden to being placed there.'

Eadulf's eyes widened. Then he was more amazed to hear Fidelma break into a soft chuckle. She paused by the light of a tavern and held out something for him to see.

He peered closely at it. It was a tiny silver coin.

'I found it tucked away in a corner of the bag. It had been overlooked.'

'What is it?' demanded Eadulf.

'A coin of Ailech, the capital of the northern Uí Néill kings. It is called a *píss*.'

'What does it mean?'

'My dear, Eadulf–' he had not heard such contentment in her voice for some days now – 'tonight has shown me the truth in this matter. My mentor, the Brehon Morann, once said that if you eliminate the impossible, whatever remains, however improbable, it must be the answer. I know who is behind the assassination and conspiracy. In spite of attempts to mislead me and, indeed, to lay false trails which, I confess, did confuse me until this evening, I have sighted the fox!'

Chapter Twenty-Three

The Great Hall of Cashel was crowded as Fidelma entered with Eadulf. Everyone was dressed formally for the occasion. Even Eadulf was wearing his best apparel and carrying his pilgrim's staff which he now used to enhance his status. It was an egocentricity on his part.

Eadulf smiled at Fidelma as he turned to take his place with those members of the court who were there merely as observers. Great importance was attached to procedure in the Irish courts and Eadulf had come to understand many of what he had regarded previously as mysteries.

Fidelma had crossed to the centre of the hall to take a seat alongside Solam, the *dálaigh* of the Uí Fidgente. He sat next to Donennach, his Prince. Litigants always sat with their advocates in what was the *airecht airnaide*, the court of waiting.

Directly opposite and facing them were three chairs behind a long, low table on which were piled several law texts. These chairs were reserved for the Brehons or judges. They constituted the *airecht*, the court itself. Behind the seats for the judges, on a dais at the head of the hall, was Colgú, seated on his ornately carved chair of office, and next to him, on his right-hand side, was Ségdae, who sat not as abbot but as bishop and Comarb of Ailbe, the First Apostle of the Faith in Muman. On the left-hand side, sat Colgú's *ollamh*, Cerball, his chief bard and adviser. These three, the foremost men of the kingdom, were known as the *cúl-airecht*, the back court, overseeing that justice was done.

To the right of the King's seat were benches on which sat the *táeb-airecht,* the side court, which constituted scribes and historians who were to record the events, together with the petty kings and nobles, led by Donndubháin, the *tanist*, Finguine of Cnoc Áine and others who were to witness the proceedings to ensure that the kingdom acquitted itself properly and according to law.

On the left-hand side was the *airecht fo leithe*, the court apart, in which were gathered all the potential witnesses. Here was seated, among others, Brother Mochta. It had surprised Eadulf to find that Brother Mochta had been named by Solam as his principal witness against Muman. Even more surprising was the fact that the reliquary of Ailbe had been placed under safekeeping. Brother Madagan was also seated, ready to be called as a witness, as were Brother Bardán, Nion the *bó-aire* of Imleach, Gionga and Capa.

Eadulf saw that the appearance of Mochta and the reliquary did not surprise Fidelma. She had assumed her seat quietly and sat, hands folded in her lap, gazing before her without focusing on any one object. Eadulf felt annoyed with her. Since she had revealed that she believed she knew the answer to the mystery, she had steadfastly refused to explain anything further to him. He felt unhappy. These last weeks he had the sense that Fidelma was becoming more irritable than usual, less open to confiding in him. He had come to regard himself as her 'soul friend', an *anam-chara* which every religious of Éireann had to discuss their temporal and spiritual problems with. It made him unhappy when she did not confide in him.

Colgú's steward came forward with his staff of office and banged it three times on the floor to bring the court to order. It drew Eadulf from his sad speculations.

The Brehon of Cashel, Dathal, was the first of the judges to enter the court, according to protocol, because the court was sitting in Cashel. Dathal was not known as the 'nimble one' for nothing. His nickname applied to the quickness of his mind in legal matters. He was not a young man, but his hair had not yet turned grey. His dark eyes were penetrating and moved rapidly around, missing nothing; if they looked directly at you they seemed to penetrate right through. He was thin, lean and almost sallow. He was quick to anger and he did not accept fools gladly, especially if they were advocates pleading before him. He moved rapidly to the judges' bench and took his seat on the right-hand side.

Fachtna, the Brehon of the Uí Fidgente, followed quickly, taking his seat on the left. He was a little older than Dathal. He was also tall and almost emaciated in his appearance. His flesh was drawn tightly over his bony features so that it resembled more of a skull than a face. His skin was parchment-like with a crimson slash on both cheekbones. The eyes were grey, restless, and his lips were a thin slit of red. His hair was grey, parted in the centre, and drawn smoothly back and gathered with a ribbon. He gave the appearance of being in need of a good meal.

Last came the Brehon Rumann of Fearna who took the central seat. Indeed, he would not only be chief of the judges but would undoubtedly make the decisions, for it seemed likely to all who gathered in the Great Hall that the judgements of the Brehons of Cashel and the Uí Fidgente would be biased to reflect the wishes of their respective Princes.

As the Brehon Rumann moved to his seat, he did not look like a judge at all. He was short in stature and corpulent in his face and figure. He wore his silver hair long so that it fell in curls around the nape of his neck. The flesh of his benign features was like the fresh, pink skin of a child, newly scrubbed. The lips were red and full as if he were given to enhancing them with berry juice. The eyes were hazel yet with a brightness that made one think at first glance that they were of a pale colour. He had a general air of geniality about him. In spite of his companions, it was Rumann who dominated the scene. He exuded an air of quiet authority that commanded silence.

When he had seated himself and a hush had fallen in the Great Hall, the steward banged once more on the floor with his staff of office. Abbot Ségdae rose. He raised his hand, holding up his first, third and fourth finger to represent the Holy Trinity. Eadulf had almost grown used to this difference to the Roman usage where the thumb, first and second finger were held up in the same symbolism.

'*Benedictio benedicatur per Jesum Christum Dominum nostrum. Surgite!*'

The blessing and the instruction to the court to 'rise' marked the beginning of the proceedings.

The Brehon Rumann duly banged the table before him with a small wooden gavel. His voice was soft but commanding.

'The five paths of judgement are embarked upon. This day was fixed for this hearing and the proper path of judgement was chosen. The securities have been given by the King of Muman and the Prince of the Uí Fidgente. Before we come to the *tacrae*, the opening statements of the advocates, I have to ask both advocates whether they are ready to proceed. It is their right at this time to make any request for a *taurbaid,* a postponement, of these proceedings.'

He looked first at Fidelma and then at Solam.

'I need not remind you that any postponement at this point must be supported by a good reason. The observance of a religious festival, an illness, a bereavement or other such matters will constitute a reasonable excuse.'

When he paused, Solam smiled officiously. 'We stand ready to press our case,' he announced.

'And we are ready to respond to it,' replied Fidelma.

'Excellent. As you may have realised, I shall be the voice of all three judges here today. You will address your remarks to me. As neither of you have appeared in my court before, I feel that I must tell you how I expect you to behave. I do not tolerate bad pleading in my court and I adhere to the letter of the *Cóic Conara Fugill.*'

Eadulf knew well that this was the main book of instruction on procedures known as 'the five paths of judgement'.

'I will order any advocate to pay a fine who speaks in an undertone so that I cannot hear clearly what has been said; any advocate who tries to incite the court, or who loses their temper, or who argues in too loud a voice and abuses anyone; any advocate who opposes a known fact or starts to praise themselves. The fine for all such offences will be as prescribed by law – the sum of one *séd*.'

A *séd* was the value of one cow. It was a harsh fine. Inwardly Eadulf groaned. The Brehon Rumann was not going to be an easy judge before whom to argue.

There was almost a breathless silence in the court now.

'Let the *tacrae* begin.'

Solam rose to his feet, nervous, birdlike in his motions. 'Before I begin my plea, I must raise a protest.'

The hush that had fallen was like a moment of calm before a storm breaks with all its fury.

The tones of the Brehon Rumann became icy. 'A *protest*?'

'It is ordained in the procedures governing a court that litigants should sit with their advocates. Next to me sits the Prince of the Uí Fidgente, who is the plaintiff in this case.'

A scowl passed across the cherubic-like features of the Brehon, turning that soft, chubby countenance into a hard, angry glare. 'Is there a point to this?'

'Behind you sits the other litigant in this case, the defendant, who is the King of Muman.'

Behind the judges, Eadulf could see Colgú stir with embarrassment. The King was not allowed to speak during the proceedings except in exceptional circumstances.

Brehon Rumann's eyes had widened. For a moment he seemed about to protest and then Fachtna, the judge of the Uí Fidgente, with a sardonic smile of approval towards Solam, leant across to Rumann.

'The advocate has a strong legal point in procedural rules. A litigant must be seated with his advocate. No exceptions are made in the texts. As defendant the King should be seated next to his *dálaigh*.'

'Yet the same rules stipulate where the King must sit,' pointed out Dathal from the other side of Rumann. 'We are in the kingdom of Muman and at the King's seat of Cashel. How can the King not sit in the place ordained by law?'

'Yet the law says that his place, as defendant, is with his advocate,' insisted Fachtna with his irritating smile. 'The King is expected to observe the law with the meanest members of his kingdom.'

Rumann raised his hands as if to pacify his fellow judges. 'I would argue that one cannot impose law on the King. I can refer to heptads and triads of the ancient law books which advise that no one can stand in surety for a King for if the King defaults then the person standing surety has no means to secure compensation, for the King's honour is more important than any claim.'

'Are you saying that the Prince of the Uí Fidgente is incorrect in bringing a legal claim against the King of Muman?' demanded Fachtna, his voice brittle. 'Are you saying that no legal claim can be made against a King? If that is so, we are wasting time sitting in judgement here. No, I cannot agree to that argument.'

Fidelma rose and cleared her throat.

'You wish to add something, Fidelma of Cashel?' asked the Brehon Rumann, watching her with interest.

'Learned judges–' Fidelma bowed her head to the Brehons – 'while, of course, the Brehon Rumann is correct in that the law advises that people should not stand surety for a King, it does not forbid it.'

Fachtna actually smiled broadly. 'Do I understand that the advocate of Cashel agrees with me? That the King must be recognised as a litigant, as the defendant in this case, and must sit before the judges and not behind them?'

'There are three questions there, Fachtna,' replied Fidelma solemnly. 'If you are supporting Solam's protest then my answer is – no, I do not agree. And your last question does not therefore follow from your first question.'

Fachtna was puzzled, not sure as to where Fidelma was leading.

Rumann made a curious hissing of his breath demonstrating his vexation at not understanding her answers. 'The advocate for Cashel should make herself clear. What is she saying?' he grumbled.

'May I remind the learned Brehons,' went on Fidelma, 'that the law texts do describe the method of balancing a King's honour with his legal accountability?'

Rumann's eyes narrowed in his chubby face. 'Remind us,' he invited shortly. There seemed a hidden threat in his voice.

'It is given in a text on the four divisions of distraint. For legal purposes the King may be represented by a substitute, the *aithech fortha*, and through the substitute it is possible to make a legal claim against the King without the King having to endure the dishonour of removing himself from office or suffering distraint.' Fidelma smiled serenely at the Brehons. 'I would have thought, instead of making a protest at this time, before this case came before you, the learned Solam would have, on behalf of the plaintiff, ensured the King was so represented here; that a substitute be appointed to sit in this chair–'

she indicated the empty chair where the defendant should have sat – 'as symbolic of representing the King.'

A ripple of amusement went through the great hall in support of Fidelma.

Solam was flushing in anger. He began to rise.

The Brehon Rumann gestured for Solam to remain seated while Brehon Dathal was clearly delighted.

'Does anyone in the court object to a substitute being seated in the chair of the defendant?' he asked. 'Does anyone object to a substitute who will be the physical representative of the King being seated before us?'

Brehon Rumann sniffed in annoyance. It was clear that he had not recalled the law and while Fidelma had scored a legal point, Eadulf could see that it had not placed her in good standing with the Chief Brehon. The displeasure of the Brehon Fachtna was obvious to everyone.

'I see no reason to simply place a body in the chair. We may proceed on the grounds that the empty seat is symbolically representing the kingship of Muman.' Rumann's voice was peevish. 'Now, are there any other protests or counter-claims or may we proceed to the substance of these proceedings?'

Solam cleared his throat and rose again hurriedly.

'I am in accord with you, noble Brehon,' he began, forcing a smile, as he attempted to pour oil on the troubled waters he had raised. 'I believe in the formality of these procedures for which you argued in your opening address to this court. Correct procedure is no cause for levity.'

'We are so pleased that you agree with the court's ruling,' interposed the Brehon Dathal sarcastically.

Brehon Rumann's face had assumed a stony composure and it was not clear whether Solam's attempt to mollify his irritability had succeeded or not.

There was a pause and when Rumann did not say anything further, Solam continued.

'Learned judges, this is a serious matter that I bring before you. It is no less than a case of attempted *duinetháide* of assassination of the Prince of the Uí Fidgente. The charge is made against the King of Muman and those acting on his behalf and at his request. We allege that Colgú of Cashel conspired with others to kill Prince Donennach!'

Solam paused and glanced around, as if expecting some reaction to his opening statement. The silence in the Great Hall was marked. There was no reaction. Everyone in Cashel knew what the hearing was about.

Brehon Rumann was still snappish. 'You will doubtless proceed to tell us the facts behind your charge?' he asked acidly.

Solam adjusted his composure. 'Learned judges–' he paused and cleared his throat, then pressed on – 'it was on the feastday of Ailbe, the patron of this kingdom, that my Prince, Donennach, came with a small party to Cashel to discuss ways and means of cementing the friendship between his dynasty of the Dál gCais and the Eóghanacht of Cashel. Colgú of Cashel had met Donennach at the Well of Ara with a small retinue and conducted him and his party to Cashel. Donennach came in peace and friendship and in innocence.'

Solam's excitable voice grew in strength. He flung out his arm for dramatic effect.

'The Prince's party rode into the market square in the town below this castle's walls. Unsuspecting of the fate that had been planned for him, my Prince rode forward. Without warning, the arrow from an assassin's bow struck him. God be praised! The bowman's hand was ill-guided. Perhaps the breath of God blew on the flight of the arrow . . . perhaps the eye of the Almighty One . . .'

Brehon Rumann raised a hand in exasperation. 'I would suggest that the advocate leaves aside speculation on the actions of God in this case and concentrate on the actions of men,' he advised.

Solam swallowed hard, his Adam's apple bobbing nervously.

Fidelma lowered her eyes and compressed her lips for the sight of the blinking, confused Solam was comical.

'Er, just so. Just so. The bowman's hand . . . the arrow did not strike its intended target. The arrow hit Donennach in the thigh. A bad wound, yes, but not life-threatening and, as you see–' he gestured to where Donennach was sitting impatiently in his chair – 'my Prince recovered.'

'Well, it would seem obvious that he did not die,' remarked Brehon Dathal loudly. A ripple of amusement spread through the Great Hall.

Solam paused and blinked. Then he struggled on.

'There was pandemonium. Donennach had fallen from his horse and thus prevented the assassin getting a further shot. Gionga, the captain of Prince Donennach's bodyguard, ever alert, had seen the direction from which the arrow had been fired. He rode his horse across the market square and found two assassins who had placed themselves on the roof of the warehouse. They were attempting to escape to their horses. Gionga, faced with two implacable enemies, was forced to cut them down with his sword.

'The two bodies were brought before my Prince, and before other witnesses. The truth of the identity of the assassins was to be seen on their bodies. One of them wore the collar of the Order of the Golden Chain which everyone knows is the élite bodyguard of the King of Cashel . . .'

Solam was apparently fond of dramatic pauses but again he was met in total silence for nothing he had said so far was new to anyone in the Great Hall.

'The second man was a brother of a senior cleric of the abbey of Ailbe, the primacy of this kingdom. This man carried with him one of the Holy Relics of Ailbe, the Ailbe crucifix, to be precise. Our contention is that the Keeper of the Holy Relics had given the crucifix to him, for this Holy Relic was to be symbolic that this assassination had the blessing of the Comarb of Ailbe. I shall demonstrate that the assassin carried this crucifix during this nefarious work as a talisman. The Holy Relic could only have left the abbey of Imleach with the approval of the Comarb of Ailbe. This compounds that both the King and his religious head were involved in the assassination attempt on the Prince of the Uí Fidgente.'

This time there was a murmur of mingled anger and surprise from the people. Abbot Ségdae gave an audible gasp and started to rise from his seat. Colgú reached forward and laid a hand on the elderly abbot's arm, shaking his head in warning not to interrupt the proceedings.

The Brehon Rumann rapped the table with his gavel to call for order. 'Continue,' he instructed Solam.

Solam gestured nervously. 'I have little more to add in this opening statement. All I can say is that Muman never wanted peace with the Uí Fidgente and sought to eliminate its Prince, perhaps to send an army into the country of the Dal gCais in the wake of the turmoil that such an act would provoke. They would take control of the Uí Fidgente and exert the vain claims that Muman have maintained over the centuries – that they are Kings, by right, over our people.'

He sat down abruptly.

The Brehon Ruman turned to Fidelma. 'Are you prepared with your opening counter-plea, Sister Fidelma?'

Fidelma rose. 'I am. Learned judges, it is my intention, during these proceedings, not only to reject the claims of the Uí Fidgente, but to demonstrate where the real culpability lies.'

'Are you challenging the facts that Solam has laid before us?' Rumann asked in an unfriendly tone. 'Do you question his truth?'

'At this stage, I will say,' replied Fidelma, 'that Solam has told you only one aspect of the truth but not the entire truth. He did not relate to you the fact that when the King of Muman and his guest, the Prince of the Uí Fidgente, rode into the market square of Cashel, the first arrow fired by the assailants was fired at the King of Muman. It would have struck him in the heart had he not suddenly bent forward to greet me as his sister. Because of that lucky action, the arrow struck him in the arm and badly wounded him. Why did Solam not mention this?'

Solam sprang to his feet, his face flushed and sneering. 'I am here to represent the Prince of the Uí Fidgente,' he snapped in his excitable fashion. 'Fidelma will speak for her brother.'

'Did you know this fact and withhold it?' demanded the Brehon Rumann, showing disapprobation.

'I knew the fact but also knew that Fidelma would make it known. It is not incumbent on me to present her arguments for her.'

Solam's excitable temper was working against him for the Brehon Rumann began to frown. 'Sometimes economy with truth is no better than a lie, Solam. Be warned. I shall not tolerate a half truth.'

Solam bowed his head penitentially.

Fidelma surprised everyone by saying: 'I do not blame Solam, learned judges, for attempting to find his truth by leaving aside what he feels unnecessary to state. Would we could all find truth as easily as we can uncover untruth.

'However, the facts are that the King was also injured and was struck down first in the attack and in the furore that ensued may lie the true reason why the assassin was not able to find a fatal target in the body of the Prince of the Uí Fidgente. Or, perhaps, he did not want to?'

'That is a conjecture!' cried Solam, springing to his feet. 'It is an insult and a charge against the Uí Fidgente!'

'No more a conjecture than Solam's interpretation,' rejoined Fidelma calmly. 'Further, it is true that Gionga, captain of Donennach's bodyguard, chased after the assassins. But so did the *tanist* of Muman, Donndubháin. Both men had a hand in the death of the would-be assassins.

'My contention is that there was no plot by the King of Muman to assassinate the Prince of the Uí Fidgente. This I shall prove.'

Solam was once again on his feet. 'That proof will be interesting. I will now add to my initial outline of the case against Muman. I have shown that one of the assassins was a member of the élite bodyguard of the King of Cashel . . .'

'You have shown no such thing!' Fidelma challenged. 'The fact that he carried the emblem of the Golden Chain does not make him a member of the Order.'

'We will judge that in the weight of the evidence,' Brehon Rumann assured her.

'The evidence will show another link,' went on Solam triumphantly. 'I have said that the other assassin was the brother of the Keeper of the Holy Relics at Imleach. On the evening before the attempted assassination, the Keeper of the Holy Relics disappeared from Imleach with the Relics of Ailbe. He faked his departure from the abbey so that it looked as if he had been carried off by enemies. He was to make it appear so, in order that blame was put on the Uí Fidgente for this action. Learned judges, I have managed to secure the person of this conniving religieux, Brother Mochta, whose twin Baoill was the assassin to whom I refer. He sits waiting to be called as a witness and, I am pleased to say, that Gionga of the Uí Fidgente recovered the reliquary of Ailbe, hidden here, in Cashel, whose theft was going to be blamed on the Uí Fidgente.'

Fidelma was on her feet, flushed and angry. 'Learned judges, this is a travesty of the truth.'

Solam was equally excitable. 'Truth? The *dálaigh* of Cashel has much to tell us of truth. Can she tell us why she also hid Brother Mochta and the Holy Relics? Why she smuggled Mochta and those Relics, without telling anyone, from Imleach to Cashel and tried to hide them in the house of a well-known prostitute of this town? A prostitute?'

There was uproar in the court as everyone now, finally, responded to Solam's dramatics.

'Is this true, Fidelma?' demanded the Brehon Rumann after he had called for quiet.

Eadulf groaned for he knew what Fidelma would have to answer.

'The facts are true but . . .'

Another burst of noise drowned the rest of her words.

'Furthermore, furthermore . . .' cried Solam quickly, without allowing her a moment to finish the answer when the clamour died away. 'Furthermore, another plot to discredit the Uí Fidgente is revealed. A band of mercenaries were hired to attack Imleach, to cut down the sacred yew-tree there and put blame on the Uí Fidgente by carving a boar on the trunk, the symbol of my Prince.

'In all these things, I say that the hand of the King of Muman is there. The purpose is to discredit the Uí Fidgente in order to have an excuse to destroy them. I say that all the Eóghanacht are involved in this plot from the King and his sister, who purports to be an unbiased advocate on his behalf, to the Princes of Muman to the Comarb of Ailbe himself.'

He sat down abruptly amidst the fury and anger of the Great Hall.

The Brehon Rumann waited until order was restored before turning his sharp gaze on Fidelma.

'These are the gravest charges that I have heard; charges so grave that no *dálaigh* would make them unless he had the strongest grounds for doing so. Before we start to hear the proofs which Solam will offer up, it is my duty to allow you to make your counter-plea, Fidelma. As you do so, I will have to bear in mind that you, yourself, have admitted the truth of the particular charges which Solam levelled against you. Will you speak?'

Fidelma rose. There was a complete silence in the Great Hall as all strained forward to hear her.

'I will, learned judges,' she began. 'Allow me to say that I admitted the facts but not the interpretation placed on them by Solam.'

The Brehon Rumann frowned quickly. 'The facts seem to speak for themselves,' he observed. 'We are all imprisoned by facts and facts cannot be altered.'

'With respect, learned judge, a fact is many-sided. A fact is like a grain bag. Does a grain bag stand up when it is empty? No. You must fill the grain bag with grain. Only then will it stand up. The fact is like the empty grain bag. It, too, cannot stand up unless it is filled. The fact must be considered with the reasons which cause it to exist.'

The Brehon Rumann was about to reply when he realised the meaning of what Fidelma said. 'I see. You doubtless intend to fill our grain sack for us?'

'I do, learned judge.'

'I presume that your argument against Solam is that the Kingdom of Cashel is not culpable in any conspiracy to discredit the Uí Fidgente? That it is, in fact, the Uí Fidgente who are conspiring against the Kingdom of Muman and the Eóghanacht.' Rumann sat back. 'Am I correct in that?'

There was a brief pause.

Then Fidelma said: 'No, learned judge. You are not correct.'

There was a stillness. The Brehon Rumann stared at her as if he had not heard her correctly. His colleagues, Dathal and Fachtna, were similarly confounded.

'I am not sure that I understand you. I repeat, your argument against Solam is surely that the Eóghanacht are innocent of conspiracy which therefore follows that the Uí Fidgente are guilty of conspiring against Cashel.'

'Learned judges,' said Fidelma clearly and slowly, 'the Uí Fidgente are innocent of conspiring against Cashel.'

The silence was now almost oppressive.

'Furthermore,' she went on, 'I cannot absolve the Eóghanacht from responsibility in a conspiracy to cause strife in this kingdom.'

'Fidelma! What are you doing?' Colgú was on his feet, his face ashen. His voice cracked like a whip across the horrified silence of the Great Hall. 'You have betrayed me!'

Chapter Twenty-Four

Pandemonium erupted in the Great Hall after the silence which met the King's outburst. Cries of anger from the nobles of Muman mingled with those of outrage from the people. Threats were hurled against Fidelma from all sides as she stood there calmly before the judges.

The Brehon Rumann looked disconcerted. It was against all protocol that a King should disrupt the proceedings with such an outburst. It was against all proceedings that a defending counsel should turn prosecutor against those whom she represented. The clamour in the Great Hall was deafening. Rumann's gavel alone could not restore order. The steward found that it took some time, banging with his staff, before the noise ebbed away to an uneasy muttering.

'Colgú of Cashel–' Rumann turned sternly to the King – 'you must resume your seat.'

Colgú, looking distraught, unable to believe what his sister had said, hesitated and then was helped back to his seat by Cerball, his bardic adviser. Abbot Ségdae had not moved. He was looking pale and utterly shocked by what had happened.

The Prince of the Uí Fidgente exchanged a triumphant smile with Solam.

The Brehon Rumann, having restored some order, turned back with an angry frown to Fidelma.

'Fidelma of Cashel, I have granted you a great deal of freedom in this hearing. I can no longer do that. In opening these proceedings I told you of the standards I expected in this hearing. No advocate can change their plea and betray their client's interest. You are guilty of affronting the procedures of this court and fined . . .'

'Brehon Rumann!' Fidelma's voice was so sharp that it halted the Chief Brehon in his tracks. 'I have not changed my plea nor have I betrayed the King of Muman's interest. I must explain.'

Rumann gaped stupidly. 'You have changed your plea most certainly, for in your opening address you said, quite clearly, before witnesses . . .' He picked up a paper handed to him by one of the scribes. 'You said that there was no plot by the King of Muman to assassinate the Prince of the Uí Fidgente. You stated quite clearly that you would prove it. Now you say that it was a conspiracy by the King of Muman.'

Fidelma shook her head.

'No. I use language very precisely as I expect this court to. I said that I cannot absolve the Eóghanacht from responsibility. I never said that Colgú was responsible. Learned judge,' continued Fidelma. 'Let me present the resolution to this matter in my own way.'

The Brehons Dathal and Fachtna leant close to Rumann and all three judges held a whispered conversation. Then Rumann addressed her: 'Your request is unusual; nevertheless, as this matter hinges on the peace of this kingdom, we will grant you some licence to present your arguments.'

Fidelma sighed with relief. 'This has been no ordinary case. Indeed, I was confused for some time by another matter which I thought was pertinent to its resolution but which was no more than a series of unrelated events crossing the path of one of the most horrendous plots to destroy the kingdom of Muman.'

There was a clamour among the people and Rumann banged his gavel several times.

Solam was on his feet again. 'Is she now saying that we plotted to destroy Colgú's kingdom?' he snapped. 'I am at a loss, for she seems to be saying one thing one moment and another the next moment!'

Fidelma held up both hands. 'Learned judges, there is no short route to the truth other than to allow me the time to explain in my way.'

'You have been given that licence,' Rumann confirmed. 'There must be no further interruptions until the counsel for Cashel has done.'

Solam returned reluctantly to his seat.

'Very well,' said Fidelma. 'I do not have to explain that there are tensions between Muman and the northern kingdom of Ulaidh. The Uí Néill and the Eóghanacht have been in disagreement since this land was first divided between them, that time almost beyond time when Eremon ruled in the north and Eber Fionn ruled in the south. The descendant of Eremon, the Uí Néill, like Eremon himself, believe they should rule all five-fifths of Éireann. That has been, and is, the cause of the tensions in this land. Even now, when we have left our pagan past behind, the chiefs of the Faith have divided on those political lines. The Comarb of Patrick in Armagh supports his King, the Uí Néill; while here in Muman, the Comarb of Ailbe gives allegiance to the Eóghanacht.'

'History!' sneered Solam, almost under his breath. 'Is our time to be wasted with history? What need do we have of such obscurity?'

Fidelma wheeled angrily on him. 'Without history we would be condemned to remain children, not knowing who we are nor where we come from. Without knowing the past, we cannot hope to understand the present, and not understanding the present, we cannot shape a better future.' She turned back to the judges. 'Learned judges, remember those historic tensions, for they are important.'

She paused a moment. There was now no sound. Everyone recalled the friction and jealousies that she had outlined. Not least the Uí Fidgente, who had several times been supported in their attempts against Cashel by ambitious Uí Néill monarchs.

'I will now turn to the specifics. Let me start by saying that there is a young Prince in the kingdom of Muman who is possessed of a burning ambition. He seeks power and to achieve power he is not concerned with law nor morality.'

'Name him!' came an immediate cry from several people.

'Name him I shall,' replied Fidelma calmly. 'But in due course. This young man, in the pursuit of power, decided to bring Muman down so that he could step into the power void. Muman is a large and strong kingdom. But where is the weakness of Muman?'

She turned to Donennach, the Prince of the Uí Fidgente. He flushed and scowled.

'It is known that the Uí Fidgente have long claimed that they should sit in power in Cashel,' she said.

'I do not deny it,' Donennach replied defiantly. 'It is history. As you have so eloquently emphasised – it is history.'

'Just so,' smiled Fidelma. 'The Eóghanacht have fought many battles with the Uí Fidgente over the centuries. The spoils have always been Cashel. Now this young man, whom, I should now tell you, is a Prince in this land, devised a cunning plot to create dissensions in Muman. He would organise an assassination. An assassination of the King of Cashel. The attempted assassination of the Prince of the Uí Fidgente was a blind to the real purpose . . .'

She had to pause because the uproar became deafening. Both Solam and Donennach were on their feet shouting while the Uí Fidgente warriors led by Gionga were standing stamping their feet on the ground to show disapproval. In the great halls, during feasting or during a trial, no one was allowed in without leaving their weapons outside. Eadulf, following the drama being enacted before him, knew that had Gionga and his men had weapons in their hands, there would have been serious trouble.

The Brehon Rumann fought for control and by the sheer weight of his personality succeeded in restoring order. He was about to speak but Fidelma resumed her summary.

'This prince, to encompass his plan, and knowing that the Uí

Fidgente would come to Cashel on a certain day, sent a trusted messenger to the Uí Néill of Ailech to reveal his plan and ask that equally ambitious King for assistance. That assistance was forthcoming. There was a Brother Baoill at Armagh who shared the belief that the Uí Néill and Armagh should dominate the five kingdoms. It so happened that, by a curious coincidence, Baoill was the twin brother of Brother Mochta, the Keeper of the Holy Relics of Ailbe.

'At this stage the plan became intricate. The idea was not merely to assassinate the King of Muman but to throw Muman into complete chaos by attempting to steal and hide the Holy Relics of Ailbe. There is little need for me to explain that the Relics are not just a priceless icon but the political symbol of the entire kingdom of Muman. Ailbe was our spiritual guardian. The disappearance of his Relics would cause great alarm and despair among us. Just think of that combination! The death of our King, the loss of the Relics.

'Even so, the conspirators were not contented. In case of failure, the Uí Néill of Ailech sent a band of his men into this kingdom. It is not the first time that this has happened. It was that band of mercenaries who attacked Imleach and cut down the sacred yew-tree.'

The Brehon Dathal learnt forward. 'Yet the boar rampant, symbol of the Uí Fidgente, was carved on that tree by the raiders.'

'In order that the Uí Fidgente might be blamed. I began to suspect as much when I saw that the raider we had captured, and who was, unfortunately killed, carried a sword that I had seen in my travels north. This was a *claideb dét*, a sword decorated with animal teeth. It took me some time to remember that it is only made in the territory of Clan Brasil. The same style of sword was carried by Baoill during the assassination attempt. Armagh lies in the territory of Clan Brasil.'

Solam had turned to her in astonishment as he began to see what she was driving at. 'Then are you saying that the Uí Fidgente are an innocent party in all this? That you are not seeking to blame Donennach and claim he was a conspirator?'

She smiled swiftly. 'I am afraid the actions of the Uí Fidgente were not helpful in supporting their innocence from the time Gionga blocked the bridge over the Suir with his warriors. But that action was not the only thing which misled me. What misled me for a while were events that were almost wholly unconnected.'

'Which were?' demanded Solam, now relaxing back in his seat.

'The involvement of Samradán in this matter. I will return to this in a moment. Let us continue with the main story. The ambitious young Prince now awaited help from Ailech. His messenger to Ailech was the man we know as the archer, Saigteóir. To Armagh, and to the Comarb of Patrick, he set Samradán. The archer was, of course, the man who tried to assassinate Colgú. What his real name was is only known to the chief conspirator. It was this chief conspirator, the ambitious young *rígdomna*, who gave the archer the emblem of the Golden Chain with instructions to leave it when he escaped after the assassination.

'The archer had come back to Muman with Brother Baoill. Baoill had been sent by the Comarb of Patrick from Armagh because he knew about Baoill's relationship with Mochta. Baoill tried to hide his tonsure of St Peter by letting his hair grow. But there was not time enough to completely hide it. Brother Mochta was contacted at Imleach. At first, Baoill tried to sound out his brother to see if he could be persuaded to join the conspiracy. When he did not, Baoill attempted to get the Holy Relics by guile and then by force. He succeeded only in getting Ailbe's crucifix.

'Brother Mochta was wounded in that affair and, having told the story to his companion Brother Bardán, and realising that there was some conspiracy afoot, it was decided that Mochta would go into hiding with the remaining Holy Relics until such time as Bardán could find someone to trust and confide in.'

'Why not confide in his abbot?' demanded the Brehon Dathal.

'As he told me, the abbot was an honest man and would insist that the Relics be returned to the chapel. Mochta and Bardán realised, from what Baoill had threatened, that warriors would be sent to attack the abbey to get hold of the Relics. If Mochta and the Relics had disappeared then, they believed, there would be no reason for any attack on Imleach.'

'But an attack did take place,' interposed the Brehon Rumann.

'Yes, but not on the abbey itself. Baoill and his archer companion had already set an alternative plan in motion. Don't forget the main purpose of these actions was to cause dismay and alarm among the people of Muman, so that the kingdom would split. The attack to cut down and destroy the sacred yew-tree of the Eóghanacht would be equally devastating to Muman. Once it was known that the Holy Relics and Mochta had disappeared from the abbey, the great yew-tree became the obvious target. It was the only other thing which would cause such dismay and alarm in Muman.'

The Brehon Fachtna intervened for the first time in this recital. 'You tell an interesting story, Fidelma of Cashel. You have exonerated the Prince of the Uí Fidgente from this matter. Your story will become more interesting if you tell us who your chief conspirator is. Who is behind this conspiracy?'

'It was a driver of Samradán who first put my feet on the right track.'

Brehon Dathal frowned. 'Samradán the merchant? You say he was a messenger to Armagh, to the Comarb of Patrick?'

'He actually told me that he had been twice to Armagh during the last two months. He was so guileless that I realised that he probably did not even know what he was involved in. He was only concerned about his illegal activities.'

'His illegal activities?' queried the Brehon Rumann. 'Is the man in this court?'

'No. He was murdered the night before last. He was killed because it was thought that he might lead me back to the chief conspirator.'

There was an audible ripple of surprised voices through the Great Hall.

'Samradán was a merchant who was mainly engaged in illegal trade. He and his men had found a small silver mine close by Imleach. The land was part of the abbey lands. The silver mine was not Samradán's to mine. As he was under the patronage of our chief conspirator – remember he is a powerful noble – that same Prince encouraged him to mine it and took a percentage of the spoils. There was another person in that mining conspiracy . . .'

Nion the *bó-aire* of Imleach was trying to leave the hall surreptitiously.

'Capa!' called Fidelma, pointing to the smith.

The burly captain of the bodyguard of Colgú held the smith with a surprising force, forcing him by the shoulder to halt.

'Bring him here into the court,' instructed Brehon Rumann.

Nion was pale. 'I had nothing to do with the conspiracy to overthrow Cashel,' he gasped.

'Do you admit you were involved with this . . . this merchant, Samradán?' inquired the Brehon Rumann.

'I do not deny that. I dealt only with him because he brought me the ore from the mine. I extracted the silver and sometimes worked it.'

Fidelma was nodding. 'Yes. I believe that you sometimes made excellent little solar-symbol brooches with it. Unfortunately the raiders destroyed your forge so that, on the day following the raid, Samradán had to leave the mine taking only one sack of silver which you had extracted but also a sack of unprocessed ore.'

'My forge could not deal with it,' agreed Nion.

'Did you ever see Samradán's patron?'

'Never. I was not involved in any plan to overthrow Cashel . . .'

Fidelma turned to the judges. 'There was my confusion,' she admitted. 'For a while I thought that Samradán and his illegal mining were the key to the problem. Especially when I found that the mine was in the same complex of tunnels in which Brother Mochta and the Holy Relics were hidden. It was merely coincidence that Brother Bardán, while going to find Mochta, stumbled onto Samradán's mining operation and was taken prisoner by him and brought to Cashel. Samradán could not take responsibility for the death of a Brother, so he hid Bardán beneath his warehouse, waiting for his patron to make a decision. That Prince decided that both Samradán and Brother Bardán would have to be killed. He suspected that they would lead me to him. Samradán was dead when I reached him. Luckily, I'd already released Bardán from the warehouse. He is in the court as a witness.'

'You said, however, it was Samradán who set you on the right track. Yet you say he was dead when you reached him. How could a dead man speak?' asked the Brehon Rumann.

'No, I mentioned Samradán's driver,' corrected Fidelma. 'This driver was coming to see me to give me some information about the archer and Baoill. You see, the driver, whose name we never knew, had no knowledge about his master's involvement in the affair nor, even, that his master had a patron. Samradán thought he was coming to betray the illegal mining operation for I had stupidly alerted Samradán that I knew he was involved in such an activity. I had asked him whether he dealt in silver and he denied that he did. Samradán mortally wounded the driver. Before he died, the man was able to tell me, in front of the witness of Brother Eadulf–' she nodded towards where Eadulf was sitting – 'certain things, which led me to Brother Mochta. More importantly, he told me of the time when the archer, who was staying at the same inn, had met with a man he could not identify. A young man, in a cloak. It was night time.'

'If he could not identify the man, how could that lead in any meaningful direction?' inquired the Brehon Fachtna.

'The archer addressed the man as *rígdomna* – Prince – giving an indication of the rank of the man. This was the chief conspirator. Brother Bardán heard the raiders speaking to Samradán and he also heard that this *rígdomna* was conspiring with a Comarb.'

Fidelma looked to where Nion was still standing with Capa keeping a close watch on him. Then she swung round to where Finguine, the Prince of Cnoc Áine was sitting.

'Let Finguine come to stand before the judges,' she called softly.

A new wave of whispering echoed round the great hall.

Finguine stood up, his features suddenly creased in anxiety. He hesitated.

'Come forward,' rumbled the Brehon Rumann. 'Come forward, Finguine.'

The young Prince of Cnoc Áine came slowly forward.

'You arrived at Imleach just after the attack on it?' asked Fidelma.

'I did.'

'At that time, you were certain it was an attack by the Uí Fidgente?'

'Yes. Nion believed so. There was also the carving on the tree and the fact that the raiders went north after the attack. Everything pointed to the Uí Fidgente.'

'As it was meant to,' agreed Fidelma. 'With, of course, one exception. The raider we had captured.'

'Yes. But he had been killed before we could identify who he was . . .' began Finguine.

'The night before you left Imleach, Brother Bardán approached you in the chapel and confessed that he knew where Brother Mochta was hiding with the Holy Relics.'

Finguine indicated the witnesses. 'Brother Bardán is seated there. He will tell you as much.'

'He arranged to bring Mochta and the Holy Relics to you?'

'Yes.'

'Do I presume then that it was coincidence that Solam joined you that morning?'

'It was as I have already told you. I was compelled to give him an escort to Cashel. But we had been delayed because I had given Bardán my word and he had not turned up. I told Solam as much as I felt it necessary for him to know. Later I discovered that you had been seen on the road to Ara's Well with the Saxon and with Brother Mochta. You were described as carrying something which could only be the reliquary. As for Bardán, well, he had disappeared.'

'How did you discover where I had hidden Brother Mochta and the Holy Relics?'

'Nion saw you leave the house of Della. It took no imagination to make inquiries and find out how friendly you were with her.'

'That is why you went to Della's house and took Mochta and the reliquary away with you? One thing is puzzling. You have proclaimed your suspicions of the Uí Fidgente on more than one occasion. Why, then, did you take Gionga of the Uí Fidgente to ransack Della's house?'

Finguine glanced nervously at the judges. 'Action needed to be taken immediately when Nion reported the matter to me. I was in Solam's company at the time Nion chose to speak to me. Solam insisted that Gionga accompany me. He was suspicious and wanted an Uí Fidgente witness. I did not have time to send for my warriors and so I had to trust Gionga.'

Solam turned and nodded agreement. 'That was so, Fidelma.'

'Having discovered that I had brought Brother Mochta and the reliquary to Cashel, Finguine, why did you think it necessary that they be removed from my safekeeping?'

Finguine looked uncomfortable and then he held her eye for a moment. 'Because we believed it was you who was behind the conspiracy against Cashel.'

Fidelma was not often given to an astonishment in which she became speechless. This time she was.

Her silence encouraged Finguine to continue.

'You have only just come back to this kingdom after years away. When you were young you went and studied with the Brehon Morann at Tara. Then you went to Cill Dara and were many years in that abbey. You have been abroad, to Oswy's kingdom in the land of the Angles and to Rome. How could we trust you?'

'I still do not see why you felt that I was part of such a conspiracy?' Fidelma finally voiced her astonishment.

Nion came to Finguine's defence. 'I told Finguine what I had heard from Samradán. He once boasted that his patron was powerful. Someone who was very close to the King of Cashel. He never mentioned whether the patron was male or female. It is only now that we have heard that the patron was addressed as a *rígdomna*.'

'And *rígdomna* being male and not female?' Fidelma reacted with a soft chuckle.

'It is no laughing matter,' cut in the Brehon Rumann irritably. 'You had almost argued yourself into the position of your prime suspect.'

Fidelma suddenly grew serious. 'Then I had best come to the point, learned judge, before you find me guilty of the conspiracy. Oh, one more question, Finguine. What were you doing at Samradán's house the other night?'

Finguine frowned. 'The other night? I was looking for Samradán as I wished to ask him some questions. I rode up to his house but there was no response to my knocking.'

'You didn't go in?'

'I didn't even get off my horse. I merely rode up to the door and knocked. When there was no response, I turned away. Then the next day I heard the news that Samradán was dead – murdered.'

'In death, the answer still lies with Samradán,' observed Fidelma. Once more an icy silence descended and everyone leant forward to catch her words. 'I mentioned that I had unwittingly asked him if he traded in silver, having been told he did. He had denied it. This was because his trade was illegal. Outside of his co-workers and Nion who extracted the metal from the ore, only his co-conspirator knew of his mining in silver. That same co-conspirator was the *rígdomna* who sought to overthrow Muman.

'That man, that young *rígdomna*, when he rode into Cashel that morning, was the one who raised his hand to give the signal for the assassins to shoot at Colgú. Only Colgú leaning forward suddenly to greet me made the assassin miss his target. The second arrow struck where it was supposed to. A bad but not serious wound for Donennach. Then Gionga, having spotted the assassins, galloped forward.

'The last thing this man wanted was his conspirators to be captured alive. If they were dead the plot could still work. He had given one of them the emblem of the Golden Chain and told them to drop it at the spot. He had not realised that the other man, Baoill, still carried the crucifix of Ailbe which would mark the start of the trail that led to the conspirators.'

'Are you saying that Gionga acted wrongly in killing the assassins?' Solam interjected.

'He did what he thought was right. He killed the assassins believing that he might be in danger. Probably, if he had hesitated, the chief conspirator, who had ridden after him, would have ensured that both men were killed on some pretext before they could talk. As it was, both men were killed. But, no, Gionga is not to blame.'

Gionga was standing with his brow wrinkled as if deep in thought. He was remembering the incident more clearly in the light of what she was saying.

Fidelma glanced encouragingly across the hall to him.

'I'll take a bet with you, Gionga. The same person who came hot on your heels and ensured you killed the two men at Samradán's warehouse was the same man who suggested that I was determined to conjure evidence to incriminate Prince Donennach. Is that not so? Didn't he suggest that you would be wise to send warriors to block my way to Imleach? To put a guard on the bridge?'

Gionga's face lightened. He nodded rapidly. 'That is so. But he . . .'

'You did not realise that you fell into his trap because, by sending your warriors to prevent my leaving Cashel, you immediately brought down more suspicion on your Prince. Your behaviour seemed to compound the guilt of the Uí Fidgente.'

Gionga raised a hand to his forehead and groaned. 'I did not think of that.'

'Who is this man?' cried the Brehon Rumann in frustration. 'Enough innuendoes. Name him.'

'What man raised his hand when the bodyguard of King Colgú entered the market square that morning?' asked Fidelma. 'We all thought it a signal to his horsemen but it was a signal to the assassins. What man immediately galloped after Gionga? What man told Gionga to set a guard on the bridge across the Suir? What man told me, in an unguarded moment, that he had traded a certain silver brooch from Samradán when Samradán kept his silver dealing such a dark secret that the only person outside of Nion who would know of it was the man who was his partner and protector?'

Slowly, Donndubháin had risen in his place and walked forward to face Fidelma before the Brehons. Throughout the proceedings he had remained silent. He had sat in his seat without responding to events, with no emotion on his stony face. He had simply stared ahead of him, looking neither right nor left. Now the moment had come when everyone finally knew whom Fidelma was accusing. He left his seat and stood a few feet from Fidelma. Even then, he managed a good-natured expression on his features.

'What are you trying to do to me, cousin?' His voice was pleasant. Yet the eyes were hard and unblinking.

'Do – to you? You are the architect of an evil conspiracy, cousin. You were angry and jealous when Colgú was elected as *tanist* and became King of Muman when you considered that the kingship should have been yours by right. Even when *you* were elected *tanist*, heir-apparent, to Colgú, it was not enough. Colgú was young and bar an unforeseen accident, you could never hope to be King. So you decided to make that "accident" occur.

'Colgú would be assassinated. The Uí Fidgente would be blamed. Disorder and turmoil would rip Muman apart and you, dear cousin, would come forward and claim the crown, promising to unite the kingdom once again. You would have the support of the whole kingdom behind you when you marched to destroy the Uí Fidgente and from the ashes of that land you would give the Uí Néill tribute, allowing Mael Dúin of Ailech to once more reach out his blood-red hand to take control of our kingdom.'

Many had risen in the Great Hall and began to crowd towards the spot where the drama was being played out. Eadulf felt himself pushed from his seat and urged forward in their forefront. He clung on desperately to his pilgrim's staff as a means of keeping his balance in the throng.

He found himself near Donndubháin and Fidelma. He did not like the expression that was changing the *tanist*'s face from its handsome pleasant features to a mask of uncontrolled hatred. It was clear that Fidelma's truth had struck home.

The *tanist* of Cashel was trying to assume a smug expression as he made another attempt to deny her accusation.

'The Brehons want proof and not supposition, cousin,' he said, clearly trying to sound amused but not succeeding. 'Where is your proof for this outrageous nonsense?'

'You do not think I have given you proof enough? There is Gionga. He will tell how you persuaded him to send his warriors . . .'

'What if I did? You have no proof of anything else. Baoill and Fedach are dead and . . .'

Fidelma's broad smile stopped him. 'What name did you say?' she asked softly.

'Baoill and . . .' He suddenly paused, realising the slip he had made.

'I think the name that you gave to the archer was Fedach? Did I not say that no one knew his name? That the only person alive would be . . . ?'

'That is not proof enough. I might have heard it from someone else and . . .'

'When you decided to kill Samradán the other night you made your fatal mistake. Without that killing, the jigsaw puzzle, our game of *tomus*, with which we played as children, would not have come into place within its frame.'

'But it was I who led you to the assassin's horses which had been hidden at Samradán's stables,' protested Donndubháin. 'Would a guilty man do that?'

'Yes. You hid the horses there yourself. Samradán was in Imleach at that time. Those horses had been kept elsewhere. Perhaps in your own stables. Then you took them to Samradán's the very evening you killed him in order to close the circle so that a dead man would take the blame. You made a mistake in showing me those horses in your eagerness to throw me off your track. They were still hot and sweaty from their run from the place where they had been these last days. We will probably find which of your servants hid the horses on your instructions. From your own lips we have learnt the name of the archer – Fedach.'

'Nonsense! The name proves nothing.'

'You removed all items of identity from those horses, except for the Uí Fidgente symbol on the saddle by which you hoped that I might still be persuaded to blame Prince Donennach. You had emptied the archer's purse, which was a stupid thing to do for it showed most clearly that everything had been tampered with. But you overlooked a single coin, however. A *píss*, an Uí Néill coin of Ailech.'

She held it out.

'It showed me that the archer had been in Ailech recently.'

'But it does not show that I was in Ailech's pay,' Donndubháin said. 'Nor does it prove my guilt.'

'No. But the death of Samradán showed me that you killed him. Where is your silver brooch, the one you said that you had traded from Samradán, the one that came out of your illegal mining activity with him? The one he asked Nion the smith to make especially for his patron with its five red garnets?'

Donndubháin's hand went automatically to his shoulder. His face went ashen.

Fidelma was holding out the brooch that she had taken from Samradán's dead grasp. She held it up for everyone to see.

'I found it clutched in Samradán's hand. He tore it from Donndubháin in his death struggle along with the cloth you see attached to it.'

'You can't prove it is mine. A silver brooch with a solar symbol and red garnets on the ends,' sneered Donndubháin. 'I have seen others like it. Look!'

He pointed to where Nion was standing. It was true that the smith wore a similar solar emblem with red garnets.

Donndubháin swung round angrily to Finguine.

'And look! He wears one exactly like it.'

Fidelma shook her head. 'Yes. Finguine's solar emblem was also crafted by Nion. That is why they are so alike. Those brooches were made by the same craftsman who made your one. But whereas the emblems worn by Nion and Finguine carry three red garnets, this one was made especially for you. It has five red garnets. I saw you wearing it on the day of the attempted assassination. Maybe it is meant to represent the five kingdoms of Éireann. Is your ambition so high, Donndubháin?'

Donndubháin acted so quickly that it was over in a moment. He slid one hand into his shirt and drew forth a short dagger, hidden in his waistband. At the same time he reached out a hand and grabbed Fidelma. She had not been expecting such a move and the next moment she was pressed, back against his chest, with the knife at her throat.

'Donndubháin!' cried Colgú, springing forward from his place. 'You fool! You cannot hope to escape!'

The Great Hall had burst into chaos and there were cries of alarm.

'If I do not, then your precious sister dies with me,' shouted the Prince across the heads of the crowd.

The knife was so close against Fidelma's neck that there was a faint spot of blood oozing along the knife edge.

'Tell Capa to saddle me a fast horse. No tricks for Fidelma is coming with me . . .' ordered Donndubháin.

He began to edge backwards from the pale-faced judges, and the anxious eyes of those gathered in the Great Hall.

There was a dull thud. The knife hand of Donndubháin trembled and then the knife dropped from the senseless fingers to the floor. A moment afterwards it was followed by the unconscious body of the *tanist* of Cashel.

Fidelma swung round, eyes wide, heaving for breath.

Eadulf was standing there looking concerned. He held his pilgrim's staff in two hands. He suddenly smiled as his eyes found Fidelma's.

'What works for a *canis lupus* can work for a human wolf as well.'

Fidelma threw back her head and laughed with relief as she embraced her companion.

Epilogue

Fidelma and Eadulf had paused on the south-west corner of the battlements of the walls of Cashel. Their eyes were on the westward mountains. It would not be long before the bell tolled the hour for the evening meal. It seemed peaceful and quiet now that the palace grounds were almost deserted and the town below the great seat of the Kings of Muman was emptying of its visitors. They had come for a spectacle in the court of the Brehons and had not been disappointed. Conflict had been averted, the guilty found and punished. Tomorrow morning, the Brehons would be departing and within a few days the Prince of the Uí Fidgente would return to his own land, having sworn a treaty of peace with Cashel.

It seemed that the month was going to end, as it usually did, with another period of fine, warm weather. The sun was lowering rapidly, a bright golden ball heading towards the western mountains in a splash of soft, rose-redness. The clouds, what few there were, lay in thin, long strands of darkness, tinged along the top by the rays of the light from the setting sun.

'It will be a fine day tomorrow,' Fidelma observed almost sleepily.

Eadulf nodded morosely.

'You seem despondent.' Fidelma caught the mood of her Saxon companion.

'There is one mystery in this matter that has not been resolved,' he said. 'At least, I cannot find the answer.'

'What is that?'

'Who killed the raider in Imleach? Was it Samradán? That does not make sense.'

'No. The death of the raider was almost superfluous, if death can be so described. He was killed, as I first suspected, for the most common of motives. Vengeance.'

'You mean that he was killed as we suspected by Brother Bardán?' Eadulf asked. 'Vengeance for Daig's slaughter?'

'No. He was killed by Brother Madagan whose eyes betray his unforgiving nature. Madagan simply wanted vengeance for being struck down by the raider outside the gates of the abbey. The next day, Madagan took the purse of the raider, filled with coins from the King of Ailech, and donated them to the abbey as compensation. Ségdae showed me the coins before I left Imleach. They were the same type as the one I found in the assassin's bag at Samradán's stable.'

'Does Abbot Ségdae know?' gasped Eadulf.

'Yes. It will be for him to pursue the matter if he wants to and for Madagan to come to terms with his own conscience. At least the raider's coins as a gift to the abbey is some recompense, I suppose. But not for Madagan. He has to find his own salvation.'

They fell silent awhile.

'I was also thinking how close you came to death and by the hand of your own cousin no less.'

'A pilgrim's staff is good to have to hand.' She smiled softly. 'At least your aim was true.'

'What if it had not been?' Eadulf grimaced and shivered.

'But it was and here we are.'

'Tomorrow the Brehons will have departed. But will Muman be safe again?'

'The Uí Fidgente have come to a peace accord with my brother. The Brehons will make their findings known and Mael Dúin, the Uí Néill King of Ailech, will be given warning to desist from plotting against Muman. So will Ultán, the Comarb of Patrick. I believe that there will be peace here for a while. I am also told that Colgú will be proposing my cousin, Finguine, as his new *tanist* when the *derbfhine* of our family next meet. I think the choice will be a wise one.'

'And what now?' asked Eadulf. 'This matter has been an exhausting one. I have never been so confused in my life. I was wondering whether you could have proved Donndubháin's guilt had he not condemned himself by his action.'

Fidelma gazed at Eadulf in mild rebuke.

'Surely you know me better than that? I do not believe in chance. However–' she smiled ruefully – 'it would have taken some time to examine all the witnesses and the evidence. Some might have become confused with it. I don't think so, though. In the end, the evidence would have been clear to anyone.'

'So what are you planning now?' pressed Eadulf. 'I have seen that meditative look on your face once too often not to realise that you are working something out.'

Fidelma smiled sadly. She had, indeed. It was going to be difficult. 'Do you know how our scribes mark the end of a manuscript as they finish work?'

Eadulf shook his head, wondering what she meant.

'*Nunc scripsi totum pro Christo, da mihi potum!*'

Eadulf found himself smiling in response as he translated. 'Now I have written so much for Christ, give me a drink!'

Fidelma nodded slowly. 'Or as I would translate, now that I have worked so much for my brother, and the kingdom of Cashel, give me some rest,' she averred.

Eadulf shook his head. 'Rest? You?' He sounded dubious.

'Oh yes. Do you remember when we arrived at Imleach there was a band of pilgrims there?'

'I remember; they were journeying to the coast to set out to sea on some pilgrimage.'

'That's right. To the tomb of St James of the Field of the Stars.'

'Where is that?'

'In one of the northern Iberian kingdoms. I would like to go on that pilgrimage. Many here in the five kingdoms do so. Such pilgrimages set off from the abbey of St Declan at Ard Mór, which is not far to the south of us. I have a mind to set out soon for Ard Mór.'

Eadulf was suddenly miserable at the thought of her leaving. It reminded him abruptly that he had delayed too long in Muman for he had been sent there only as a special envoy of Archbishop Theodore of Canterbury. What Fidelma was actually saying was that the time had come to say farewell.

'Do you feel that it is right to leave Cashel at this moment in time?' he asked hesitantly.

She had made up her mind. For some time now Fidelma had felt a dissatisfaction with her life. When she been away from Eadulf, when she had left him in Rome to return to Éireann, she had experienced feelings of loneliness and longing, as if of a home-sickness even though she was home among her own people. She had missed the arguments with Eadulf, the way she could tease him over their conflicting opinions and philosophies; the way he would always rise good-naturedly to her bait. The arguments would rage but there was no enmity between them.

Eadulf had been the only man of her own age in whose company she had felt really at ease and able to express herself without hiding behind her rank and role in life, without being forced to adopt a persona, like an actor playing a part.

She had missed his company with an acuteness she could not explain. It had now been ten months since Eadulf had come to her brother's kingdom as an emissary of Theodore, the Archbishop of Canterbury. Ten months during which they had shared several dangers and had been close. Close like a brother and sister.

That was just it. Eadulf was always impeccably behaved towards her. She found herself wondering whether she wanted him to behave in any other way. Religious did cohabit, did marry and most lived in the *conhospitae* or mixed houses. Did she want that? Her old mentor, the Brehon Morann, had once told his young pupils that marriage was a feast where the *gratias* was better than the food.

Unable to really come to a decision herself, she had almost been relying on Eadulf to make the decision himself. To suggest something to her. He did not. Yet if he wanted marriage, he would surely have spoken of it long since. What was it that was written in the *Book of Amos*? Can two walk together, except that they be agreed? It was obvious that Eadulf was not interested in such a partnership. He had never raised the prospect of such a relationship nor did she feel she should if he did not. The closest she had come to the subject was when she had asked him if he had heard the old proverb that a blanket was the warmer for being doubled. He had not understood.

'Do you feel that it is right to leave Cashel at this time?' he asked again.

She roused herself from her thoughts. 'Yes; just for the rest, as I say. There is an old saying that to rest the eyes and the mind, it is sometimes best to change the silhouette of the distant mountains.' She looked at him seriously. 'You have been away a long time from your home in Seaxmund's Ham, Eadulf. Don't you ever feel the need to get back to your people and change the silhouette of these mountains? You have a duty to Archbishop Theodore.'

Eadulf immediately shook his head. 'I can never be tired in this land and with . . .' He flushed and did not finish what he was going to say. He was confused. There was a saying among his own people. Do not bring a reaping hook into someone else's field. It was clear that Fidelma did not feel the same way as he did otherwise she would not have suggested his return to Canterbury. She had not apparently even noticed that he had left his sentence hanging in mid-air.

'Your Archbishop must need you back. You cannot delay your return much longer. What better time for both of us to leave Cashel – you to your homeland and I to seek out those new mountains?'

'Is it right, at this time?' Eadulf pressed yet again.

'Someone once said that there is always a time to depart from a place even if one is unsure where one is going.'

'But there is a permanence here, Fidelma,' protested Eadulf. 'I have come to feel at home. I would find a means to stay in spite of the demands of Canterbury. These are the mountains I wish to continue to see. The river down there is the water I want to rest beside, to daily bathe my feet in.'

Fidelma waited, finding herself hoping to hear him say that which she wanted him to say. When he did not, she smiled sadly.

'Heraclitus said that you cannot step twice into the same river for other waters are continually flowing into it. The only thing that is permanent, Eadulf, is change.'

She stretched her arms and yawned, her face turned towards the setting sun. It stood poised for a moment or two, an oval glow on the horizon before abruptly vanishing and sending a flood of dark shadows across the land. She shivered slightly at the sudden chill that swept over the great Rock of Cashel.

'*Incidis in Scyllam cupiens vitare Charybdim,*' muttered Eadulf. 'You fall into the Scylla in trying to avoid Charybdis.'

Fidelma raised an eyebrow. 'You think that I am trying to escape from something I consider bad and will fall into something that is worse? No. I just need a change, that is all, Eadulf. There is boredom in permanence.'

A bell began to toll solemnly in the background.

'The evening meal, Eadulf. Let us go in and change this evening chill for the warmth of a good fire.'